RAMPAGE

RAMPAGE

WILLIAM P. WOOD

St. Martin's Press
New York

St. Martin's Press titles are available at quantity discounts for sales promotions, premiums or fund raising. Special books or book excerpts can also be created to fit specific needs. For information write to special sales manager, St. Martin's Press, 175 Fifth Avenue, New York, N.Y. 10010.

Mass market edition/May 1986

ISBN: 0-312-90306-5
Can. ISBN: 0-312-90307-3

Grateful acknowledgment is made for permission to reprint material from the following:

   "The Two Trees" by W. B. Yeats, reprinted with permission of Macmillan Publishing Company from *The Poems of W. B. Yeats* by W. B. Yeats, edited by Richard J. Finneran. Copyright 1916 Macmillan Publishing Co., Inc., renewed 1944 by Bertha Georgie Yeats.

   An extract from "To a Child Dancing in the Wind" by W. B. Yeats, reprinted with permission of Macmillan Publishing Company from *Collected Poems* by W. B. Yeats. Copyright 1916 by Macmillan Publishing Co., Inc., renewed 1944 by Bertha Georgie Yeats.

To my family
PRESTON, ELEANOR, and MARK
with love and admiration.

Now 'tis evident that in the case of an infection there is no apparent extraordinary occasion for supernatural operation, but the ordinary course of things appears sufficiently armed and made capable of all the effects that Heaven usually directs by a contagion. Among these causes and effects, this of the secret conveyance of infection, imperceptible and unavoidable, is more than sufficient to execute the fierceness of Divine vengeance, without putting it upon supernaturals or miracles.

—Daniel Defoe, *A Journal of the Plague Year*

Neither the city nor the people described in this story are real. They have no actual counterparts and must not be seen as depictions of real places or real people. They are, from first to last, imaginary.

Likewise, no actual crimes are presented in this story. The crimes and consequences that occupy these fictional people are absolutely without connection to any true events.

Finally, let me be specific about the legal setting of this story. While I have drawn on my knowledge of the law and experiences as a lawyer, I have not used real people involved in criminal law as models for characters, or real events for stages on which to set the action of this story. Because this is a story about violent and bizarre crime, it necessarily includes characters who are judges, lawyers, psychiatrists, and members of law enforcement agencies. These are also people of the imagination, as are the other characters, and not actual judges, lawyers, psychiatrists, or policemen.

RAMPAGE

PART ONE

CHAPTER I

ONE

On Wednesday, near ten in the morning, the Eastgate Mall bustled. The Christmas shopping fever was building, with only two weeks left before the holiday. Shoppers eddied briskly through the parking lots toward the stores, and the steady clanging of Salvation Army bells mingled with sprightly music piped throughout the mall. He left the white Chevy at the edge of the mall and walked back a block to Mission Drive, and at least a few of the women shoppers stared at him momentarily before he turned the corner and was lost from view.

He walked canted a bit to one side, then righted himself and walked on. He was a tall, gaunt young man in dirty blue jeans. His face was pinched, as if pushed in from either side, and his black hair hung limply down to his shoulders. It flapped in the light breeze over his forehead and ears.

Although the day was California bright and sunlit blue, the December cold penetrated the red nylon ski parka he wore over a gray sweat shirt. His black sunglasses formed the dark upper half of his face; the lower half was made up of a small beard and unshaven cheeks. He moved more slowly as his eyes searched along the houses on Mission Drive. He looked at each home, tilting himself suddenly to one side, swinging back upright again, buffeted by an unseen wind that stirred no trees or leaves.

Several times he paused in front of a house. But then, each time, he walked on. Ahead, halfway down the block, he saw a young woman in yellow knit pants get out of a car, trundle some bags to her door, and go inside. At once his walk quickened. He listed over, swung upright, planting one foot in front of the other without taking his gaze from the stucco-fronted house down the block. Hands

3

fumbled in the pockets of the parka to make sure everything was still there, and now he was almost at a trot, still wobbling, still staring. He was at the front door.

He pushed the doorbell. It sounded inside. He stood still and waited.

When the door opened, it framed an old woman, a baggy gray one with coiled white hair and a musty smell, as though she'd come straight out of a cedar chest. "What can I do for you?" she asked. Her look of courteous curiosity faded to an expression of concern when she registered the odd appearance of the young man in front of her.

"I'm collecting old clothes for charity," he said softly, as though it would hurt his voice to raise it.

"What? I couldn't quite hear you." She leaned forward, hands still on the door, ready to close it.

"I'm collecting for charity. Old clothes, if you have any."

"No, no thank you, we don't." She smiled faintly, retreating into the house, an old turtle pulling herself back into the safety of her shell.

He stepped forward. He was partway inside.

"How about cans? I'm collecting cans and bottles. You know, soda cans."

Behind the sunglasses, his pulpy eyes regarded her.

"No thank you," and she pushed against the door.

He stepped inside, and she was shoved back, her thick white arms flailing. "Get out," she said, but instead he shut the door behind him.

"Sit down," he told her. He took a small gun from his parka and pointed it at her.

She squealed and her face bunched together. "Sit down," he repeated, shooting her in the face. In the living room the sound was a crack, like a yardstick snapping. The old woman pitched part way back onto a sofa so her head rested on the cushions. A small red hole just above the bridge of her nose gaped and dripped.

He made a tiny whining sound and headed toward the rear of the house. Someone else had to be home. He'd seen the young woman go inside. He clumped awkwardly through a hallway, then into the brighter kitchen. An old man and the young woman were at the sink.

"I'm collecting for charity," he said to them.

4

"What was that noise?" the man demanded harshly, and the woman stood still, a head of lettuce in her hands with water sluicing over it.

Instead of answering, he made the gasping whine and aimed the gun, his body suddenly pulled off to one side again. The young woman trembled and dropped the lettuce into the sink.

"Go into the bedroom," he said. The voice remained soft, even though he was sweating. He lunged and pushed the old man, who put his hands in the air.

"I'll tell you where the jewelry and my wallet are," the young woman said in a high voice, "and we won't call anyone. We won't."

"Go into the bedroom." He shoved again. The old man and the woman walked slowly out of the kitchen and into the dark hallway in front of him. "Where's my wife?" the old man asked abruptly. He was a paunchy old man in a cardigan and pastel slacks. His moustache was pure white.

They were almost at the bedroom. He stepped up behind the old man, put the barrel of the gun against his head, and fired. The old man fell forward onto the woman because they'd been walking so closely together. She screamed and tried to run ahead. He leaped over the old man, who'd toppled face forward to the hall carpet, and grabbed her by the arm. For an instant she stared right at him, her face drained of color, twisting in his grip, screaming. He screamed, too. He shot her first in the chest. She fell back into the bedroom, gasping and bleeding on the floor.

He crouched over her and shot her on either side of the head. Satisfied that she would stay silent, he went back to the hallway and did the same to the old man. Then he went into the living room and looked at the old woman bleeding on the sofa. He shot her again on either side of the head, reloading the gun afterward.

The living room had a picture window, framing a green-curtained vista, a serene square lawn, the sidewalk, and the street, lined with houses identical to this one. He got down onto his belly, slid across to the draw cord attached to the curtains, and pulled it so the window was covered. The room was now in murky green dimness.

On his hands and knees, he crawled back to the old woman. The cushion under her head was dark red and wet. He pulled her down onto the floor and put his hands under her arms, dragging her slowly toward the rear bedroom, her clothing making a sibilant sound on the carpet. She was heavy, moist and solid. He panted and gabbled, his fleshy lips pouting as he moved backward until his heel kicked the old man. Breathing fast, although not entirely from exertion, he hefted the man into the bedroom. He came for the old woman next, taking her by the arms, dropping them with a thump when the body was partly in the bedroom. Her floral-print dress had torn.

He stripped off his parka, flinging it roughly to the bed. This room had a bluish tint—blue filigreed wallpaper, blue curtains, pale white dressers. With a quivering hand he wiped his face up and down, up and down, and tugged off his jeans, crying with frustration when they caught on his sneakers, pulling and jerking until they came free. He tossed them on the bed. He flicked his head from side to side, deciding exactly what came next. He wore no underpants.

He stepped over the bodies and got his gloves from the parka on the other side of the bed, slipping them on. Off came the dark sunglasses. He padded quickly to the kitchen and pulled out drawer after drawer, keening loudly, trembling as he dug into the silvery utensils and egg timers, finally pulling out one thing and sighing. It was a long carving knife with a weighted handle, a steel knife used for family gatherings and holidays.

He carried the knife back to the bedroom. Briefly he knelt over the old woman, but he had to jump up and hurry back to the living room to grope in the murky light for his gun, which he had dropped near the sofa. He brought it with him to the bedroom and put it carefully away before turning again to the old woman. What a body, what an immense, flabby white body, wrapped in its torn dress. Kneeling again, he tore the dress all the way open, yanking it back and forth, rolling her slightly until it was off. He slit her undergarments, and she lay on the floor, inert. He began to work with the knife.

All the time he worked his hands flew faster and faster until they nearly danced over the old woman, flying here and there, pulling and turning, yanking and poking. He was soon covered in sweat beneath the sweat shirt, so much sweat that it trickled down his thin legs. Organs and shiny tubes, red guts in purple iridescence lay before him. He was on known ground now. His hands flew again, and a pile grew beside him as he worked, snipping and cutting.

Enough. He tried at last to drink from the red openness, bending his body lower, but this didn't work, and he sat back, breathing heavily, whining on his haunches, and cupped his hands together in the fashion of a communicant. He dipped downward again, but the results were not pleasing. He jumped up, shaking and gabbling to himself. Back to the kitchen and, casting around, his roaming eyes found a measuring cup half full of flour. With frantic delight he emptied it and took the cup back to the old woman where he knelt, scooping and drinking eagerly.

He kicked the old man when he got up, idly at first, then again, harder. Now he went to the other woman on the floor of the bedroom. He lifted her onto the bed and clumsily got her clothes off. When she was naked he turned her onto her stomach. He grew excited. This was different, this was vastly, wonderfully different from the pale sickliness of the old woman.

He forced himself into her. The noises he made, high-noted and constant, counterpointed the squeaking of the bed as he bounced, driving himself into her without restraint, his face contorted with effort and excitement, his hair jiggling around his head like a hundred maddened gnats. He grunted once and then lay back over her, mewing softly to himself.

He lay there for a while in the perfect stillness, then slowly got off her and rolled her onto her back. Her mouth had fallen open a little; her eyes glared dully upward. He did one thing more to her open mouth.

With her, he was less dexterous using the knife, but no less thorough. The pile of organs grew again. He fetched the measuring cup once more, setting it down gently on the night table beside the city phone directory and a forest-green bedroom telephone when he finished.

It was almost time to go. From his parka he managed to yank out a large black trash bag, folded into eights. He unfolded it, muttering distractedly, and started stuffing his pile inside. Each addition made a soft plop as it fell into the bag. It was a quarter full when he was done. The bag slithered warmly in his hands, as if with a dumb life of its own. He wiped his head on his sweatshirt sleeve, leaving a dark stain, like the trail of a mollusk.

Almost skipping with haste, he took the knife into the kitchen and ran it first under hot, hot water, then cold, shaking it in the air like a sputtering Fourth of July punk to get the drops of water off. He deposited it on a plastic tray where dishes and pans lay drying.

He hurried to the bedroom, and pulled his pants on quickly, then zipped himself up. The room was dank with the smells of sweat and blood. Around him in the bluish light lay the bodies, split redly open. One final check to make sure he had everything, sunglasses on, and he hoisted the trash bag, going out to the kitchen. A small alcove with a washing machine had a side door. He opened it.

In front of him, in the neighbor's yard, was a woman humming to herself as she hung wet clothes to dry. The sight terrified him suddenly, and he whined, ready to run. Almost as swiftly, he caught himself. The woman looked up at him, still humming.

"Collecting old cans," he said, tapping the bag over his shoulder.

"I have some," she said.

He shook his head and waved his free hand. He stepped out and closed the door behind him, and when he was around the house, out of her sight, he loped to the sidewalk, lugging his trash bag, tilting and wobbling, the red parka flapping about him like the terrible edges of a wound. He was a silent specter capering down the street with his burden, his hair streaming, red nylon flapping.

When he returned to his car, the bag went alongside him in the front seat. He checked his watch. The clanging bells from the mall sounded like alarms, and he started the car, while over the bells the music of "God Rest Ye Merry Gentlemen" floated out.

TWO

Fraser dropped his armload of thick black notebooks onto the imitation-oak counsel table with a bang.

The loud noise set the crowded courtroom chattering; all

the defendants and their lawyers and friends tensed like nervous animals. Wearily, Fraser put his hands over his eyes for a moment.

"No talking when court's in session," shouted the bailiff.

From the bench, Judge Donelli noticed Fraser. "I see we've got everybody together on the Yamato matter. We'll take that next."

A defense attorney, wearing a gaudy three-piece suit checkered in mauve and green, took his place at the railing around the heavy steel door to the holding cells, the tank, from which prisoners were delivered into Department 3 of the Municipal Court. It was the first of many courtrooms most of the defendants would see as their cases proceeded slowly to final dispositions.

Restlessly, Donelli's eyes bounced around the courtroom, lighting briefly on Fraser and the other lawyer, then hovering somewhere about eight feet off the ground. Donelli was short, round, with dark features and a snappish manner. Courthouse wisdom regularly held that he was too smart for the municipal bench but was unable to make enough highly placed friends to rise farther. Donelli himself agreed with this assessment, and it did little to improve his temper. He seemed to be staring off into space at the moment. "You look tired this morning, Mr. Fraser," he said.

"I am tired, your honor." He was more than tired. He no longer cared very much about all this. It was an effort just to stand there.

The judge was going to say more, but the bailiff had pushed the buzzer at the tank door, a heavy armored contrivance, and said, "Yamato," to the deputy sheriff who stuck his head out. A moment later Fraser watched a diminutive man in rubber sandals, blue jeans, and an orange sweat shirt stenciled front and back with the initials of the county jail, step cautiously through the door and over to his lawyer.

Fraser took a deep breath. It began again.

"All right," Donelli said rapidly in his auctioneer's style, swallowing and gargling syllables, "the record will reflect this is case number six-one-seven-seven-four. You are Martin Yamato?"

The man in the dock blinked rapidly. His lawyer answered with lumpish gravity. "Pardon me, your honor, his full and correct name is Dr. Martin Yamato."

"Just a moment, counsel. Isn't that his occupation? That's not his name."

"I wanted to interpose that for accuracy, your honor."

"With all respect"—Donelli managed to sound impatient, angry, and bored all at once—"let me get this record straight, and then you can make your comments. Now then, is your true name Martin Yamato?"

"Yes, sir, it is."

"And Mr. Killigrew, you are retained to represent this defendant?"

"I am, your honor," Killigrew said gravely. He cleared his throat, his heavy face assuming a jowled severity.

The man was deaf and dumb, Fraser saw that. With a little effort Fraser could tie him up hand and foot. But it didn't seem to matter anymore whether Killigrew was brilliant or ridiculous. Fraser was deadened. It didn't even seem to matter that Yamato was a murderer.

"The People of California are represented by Mr. Fraser of the Santa Maria District Attorney's office."

By rote Fraser replied, "Yes, your honor."

"Now then, we're here because Mr. Killigrew put the matter on calendar. You have something to bring before the court, Mr. Killigrew?"

Fraser recognized Donelli's tone. In a minute the judge was going to tear the defense attorney to pieces.

"If it please the court," said Killigrew glancing out at the large audience, "my client wishes to enter a new plea today."

Donelli's small eyes squinched smaller in annoyance. "He's already entered pleas of not guilty last week."

Killigrew gave a courtly nod. "That's true, your honor. He will again enter pleas of not guilty, and not guilty"—he paused as if announcing an event—"by reason of insanity."

He stopped talking and stood expectantly.

Donelli smiled very slightly.

"Do the People wish to respond before the court does, Mr. Fraser?"

He barely heard the judge's question. He was staring at

a black-haired woman and her small baby, perhaps a year old and dressed in bleached blue clothes, sitting in the middle of the courtroom. He couldn't take his eyes from them. The woman's smile unnerved him. It was a vague, vacuous look. Every so often she cooed at the baby. Fraser saw that the baby's eyes were reddened, and it was coughing, thrusting its small arms out to push something unseen away.

"Mr. Fraser?"

The empty-eyed mother bounced the baby and rearranged its clothing, holding it by the waist. At each wrenching cough, the tiny eyelids squeezed shut. . . . Sweet Molly, Fraser thought, sleeping on a bed of mist. Carried away while your father cross-examined a murderer's brother. He hadn't been worried about Molly. The danger was past, and when he saw her that last night in the hospital she was asleep in an oxygen tent, the sides all frosted and misted. She looked small in there, much smaller than she was really, sleeping so profoundly in a cloud. He'd gone to court the next day, and she had died. Kate had stayed with her. At least there was that comfort. It was, he knew, one of the reasons he and Kate were drifting apart. The message from her about Molly got to him during the afternoon break, which made it very convenient. Molly Fraser, two years, seven months . . .

"Do you wish to be heard, Mr. Fraser?"

He looked up at the judge. "I'm sorry, your honor." He fumbled for a moment. "Yes, I do want to be heard. Mr. Killigrew doesn't have the slightest idea what he's doing."

Donelli coughed, and Killigrew said loudly, "That's uncalled for, your honor. Please tell the district attorney not to say things like that."

"A legal ground would be more appropriate," Donelli said.

"The obvious ground, your honor, is that Dr. Yamato cannot enter a plea of not guilty by reason of insanity in Municipal Court. The law doesn't allow it."

Killigrew bristled. "From the time of the Magna Charta and the foundation of Anglo-American jurisprudence, your honor—"

Donelli cut him off. "Please don't give me a history

lecture. I agree with the People's representative. Tell me where you read you can enter this plea here."

"I assumed a man is always entitled to his rights—"

"That's not the point," Donelli said. "We have laws, and they state you may only enter a plea of not guilty by reason of insanity in Superior Court."

Killigrew gathered himself together. "Then we will do so." His client blinked at him several times.

"Anything more you want to add?"

"No, your honor," Fraser said. He watched Killigrew, who was leaning over the railing to murmur to Yamato. It might be enough if he just didn't look back at the woman and her baby. He could finish and get out of the courtroom relatively intact. But there was one more thing to do, and he knew it would fluster Killigrew and annoy the judge. If he'd been more alert, if he'd cared, it would have been done last week when Yamato first appeared in court. Now it came late, straggling along, a reminder of his weariness, his terrible indifference.

Donelli denied Killigrew's motion, scolding him. Fraser roused himself when he saw the judge scanning the calendar, about to call another case.

"Anything more, gentlemen?"

The bailiff was taking Yamato back to the tank, and Killigrew was stuffing notes into his checkered coat. Fraser spoke without enthusiasm. "I do have one matter."

The judge looked up, as Yamato hung between the courtroom and the holding cell.

Fraser went on. "I'm moving at this time for a re-evaluation of the defendant's bail, your honor. It slipped my mind, but the People never intended that his bail should be so low. It is the People's position that since this is a death penalty case, murder in the first degree with special circumstances, it is improper for the defendant to be on any bail at all. His bail should be revoked."

Donelli tightened visibly. The judge hated surprises in murder cases with reporters watching.

"What are you specifically pointing to, Mr. Fraser, when you urge this on the court?"

Fraser flipped open one of the black notebooks, the collected case against Yamato. This was a mechanical operation, the meticulous listing of all the things that made

Yamato a flight risk—his lack of ties to Santa Maria, his actions after his wife's body had been found, the guns he had when arrested. Fraser said it all as a matter of duty.

Killigrew countered with a litany of Yamato's friends in Santa Maria and the defendant's ardent desire to resolve the charges pending against him. Indignantly, Killigrew said, "The district attorney is clearly trying to strip a poor, muddled man of his bail, a thing to which every defendant in Anglo-American jurisprudence is entitled."

"Not in a capital case," Fraser broke in.

"The court can handle this matter, Mr. Fraser," Donelli said irritably. "I'd have preferred you made your motion in a more orderly fashion."

Killigrew nodded vigorously. "It was without precedent."

The judge sighed. "However, I see the People's position. I'm going to increase bail from four hundred to seven hundred fifty thousand dollars. I do think Dr. Yamato's past associations count for something, even though he has a good reason to leave now. He'll be remanded unless he can post that bail."

Fraser closed his notebooks as Donelli called him to the bench.

Leaning over, his bulky body tensed, the judge whispered, "Don't throw me any curves like that again, okay?"

"I'm sorry, judge. I didn't have a chance to tell you this morning."

Donelli was not pleased. "Okay. Let's get our signals straight from now on? Let's figure these things out in chambers next time you want to lift bail. I'll even supply the coffee." He peered at Fraser. "You look rocky."

"I'm just a little under the weather. It isn't serious."

Abruptly, Donelli's eyes indicated Killigrew, now in the back of the courtroom in earnest conversation with several Asians. "Who's idea was he?"

"The family got him through some club Yamato belongs to. He's from Los Angeles. This is his third trial."

The judge grunted at the news and flopped back in his chair. The audience was over. Fraser managed to leave the courtroom without seeing the woman and her sick baby. He brushed by the relatives who were trying to get one last

13

glimpse of Dr. Yamato in the tank doorway. The buzzer sounded behind Fraser, Donelli called another case, and the metal door thudded shut.

He broke quickly away from the TV crews and reporters waiting for some comment on the morning's activities. He had another appearance to get through at eleven, a hearing in Superior Court. One more, and that was all for the day. It was another murder case.

One more to go, he told himself again and again in the elevator, just one more to go.

THREE

Wednesday was his first day off in two months, and Gene Tippetts was glad it had settled down after a bad start. A day doesn't get off on the right foot when you go outside with a bowl of dog food and find out the dog isn't in the backyard. Hattie—that was the puppy's name—had run away again. Her small chain and collar lay on the ground, but she was long gone. Gene's heart sank. He could have predicted what Eileen said when she found out.

"Andy cried for hours the last time Hattie was gone. I can't take that today . . ."

He had tried a little tender persuasion, but she was more or less right, and not interested in persuasion anyway. Sitting at the kitchen table in her bathrobe, Eileen had been annoyed because the bathroom scale said she'd gained a few pounds. Gene always told her it was a waste to weigh yourself every damn morning, but she did, every damn morning.

Now he tried to keep one eye on Andy and the other on Aaron as the boys roamed through the furniture displays in the store, while Eileen talked to a salesman. Gene sighed. They couldn't afford a dining-room set. Not now. Maybe next year, but he didn't have the money now. Eileen motioned him over. He told Andy to stop hiding under a great four-poster bed.

This was better than earlier that morning, when he'd thrown on his scruffiest clothes to go looking for the dog. Now it was plain that neither boy minded very much Hattie's being missing in action. A couple of hours ago, saying he'd look for the puppy seemed the easiest way to keep the peace, even if it was his day off.

And he'd gone out into the chilly morning. Where did you start looking? He had stood uncertainly in the middle of the block. The whole neighborhood was quiet, beautifully quiet at six-fifteen, except for that thrumming noise up the block. It was the gas generator at the Reece place. Day and night it thrummed, and most of the time nowadays he didn't even notice it. But in the early morning quiet Gene looked toward the Reeces' white house up the block, and without thinking he found himself walking toward the noise.

If the puppy was missing, he had an odd notion that Mrs. Reece or her screwy son would know about it. He walked with his hands deep in his pockets, the air misting in front of him. Overhead the sky was changing slowly from black to deep blue.

The gas generator droned, drawing him on like a chant. The house was funny, too. For years an old couple named Jelicoe had lived there; then they were gone and the place was empty, a kind of sullen empty, with the windows all open and black. Then one morning a few months back, all the windows were curtained in white and closed, and there was a scroungy white Chevy parked in the driveway. And within a week the gas generator had appeared, spluttering to life. The son put it together. He was good with things like that, always fixing the car, tinkering with the generator. Gene saw the house in front of him. Funny. It was as if something had come scuttling along one dark night, looking for a place to hide its soft, jellylike body, a marine thing that had spied the empty Jelicoe house and pulled the old place gratefully around itself.

It was a cloistered little yard, apart from the rest of the street.

He knocked on the front door. The house seemed deserted. He stepped back. No movement anywhere. He knocked again more forcefully. A dog barked arrogantly, far away.

He was about to use the bell when the door opened slightly. Acrid, cool air came out, and in the crack of the door he saw a short, thin woman with an aureole of reddish hair. Her face was heavily furrowed, and her eyes seemed to have trouble focusing on him. She wore a pink fluffy robe.

Her breath rasped, and tiny hands pulled the edges of the robe more tightly closed. "Mr. Tippetts," she said. "What is it this time?"

He felt a twinge of foolishness suddenly. "Our puppy got out, or maybe someone let her out last night, Mrs. Reece. She's a little boxer puppy named Hattie. Have you seen her around here?" He tried to keep his voice pleasant, but he hated talking to the woman.

"Oh, come on, you're kidding. You woke me up because your dog got out?"

"I just wanted to know if you saw or heard anything this morning."

Naomi Reece made a disgusted sound and waved her skinny arm at him. "I've been asleep. I didn't see your dog. I don't know anything about your dog." She started to close the door.

"Is Charlie home?" The hard tone in his voice made her pause.

"He went out yesterday, maybe last night, I don't know. I don't know if he came home from work." She backed away. "I'm going back to bed."

"You're sure Charlie wasn't home last night?" Gene put his hand out and stopped the door from closing. Naomi stared at him, breathing noisily.

"Can't you leave us alone?" she cried out, the words echoing in the deserted street. "Why don't you leave us be? I told you Charlie's been gone all day and last night. That's all."

Gene pushed closer, forcing the door against her, opening it wider. "I want to check your house."

"Leave us alone," Naomi repeated loudly. "I'm not bothering you. Charlie hasn't done anything. You're always suspicious, making Charlie nervous, upsetting him. Now just go away, Mr. Tippetts, go away before I start calling the police because you're on my property without permission. See, I can do that, too. I can call the police on people who come on my property." She husked at him angrily, her little face contracting.

Gene let go of the door. The driveway was empty.

Maybe she was telling the truth. "Okay, I'm going to leave, Mrs. Reece. I'm sorry I bothered you. But you know damn well this is the first place anyone in the neighborhood is going to come when funny things start happening. Your son's been caught fooling with four dogs we know about, so don't tell me I'm out to get you. I don't care what you and Charlie do, as long as you leave the rest of us in peace."

"Charlie didn't have anything to do with that business."

"I'm not going to argue with you."

"He wasn't arrested. Nothing happened."

Gene came closer to her. The room behind Naomi was dark, and a faint smell drifted out from it, a clinging stink he couldn't place. "Well, so there's no mistake, Mrs. Reece, if I find out Charlie had anything to do with my dog getting out, or if he took my dog, I'm going to the police. Maybe the others didn't want to, but I will. So you tell him that, if he's thinking about doing anything in the future."

"I've got to close the door. I can't breathe." She rasped heavily, and he let the door shut. Inside, the lock was bolted.

For a little while Gene checked around for the puppy, making silly noises to attract Hattie's attention. He was ticked off at Naomi Reece, but that was nothing new. She was a bad neighbor, plain and simple. His mood was crappy as he walked home. Some day off.

Before going in to breakfast, he studied the backyard-door latch and Hattie's collar. There was no way the puppy could have gotten through the latched backyard door. He thought of Charlie again, but decided not to mention any of it to Eileen.

"No luck," he told her, and they had eaten a reasonably pleasant breakfast.

His crappy mood had dissolved as the day became brilliant, blue and crisp. Andy, his oldest, soon stopped crying, and Aaron hardly noticed the puppy's absence. When they got to the stores, Eileen brightened, and the day took on a wholly fresh feeling.

The problems right now were to keep the kids together, to pry Eileen away from the furniture salesman, who kept insisting she just sit down at the mahogany dining table, and to do a little grocery shopping. With the kids scampering around them, she was trying some soft sell. "It could be an early Christmas," she said, holding his arm tightly, "and you could count it as my birthday."

"We can't swing it this year, babe, even if we counted everyone's birthday." He grabbed Andy to keep him from hitting Aaron. "Next year maybe. This year we paint the house."

They had lunch out, with a minimum of arguing between the kids about who ate what, and when they got home in the early afternoon the biting winter air made them all frisky. He found himself holding Eileen more often than usual, and he wrestled with the kids on the floor.

There was an old movie on TV, and Gene watched it from the couch while Eileen put the groceries away. He'd promised all hands another patrol for Hattie after dinner— and that he would put up a couple of signs around the neighborhood if she still wasn't found. Andy took out the garbage. It was his newest chore. Gene thought the day off had turned out pretty well until he heard the frantic running feet and Andy's babbling cries. Now what? He found Eileen soothing Andy, trying to stop his hiccupping, frightened crying. She looked up, bewildered.

Gene went out to the garbage pails, the sounds of the commotion trailing after him. The bundle of papers Andy had carried lay scattered on the ground in the alley, and the metal trash-can top, glittering in the harsh afternoon sunlight, was beside it.

The puppy's body was on top of the old bags of garbage. Its severed head, eyes open and filmy, the pink tongue stiff, had been tossed casually onto a torn-open box of shredded wheat cereal, like a grim offering plate to a god of offal.

CHAPTER II

ONE

Fraser didn't get out of court until three in the afternoon. The notebooks he carried were uncomfortable under either arm, but he resigned himself to the annoyance for the short walk from the courthouse to his office.

Just outside the courthouse, on the broad plaza, was a small party, cameras clicking, people laughing and hugging. There were brightly colored formal dresses and corsages. A dark-haired bride and groom, at the center of the loudly talking group, kissed again to applause.

Fraser heard them mixing Spanish and English. He tried not to stare at them as he passed. The stocky groom was rumpled in his rented, apricot-colored tuxedo. He had one arm firmly around his new bride, who kept putting her hand to her mouth as she giggled. It was not at all like his own wedding to Kate. Her father, one of the largest rose growers in the state, had wanted a big wedding. Kate had wanted it, too. She had probably never considered anything else. The idea of a civil ceremony, a busy clerk handing over a certificate, and then the brief flurry of fun in the shadow of the courthouse, wouldn't have entered her mind. She came to him in a church, in a crush of yellow and red and white roses, perfuming the air. It was a very big wedding, with an equally big reception afterward, and by the time it was over Fraser and Kate had gifts enough to fill three cars, including her father's Cadillac. Fraser was very happy with Kate. She was very happy then too, because she didn't know that this bright young lawyer was going to join the district attorney's office in a few months. Kate undoubtedly had a different picture in mind, and Fraser hadn't said anything to make her think she was wrong. That was his fault, he realized. She had thought he was going to be like his father—a member of a respected civil law firm, a partner after five or six years, settled in with an income and prestige. It took her by surprise when Fraser turned down his father's offer to join the firm.

Perhaps that initial misunderstanding between them had been crucial, had tainted everything that came afterward. He didn't know. All he could do was chart the descent. Perhaps love was like the idea of justice—spontaneous devotion to either one declined gradually into an obligation, and then, one day, became onerous beyond words. The prospect terrified him. A union sanctified by as much expense and ceremony, and with as many patrician dreams as theirs, had to last forever. But it wouldn't. Fraser walked a little faster. It wouldn't.

He knew that the groom was watching him warily, and the bride looked quickly away. Does he have a record? Maybe, Fraser thought. Maybe they think I can sense these things and read their minds. Under his feet, as he hastened by, in the cracks of the sidewalk, were old dried bits of rice, the remains of countless civil ceremonies at the courthouse, marriages sent out with as much hope as his had been.

The building that housed the offices of the District Attorney of Santa Maria County was sludge-colored and soared monotonously for five stories that were like segments of a tapeworm.

Workmen had scraped the name of Gleason, the outgoing district attorney, from the glass doors where it had sparkled in gold-leaf lettering for sixteen years. Fraser had lost an old friend and ally when Gleason had been defeated in the last election. But more than that, Gleason's departure had meant that one more part of Fraser's life was being uncoupled from the rest. It was as if he was being suddenly, inexplicably, separated from the most important things in his life. With Gleason gone, he didn't even know what would happen to his job.

The workmen were carefully putting in the name of the new man, Spencer Whalen. Fraser counted four small hand trucks carting off the old D.A.'s files and mementos, while dollies smoothly wheeled Whalen's to the fifth floor.

He caught his own reflection in the glass doors. Outwardly, he looked severe in a gray pinstripe suit, black shoes, a navy blue tie—a man as solidly filled out as he'd been in the days when he'd played baseball in college. His hair was marked with gray already. He moved without hesitation, but without lightness, either. No wonder the bride and groom were nervous when I passed, he thought. I look like a small-town cop.

He was the supervisor of the Major Crimes section. He took the stairs to the section's offices on the third floor, behind a county subgroup that handled dental insurance records. The signs to the offices were unintentionally misleading, yet Fraser had never really wanted them fixed. Like him, those who needed to find their way to Major Crimes always would.

In Major Crimes he dealt exclusively with murder. Every intentional killing of a human being committed in the county came first to Fraser for appraisal. He and his attorneys decided whether the killing became murder, or something else. He made order out of violent chaos.

He nodded to Sally Ann as he walked in. Things didn't look quite right. She was sitting at her desk, barricaded, as usual, on three sides by files and telephones, but there were two men he didn't know lounging in chairs outside his office. The door was closed. He put his other pains aside for the moment.

"Hey, Tony, you can't go in."

Fraser paused, his hand on his office door.

Harry Ballenger, an older lawyer in the section and his former supervisor, came loping up. "You can't go in for a while."

"Somebody in my office?"

Sally Ann hooted loudly.

Ballenger drew him away by the shoulder. "Let's get away from the door." He smiled at the men. "In a minute, gents."

Fraser let himself be pulled to the other side of the room. A small Christmas tree decorated with ornaments and lights stood in a corner. Sally Ann had hung a little banner over it: "It Better Be Merry!" Fraser put his notebooks down on a table, glad to be free of their weight. Ballenger assumed a serious pose. "I had to borrow your office, Tony. You were out. It was the only one available."

"Who are those guys?"

"Federal narcs."

"Who's in my office?"

"Cardenas. The narcs are going to talk to him after I'm through."

"Cardenas is going to talk to you after three months?" Fraser was surprised. Cardenas was Mexican Mafia, and he had refused to say anything to law enforcement about his role in the assassination of a counselor in a federally funded drug-rehabilitation project.

"He's already talked."

"What did you give him?"

"Nothing. I didn't give him anything."

"Great. Let me have my office back." He was puzzled by Ballenger's reluctance to let him go.

"I can't. Give me twenty . . ." He looked quickly at the wall clock. ". . . no, fifteen minutes, and you've got your office."

Again, Fraser heard Sally Ann's derisive hoot. "Okay, Harry, give me the rest of it."

"What? Cardenas is using your office. He'll be done in fifteen minutes. Why don't you go out, get a cup of coffee? Go upstairs and pay your respects to Whalen. Kiss his ass or whatever he wants."

Fraser turned toward his office. Ballenger caught him by the arm.

"You'll screw up my deal," Ballenger pleaded.

The feds looked with bovine interest at Fraser.

"I've got a lot of things to do," Fraser said, "and I don't feel like having some con keep me out of my office. What's he doing? Making unlimited long-distance phone calls?"

"No . . ."

"What's he doing?"

"He's got his wife with him."

Fraser finally chuckled. "They're both in there?"

"I promised Cardenas a contact visit if he talked to me. He talked. So I gave him his visit."

"What's going on now?"

"Well, they're inside, I guess," Ballenger looked at the clock again, "and contact has been made by now."

"On the couch, I hope, not my desk."

"Cross my heart, Tony, I told Cardenas to keep the place clean. Really. I told him."

"What's she look like?" Fraser asked.

Sally Ann looked over at them with faint amusement. "Not your type, I swear. She doesn't look a *bit* like me.

22

All's I saw was a lot of eyeliner and a hell of a lot of hair.''

"That's my office you're using as a trick pad," Fraser said to the feds. "I guess you guys don't get duty like this very often."

The feds laughed. "This is the first time."

"Well, I'm going to pull the plug now."

"Suit yourself. They've been real quiet in there." One of the agents looked quickly at Sally Ann to see if she was embarrassed.

"You can't shock her," Fraser said. "She's been here too long. Sally Ann, would you ring my office?"

"Tony," Ballenger said, "just a little longer."

Sally Ann dialed, and they heard the phone burr behind the door. The feds waited expectantly for the show. Fraser felt obliged to keep everyone happy, but all he really wanted was to get Cardenas out of his office. He wanted to go to sleep in there.

"He's been inside for a year, Harry," Fraser said, taking the phone from Sally Ann. "I don't want him to wear himself out. And we've got to think of that poor woman, too." One of the feds laughed without opening his mouth.

Ballenger sighed. "Nobody ever gives the old master a chance anymore."

"Mr. Cardenas?" Fraser said into the phone. "The game has just been called. Time's up. Please arrange yourself and come out, because I'm coming in."

A moment later, his office door opened. A short, black-haired man stood there fastening his belt. Behind him stood a woman.

"Thank you so much," Fraser said.

Cardenas looked at Ballenger and the clock. "I got ten minutes coming."

"It's out of my hands," Ballenger said.

The feds gathered Cardenas up. His wife came out, and the two embraced. They spoke softly to each other. The feds separated them and took Cardenas. Ballenger spoke to him and the man shrugged. His wife didn't look up after he had gone. She walked out quickly, her eyes downcast. Fraser let her pass by. He envied Cardenas and the woman. They were reduced to hurried intimacies in a strange office while guards joked outside, and yet that had been the best Cardenas could expect for talking. He accepted it. And the woman: She had come to him, knowing what it would be like. That was devotion or loyalty or love, whatever name was attached to the bond between them. He did envy them, and wished he hadn't been reminded that an undamaged bond such as theirs existed.

TWO

"Help me clean up, Harry," he said, and Ballenger followed him into the office.

"There's nothing to clean up," Ballenger said proudly. "I told you they'd be careful."

Fraser fixed a cushion that had fallen to the floor and made sure his desk was still locked. "I told them not to touch anything," Ballenger said when he saw Fraser jiggling the drawers.

Fraser sat down heavily and rubbed his eyes.

"You want me to tell you what came in?" Ballenger pointed at the clipped reports on the desk.

Every day, detectives from police agencies strolled in with new murders for Fraser to evaluate, assign or reject. He didn't feel like reading this latest batch. "Go ahead and tell me what we've got."

"Two homicides. One's a stabbing, one's a shooting. And a couple of supps."

"Anybody in?"

"One guy. Arrested right after he shot his best friend for twenty-five dollars and eighty-two cents. The other homicide, a woman stabbed her neighbor."

Fraser could already see the final dispositions. The shooting would become voluntary manslaughter. The stabbing would be anything from second degree down to a pat on the back, depending on how wretched the deceased neighbor had been.

"The supps are on the nightrider shootings. Couple of weeks ago, and then two, no, three days ago. You remember?"

"The man who was jogging and got shot from a passing car?"

"That's it."

"What came over?"

"The cops found a witness to a similar shooting. A guy was parking his pickup one evening and this beige or white or maybe off-white Chevy drove by. Ping, ping. He ducked and got nicked in the ankle. Anyway, he gave a tentative ID on the car. Dented and scratched, older model."

"That's not very good."

Ballenger nodded. "But when you put it together with the last shooting, we've got the same car. Witnesses say the guy was shot at from an older-model, white Chevy-type car."

He tried to match Ballenger's interest in the puzzle. How did Ballenger find the enthusiasm year after year, case after case, when motives and brutality were confounded with each other? If anyone should be weary, it was Harry Ballenger. Fraser often felt sorry for him. He was older. He had been Fraser's supervisor when he first joined the office, and now Fraser was his. Ballenger had been passed over for every important assignment in the last three years, and the meaning of that was clear. Major Crimes, for better or worse, was his last stop.

It might be his reckless manner or the rumored laziness of his lawyering that had frozen him. When Ballenger had been sent to the hospital for ulcer tests, which proved positive, some enterprising law student working in the section had ventured into the dark, wild clutter of Ballenger's office. He'd found stacks of old files stretching back to before Fraser's time, files stuffed into drawers, spilling off the desk, hidden behind bookcases. When Ballenger returned and found his office cleaned up, he roared that it had taken him years to collect those files. He called them his reference materials. Office gossip toted this up with Ballenger's long lunches and his early departures and said he was too lazy to close out old case files, but Harry hinted mysteriously that he had his own filing system. He said vaguely that he'd reveal it someday.

Fraser was glad Ballenger didn't seem to mind having him as the section's supervisor. He liked Ballenger, and found that Harry often had an unusual and useful perspective on a case. He was one of the few people, along with Sally Ann and Gleason, that Fraser trusted. But he didn't trust Ballenger enough to tell him what was happening.

Instead, he said, "It still sounds like kids taking pot-shots from their car and hitting this guy by accident. I don't think it's anything else."

"There's only one person in this car. The driver is the only one."

Fraser didn't have the energy to pursue it. He gave up. "I could be wrong."

Ballenger stretched, his vest and shirt drawing tightly over his round shoulders and stomach. "You look pretty beat up."

"The Yamato and Willis hearings took longer than I thought. Maybe I'm coming down with something."

"How about a little relaxation later? I can clear out a little early today."

"You can clear out early every day, Harry. Sure. I'd like that. Stop by before you go." At least Ballenger could get him away for a while, and that was better than nothing. He didn't want to admit it, but a sense of panic lurked very near now. It was only just kept in check.

When he was alone, Fraser puttered around, filing notes from the hearings, arranging the notebooks. It was the routine he fell into now when the outcomes of the cases no longer interested him.

On his desk was a red-bound book, poetry by Yeats, a gift from George Sutton Fraser to his son Anthony on the occasion of his graduation from law school. He hadn't read it until a month ago, when the strain with Kate had grown almost palpable. His father, as far as he knew, was unfamiliar with poetry in general, and yet his gift was a book of Yeats. It was as if George Fraser knew his son would need to read it someday, and the words a cold old lawyer couldn't say would be there. *"For all things turn to barrenness,"* and Fraser heard his father in those words. It was like his father to speak through a third party.

Fraser put the book down. He was tired. If only he could sleep better; perhaps it was that simple. He had gotten four hours the night before, and five before that, and the nights stretched behind him for months that way. He couldn't count the nights Kate had found him wide awake at three in the morning. She slept very lightly, and he tried to get out of the bedroom without waking her, but almost never did. It had grown worse lately, and often he lay in bed feeling alone, too tired to stay fully awake, too alert to go to sleep. It was as though he was waiting for something in those long, dark hours of the night.

Kate knew something troubled him, but he couldn't admit her to the jumble in his head, or tell her about the feelings that picked away inside him like small animals. He drifted beside her, aching and sleepless and waiting.

> *For all things turn to barrenness*
> *In the dim glass the demons hold,*
> *The glass of outer weariness,*
> *Made when God slept in times of old.*

It may be one of the reasons they were drawing away from each other. It wasn't Molly, or the separateness in their lives that poor Molly's short life had concealed for a time. It was hard to stay with a man who seemed to be far away, listening to something you couldn't hear, waiting for something you would never see.

But, for all the feelings he still had for her, he wasn't sure Kate would ever understand. She unhappily accepted his decision to become a deputy district attorney, consoling herself by imagining his work as a sort of chivalrous battle. Later, she discovered the violence, the gore, the things he did, and tried to avoid talking about his work. They rarely discussed it. When he came home they pretended the world revolved around anything but the people and things he saw every day. It was better, infinitely and beautifully better, when Molly took up their time and talk and thoughts. But Molly had been dead for six months.

Fraser put his head down on the desk. He didn't want to lose Kate, too. She was bright, sensitive, with a fragile insouciance about life. He knew that it terrified her, this looming possibility of hostility between them. However strenuous his efforts to anchor her to his life, Fraser feared she would leave. Like Molly, gone forever.

That's why I'm panicking, he thought, I can't stop any of it. I see it. I know every minute what's happening and I can't change it. He imagined a crab with its legs torn off.

I don't have any choice.

Sally Ann laughed raucously outside. Her laughter and benign flirtations were part of the familiar but no longer comforting landscape of his life.

He reached behind him into the Yamato notebooks and found a thick envelope, taking a large stack of photos from it and spreading them in front of him. They were scenes of the Yamato house taken by the sheriff's crime investigators. Dr. Yamato, an orthodontist, had strangled his wife of fourteen years and then partially dismembered her. The pieces he'd stuffed in clear plastic bags. These he had hidden poorly behind cement bags in his garage. After five days, her friends grew worried. Mrs. Yamato's disappearance, and her husband's sudden departure with their children, were reported to the police. It didn't take long to find what remained of the woman. There had been a small heater in the garage, and the doctor had left it on for some reason.

Most of the pictures in front of him showed the garage interior. Some included measuring sticks to show scale. They recorded an utterly ordinary assortment of tools and junk, skis and sleds, boxes, lawnmowers, a washing machine with its lid up, broken chairs, a rusted barbecue on two tilted legs, a snappy picnic umbrella of orange and white. The rest of the pictures were detailed shots of the cement bags and the plastic bags. In the murky bags could be made out shapes and colored liquids, suggesting the distended embryos of a creature long vanished from the face of the earth. These were its forgotten eggs, and the discernible parts, those fingers pressed against the plastic, a mass of hair splayed out like a mermaid's drifting on the ocean, were the yet unborn taking shape. That was what Kate would choose to see, he thought. But these bags wouldn't hatch, he knew that; though they did vomit out their contents at the coroner's office, lying under white lights, on metal tables with gutters. That was the final series of pictures.

Here the truth was revealed, stripped of romanticism and imagination. A still recognizable face, the eyes clotted open; a hand curled in a twisted gesture that suggested disdain; some of her clothing—all of it demonstrated that this had been a woman and not some mythical beast. The rest of her body, as it ended below the face or above a wrist, had turned to sloshing jelly in the garage's heat.

Fraser would show these pictures to the jury in the trial of Dr. Yamato. The defense would object—Killigrew would puff and make absurd noises—and then the jury would see these things. Fraser knew how the jurors would react. He wondered what his father would have done, a man who considered himself tough as well as sophisticated. The old man was no more capable of seeing these pictures than was any gentle housewife. As for the jurors, some of the men would stay oddly stony, their jaws tight, some women would cry, one or two always gagged. Somebody might even faint. Most would merely wince. But all of them, all of the accountants and housewives and retired electricians, would see and remember for the rest of their lives something previously unimaginable.

Fraser looked at the whole series of pictures without flinching. He wasn't a medical man, so he couldn't even look clinically at this wreckage of a human being. He had only an amateur's conception of what the various anatomical sights meant. He was otherwise just like the jurors. The difference was that he didn't mind these sights anymore. He could look at the photos for hours without effect.

The other evidence of his profession filled his large office. Besides piles of photos there was a tan mannequin with black dots and arrows marked on it. These indicated bullet entry and exit wounds. Charcoal and watercolor sketches from his trials were hung on the walls, gifts from television stations that had covered the stories. Below the sketches, in boxes and draped carefully over books, were clothes, tennis shoes, shirts, a pair of hiking boots, a pair of brown pants cut up one leg to the knee, all identified by evidence tags, the leftovers from an acquittal. A victim's clothes. Fraser lived with it all.

The farce with that clown Killigrew, the sad little game with Cardenas, that's what his pursuit of justice had turned into. How long could he keep up the pretense of interest, the appearance of righteousness? Through the Yamato trial? The one after that? How long, finally?

Fraser saw one poem in the Yeats book. *"Dance there upon the shore/What need have you to care/For wind or water's roar?"* The title leered at him. "To a Child Dancing in the Wind."

Without thinking, he tore the page from the book.

THREE

In the beery, dark, warm sanctuary at the back of the Pine Room, Fraser drank with his coat hung behind him on his chair and his shirt sleeves rolled up. It was noisy and smoky, and he could barely see into the rest of the bar, where a band of Irish patriots was bellowing out a hymn to the grand old country. Ballenger sat across from him with his tie loosened, talking loudly.

"Can I go on with my story?"

Fraser nodded. "Sure."

"I don't want to hear any more about your screwed up marriage."

"Falling-apart marriage. There's a difference." Fraser drank. "Sorry I mentioned it."

"Okay. So . . ." Ballenger smacked the table. "So old Leydig comes sauntering in, and he says, do you have the ducks? I say, no, it's a case of shooting ducks out of season, and I've got this game warden ready to say he saw old mister hunter shooting his ducks. But Leydig has his eye on a golf date or something. No ducks, no case, he says to me."

Fraser managed a genuine smile at Ballenger's antics. They didn't fit a man who was nearly sixty and heavyset, with a hearing aid plugged not very well into one ear. He had been a lawyer for thirty years and a deputy D.A. for most of that time. When he told stories, he leaned backward a little, like a comic inviting a pie in the face. He was the only man Fraser knew who wore suspenders. Every so often he dipped his fingers into the glass of stale club soda in front of him.

"I don't remember Leydig," Fraser interjected sloppily. The drinking was muffling him without deadening any of the pangs he had felt all day.

"He's been dead for years. Shut up now. So we go through this whole damn court trial, and the old coot hunter gets Leydig thinking he said blow job. Judge cups one ear, did you say you were giving this court a blow job? Naw, naw the old coot turns red, I said the D.A. is giving you a snow job. But Leydig is pretending he didn't hear. He gets mad. You can't give this court a blow job, he hollers, and fines the old coot."

Fraser laughed more loudly than he had intended to and tried to think of a war story. Ballenger waited expectantly.

"I can't think of one," he said after a moment. He tried to summon up one incident from over a decade as a lawyer. It was all hidden away.

"Leydig was a character." Ballenger worked to keep the conversation alive, as he had for hours. "He was down doing traffic court."

Fraser finished his glass. "I don't want any more Leydig stories, Harry." He called for another drink and sat back in his chair.

Right behind him, at the only other table in the cramped rear of the bar, he heard Judge Strevel say, "You guys hold it down. Phantom and I are locked in mortal combat."

Fraser squinted. Phantom was a squat old lawyer in a red sport coat and gold tiepin. Strevel, glasses cockeyed, had wangled him into a dice game. Phantom had earned his nickname by being hard to find around the courthouse, either by judges, bailiffs, or clients. Fraser patted his arm genially.

"He cheating?" Fraser asked, pointing at Strevel.

"I haven't caught him."

"Let's go, Phantom," Strevel said, lighting another cigarette. "Let's go."

"I bet he's cheating," Fraser said. "You better watch him."

The judge paused and poked his glasses to get them on his nose correctly. "Holy moly me," he exclaimed, "by all the little saints, here's Master Fraser out and about at this hour. Why, it's nearly nine. He's been here, what? Four hours? What's the world coming to?"

"Since three-fifty and counting," Fraser corrected, holding up his new glass, the ice in it hard and silvery.

"Well, I don't know what's happening. Here's a man you could set your watch by. I've seen punctual guys when I was at Justice, but this man was so regular you could set court recesses by him." The judge kept a vigilant eye on Phantom's jangling dice tosses. "You tell him to file motions an hour before a hearing and he files them one precise hour before the hearing."

"He is cheating," Fraser said again, with an edge in his voice.

"Lunch time rolled around, and regular, punctual Fraser was coming out the door at the D.A.'s office right at twelve, not before, not after. If you told him to be in court at eight-thirty to go over instructions, he'd be there at eight-thirty with a couple more instructions and some motions and maybe a couple of memos on the law for you. I got there at nine, of course." Strevel's face was hazy in its shroud of smoke.

"He's keeping me company," Ballenger said. "I had to get out a little early."

"I think it's a sad state of affairs when I can't even count on Master Fraser anymore. I mean"—the judge avoided Fraser's eyes—"what's happening to our safety if he's not at work the entire afternoon and into the evening? Who's protecting us? What will he be like in the morning? What will his wife say about his sudden new hours?"

"She won't say anything," Fraser said.

"Whoops. Pardons." The judge grinned. "Touchy subject, I guess."

Fraser grabbed Strevel by his soft shoulder and swore. His anger built suddenly and whitely.

With uncharacteristic speed, Ballenger got between the two men. "Take it easy." He pulled at Fraser and glared at Strevel, who sat still, his cigarette fixed languidly in his fingers.

The judge smiled at Fraser. "You don't want to bust me. I can still beat your ass."

Fraser leaned forward but Ballenger tugged him back. "We're calling it a night, Tony," Ballenger said hastily. "See you later, Pete." He hoisted Fraser up, pulled his coat roughly over one arm, and marched him off.

"Night, gentlemen." Strevel ground out his cigarette and went back to berating Phantom for cheating.

Fraser let Ballenger push him through the bar. "You don't have to hang around."

"I like breaking up fights between old friends."

Ballenger hung on stubbornly as the two of them walked out past judges and lawyers they knew, packed into various corners. The Irish wailers looked maudlin as Fraser weaved by, sighing wetly in their beers. Like Yeats, he thought bitterly, and then he and Ballenger were out in the cold, on the street.

"Let's get out of here."

"Take it easy." Ballenger struggled into his coat. He rubbed his hands together briskly. "Okay, where to?"

But Fraser was at an impasse. He didn't want to go home and face Kate and risk embarrassing her. He was angry and ashamed at the same time about that. No, he couldn't go home. He didn't want Ballenger clinging protectively to him, either. "Why don't you go on, Harry? I'm okay now."

"No, no, I don't have to be anywhere. Sheila doesn't mind where I am tonight."

"I don't need a baby-sitter."

"How you going to get around? Take a cab?"

"Yeah, I'll take a cab."

The remark sounded peremptory, and he regretted it. "I'm sorry. Didn't mean that." He licked his lips. It was very quiet outside the bar. The street was deserted. A neon NOEL in red, white, and green was the only color he saw.

"It's okay," Ballenger said easily, "you've been wound a little tightly lately. Hell, you haven't taken a vacation in a coon's age."

"I've got to do something, Harry. Things aren't going too well right now."

Ballenger shoved his hands into his coat pockets. "Soon as you find out how you stand with Whalen, I think you and Kate should just take off for a couple of weeks."

Fraser shook his head. The air refreshed him a little. He tried to imagine the healing powers of a few weeks' vacation. It wasn't enough. It wasn't enough by a very long way. "No, it's more than that," he said.

"What're you going to do? Change jobs? Go with some private firm? Start back ten, twenty grand and do goddamn insurance defense work?"

Fraser wanted Ballenger, more than anyone else right now, to know the sense of loss and fear he felt.

Ballenger went on. "Look, Tony, you're a trial lawyer. I'm a trial lawyer. We're both lifers in the office. I've been in trials so long I wouldn't trade it in even if I could." He was excited and it gave him a slightly manic look. "I've been in trials so long I've got colitis, spastic bowel off and on, let's see, what else? A couple of ulcers, a slight heart murmur, my eyes aren't worth shit anymore, and before we call a jury panel in, even now, I've got to take a piss so bad I could cry. It doesn't sound like it's worth it, but it is. I know I couldn't do anything else."

"It's not worth it."

"I don't see *you* doing anything else."

Suddenly, Fraser felt sick to his stomach, partly from the liquor, but largely because what Ballenger said was true. Ballenger looked at him. "I'm going to take you home. Take a couple of deep breaths, and tell me if you're going to upchuck before we get to my car."

He swallowed and breathed. "I can make it."

FOUR

Ballenger knocked on the front door after hauling Fraser up to it. He leaned Fraser against the house. "Well, this is as far as I go. I don't think Kate wants to see both you and me. You're bad enough."

"Come on in if you want to." His tongue was thick, and his voice sounded distant. "She's kidding, she's only kidding about you."

Ballenger was already heading back to his car. "I've had my fun for the night." He waved good-bye.

The door opened as Ballenger drove away. Kate, in jeans and one of Fraser's old shirts, looked out. "Hello, stranger. Do you need a hand?"

He nodded heavily.

She took his arm and put hers around his waist, guiding him inside and toward their bedroom. He felt ungainly against her graceful body. He was shorter, heavier beside her swimmer's delicately toned firmness. In summers past in Monterey she had teased him about his puffing efforts in the cold opaline water while she swam easily and beautifully, her ash blond hair swaying in the ocean. That was years ago. That was an age ago. He'd thought she was fragile then. Even now her dark eyes went to him every step or so, and he thought he still saw the shy, too-innocent child she must have been. Kate wasn't fragile. She was bruised now, he thought; she'll get better. He covered his awkwardness by being bluff.

"Harry brought me home. That was pretty nice of him, wasn't it? He's a pretty nice guy. You ought to like him."

"I suppose I should." She grunted as he slowed down. "Try one foot after the other; one down, then the other."

He rested his head against her. "You're getting good at this."

Kate eased him over to the bed. "I didn't know I'd get so much practice."

"You worried?"

"I didn't know where you were. I called your office around five and they said you were gone."

"Long gone, long gone."

"We could have celebrated together."

"Wasn't a celebration."

"Then what was the occasion?"

He fumbled as she slid him down on the bed, swinging his heavy, lifeless legs over. "I don't know. Guess it *was* a celebration. I raised bail on someone."

She doesn't laugh anymore, he thought. I can't remember what that sounds like now. Kate was a very good mimic who saw surface mannerisms and caught tones quickly, playing them back again in accurate yet silly ways. She used to double him up with renditions of the pouty, affluent girls at the private school she'd gone to before college. Her depiction of the bickering Mahons, when George and his wife were publicly airing their differences no matter in whose home, was funny because it seemed, at the time, so wildly improbable that anything as comic-operatic could ever happen to them, too.

She worked over him coolly, undoing his belt, loosening his tie. He heard a little of what she said, but it came intermittently across a darkening, deepening chasm. "Do you want to get undressed?" She was unbuttoning his shirt.

"I know what you're up to." He sat up awkwardly and laid his hand across her breast, trying to kiss her. He was aware that she was turning from him.

"I don't think either of us is up to anything now." Gently she pushed him back on the bed.

"Missed you all night. Almost punched a judge because he made a crack about you."

She looked at him, one hand on his chest. "What crack?"

"Nothing. Forget it. He said you wouldn't care, that's

all. Didn't care, something like that. Almost hit him. Harry stopped me. Old Harry.''

Kate knelt by his feet and untied his shoes, slipping them off. "I do care, Tony. I wish I knew what was happening to us now. I wish I knew that more than anything in the world.''

Grimly, he sat up again and put his face against her cheek. There was a spark of warmth where their skin touched.

"I'm sorry,'' he said.

"For what?''

"Making you stay here. I don't know what's going on. It just goes and goes and goes.''

She had gotten him as ready for sleep as she could. She unfolded the thick comforter at the foot of the bed and pulled it over him. "I know it does,'' she said gently. "My knight.''

Kate stood and turned off the light.

"Where are you going?'' He spoke so quickly the words sounded imploring.

"I'm going to read for a while. It's only nine-thirty.''

He could barely make her out, silhouetted in the doorway, slim and sad.

"Come back.''

"I think I'll stay in the guest room, Tony. You're a little ripe for me in here.'' She said it without recrimination.

He closed his eyes. A revolving wheel spun him around and up and down and around in the still blackness. The room was dark as well when he opened his eyes again. Kate was sliding into bed alongside him under the covers. It was after midnight.

"I'm sorry,'' he said.

"You don't have to keep saying that.''

"Yes, I do.'' His hand moved to hers and held it tightly. She touched his cheek and kissed him.

"Go to sleep. You can let it go for once, Tony.''

He did feel the fatigue enfolding him, humid and impenetrable. There was something he had to tell her, though. He had to tell her about Donelli's courtroom. "I saw Molly today,'' he said.

"What?'' she whispered, turning on her side to face him in the darkness.

"In court I saw Molly when she was little. It was her. I did see her.'' He looked at Kate. "I really did.''

She didn't answer, but she hadn't moved since he said it. He could feel the tension in the body so close to his. She didn't even breathe. Then she said, "I see her too, sometimes."

Kate put her hand on his face, stroking it. "I didn't know we both did. Poor Tony." She said it very softly.

Then she turned away again and his eyes fell shut of their own awful weight.

The telephone rang at four in the morning. It always rang at four in the morning, and Fraser suspected it would continue to ring at that hour.

The voice buzzed incoherently in his ear. He swallowed against a dry, gummy tongue and felt an ominous churning in his stomach as he sat up in bed. Kate was awake. Again the voice buzzed.

"Hold on, wait a minute," Fraser said with his dry, gummy tongue. His words were almost chewable. "I can't understand you at all."

"Sorry, Mr. Fraser, I guess I expected you to wake up right away. You awake now?"

"I'm awake."

"Okay, this is Mel Sanderson. We met a couple of times. I'm working Homicide-Assaults now."

"Sanderson? At SMSD?" He rubbed his eyes with his free hand. "You're Hopalong, right?" Fraser pictured a heavy, red-haired man. Sanderson had killed three men during a riotous summer. He was with the Sheriff's Department.

"That's right." Judging from the voice, Sanderson didn't like the nickname. "We met a couple of times over in court."

"Well, that's fine, Mel, that's fine. What can I do for you?"

"See, Mr. Fraser, we got something here, and I figured someone from your office, maybe even Mr. Whalen himself, should be in on it, kind of, so you can call the shots if you want to, when we catch this guy." Sanderson sounded cautious, and Fraser wondered if he was with someone. The room turned slowly about him, like a Ferris wheel coming to a stop.

"What have you got?" he asked, with as much snap as he could muster.

"Triple homicide, Mr. Fraser."

"I'm not the normal Major Crimes deputy on duty tonight, Mel. I think you should be talking to the regular night call deputy."

An almost imperceptible pause at the other end. "I know you're not the normal one. You're the supervisor. That's why I called. I'm going to give you the address, and I think you should come over before we move things around too much. It's a triple homicide, two women, one man. All shot. But it's worse than usual, and that's why I called you. You'll want to see this. There's going to be a lot of noise on this one."

"What is it? Gang? Anybody prominent involved?"

"Nothing like that, Mr. Fraser. You better come over here and see for yourself."

Kate whispered something to him.

"I've got to go out," he whispered back.

Sanderson went on talking. "I've never seen anything like this, ever. Nobody has."

"Where are you going?" Kate asked. "Do you feel all right?"

He shook his head, trying to hear what Sanderson was saying. "Repeat that again."

Fraser knocked over a lamp when he tried to turn it on without taking the receiver from his ear. He swore. He found a piece of paper and wrote down the address on Mission Drive that Sanderson slowly repeated.

CHAPTER III

ONE

By the time Fraser got to the coroner's office, set on a quiet street under shade trees, the sun had been up for several hours. Earlier he had watched, from that house on Mission Drive, as the dawn enlarged from a streak of orange piping at the horizon to an eruption of white and blue. It matched the still small blaze newly ignited in him. He was light-headed, amazed and yet pleased by the speed and vigor with which the thing had captured him. He had never expected to feel this exhilaration again.

"I'd like your first impressions of the victims," Fraser said when Dr. Mahon pattered softly back into the office, handing him a plastic cup of coffee.

"Did you see them?" Mahon blew carefully on his own coffee.

Fraser nodded. "At the house a couple of hours ago. A sheriff's detective called me."

Mahon clacked his dentures nervously. He wore a tweed coat with elbow patches. He had a soft handshake and pouched eyes and he looked like someone who should hold a volume of Hawthorne rather than a cadaver's liver. He seemed to be a professor of American literature lost in a morgue. But he was indeed a pathologist. When Fraser had met him for the first time six years before, he had noticed a medium-size bottle on Mahon's desk, alongside his calendar and silver-edged framed photographs of his first wife and grandparents. The bottle, as far as Fraser could tell, had clear fluid in it in which something pale white floated. He made out the hint of a cuticle, and it was with a little disgust that he asked Mahon if the thing, however improbably, was a toe.

"This has great sentimental value, Mr. Fraser." The pathologist picked up the bottle. "It's like the first dollar a man makes in his business. I've had this since my first autopsy."

"*Is* it a toe?"

"It's a big toe. I assumed it would be the least likely thing anyone would miss." He shook the bottle gently. "The damn thing should last forever."

Fraser soon came to realize that Mahon's appearance was a poor guide to the man. The soft edges were a disguise. His intelligence and judgment were keen and well respected, and over the years, Fraser had cultivated Mahon and his wife. He and Kate were Mahon's first friends when he came to Santa Maria.

"It's atrocious all the way around," Mahon said. "I operate on the assumption that I've seen it all, and I probably have, in the sense that it takes some to get to me now. But I'll tell you, that atrocity got to me."

"It's almost unbelievable."

Mahon nodded, frowning a little. Fraser knew him well enough to see that Mahon was shocked not only by the ferocity of the murders, but by being confronted with something that defied every precise measuring device in his laboratory. There was no scientific standard to help him deal with this.

"From the top," Mahon said. "The victims were all killed in the same fashion. The cause of death is fairly obvious, gunshots to the head, small-caliber bullets, probably a twenty-two is my guess right now. The victims were killed almost execution-style; one shot, then two afterward."

"The other wounds didn't kill them?"

"No, they were not the cause of death, at least I don't think so. The head wound came first, then the others."

"The man, Henderson, he was no different from his wife or Mrs. Ellis?"

"They all died in the same way, and about the same time. The male victim was not mutilated. I think Mrs. Ellis may have lived for a short time before she died, but I don't know now."

"I think that's important down the road, George. If she lived while the mutilations were going on, that's another charge I can add."

"You're thinking a little ahead of me."

"What about the other wounds?" Fraser was impatient. He needed to learn as much as he could, in simple terms, about the complexity that had confronted him a few hours before.

Mahon's dark eyebrows drew together. "Well, preliminarily, the two women were severely mutilated. You saw that. Both Mrs. Ellis and Mrs. Henderson had their breasts cut off. Mrs. Henderson was mutilated in the vaginal area, too, but Mrs. Ellis wasn't. The eyes of both women were damaged. Mrs. Ellis was sodomized."

"I didn't know that."

"She also had a mass of excrement in her mouth."

"Human?"

"I don't know that yet. I'll be able to tell you by the end of the day. These women were eviscerated in a crude fashion, butchery really. I don't envy whoever gets this case in your office." Mahon watched Fraser and slowly drank his coffee.

"I don't know who's going to get the case." Fraser didn't want Mahon to know how fascinated he was already. Almost from the moment he walked into that house and saw the bodies, he felt a jolt, electric and riveting. Something beyond the horror had beckoned to him seductively.

"Isn't it going to be yours?"

"We've got a new boss, George, and Spencer Whalen may have different ideas about who should be doing things in the office. I don't even know if he's going to keep me on as Major Crimes supervisor."

"You're the obvious candidate for this one. You've handled all the other big trials in the last while."

Fraser managed a thin smile. "Times change."

Mahon nodded and said, "Well, I've got all sorts of evidence, once you find this bastard." He hit the word hard. "You'll have a damn good circumstantial case. I haven't done eliminations from the victims yet, but I believe we've got the killer's hair. We've got semen samples from the Ellis woman. We've got saliva from her, too, because he drooled on her back. There's a partial footprint in blood. You should be able to tie him up very nicely."

"I'd like to do something more than tie him up." Fraser began tapping a pencil, tap, tap, tapping, thinking of what he'd seen.

"That's the problem with being civilized." Mahon's lusterless eyes were ironic. "I take it there isn't anything to suggest a burglary or a robbery?"

"No. The house was undisturbed, except for the bedroom and some blood in the living room. I don't think this was a robbery that went sour, and I don't think it involved anybody the victims knew."

Mahon, for some reason, looked at him sadly. "No, well, I didn't think it was anything like that. That's why I don't envy whoever gets this case. You've got a crazy man—and with this kind of evidence, one who can make an insanity plea really take wing."

Fraser stopped his pencil-tapping. "If I get this case, believe me, there isn't going to be any insanity verdict. Not after what this man did."

"Then you're going to have a very tough row to hoe, Tony. These women were missing organs, for example. It varies for each victim, but the hearts, lungs, pieces of the liver, and kidneys were removed. That sounds an awful lot like out-and-out lunacy to me."

"They weren't brought over here?"

"No. Nothing."

It was still drawing him on as Mahon described the full extent of the acts, that new presence, as yet indefinable and without definite form, but beguiling, whispering to him alone, apparently, because even a man like Mahon saw only the outward signs. Fraser experienced something much deeper. He couldn't say precisely what it was. "Couldn't the organs have been displaced when the victims were cut open? Accidentally?"

"Well, that's the whole point," Mahon said, finishing his coffee in one long swallow. "The bodies were cut open to get *at* these organs, God knows why. That was the reason for the massive wounds." He watched Fraser again. "I honestly hope you don't get tapped for this one."

"Why?"

"I have a theory about crimes," Mahon said, "big crimes with a lot of publicity and crimes of special ferocity. I think they're destructive. I think they taint whoever comes close to them. They distort and twist the police, the judges, the D.A.s, everybody. I really don't think that truly terrible crimes can be handled by our legal system."

"We do it every day," Fraser said. "You can't just give up."

Mahon shook his head sadly. He seemed distressed. "No, I know that. I wish there was some other way out."

"Summary execution?"

"Well, as I said, that's the problem with being civilized. You narrow your choices." He sighed. "How's Kate holding up, by the way?"

They had gotten to the door. Mahon opened it, and the subdued clinking, tinkling, bustling murmurs of the lab came in. How was Kate holding up? It was understandable that Mahon should have thought of her, and of being civilized, almost together. "She's fine. Busy as usual. Why don't you see if you can't swing dinner with us next week?"

"I'd like that," Mahon said. He shook Fraser's hand. "I really hope someone else gets this one. Let him get mired in this thing."

TWO

For a short time after he left the coroner's office, Fraser was uncertain where he should go. He drove toward his office, then changed his mind and turned toward home. He was tired again, and kept slipping back in his mind to that house last night. The place had been unusually animated for four-thirty in the morning. At the edges of the darkness neighbors and gawkers in motley clothing were being held back by a couple of deputy sheriffs. Eight squad cars and a large crime-scene van, their blue and red lights pulsing slowly, seemed to talk to each other over their radios, the voices echoing softly from car to car. Fraser parked nearby. Still in a boozy fog, he walked past cars that crouched around him in the dark, like big cats with feral eyes. Then he was in the house. He had remembered his gold badge, and he pinned it over his coat pocket.

The house was ablaze with lights, shafts streaming wildly, crookedly out of the windows and the open front door. Men in various uniforms—deputies, city police, coroner's assistants—crept through the living room, flashes scattering light as still pictures were snapped of every part of the room, the sofa, the floors, the stains. Like archaeologists, ID techs from the sheriff's department brushed dark powder on window frames and doorways, on a coffee table, then bent over to examine the latent marks, while others measured with steel tapes. One man dug carefully at a bullet hole in a sofa cushion.

Fraser spoke to the men he recognized. They pointed him toward the bedroom.

Inside, he saw the old man, then the two women. He took the sight calmly at first. Sanderson greeted him and began talking about what they'd found. No signs of forced entry. Nothing missing. Still checking the victims' clothing.

Apparently a freshly washed knife in the kitchen might have been one of the murder weapons. Sanderson led him into the bedroom itself.

It was in there, like a flash going off in his face, that he first noticed how special, how very different this crime was.

Five or six men were crowded into the small bedroom. He watched them muttering to themselves, shaking their heads, their faces unnaturally pale. He noted that it was a blue room, as though he sat in an empty swimming pool painted blue at the bottom. It surrounded him, that blue. As Sanderson talked, Fraser saw a small suitcase on the floor. Almost at once he trembled deep inside himself. Back from a business trip and walking into the blue room, without any warning, without any protection. The young woman, Ellis; her husband had come back from a business trip carrying that suitcase. Fraser imagined the convulsion that must have ripped the man right out of the room at the instant he saw what was on the floor. Back from a trip. Expecting nothing. I've got years of it for armor, he thought, but that guy was naked. He came naked to it.

Sanderson pointed to things, to the bloody measuring cup, a ghastly bit of normality alongside the telephone. He pointed to the tracks in blood along the carpet. He was eager to show and to please Fraser. But Fraser saw and heard something else.

The bodies were vivid red splashes that clashed jarringly with the blue room. In their loosely draped arms and gaping wounds and holes, more than mere chance lay slyly before him. If he could go beyond the poor dead women, with their dreaming dead expressions, a pattern would reveal itself. An orderly arrangement existed for him to see. He sensed its force, its tangibility. There was more here than the dead bodies, the blood, the blueness. Here were the thing's leavings and its track tantalizingly laid out. Here was a command left to him, written in flesh and death. Explain this, it whispered, make sense of me.

The bodies were covered, then taken out. He thanked Sanderson for calling. He acted composed, if a little tired and drunk. Nothing hinted to the others that Fraser felt a revelation was at hand.

From that house he had watched the dawn come . . .

When he got home it was almost eight A.M. Kate was already gone. A hurried note was pinned to the kitchen table saying that she had a million places to be, meetings, lunch, and would be home around seven. That was fine. He would be undisturbed all day. Usually he was at work by seven-thirty at the latest. He called Sally Ann and told her he was under the weather and wouldn't be in. He undressed, took a shower, and got into his pajamas. The bed was neatly made and he slipped gratefully but cautiously into it, as one would put a secret letter into an envelope. The house around him was full of creakings and groanings in the winter morning. He ignored them and went to sleep. It was a deep, perfect sleep, the most complete he'd had in a long time. When he woke up it was nearly evening, already dark, and he hadn't dreamed at all.

"Tony?" Kate called. He heard her putting down grocery bags and jingling things. He wanted to see her, yet even so, Fraser was resentful. He needed to be alone.

"I didn't think you'd be in bed," she said. She was dressed stylishly in a gray and black outfit. If she had been standing nearer . . . Fraser imagined his hand moving up her thigh. He had done little more than imagine the last few months.

"I've picked up something."

She sat next to him and felt his head. "No temperature. Is it the flu or a cold, do you think?"

"I don't know."

Kate kissed him, then got up and went to the dresser, checking her hair and makeup in the mirror. "It was a hectic day." She found something imperfect at the corner of her fine mouth and began delicately smoothing her lips, her eyes focused with determined interest on the operation. "I ended up spending four hours at the Cities League and we had a big, big debate, I guess you'd call it, about the City Hall plaza. I had the debate," she laughed slightly, still correcting her mouth, now moving upward to her eyebrows, smoothing them with quick, expert brushes of her fingertips. "Did you ever meet Bob Hollis?" She turned halfway from the mirror to look at him.

"I don't remember. I don't think so."

"Well, he's the planning man. He tells us how the plaza will look, how everyone will love it; he likes to just order you.'' She ran her hands back along the tan length of her neck to her shoulders in pleasurable fatigue. ''So today he tells us that the access paths will not be planted with trees. That was it. I said, Mr. Hollis, do you think Santa Maria should have a plaza around its City Hall just barren in the summer and depressing in the winter? I said it pleasantly, but he got my message.'' Kate turned to face him. She went on, her finger poking the air. ''I've asked you about these trees, I said, for two-and-one-half months. You can try and put me off until the next meeting, but I'm going to come after you on this until you do what's right.''

Fraser nodded automatically, watching her reenact her victory.

''I think that's what turned things around, Tony,'' she said. ''We took another vote and the trees are in.''

''I'm glad you got what you wanted, Kate.''

''It's just because I had the best idea,'' she said. ''One thing I learned at home was to be persistent. The times I went to dad's office, watched him do things with people, he never raised his voice. But he always got what he wanted.'' Now Kate looked at him intently for the first time. ''Did you feel this bad at work?''

''I've been in bed all day.''

He saw concern flash over her. ''You should have called me.''

''I didn't know where you were. Besides,'' he tried to lighten it, ''this Hollis guy might have gotten away with it if you left. It's nothing much.''

''Nothing? Tony, I can't think when you last took a day off. You must feel terrible.'' She sat next to him again. ''What can I do for you?''

''I need to get some rest, that's all. I'll feel better later.''

''Should I make something light for dinner?''

Fraser shook his head. ''Nothing for me.''

''I was going back out,'' she said, ''but I can stay with you.''

''Don't screw up your schedule, Kate. It'll be quieter here if I'm alone. I can sleep.''

She stood up abruptly. ''You don't want me to stay,'' she said in a voice he had heard too often in the last acrimonious winter months.

46

"There's nothing you can do." He answered as her voice required. It was becoming a demeaning ritual that neither of them sought.

"You'd rather I wasn't around, in your way, talking all the time, spoiling everything. You'd like me to just walk around here with my mouth zipped shut. You don't have to listen to Kate. She can't shut up and she can't do anything."

"Will you calm down? I didn't say anything like that. I said it'll be quieter. That's all I said."

She went to the closet, opening the door with one hand, her arm stiffening. The door swung wide from the force she used. "You never *say* anything, Tony. It's the way you look at me." She roughly changed her shoes and took a heavy beige coat off its hanger with a single hard pull. "I have some importance, you know. I'm here. I exist."

"I never said you didn't. I just wanted it quiet. I guess I just need to be alone."

Kate stood at the bedroom doorway. "Fine. You will be." She turned and seemed to dissolve into the blackness of the house beyond the door. Fraser listened to the distant, muffled sound of the car as it drove away. For a little while he lay in the darkness, hearing the night wind brush the skeletal branches of trees across the rooftop. . . .

Near one in the morning, he woke in darkness. Kate was asleep beside him, the wind sighing faintly and dissonantly around them. He barely made out her features, softened like a child's who has cried itself to sleep. Now, with new cunning, he managed to get out of bed without waking her. He was suddenly very hungry and he made himself a sandwich, wolfing it down, then got back into bed. His mind was working now. He felt at peace. What he had waited for had now come to him. It's mine, he thought. My case.

My case.

Kate's light, tense breathing and the faint wind mingled and Fraser slept.

Cold morning air filled the kitchen when he went to Kate. She was making breakfast for them both.

"I'm staying home again today," he said.

She stopped scrambling eggs. "Tony, I'm sorry I got angry last night. I didn't mean it."

"I know," he said untruthfully.

"Do you want me to call the doctor? He might be able to give you something."

"No, I'll be okay." He turned to go back.

"There was a story on the radio."

He stopped.

"Three people were murdered, and they kept saying it was very brutal. It was a horrible thing, they said." She started scrambling the eggs again. "Did you hear about it?"

"I went there. That's where I was yesterday morning."

"I suppose you'll get it?"

"I think so."

She came over to him. Her hair was uncombed but it hung almost neatly on her shoulders. Her face was unlined and clear.

"It's not fair," she said vehemently. "They've got other people. Give it to Ballenger, or anybody else. I know what's going to happen if you keep it. You won't think about anything but the case. I'll be living here by myself, Tony, just like after Molly died. We don't need that all over again."

"It won't be that way. Believe me."

He stepped toward her, but she was ready for him. "How can it possibly be different? Haven't you as much as told me that it's the goddamned murderers who kept you from falling apart when she died? Do you know how that makes me feel, Tony, when you say things like that, when you tell me being away from me, being all wound up in a murder trial, is what saves you? I'm not even part of your . . . your prescription? I'm nothing?"

Fraser tried to touch her, but she stepped back, bumping into a chair that grated over the shiny floor. "I need more comfort than that," she said. "I deserve more."

"Yes, you do. I never said you didn't."

"Then give this case to someone else."

"No," he said. "I have to keep this one."

"Other men don't have to keep hurting people they say they love."

"It's my responsibility," he said, his anger finally rising to meet hers. "You apparently don't understand that as well as I thought you did."

"I wish you thought about your responsibilities to me. You didn't think about your responsibilities . . ." Her hand clenched suddenly. She stopped and put her hands slowly to her mouth. Her eyes were closed for a moment. "Just say it. Say you want this case, the one they said was brutal."

"I do want it. I wish I could explain it to you." He felt drained as he approached the mystery. "The best I can do is say it's very important for me to win this case. I know that sounds strange. Nobody's been arrested. We don't know anything about the killer." He reached for Kate again. This time she let him put his arms around her. His words whispered in her ear. "I saw something yesterday, Kate, and it just got to me. It won't let me go."

"What am I supposed to do?"

"Bear with me. I promise you things will be different afterward. I promise."

Kate gently pushed him away and went to the range. "You just won't forgive me," she said, moving a fork slowly through the eggs. "And you won't let me do anything about it."

"There's nothing to forgive."

She laughed curtly. "Molly was my fault. I did something wrong."

"You never did anything wrong," he said fiercely. "You never did anything wrong."

"And all the little Mollys yet unborn." Kate turned off the burner. "I guess you're just not going to let me off the hook for any of it."

"I've never blamed you for not wanting kids so soon." But it was empty of honesty and the wrong thing to say.

"You can have breakfast," Kate said. She left the kitchen and Fraser waited there in a chair, his robe thin protection against a stray chill, until she got dressed and went out. He called the office and said he wouldn't be in.

He stayed in bed all day, getting up only to go to the bathroom or to bring some bread back to bed with him. The phone rang off and on for several hours. He didn't answer it and went back to dozing.

The phone woke him up again in the afternoon; it rang for a long time. He took it off the hook.

In the early evening he pretended to be asleep when Kate came into the bedroom. A moment later there was a strident banging on the front door. "Don't answer it," Fraser said, "they'll go away."

Ballenger shouted, "I can see your damn lights. I know you're in there."

The pounding went on, and Kate headed for the door. "I've got to answer that even if it is Harry."

Fraser followed her to the living room. She opened the door, and Ballenger and Sally Ann trooped in.

"Hi, Katie," Ballenger said jovially, then to Fraser, "Your phone's busted, you know. I've been calling you all day."

Distastefully, Kate turned from Ballenger to Sally Ann, and glanced at Fraser. She knew he'd only pretended to be asleep and that the phones were working. "How are you, Sally Ann?" she asked politely.

Fraser sat down on the couch. He had on an old bathrobe with tattered cuffs. Ballenger plopped down beside him. "What's up, Harry?"

"Well, no phone, no Fraser—Whalen's been getting jumpy. He's got an investigator ready to come over here. He thinks there's something wrong. Is there?"

"Everything's fine."

"Helluva long siesta," Sally Ann said, laughing at Kate's worried face.

"That's good, that's a real relief," Ballenger grunted happily, "because Whalen wants to see you bright and early. At first we told him you were out sick. Then he found out you were over at this murder scene and didn't bother to tell him. He's a little exercised about it."

Sally Ann piped in. "He's about to have a stroke." She sounded delighted at the prospect.

"I'll see him first thing." There was no way to avoid it any longer. Fraser saw Kate gamely trying to talk to Sally Ann. Suddenly, he wanted Ballenger and Sally Ann to leave. They upset Kate, especially Harry, whom she had never liked very much since finding him earthily rambunctious once after a party. Fraser wanted to at least spare her this discomfort, however minor it was in comparison to the greater one he could not. "Thanks for stopping by, Harry." He rose.

"Hey, have you folks eaten yet?" Ballenger asked.

"I don't think we could," Fraser said.

"No, not tonight," Kate agreed.

Ballenger shrugged and walked to the door with Sally Ann. "I want it noted on the record that I did my part today. He was asking where you were. He asked everyone where the guy in charge of the case was. I held him off as long as I could, but then he started talking about sending an investigator over here, and your phones weren't working, so I figured we'd better drop in. I was getting hungry, too."

"He gave the case to me?"

"Of course he did." Ballenger didn't seem to hear Kate's intake of breath. "Another thing, Tony, he wants us to call him Spence. Not Mr. Whalen or Spencer. Just Spence. Can you see Gleason doing that? Sounds like he's crew captain at a goddamn prep school."

After they had gone, Fraser told Kate, "I really don't have a choice."

"I'm going to have to get used to being really alone."

He hugged her gently. "You'll never be alone. I promise you that."

CHAPTER IV

ONE

It was a gentle kiss Gene Tippetts gave Eileen as she stood next to the car door. Andy squirmed anxiously on the front seat, banging his feet against the dashboard until Gene sharply told him to stop.

"He just doesn't like the idea of going to the dentist," Eileen said.

"I know. But he was denting the car."

She was wistful. "When you coming home? Are you just going to drop Andy off, or can you have lunch?"

"I took the morning off, hon," he said. "I better get back to work as quick as I can. I'll run him up to the dentist, get him home, and then I'll shoot over to the plant."

"Be nice if you could stay."

"I can't."

"I'm sorry you called the police the other day. There should be some other way."

She was bringing it up again. He took her hands, whispering it in her ear so that Andy couldn't hear. "Hon, we both know Charlie Reece killed the dog, and I'm not going to let him get away with it."

"You know what I mean," Eileen said. "I don't want to get them mad at us. I don't want us to have any trouble with them." She shook her head angrily. "They're not going to move. They know nobody likes them, but they still won't leave."

Gene brushed his hand over her forehead. "There's no trouble. The police will take care of everything. This is our house. This is our neighborhood. We're staying. So if Reece comes near our house again, I'll break his neck." He thought uncomfortably of the dog's body in the trash can.

Eileen pecked him on the cheek and stepped back as he got into the car and backed it slowly into the street. She waved at him, and he thought she looked tiny somehow, standing in the driveway in front of the house.

"Wave 'bye to Mom," he said to Andy.

The boy wiggled his hands in the air.

They slipped into the street and drove away.

Eileen stood watching for a moment before going back into the house. It was chilly outside, depressingly gray and misty, as if winter would never end and brightness had been banished from the earth.

Boxes of Christmas lights were stacked near the door, and she almost tripped over the plastic wreath Gene had unearthed from its year-long hiding place in the garage. Putting the decorations up was one chore she looked forward to. They would brighten things up.

Aaron was in his room, delighting in this unexpected liberation from his brother, even if it was only for a short time. She heard him rummaging around, talking to himself, his toys bonking and banging. She went to the kitchen, turned on the small portable TV that sat beside the sink, and watched a morning show while she did the dishes. Her hands dipped into the foamy water, the tapwater flushing suds down the drain with a liquid gurgle. A diet doctor was talking to a couple of overweight celebrities and advocating the heavy use of vitamin C, the more the better. He also wanted people to eat more liver. She gagged at the idea. Her fingers made the clean, wet plates squeak. The diet doctor was going on and on, about all sorts of revolting things to eat that would make you feel full of pep and energy while the pounds melted off, when Eileen heard a car easing into the driveway. She washed another dish and put it into the plastic rack, drying her hands on the towel hanging over the ''Think Thin'' notes clamped by magnets to the refrigerator. Maybe Gene had forgotten something.

She turned around. With that damned doctor laughing and talking so much, she hadn't heard him come into the kitchen. But there he was, standing only a few feet away, looking funny, different, his hair unwashed and tangled, with deep blue black whiskers and sunglasses, wearing his red parka and jeans, carrying a little brown bag tightly.

''How'd you get in here, Charlie Reece?'' she blurted out. Her voice sounded angry and fearful to her.

He made a small sound and suddenly seemed to fall part way over to one side. He might be sick. It didn't even look as though he'd heard her. He moaned slightly.

''What are you doing in here? Go on home right now. You hear me? Go on. Just go on.'' She tried intimidating him as if he were a naughty dog. He kept making that odd sound, then straightened up.

''Can't go yet,'' he said, so softly that she barely heard.

''I want you out of my house,'' Eileen said firmly. He frightened her. He was spooky, just popping up like that, making weird noises. Gene wouldn't tell her what he'd done to Hattie. Behind her was the rack full of clean dishes, clean spoons, clean forks, clean knives.

''Go on,'' he said, herding her.

''Now, look here, Mr. Reece . . .''

He took a little black gun from the paper bag and pointed it at her. He was making a whining sort of noise, his lips squashed rudely together, revoltingly, monstrously.

"Go on." He pointed toward the living room.

"Oh, please leave."

From the other part of the house, she heard playing in the boys' room.

"Aaron," she breathed.

TWO

Kate heard the clock intoning the hour. Chimes tinkled eight times, fading away into the mist and cold outside the house. It'll come in a second, she thought. A breath after the last chime fell silent, a mechanical click signaled peace for another quarter of an hour. She liked the sound of that click and waited for it. It meant an appointed task completed. It meant quiet.

Kate stood away from the living-room window. Tony had been gone for a half hour. Only eight, she thought. So much time.

She went upstairs. The hallway leading to the guest room was white and that was where Kate found herself. It was a pleasant room, filled with as much light as the gray day permitted. Light from the windows fell over the bed and dresser and small chairs, the mirror, and the flowers printed on the wallpaper. Kate sat down on the bed, her feet on a tan rug.

This was Molly's room. As Kate remembered exactly, the crib had stood where the dresser was. The diapers and bowls and bright toys alongside it were always hung and folded neatly. So many times she came in here to tend or feed their daughter, sitting with her in a rocking chair, looking out the windows as she did now, seeing the same trees, the other houses in orderly ranks beyond the trees.

Kate moved her hands across the bedspread, and the dread she had felt when holding Molly returned. A dread mixed with love and such affection for the bewildering small flesh that was part of her. I loved her as much as he did, she thought. I'm her mother. She was my daughter. The incantatory words came over and over. I loved her. I loved her, Kate thought, looking again out Molly's windows.

The last thing Kate did at night was to look in on Molly. Molly was older then, grown enough to sleep in a small bed with wooden bars where the crib had been. Kate put her head in a wedge of light from the hallway into the darkness of the room. The wedge fell across Molly's face and hair. It was all Kate could do not to shudder. I loved her, she thought again uselessly. How can a mother fear her own child? How can she fear the very idea of children?

Downstairs the clock moved inexorably and chimed; Kate listened tensely in the silence that followed.

THREE

From practice, Fraser ate in small bites, his silver fork clinking melodically on the delicate china plate. The old D.A. used to call on people unexpectedly at these breakfast meetings, and Fraser assumed that Whalen would continue the tradition. Fraser had no wish to sit there with scrambled eggs falling out of his mouth while he tried to speak.

"Has everybody been served?" Whalen asked, rising to his feet and rapping his heavy red knuckles on the tablecloth. "Go on eating, and I'll start talking. I know you all have places to be this morning."

At least Whalen got credit for improving the surroundings of the meeting. Fraser thought this dark walnut conference room, sheltered even from the muted murmurings of the rest of the El Dorado Club, was a great improvement over Gleason's coffee-and-doughnut sessions in the old training room at the office. Fraser hadn't been back to the club since the days when his father had brought the family there for holiday dinners.

This was the first formal meeting of the senior staff, and Whalen had come prepared to impress them with his competence. At his right sat the new chief deputy, Tim Infeld, idly pushing a piece of paper. He was thin and didn't eat. On his left sat Whalen's secretary, her pen poised to record every word. As they were being served, she leaned toward Fraser and said respectfully, "He's a very masterful man," with a glance at Whalen. She had been plucked from the clerical staff because of her enthusiastic support of Whalen's campaign. Fraser agreed noncommittally while she took picky bites from a sweet roll.

"The recent homicides in this county have outraged everyone. Me included." Whalen raised his eyebrows at Fraser. "We've got to be right on top now. Tony Fraser's handling the case, and he's got complete authority to act. Now you can tell anyone you meet, or anyone who asks, that when we catch this suspect, we will charge him, we will prosecute him, we will not bargain, we will not deal, we will ask for nothing less than the death penalty. Isn't that the way you see it, Tony?" Whalen put the question as if Fraser disagreed.

"That's exactly how I feel, Spence."

"You see, my friends, I know some of you didn't vote for me. I know you don't know me at all. But I promise you I intend to turn this office back into the finest D.A.'s office in the whole state. I intend to show the state—and maybe the country—how a crime like this one is handled in Santa Maria County. And I'll tell you right now, if you can't handle it or hack it, I'm not going to mollycoddle you like my predecessor. You can get off the boat right now."

Whalen went on like that for some minutes, rapping the table, raising his hoarse voice, his slate gray eyes hard on the senior staff.

"Tony, give us a progress report," he said, sitting down abruptly and waiting coldly for Fraser.

This hadn't been on the morning agenda, but Fraser had expected it. He rose easily. "There isn't much to report now. Mel Sanderson and several detectives at SMSD, along with the city police, are developing some leads. We have a description of a man, twenty to thirty years old, about six feet, weight about one hundred forty or fifty, thin, wearing a red jacket, sunglasses, unshaven, near the scene at the time of the offense. Mel is checking that out. That is more or less where we stand."

Whalen muttered impatiently, "I hope they get off their butts."

Fraser sat down, intending to use the pretext of an eight-thirty court appearance to leave. His presence at the breakfast, after that command performance, wasn't necessary. Each time he tried to get up, however, Whalen kept him there with a whisper about something, so he sat through several progress reports and a lauding of Whalen by his new chief deputy. His secretary led a spatter of applause when it ended.

Finally, Whalen motioned Fraser away from the table and over to a buffet where a large silver coffee urn stood. He busied himself. Infeld was reciting a manpower-change program for the staff's benefit.

"I have an appearance soon," Fraser said.

Whalen dumped lump after lump of sugar into the coffee. "The other day we really didn't have a chance to get acquainted, Tony, and I can't leave you with any erroneous impressions. I'm going to pass by this little bender you went on."

Fraser was startled by the bald charge. "Bender? What are you talking about? I wasn't drunk."

"Tony, I know whereof I speak. I know all about benders, believe me." Whalen reluctantly sipped the heavily sweetened brew. "And you were so drunk it took two days to sober up. Normally, I'd tip my hat to you. If you can grab it, go for it. But this case was breaking, and I couldn't find my Major Crimes supervisor. We can't have that happening ever again." Whalen's pinkish face broke into a grin.

"I don't need admonitions from you," Fraser said. "I have a very good idea of my responsibilities."

Whalen sipped again. "Infeld's outlining my staff reductions, cutting all the fat that's built up around here. Every section is losing people, Tony. Every section means yours, too."

That was it. Fraser saw the bully revealed. "Nobody's ever touched Major Crimes before. We're shorthanded now. We have too many cases."

Whalen shrugged impotently. "You've got to give up one deputy. I'm not going to debate the point." He drank his coffee and eyed Fraser over the rim of the cup. It was an odd sight for Fraser, those sausage-thick fingers curled around that thin, elaborate little china cup.

"Who?" he asked, to prod Whalen. He obviously had someone in mind.

"How about Ballenger? My summaries say he isn't pulling his weight anymore."

Whalen knew Ballenger was his oldest friend in the office. He was Fraser's soft spot. The only question was what, precisely, Whalen wanted to gain from this.

"Not Ballenger," Fraser said. "I'm not cutting him or anyone in my section."

The thick reddish wrist came up in front of Whalen's face. "Tony, you're late for that eight-thirty appearance."

"Don't play games."

"Someone has to go." Whalen put his cup down.

"What do you want? What's the point? You could have told me you wanted a staff cut anytime. You didn't have to do it here in public." His voice was raised and several people turned from Infeld's recitation to listen.

"Well, you and I can make a deal." Whalen was unaffected by Fraser's anger. "You can keep Ballenger. In fact, you can keep everyone in your section, and what's more, you can stay the supervisor. In return, you don't go on any more benders during this case, or get sick suddenly," he laid biting stress on the word, "or leave town. And you keep me informed, step by step, of what the hell is going on in your bailiwick."

The grossness of the man astounded Fraser. He was an incredibly clumsy blackmailer.

"I always intended to keep you informed. I do know my job."

"I think you do, too. You need a little bit of incentive now. This is it. You can use your loyalty to the office, or to your pal, or whatever you want, but whatever it takes to get it from you, I'm going to get a goddamned prosecution from this horror story, and I mean a prosecution that'll be talked about."

An explosion of anger filled Fraser, worse than what he'd felt toward Strevel. He was going to hit Whalen or resign.

No, he wasn't. The case was his, and he would not give it up for anything, even Kate's saying he should. Whalen, of course, didn't know that. He was a political animal who felt insecure unless he had some chain wrapped around anyone in his view.

Fraser mastered his anger. His lips were dry and he felt tight in the chest. He had picked up one of the coffee cups without thinking. Now he put it down so gently in its china saucer that the two exquisitely brittle and bright surfaces barely tinkled.

"I know my job," he said without raising his voice.

FOUR

The dentist's waiting room had the antiseptic, rubber odor of all waiting rooms, and Gene tried to ignore it as he picked up the morning newspaper. The young receptionist had closed the frosted glass of her cubicle so he couldn't see her, and there was no one else waiting with him. He flipped the pages. Had to get past that headline, TRIPLE MURDERER STILL SOUGHT. City seemed to be full of nuts suddenly. Charlie Reece killing dogs in his neighborhood. Some guy chopping people up in the east part of town. Spoiled the Christmas season.

Gene was proud, though, the way Andy had gone in like a trooper, no whimpering, just right in with the dentist and right into the chair. Tough little guy when you actually came to it.

He looked at his watch again. Almost an hour. That meant a cavity, or two. He yawned and wished he had the day off. He'd take the kid home, he'd lie around, he'd do nothing. It was a nice picture.

From inside the frosted glass, from an area of whiteness and sluicing taps, buzzing drills, and all manner of silvery, terrible instruments of torture, he heard a whining noise as some mechanical monster started up. He imagined poor little Andy bravely sitting in the confines of the chair, mouth pinkly open, the bright lights blazing, and the dentist bending over him, bringing the whining, steely instruments closer, until the spinning drill tip, flashing so fast it couldn't really be seen, touched the tooth and started vaporizing enamel.

Gene winced at the thought. He hated the idea of pain.

FIVE

"I hate the idea of that knife. Don't like it at all." Judge McKinsey sat on a couch in his chambers with the lights dimmed to a funereal gloom, an old afghan tossed over his legs.

"The alternatives aren't very good," Fraser said. McKinsey, he'd found out, was set for an argument, and he happened to be handy.

"My friend, I've been in more hospitals than your father and your father's father stacked together. I've had it. I don't want them cutting on me anymore. Now, isn't that my decision?"

"Sure it is. I just think you shouldn't be too quick to make it."

The judge spat tersely and tossed a cigarette butt into a full ashtray balanced beside him on the couch. He calmed down very quickly. It was a mark of his temperament. McKinsey had sworn Fraser in as a deputy D.A. The brief ceremony had taken place in these same chambers, only the two of them present, McKinsey putting on his robe, raising his hand, reciting the oath rapidly, and shaking Fraser's hand. Then, as he got out of his robe with the dexterity of a quick-change artist, he'd advised, "And remember, pal, when you've got them down, kick them in the ass."

Fraser thought highly of him. He was a roughrider and one of the last of his kind. As a kid, McKinsey had gotten into trouble, and even spent sporadic days in the old city jail. He was, in those days, regarded as a brawler and a braggart. Fraser's father, who rarely got into court, thought McKinsey's appointment to the bench was a mark of favoritism over ability. But McKinsey had always been able. He'd gone into the army during the war and had gotten a Purple Heart. When he came back to Santa Maria, he'd gone to law school at night and, to everyone's surprise, became a deputy district attorney. The office only had three lawyers in it, and McKinsey was commonly thought of as the first among them. After prosecuting for several years, he became a public defender, the only one, and he stayed at it until appointed to the bench. McKinsey liked making his own decisions. He was universally pegged as being independent.

"I don't want to talk about it anymore," he said, snatching another cigarette from the nearly empty pack. "Tell me why young Whalen's giving you a hard time."

Fraser had told McKinsey about the display that morning. "I can't really understand it. It makes some sense because I'm part of the old guard, the tired bunch he campaigned against. On the other hand, if I do a good job on this thing, Whalen can take the credit. I think he wants that more than anything. He wants me on a leash. And if I fumble, well, he's got a fall guy. He can wash his hands of me."

"That, my friend, is how the guy's acted all his whole damn life."

"I'm not going to make any mistakes," Fraser said. "If this case goes to trial, I'm going to win it."

The judge grunted. "Sure you are. I don't know any D.A. who wants to lose one. But a conviction off this booby, if the sheriff ever hauls him in? I don't think there's a judge or jury in this country that'd convict him. He's got a built-in insanity defense." McKinsey coughed again.

"George Mahon said the same thing. Who was that talking, judge, the former D.A. or the former public defender?"

"It's the lawyer. It's an impossible case, pal. Look at them." McKinsey pointed his glowing cigarette at a photograph squirreled away in the corner of his bookcase. It showed two neatly dressed young men with cardigan sweaters and crew cuts, flanked by two older men, both in suits, one of them a trimmer and more confident McKinsey. "The Rainier boys, Tommy and Kevin. Pretty good kids most of the time. They had jobs, no real records."

"They look like Ozzie Nelson's kids."

"I put sweaters on them to hide the tattoos. But they didn't need much cleaning up. We went to trial because these two charming children had gotten an old woman, an aunt, I think, and tied her up with electrical cord. Then they tied it so she'd strangle, putting the cord around her neck and feet. Then they left her on the living-room floor, hog-tied. Then they both sat there and watched."

"What was the defense?"

"There's the kicker. I defended Tommy. This was back before there were shrinks all over the courtroom, and all this exclusionary crap about evidence, too. Almost everything came in. We were in front of Ullrich, Teddy Ullrich, and he was such a rollover, he'd let us bring in the Brooklyn

61

Bridge. I put on a couple of shrinks, but they were for show. What really turned the trick was the D.A. He did it. He proved, I mean he *proved,* that it took this old lady about forty minutes to lie there and choke to death.''

Fraser listened closely, because McKinsey might as easily be talking about his trial.

"I got up and repeated what my shrinks said," the judge flourished his cigarette, "and made that jury remember how long it took this woman to die. They came back in three hours. Not guilty by reason of insanity for both the little charmers.''

"Psychiatric testimony isn't going to save this killer," Fraser said emphatically.

McKinsey coughed onto the back of his hand as he shook his head. "Buddy, I'm telling you that my jury came back and set these two loose because they couldn't believe that anyone in the whole wide world would sit and watch an old lady choke to death for forty minutes unless they were insane. You've got a guy who makes these kids look saintly. I don't even think the jury will leave the box before giving you an N.G.I. verdict.''

"I'm not going to make the mistakes the D.A. did in your case. I can get a conviction.''

"Means a lot to you?''

"Maybe a lot more than it should.''

"Sorry to hear that.''

The telephone buzzed, and one of its small lights flashed in the semidarkness.

"Jesus, Mother Mary," muttered the judge, flipping off the lap blanket and heaving himself upright. He walked to the phone, which sat behind his large, crowded, and disordered desk. He had a pugnacious walk, chest thrust out, hands dangling loosely, even though he was thin in the legs and had a large drinker's gut and his sparse hair was gray white. There's a lot of fight left, Fraser thought, no matter how much he complains.

"Yeah," the judge snapped into the phone. "Sure, sure.'' He held it out to Fraser. "Some guy for you.''

"I told the office I'd be stopping by here, judge.'' He took the phone.

"This is Sanderson, Mr. Fraser. I think we've got another one.''

Fraser felt an icy tingle uncoil, but he said calmly, "I'm with Judge McKinsey. I can't talk right now."

McKinsey swore and shambled out. "Hell, you can have the damn place. I'm not getting any more of a nap." He paused. "But keep an eye on old Spence Whalen. He may be too big to settle for just D.A. of Santa Maria County. In the fifties, when his old man took him to the cathouses on Ninth and Arroyo, Spence'd check to make sure he had ways to get out if there was a raid. He found every exit. He covers his ass."

"I'll keep my eyes open."

"Tell whoever that I'm up in the cafeteria for a cup of coffee, and if they send me any half-day divorces, I'm going home."

Fraser waited until the door closed. "All right, Mel, what's the story?"

"Twenty or twenty-five minutes ago a man named Eugene Tippetts brought his kid back from the dentist. He found his wife in the bedroom. Shot three times, small caliber, mutilated like the others."

"Had she been sexually assaulted?"

"I think so."

"What about the house?"

"Entry apparently through an unlocked back door. No signs of forced entry on any of the doors or windows. The bedroom was ransacked."

It was the same. It came in broad daylight, on quiet streets, in pleasant neighborhoods. Evil didn't announce itself anymore by strange omens or signs. It simply walked in.

"Where are you now?" Fraser asked.

"I'm still downtown. I'm going out to the Tippetts place as soon as I hang up. I wanted to let you know first".

"Good, Mel." Sanderson was obviously trying to win points with him, which was fine if it produced immediate results. Sanderson hoped to be useful, Fraser thought. He had ambitions like everyone. "Call me at the office right away when you've looked around at the scene."

"There was one additional thing." Sanderson hesitated briefly. "We're still checking it out. Tippetts says he has another son, about five. He was with the mother. He isn't at home right now. We're checking to see if she might have taken him to play with a neighbor or something like that. It could be a false alarm. The only definite thing is that he's not anywhere in the vicinity of the house.''

''My God. What could he possibly want with a little boy?'' The memory of the blue room mocked his question. Five years old, just about twice as old as Molly. They might have played together someday. Now she was dead and the little boy was missing. My God, he'd said without thinking. There was no divinity that could permit this to happen. ''I want to be informed, Mel. Call me no matter what you have.''

''Will do.''

Fraser hung up. There was another framed photograph near the telephone, a much younger McKinsey, an impossibly young McKinsey slogging through the snows of Germany in his fatigues and rucksack with a squad of other grinning young GI's.

The same God who allowed the Nazis to exist, who sat by while the fires were lit, watched from some great distance while McKinsey and others put a stop to that evil. No, you can't call on anything but yourself. His weapons lay in the law, his experience, whatever strengths he had on his own. McKinsey proved that years ago.

Fraser could prove it now.

CHAPTER V

ONE

No one at the office had a clear idea where Whalen was. Infeld suggested he might be at the El Dorado Club, holding a meeting with friends. His secretary speculated that a luncheon downtown had run late. But Fraser gave up trying to find him at that point. He'd let Whalen read about it.

His phone rang about an hour and a half later. He picked it up hungrily.

"Sanderson, Mr. Fraser." The detective's voice was tight with excitement. "I've been out here for a while and I've got some news. I think we've got a suspect. It's a little soft right now, but my gut feeling is that it's very good."

Fraser slipped a pen and pad from his desk, suddenly as breathless as Sanderson. "Go ahead."

"We've got a neighbor here named Frawley who saw a white Chevy pull into the victim's drive. He saw the driver, described as a white male adult, twenty to thirty, long black hair, six feet, six-two, one-fifty to one-seventy. Clothing described as old blue jeans and a red ski-type parka. He had on sunglasses."

"That's him. That has to be him."

"Now, the best part is that the witness knows this guy. He's a neighbor of the victim."

"He's what?"

"He's a neighbor, too. He lives at the end of the block. His name is Charles Edward . . . excuse me, Edmund Reece. Witnesses say he lives in a house down there with his mother. No one else."

"Where's the car?"

"It's not in the area. Nothing at the house, either. Witness didn't see it leave, he just caught it driving up. He thought it was strange because the victim and her husband have been having problems with this Reece guy for several months. The husband even reported Reece to SMPD for killing their dog a couple of days ago."

"Is the house covered now?"

"I've got two units on it. It's all quiet."

"How many units do you have out there?" Fraser began doing rapid logistical calculations.

"Six, two more on the way. If I need more, I think I can scrape them together fast. I've got twelve men right now."

"Have you got a want out for this Reece?"

"Done. Witness says he's got a job at a gas station someplace around here. I'm having them checked."

Of course he'd done that. Sanderson was a conscientious detective. Fraser asked for his own satisfaction. He wanted to hear that men were looking, places were secured, witnesses located. He wanted to be steadied by the routine.

There was a larger, more worrisome question, though. He doodled quickly on the pad. No time for reflection. "We've got a problem," he said. "Do you go into the house now or wait for a warrant?"

"That's the one," Sanderson agreed, not venturing any further. Fraser knew his own choice.

"Do you have anything more?"

"You've got it all."

The decision had to be made on this information then, and no more.

"Even rushing a search warrant through will take a couple of hours minimum, once we get a judge lined up," Fraser thought aloud. "That's after putting the package together and getting it over here. You've got sufficient cause to arrest this Reece now if he comes wandering home. You can stop him if you spot his car. He's a suspect in one murder, probably three others."

"And this is fresh as hell," Sanderson interjected.

"And we've got a little boy missing. Our suspect presumably knows where he is. No more word from the neighbors on that?"

"Just a sec." Sanderson's voice was muffled as he put his hand over the phone at his end of the line. Silence. Then, "Nope. The victim's husband doesn't think his wife let the kid go anywhere. But that's all."

"All right." Fraser ran it through his mind. "We've got a fresh lead and a suspect, and your witness doesn't know if the suspect went home or where he is." He tried to reduce the grisly possibilities to a mathematical exercise, a decision table, a formula. "We know he isn't at home, right? Is the mother there?"

"Don't know. I was waiting to talk to you."

"Assume she is. Does it make a difference? The child is missing, in great peril, from what we know, and we can cut a hell of a lot of time by checking that house immediately."

Fraser knew the risks, and he'd gone through all the steps, and his instinct was to rush forward anyway. "Do it. Go into the house now."

"Do we have to knock-notice?"

"Mel, he's armed, so I think you can take precautions. He's got the child, too. Go in there right now."

"You're saying we can break in?"

"Get into the house," Fraser repeated. "Don't seize anything, Mel, leave everything as you find it until I get there. Just get inside."

Sanderson was elated. "I'm on it." He clicked off.

Fraser hung up slowly, then went quickly to Ballenger's office two doors down. He didn't even reply when Sally Ann tossed a ribald crack in his direction. It was like the old days, this sudden need to go to Harry for advice on a case, asking him what ought to be done, what had gone wrong. He hoped he hadn't made the wrong decision, carried along by Sanderson's enthusiasm and by his own appetite.

Ballenger was bent over a diagram showing the movements and times of a murder. His lips moved as if he was talking to a jury. He smelled of oranges and hair oil, and his suspenders were down around his waist.

"We've got a suspect, Harry."

Ballenger glanced up. "That's terrific. When'd they pick him up?"

"He's still out. They've located his house, and I told them to check it out. They're doing it now."

"No warrant?" Ballenger whistled faintly. "How come?"

He explained the danger to the missing child.

"I see that." Ballenger pulled at his suspenders. He claimed it helped his thinking. "But you may give this guy a ready-made issue without the warrant."

"I know that."

"Sanderson finds anything in the house besides that kid—stuff from the other killings, say—and you've sent yourself up the creek. The first motion to suppress, and you've lost it all."

"I'm treating this as an emergency. We may save a life. I think I can argue exigent circumstances for a warrantless entry on that alone."

"It's a bitch of a choice. You can see saving this kid, catching this guy, and maybe getting some evidence, and then down the line a judge boots it all out and tells you, hey, friend, no warrant for the search." Ballenger took a few Maalox tablets out of his pants' pocket, spilling them onto his desk. He tossed three tablets into his mouth, chewing loudly. "You did the right thing. I wouldn't worry about it."

"I wanted to hear that, Harry," Fraser said. He hadn't told Ballenger about Whalen's threat that morning. Ballenger already knew he wasn't well liked by the new administration. This latest bad news could wait.

He gathered up his briefcase, dumping pens and legal forms into it. He buttoned his coat securely.

Sally Ann called over. "What happens if they raise the skipper while you're gone? What do you want me to say to his holiness?"

"I'll talk to him when I get the chance," Fraser said on his way out.

TWO

"I never thought that meeting was going to end," Kate's laugh had a brittle edge to it, "the way Allan let everyone, every single person get up and talk, talk, talk."

Her edgy fingers played with the menu. The man across from her at the small table nodded. She noticed he was watching her closely, his hands folded patiently, one over the other, on the tablecloth.

"It's good to know I've got at least one ally on the committee, Frank," she said to him lightly.

"Always."

She made a desultory review of the menu. The luncheon crowd was thinning out, and the waiters moved slowly among the remaining diners.

"Oh, I can't decide. I'll make up my mind when the waiter comes."

Her companion smiled at her. He seemed to be smiling and watching her all the time. The attention was not unpleasant.

"I'm glad you were free for lunch on such short notice," she said.

68

He watched her eyes. "It's always a pleasure."

She smiled at him.

The meal was taken with playfulness. Both of them laughed as she imitated various committee members. Over coffee, she felt the somber mood return. The restaurant was nearly empty.

"If I didn't care for him, it would be simple." She didn't look up at the eyes that were still surely studying her. "I don't know what's happening. I really and truly do not understand why we're acting this way to each other. I'm sorry to burden you with this personal crisis."

"I'm here, Kate. You can use me any way you want."

"It just goes on and on. It doesn't get better. I think it's getting worse. We fight. I can't make him understand things anymore. You know, the way people talk to each other, they listen, they do things. He won't listen. I don't know what's going to happen to us." Her hands, she saw, were resting a few inches from his. His hands moved forward as if in a benediction, revealing gold cuff links set with blue stones, and Kate caught the tang of pine and spice from his cologne.

"I just feel so damn powerless," she said. Her words came as his dry, steadying hands rested on top of hers. She made no move to take them away.

"There, there," he said comfortingly, "there, there."

THREE

Sanderson tried wiping the grimy black fingerprint powder off his hands when he hung up the phone. The powder clung to him like iron filings on a magnet. Two other deputies and another detective, Nestade, were with him in the kitchen of the Tippetts house.

"The D.A. says we can go in. I want three guys to go in with me through the front, and I want five in the back. Tell the guys you've got watching the place to stay put. I'll be right there."

Nestade and the deputies left to pass the word. Sanderson wiped his hands futilely again. He was a stocky man who could easily become overweight, but his solidity was leavened by an oddly out of place pacific look in his eyes, and he took people by surprise when he moved swiftly. He hadn't liked the way Fraser had dredged up his hated nickname when they first talked. Hopalong. He'd spent five years living down that reputation, although it still had some uses. He was a detective now, and this case would erase all that if everything came out all right. The trouble with most people, he had decided, was that they didn't know when the spotlight was on them. They missed chances. Sanderson knew he was being watched and intended to make the most of it.

Like his misleading tranquillity, his solid frame also misled. He was aware of malleability at his core, a lack of fixed principles. But this always struck him as a strength. It made him flexible. It made him versatile.

In the living room, ID techs were still going over the floor and furniture. Sitting in a large, slightly soiled stuffed chair was the husband, Tippetts. A deputy sheriff was talking to him and writing on a report form. Tippetts sat in the chair as if he hadn't a bone in his body, limply, without any support at all.

Sanderson hated this part of investigations. It was as if you came on an animal somebody had stuck with a long spear. It wasn't dead; it kept making noises and moving, but there was nothing you could do to get the spear out. Tippetts was chattering away.

"I knew she was dead the second I saw her. I could tell. I could tell when I opened the door, it was so quiet. You get used to the noises. I didn't hear any. I knew she was dead. I knew it."

Sanderson stopped beside him. "How are you doing, Mr. Tippetts? Can I get you anything?"

Gene slowly shook his head. He sat in the same chair where he always watched TV, Aaron and Andy at his feet or curled up with him. The TV sat blankly before him.

"Are you staying here tonight?"

Sanderson regretted the question instantly, because Tippetts's face constricted. "I can't stay here. I can't stay in this house. My son can't be in this house. Thank God, he didn't see anything. Thank God, thank God."

"Are there some friends or neighbors who can help? You want us to find you a motel?"

"We don't have any family here," Tippetts said tightly. "The Hamiltons will put us up." A gray sheen covered him. "They'll do that."

"I want to make sure you're settled. I can get hold of a priest or minister if you like."

"No, no." Tippetts shook his head back and forth. "We don't have any." Sanderson thought he was finished, but suddenly and violently he cried, "Where's my son? Where's my son?"

"He's out in one of our cars," Sanderson said gently. "He's fine."

"Where's Aaron? Do you know? Where's he? Where's my son?"

Sanderson stepped back as Tippetts bolted out of the chair. Before he could get to the front door, Sanderson had him by both arms. "Simmer down, Mr. Tippetts. We're looking for him right now. We're taking care of everything."

To the deputy, Sanderson said, "See if you can find out who the family doctor is, and get hold of him."

The two of them got Tippetts back into the chair. The lack of color in his skin and his abrupt, jerky chattering made Sanderson think of earthworms he baited on fishhooks, how they writhed and twisted over and over on the impaling metal point.

He didn't know how to console Tippetts. He honestly didn't know how to console any of them. The man went on making noises and sounds so pitiable that Sanderson couldn't stay near him. "You try to calm down, Mr. Tippetts," he said uselessly. "We're going to take care of things."

Half the people on the block were gathered outside across the street, and squad cars were lined up back to back when Sanderson strode across the front lawn. One TV mobile unit was there, another was just parking. The print reporters would be making an appearance soon. The camera crew was working the small crowd, getting people to point toward the Reece house, shake their heads in dismay, make philosophical observations. The camera and microphone sensed him quickly, and even as he headed across the street to the cluster of people, he heard questions. "Can you hold it for just a second? Just need a second."

Sanderson couldn't place the name of the young Latin guy with the camera and sound man trailing him, but he recognized the face. "I'd like to. I'm sorry."

"Is Reece barricaded in his house? We heard he's got guns."

"I'm sorry, you guys are going to have to stay back here. I'll talk to you when we've secured everything."

"How about letting us follow in a squad car?"

Sanderson almost wanted to laugh. "You'll have to stay here until we're finished. We'll have a long talk then if you want."

Several deputies blocked the crew from following him as he searched among the growing crowd for their witness. "Mr. Frawley?" he called out, "will you come with me?"

A middle-aged man in a plaid work shirt detached himself from two nervous women and followed Sanderson. "We'll take the car," Sanderson told him.

They got into a squad car that drove slowly down the block to the white house near a stand of trees. Sanderson noted approvingly that the house was covered from the back and that his men were well shielded. The adjoining houses had been emptied. For all the stir going on, the atmosphere was surprisingly stagnant.

"Just to be one hundred percent sure, Mr. Frawley, that is the house?" He pointed out the car window.

"That's the one. Looks like nobody's home, but that's it okay."

"Tell me anything else about where Reece works."

"Boy, boyoboy, it's someplace around here, I can't say where. He told me he's a mechanic. Fixed my car once, scraped something out, did a dandy job. He's pretty good with cars."

"Thank you. The deputy will drive you back up the street."

Sanderson got out, and the squad car backed away slowly. He motioned to Nestade and several deputies. "We'll make the entry through the front. I'll do the talking. I want to get in there fast. If I don't hear anything inside in about one second, we break in. Give me about thirty seconds at the front, then I want you coming in. We set?'' A deputy trotted off to relay his instructions.

Sanderson waited a moment for the others to position themselves. He hoped this wasn't a dry hole, but aside from that worry, he wasn't nervous. He was juiced up, ready to go, and there was a big difference between that and nerves. This was a part of an investigation that *didn't* make him nervous about getting it right. He had a feel for this kind of thing.

He pointed silently to Nestade and the two deputies as they walked across the grass to the door. Standing off to one side of the door, Sanderson paused, listening. It was quiet in there, like putting his ear to an enormous cipher, a great zero. The only noise was the motor or generator, grumbling at the side of the house.

''Okay?'' The men nodded, signaling thumbs-up to him. Nestade stared at the door as Sanderson knocked hard on it with his fist.

''This is Detective Sanderson of the Santa Maria Sheriff's Department. Open the door.''

He stepped back as he spoke so the door would be clear. Nothing happened inside.

''Let's go,'' he said.

Crouching below the midpoint of the door, one deputy moved sideways to a window, closed and tightly curtained. Using the side of his baton, he smashed into the center of the glass, shattering it in a spray of shards. At the same time, so the sounds ran together, Sanderson heard another window breaking at the rear of the house.

Rapidly the deputy cleared the glass fragments from the window frame, using the baton to break them off. Then he jumped through the empty frame, the white curtains flapping around him. He landed on the floor with a thud. Sanderson stood with his service revolver drawn. The front door opened. He and Nestade let the remaining deputies inside.

They met the other men who had come in through the back of the house.

"Okay," he told them, "take it easy. Look for the kid and play it slow. Don't move anything if you can help it."

Gingerly, they began going through the house. Sanderson sniffed the air. It smelled heavy, unpleasantly scented with lilac, as though a ponderous effort had been made to obscure something else.

The living room was neatly kept, the spotless pale couch and chairs, the lamps and tables all gleaming, more like stiffly lacquered props in a museum than the furniture of a home. There were no books, no pictures, no personal bits of furniture or decoration. Everything looked normal enough, in the right places, yet gave the impression that no human being lived among these hard, untouched artifacts.

He went from the living room into a small kitchen. A frying pan with white congealed grease in it sat on the electric range. It was shockingly out of place, like a pimple on a beauty queen. Nothing else had been disturbed. The dishes were carefully stacked near the sink, and the Formica countertop sparkled cleanly.

"It looks like a goddamned Holiday Inn," Sanderson said.

It also looked as though no one was home. Nestade walked a few feet behind. "What if this guy's here someplace?"

"We hold onto him until we get an arrest warrant. The D.A.'s coming down so it'll all be neat and tidy."

Nestade snorted. "I hope he isn't home. I hope they grab him trying to come in. I don't want to sit here staring him down while we get a damn warrant."

Sanderson stepped from the kitchen into a hallway. He still had his gun out as he put his ear against a brass-handled door. He looked up and shook his head. The other men could be heard moving in different rooms. He put his hand on the handle and slowly turned it, pushing the door open.

It was a bedroom, dark, yet faintly lime-tinted in the exhausted light that filtered through the curtained window. A medicinal odor hung in the room, something he couldn't identify, maybe isopropyl alcohol or antiseptic soap. A canopied bed, fringed with small tufted balls, took up most of the space. On it lay a woman, her mouth pressed tautly shut, breathing torturously. She was a small woman who barely took up a third of the bed.

Sanderson went to her. Her eyes were half open, but unseeing.

"Can you hear me?"

She slept on.

"I'm going to wake you up," he said. "We're from the Sheriff's Department. We're policemen. Can you hear me?"

He sighed and put his hands on her bony, delicate shoulders. Suddenly he had a terrible fear that she would crack apart in his hands, like a sea creature too roughly handled. He shook her gently.

Her mouth flopped open and shut as she rocked on the bed to his shaking. On the nightstand were a clock and several bottles.

"Take a look at them," Sanderson said to Nestade.

Nestade held the bottles up one at a time. "She's probably out of it. These are all barbs and tranquilizers. All prescription. For Mrs. Naomi Reece."

Sanderson half pulled her into a sitting position. Her head was rolling on her shoulders. Her breathing sounded strangled, then she jolted forward. "Charlie!" she screamed, her voice raspy and thick.

She looked at Sanderson and Nestade in terror, her body thrashing in Sanderson's hands. "Charlie!" she screamed again.

"Mrs. Reece, Mrs. Reece, we're police officers, we're from the Sheriff's Department." Keeping his hands on her, Sanderson inclined his head to indicate the badge on his pocket.

She saw the badge. She saw Nestade. But instead of calming down, she screamed again. "Charlie! Charlie!" The name echoed and bounced in the room, through the house. It was a keening, animal cry.

"Take it easy, take it easy, we're not doing anything to you."

"What are you doing in my house? What are you doing in my room?" she cried, her head snapping from side to side, trying to take everything in, struggling up out of a drugged, balmy sea.

"I'm a detective with the Sheriff's Department, and so

is my partner," Sanderson replied. "There are other officers in your house now. We're looking for your son. Is he home now?"

"I'm not," she briefly put her head in her hands, her breathing shallow, noisy, and brittle. "I'm sick. I'm a very ill person and you'd better get out."

"We've got probable cause to believe your son is involved in a serious felony, Mrs. Reece, and we're looking for him. Is he here?"

"No, no, he went out. He went to work. He took the car. You didn't find him?" she asked quickly.

"Where does he work?"

"I took some medicine. I don't know. I won't tell you," she shouted. "Get out of my house. Leave us alone!"

"We're going to search your house, Mrs. Reece. You can come along with us if you want."

Suddenly she got on her knees on the bed. "No!" she shouted. "Get out, get out!"

Sanderson and Nestade held her more tightly. "Jesus. What's the deal?" Sanderson swore. She was acting like they were about to cut her head off.

A short deputy stuck his head in the doorway and saw them wrestling with Naomi Reece. "One of you guys better get down here," he said. "We got something going here."

"You found the kid?" Sanderson asked.

"Nope. But we got something."

"Mrs. Reece, is Charlie's room down the hall?"

She moaned in his hands without intelligence or coherence. "Get a couple of guys to stay with her," he said to Nestade. "I'm going down the hall. Call her doctor, too."

"It's just down here," the deputy said, pointing for him. Four other deputies, looking queasy, stood in the hallway as he walked through. Sanderson was getting used to that reaction in this investigation. These guys are really frightened, he realized with a start.

As soon as he went through the doorway, before his eyes registered anything in the room itself, the stench engulfed him, a raw death smell, unforgettable and revolting. It was palpable. It made the flesh on his neck crawl uncontrollably.

"Goddamn," he said. "Goddamn," more softly. He held himself down, turning to one of the deputies outside. "Get the ID techs in here now. I want pictures of everything."

It was a fairly large room—perhaps it had been a family room at some point in the past—and it had a bathroom connected to it. It opened onto the backyard, which was visible between the window curtains. Sanderson switched on the light.

"Goddamn."

He did a quick walk-through to make certain there were no signs of the Tippetts kid, and then he went back to Naomi Reece's room. She was on her back again, tears washing down her face and her breath laboring stertorously. "Mrs. Reece, is that Charlie's room down the hall?"

"She's out of it again. She won't say anything." Nestade wiped at a large dark stain on his pants. "We got her out of bed and she pissed on my leg. I threw her back in bed. Pissing on my leg." He dabbed at the stain. "I'm going to put some water on it."

Sanderson and another deputy stood coldly over her. "We're going to search the house, Mrs. Reece. Do you have any objections?" He wasn't asking politely.

She cried on without acknowledging him.

"That sounds like consent to me," Sanderson said. He went to the living room, barking out, "Where are the ID guys?"

"Right behind me," someone answered, gesturing toward the open front door. Three men, two in casual suits, one in uniform, came in carrying large toolboxlike cases and a camera. Sanderson took them to the son's room. At least he was a little more prepared when he went in the second time.

"Take pictures of the whole place," he said. "Then let's snag anything that's not nailed down."

Nestade came in, his pants soaking wet. "I thought you wanted to wait for the D.A."

"I'm not waiting," Sanderson said tersely. "It's all out

in plain view." He gestured at the things displayed before him. "This is the guy. This is where he lives. We don't need a warrant now." He looked sharply at Nestade. "You want to stand around here waiting for the D.A. to show?"

"If we gotta be here, I want to be doing something," Nestade said quickly.

Sanderson nodded. He had to keep busy, too, and make the world shift back into place once more.

He breathed in short gasps through his nose, and the other men followed his example.

"What the hell has this guy been doing?" Nestade said in amazement as the techs busily sifted through the room.

"He shit everywhere. He shit all over the goddamn floor." Sanderson directed as they took pictures of the dried feces on the floor, some in large mounds, indicating that the place had been used more than once. Feces had been flung onto the walls. They were even in the rumpled, half torn-apart bed.

"Get the bookshelves, too," he said. Those wild charts and drawings, the books, the little dark things squashed into corners. Record it all. Pin it down, and maybe it wouldn't seem so alien, so frightening.

"What the hell stinks so bad in here?" Nestade asked disgustedly. "I know the shit's bad, but, Jesus."

"It's something else," Sanderson agreed, looking around for the source. "Maybe it's this other crap."

The place was an incredible scramble of books and old clothes, string, hair, combs, shoes, every fragment thrown about the room without sense. He found a heavy iron frying pan, with clotted blood and bits of tissue clinging to it, sitting on a pile of books.

I've got one at home like that, he thought, same kind, same color. Lynn makes pancakes in it on Sundays.

The frying pan was corroded, deeply stained. In a tinfoil packet beside it, opened and black, lay what looked like a rotting kidney. Sanderson covered his mouth for a moment, although not because he was sick; it was an almost physical sense of shame that overwhelmed him. A man lived here, not an animal. It was a man, a man, and the place stank like the monkey house at the zoo.

They worked quietly now, swearing occasionally, trying

to finish as quickly as they could. Cages of guinea pigs, squirrels, some dead, others frantically running inside the wire mesh, were taken out. In the bathroom there was more fecal material on the floor and partly covering the bowl of the toilet. A thin layer of greasy water sat gelatinously on the sink counter. The shower stall was open, and near the drain were feces, hair, and some grayish tissue.

"That looks like brains," Sanderson said softly.

"I gotta get out of here for a few minutes," an ID tech said thickly. "This is getting to me." He wiped his face with a handkerchief.

"Go ahead," Sanderson said. "It's okay."

Little plastic bags appeared, and he ordered bits of things to be sealed in them, cataloged, tagged for reference, initialed with the date and badge numbers, all by the book, each sad remnant captured for use in court. Nobody was going to fault his procedure, Sanderson vowed; it was all going to be just the way they wanted it.

A nattily dressed ID tech with a pencil-thin moustache called out, "I got shells over here." He was pointing to a pile of clothes in the corner of the room. "Looks like twenty-twos, I think." He held up a small bullet.

"Get a picture and take it," Sanderson said. He thought of the woman up the hall, crying out for her son, and of the tormented man he'd left down the street. Both linked together by the occupant of this room. It had a neat nastiness to it.

FOUR

"I'm doing you a favor," Fraser called to the press as he showed his identification to the deputy sheriff at the door.

"Telling us we can't shoot inside the victim's place is a favor?" a reporter said.

"You'd never be able to use any pictures on the air. I'm saving you a lot of wasted effort." He held up his hand to break off the argument and was conducted back to the bedroom, noting the men watching Mrs. Reece as he went. He took in the sights and smells of the room simultaneously; it was as though he had stumbled on the idol ground of an unknown cult. He tried at the same time to maintain a detachment, in order to correctly study the cult's mysteries.

Yet he was unnerved all over again. It was this insane juxtaposition of the usual and the unusual that was terrifying. Fraser remembered a cocktail party Kate had wanted him to go to that night. Even though she had said little about it, he knew his presence would mean a great deal to her. How to draw that together with this room eluded him. They were as far apart as the moon and Santa Maria.

Sanderson was at his side. He asked the detective, "Have you found anything about the little boy?"

"Not really. There's some tissue in the shower. I think it might be brains. I don't know if it's human or what. He had animals in here."

"What about the mother, what does she say?"

"She's half dopey on tranks. I asked her if we could search, and she didn't mind."

"We won't hang our hats on that," Fraser said wryly. They both knew the consent was invalid.

Abruptly, his bile rose into his mouth. He swallowed hard.

Sanderson nodded sympathetically. "We've been taking shifts. We can't stay in here."

"I want to see anything you've found."

"Take a look at the bookshelves, check out the titles. See the stuff this guy reads?"

Books were scattered on the floor near the shelves. Fraser scanned them all. It was maddening. There was an order here, a pattern of thought and action, a meaning shimmering distantly at him, as if from a great depth.

"War," Fraser said, "a lot of Nazi material. *Rise and Fall of the Third Reich, German Made Easy*, more Nazi books. Here's one, *Mein Kampf* in English. He's not stupid anyway. *Gray's Anatomy*." He hefted the volume out of its place. "He's an avid student of medicine."

"Why?"

"Pages torn out, he's marked places. This has gotten some use. What else? Over here are some psychiatric texts. More medical books."

When Fraser looked up, Sanderson pointed to the charts and pictures thumbtacked on the wall to the right of the bookshelves.

Fraser stared, taking the images in. The first was a large anatomical diagram of the human body, the cavities drawn open to show all the organs. It was a standard diagram from any biology class in high school. He remembered an identical one hanging behind his own teacher. The open cavities were different on this one, though. He saw red and black lines drawn raggedly, snaking like rays from a brilliant sun, around the heart and liver, connected by an intricate network of arrows to the brain. The eyes of the diagram had originally been drawn closed, but they had been altered, clumsily redrawn open, staring vividly, and a third coarsely marked eye had been placed in the forehead. Swastikas adorned the spaces around the body.

"I guess he's a Nazi," Sanderson suggested.

"No, none of this had much to do with Nazis, or they're only a part of it. This is something else." His gaze was pulled to the next picture, which was drawn more violently, hastily. "I don't know exactly what."

It was a child's skeleton, the bones poorly drawn, primitively joined, the vision of a third-grader at Halloween. Rearing through the round rib cage was a great phallus, pointing its brightly painted red tip toward the leering skull. More swastikas danced around the figure.

Over this skeleton was an enormous dominating swastika and the word *yes* repeated like a woven strand of rope around the strange image.

Cultic mysteries. Another world, he thought.

"That kid's had it," Sanderson said. "If this guy's got him, he's dead."

Fraser turned on him. "No. He's not dead. We don't think he's dead. He's not out of danger," he said. "We can't admit anything like that."

He wondered how Sanderson would take the rebuke. The detective remained impassive, even sleepy-looking. He folded his arms. "I can play it any way you want."

"It's the only way, Mel. Our only justification for even being in here is that we continue to believe that child is alive." He noticed the techs and deputies fastidiously poking and collecting evidence. His stomach fell. "What are they doing?"

"Looking for evidence. We found some shells that look

like they match the gunshots to all the victims." Sanderson was about to go on but Fraser stopped him.

"I told you not to seize anything until I got here."

"What's the problem? It's all out in plain view. We see it, we can seize it."

"It's not good enough," Fraser said. "At least, I'm not sure. The point is that I told you exactly how this investigation was going to be handled. This is my case. You'll handle it the way I tell you to." All around them men were pawing through clothes and piles of debris. "Stop what you're doing," Fraser ordered. "I want you to stay put until we get a warrant to cover everything."

Sanderson shrugged and let the order stand. The men paused and waited.

"Where's the phone?" Fraser asked.

Wordlessly, Sanderson pointed and walked ahead to the kitchen. "Mel," Fraser explained, "this isn't an exercise. Your people saw things, they saw evidence, and there isn't any justification for seizing that evidence without a warrant. We can be in here, I hope, because we're looking for the Tippetts boy, but we can't seize anything. Do you understand?"

"I said I can play it any way you want."

Fraser thought this nipped the problem in the bud and a warrant now would cover any evidence already seized. It was a little tricky, a warrant to seize evidence already seized, but the only witnesses to the time differences were Sanderson's people. Probably no harm had been done. He disliked the idea, though. It savored of dishonesty and now linked them all in a small but legally significant pact of silence. He was wondering, too, about Sanderson. *I can play it any way you want.* The promise seemed boundless.

Naomi Reece, her nightgown only partly covered by a hastily thrown-on robe, huddled, weeping, in a chair.

"Arrest her?" Sanderson asked.

"Not now. She's nothing better than an accessory now. She might say something if she's not under arrest." Fraser looked at Sanderson, solid, obliging, sleepy-eyed. How far was Sanderson prepared to go in a case like this?

Fraser searched his mind for a suitable judge on the Municipal Court, one who would listen to a warrant request attentively, read the affidavits lightly, and sign a search warrant after police officers had gone into a house. In rapid order he thought of, and dismissed, name after name. Finally, he picked Jaime Zuniga, who could be persuaded, with the right combination of flattery and veiled pleading, to sign the warrant. He picked up the phone to call the court.

CHAPTER VI

ONE

It was bad luck. Eddie Muñoz couldn't call it anything else. First his cold was worse, and it was a bitch carrying Kleenex in his uniform without it looking stupid, then his partner called in sick, then he was the closest car to check out gas stations along Alta Boulevard looking for a possible, stressed possible, armed 187 suspect. Muñoz could have laughed. Use caution, make it fast, they said. He snuffled loudly. Homicide suspect hanging around a local gas station? He was a hundred miles from Santa Maria and making tracks. Muñoz blew his nose and balled up the tissue. He arced it into the tiny plastic wastebasket on the squad-car seat. Waste of time. Bad luck.

A light drizzle was coming down when he got to station number five, the Econo-Serv, and drove up. It wasn't much of a gas station—swooping yellow-wing roof, two bays for cars in the garage, three pumps. Half a dozen cars in various states of collapse parked outside. He liked cars, and before joining the police, had thought about the army or air force, someplace where they'd pay him to be a mechanic and he wouldn't have to worry about starving. But he wouldn't have wanted to end up at a place like this. Business must be real slow.

Nobody much around, either. He checked his watch. Two. Should be some kind of activity at two in the afternoon.

He pulled up in front and got out, making sure his uniform hat was on firmly. The thing came off too easily. He looked into the office, crowded with old stock-car magazines, a candy machine, and papers. No one there. He heard clanking sounds from inside the garage.

He had to blow his nose again. The sound brought someone from behind a clunker, a Rambler in better days, maybe. Muñoz quickly cleared his nose. The radio call had said caution, possible homicide suspect.

"Have car trouble?" the guy asked him.

"Nah," Muñoz said, "just stopped by. You Charles Reece?"

The guy, maybe twenties, late twenties, slender, black hair, shook his head as he wiped his oil-blackened hands and walked over to Muñoz. "Nope. He's been gone all day. Something I can do for you?"

Muñoz watched him carefully. "He's the guy I need to talk to. It's nothing important. You got a phone number or something? Any idea when he's coming in?"

"Geez, no. If he isn't here by now, I think he's out for the day."

Muñoz ran down the suspect's description. This guy could fit. Same age, right build, general features matched. But the report said the suspect was unshaven, looked wild, dressed in a red parka and jeans. This guy was buttoned up in a khaki shirt and pants, a little dirty from working on the clunker, but neat as a pin otherwise. He was calm as they came, too. No shakes when he saw a cop. No nerves.

"You the owner?" Muñoz asked.

The guy laughed. About six feet now separated them. "Hell, no. I just work here. Owner's checking another place he's got downtown."

"Any of Reece's stuff around, like clothes or anything?"

"I don't know. Me and another guy keep our gear in this locker. Might be something of Charlie's in it."

Muñoz nodded toward the locker. "Let's take a look."

The guy walked ahead slightly, and as he did, he leaned over a little suddenly to one side. A whistling whine came from him. Immediately, he straightened up.

"What's the matter?" Muñoz sneezed as he asked the question.

The guy glanced at him. "Backache. I twisted some-

84

thing when I was screwing around under that mother." He tapped the Rambler as they passed underneath it.

Muñoz was close to him now. The guy stepped away slightly. There was a look of apprehension on his face, but it faded in a moment, like a light turned out. "You got a bad cold," he said. "I get them easy."

"Don't tell me about it," he said, coughing. "Okay, open it up."

The guy knelt and opened the locker door. "Maybe you could stay away from me. I'm not kidding about how easy I get sick."

"I don't want to give this to anyone." Muñoz stepped back. He was worried about an armed homicide suspect, and this guy was worried about catching a cold. "What's your name?" he asked, as the guy peered into the locker.

"Bob. Robert."

"Last name?"

"Tippetts. Bob Tippetts."

"Just call me Ed."

The guy stood again. "Funny, I don't see any of his stuff in there. Maybe he left town."

"He did keep things here?"

"Sure. Nothing in there now. I think he's cleaned it all out."

Muñoz looked inside. There were some overalls, a pair of sneakers, all belonging to the other employee, according to Tippetts. Dank and rank, Muñoz thought, poking in the clothes. No parka, no jeans, no gun, nothing, nothing. More bad luck. At least, though, he could report where Reece worked.

"Okay, thanks a lot, Robert. Look, here's my number. Give me a call if Reece comes in today, okay? I've just got to ask him a couple of things."

The guy took the card Muñoz handed him. "Sure, sure. Say, you want me to call the owner?"

"I can do that. Thanks for the hand. Stay dry."

The guy walked Muñoz back to the squad car, keeping his distance. They exchanged a couple of tips about automatic transmissions. He seemed to know what he was talking about. He was still standing there when Muñoz got into the car. It looked a little funny, nothing great or striking, just odd to see someone standing in a light drizzle watching a cop get into his squad car, as though he was waiting to see when the cop left. Or to make sure he left.

Muñoz was about to close the car door when he saw the white Chevy parked among the other battered cars. The call had said Reece was driving a white Chevy. This guy Tippetts did very generally fit the bill, too. Muñoz got out again.

He cocked his head at the Chevy. "Whose car?"

"Mine. I'm working on it."

Muñoz nodded as if it didn't mean much. Maybe it didn't. He walked to the Chevy. It was tucked in among the other cars so nicely that if you didn't want to find it very badly, you'd never spot it just looking from the street. Someone had gone to a bit of trouble to squeeze it in there.

"Robert?"

"Yo."

"You want to open it for me? I really like these old Chevys. Used to have one like this."

The guy hadn't moved. Now he came to Muñoz slowly, almost with the precision of a man who thinks his feet are made of glass. Muñoz kept up a steady patter about his old car, how he drove it, what he bought to fix it up, and all the time Tippetts patted himself to find the key. "I think I left it in my street clothes."

"Back in the locker?"

"Nope, in the rest room. It's busted, so I use that to change and lock it up. I'll get it."

"I'll come with you." Muñoz strolled casually, but now he felt tension radiating from the guy a few feet ahead of him. As soon as they got to the men's room, Tippetts found the door key, unlocked the door, and Muñoz was right behind him. "Don't worry about catching anything," he said.

Tippetts squeezed back against the wall to let Muñoz by. The room was dark with grime. On the sink, piled up, were jeans and a red parka.

"These yours, Robert?"

Tippetts hadn't moved.

"The car keys in the jeans?"

"I'll get them." He tried to push past Muñoz to the clothes.

86

"Just stay put. I'll find them." Muñoz was feeling the parka. He pulled out a gun. A small one, maybe a .22.

Tippetts made a surprisingly fast spin and took off running.

Muñoz, shoving the gun in his waistband, shouted after him and started running full tilt. His heavy legs pounded on the concrete. Tippetts was running ahead of him making these funny squealing noises like he was giggling or crying.

Muñoz shouted again as they ran across Alta Boulevard, cutting through four lanes of traffic. Tippetts zigzagged past cars that screeched and barely missed him. Muñoz came after, his breath struggling through his congestion. He was blowing snot all over.

Tippetts was across the street, running parallel to a row of stores, and he almost plowed into a couple of kids coming out of a minimart. Muñoz shouted once more. He was gaining.

He picked up his pace, and then his hat sailed off behind him. He cursed at it.

Near an automotive supply store, Muñoz reached out and got both hands on the guy's thin shoulders. Muñoz threw him against the store; then, when Tippetts cried out, a weird kind of babbling that didn't sound human, Muñoz flipped him neatly onto the pavement.

With his hands full, Muñoz had to wipe his nose on his uniform sleeve. He was annoyed beyond words at the sloppiness.

Tippetts had completely given up. Now he was saying something.

"Don't make me sick. Let me go. I'm sick. I'm sick."

Muñoz pulled him up into a standing position, holding the man's arms behind him to put handcuffs on the bony wrists. "You're under arrest, Robert. You can say whatever you want to, but it will be used against you in court."

"I need a doctor. I'm sick. I'm in pain."

He went on like that. Muñoz walked him back to the squad car. Not bad. An armed 187 suspect, not bad at all. On the way to the car, he even managed to retrieve his hat.

TWO

By the time he left the courthouse and sent Sanderson back to the Reece house, Fraser had acquired a headache. Judge Zuniga had signed the warrant after an obligatory session of supplication from Fraser. That was Zuniga's way, and Fraser used it to get the warrant. At the same time, he had to keep an eye on Sanderson, who spoke too much and too casually.

The warrant was solid, and Sanderson had gone back to seizing evidence. Fraser's headache came from the strain of the afternoon, and his worry about Kate. The investigation was moving swiftly. They hadn't quarreled in the last few days, both perhaps chastened by the last fight. He was worried now that these new developments might break the truce. If they did, the last place he wanted to be was at a cocktail party.

But his sense of obligation and affection roused itself. She wanted him at the party. It was a small thing. Apparently he was unable to avoid hurting her, and any minor penance that could be done was worthwhile.

Sally Ann halted him frantically when he walked in and routed him to the fifth floor. "The big honcho said he wants to see you the minute you set foot in the door."

"I'll be upstairs," he said. He walked without haste. His mind was fixed on other puzzles, him and Kate, the mysterious sights and things at the Reece house. It was difficult to come back to Whalen.

He passed two things in Whalen's outer office. The first was the trophy collection, four shelves high, ranging from the law enforcement glee club award to the best mixed tennis in 1967. The second was an old investigator everyone called Huey, an owl-gray man wearing a shoulder holster and a pocketful of pens, and carrying what looked like a bundle of men's pants. He was now Whalen's personal assistant.

"Rush job," he said cryptically to Fraser.

Whalen's secretary, reflecting her boss's exasperation, saw him and exclaimed, "Oh, there you are!"

"Here I am."

"I'll buzz you through."

Whalen's door opened, held by Infeld. Beyond him,

Whalen sat behind his desk, his face flushed and damp. He half rose when he saw Fraser.

"Where the hell have you been? What the hell did you leave me high and dry for?"

He had no trousers on, only his boxer shorts.

"There've been some major developments in the investigation, Spence. I've been tied up."

"I know about the major developments. I didn't hear them from you. I heard them from everybody else, and I didn't have the slightest fucking idea what the hell was going on."

"We've just gotten a warrant for a suspect's house," Fraser began, but Whalen got louder.

"We agreed this morning that you'd keep me posted. I thought that's what we agreed, didn't we?"

"I tried to find you."

"So how does it happen that I'm sitting here with the phone going, and no information, and my Major Crimes supervisor missing *again,* while this case starts erupting all over the fucking place?"

"Nobody," Fraser looked to Infeld for corroboration, "could find you. I couldn't spend my time waiting for you to turn up."

"Shit. I was right at the club. Everyone knew that." He turned toward Infeld. "You knew it, didn't you, Tim?"

"That's what I understood," Infeld said in his laconic manner.

"So it wasn't so fucking hard to find me. I wasn't on the fucking moon."

It occurred to Fraser that Whalen was on the moon, and his own head beat painfully with each loud, sloppy accusation. Whalen's eyes were shaded in red, his face lightly covered with sweat; his shirt clung too closely to his body and an otherwise cheery alcoholic miasma encircled him. It's infuriating to have to deal with him every step of the way, Fraser thought.

Whalen lurched over his desk, scattering papers and a vase of flowers as he reached for a stack of phone messages. "Look at this." He waved them at Fraser. "Every newspaper, the TV, every goddamn reporter between here and Los Angeles asking me about this guy they caught. I don't even know his fucking name, Fraser. I had to find that out from the reporters."

The thing hit him. "Who's been caught?" His head beat in a red tattoo.

Whalen's eyes rolled in disgust to Infeld, who looked back as though Whalen was a small insect in a very small bottle. "You don't know? You don't know? You don't know?"

"Is it Reece? Is it him?"

Infeld nodded. "Earlier this afternoon. I don't know how the papers got it so quickly."

"You think I'm kidding," Whalen said. "You think this is some kind of party for your benefit. It's not. I'm telling you it's not. I'm going to have your ass—"

Before he'd finished, Fraser stepped closer, without raising his voice, stilling the blood pounding in his head. There was so much to do elsewhere, and nothing to do here.

"Let's get one thing straight, Spence. From now on, you need me. I don't need you. I'm handling this case, and I've been calling the shots since we found Reece's residence. I'm going to continue calling the shots. It's my case."

Whalen's half-lidded scowl followed him as he left the room. "Don't screw me again, do you hear that? I'll have Ballenger's fucking ass out of that section. You don't screw me again, Fraser." The voice grew fainter and tinier the farther he went from Whalen's office.

THREE

They brought him into the largest interview room at the Sheriff's Department and sat him in a chair at the head of the table, handcuffing his right wrist to the armrest. He sat quietly, looking down the table, his body tilted to one side, humming tunelessly to himself. Fraser watched every movement, heard each sound. There he is, Fraser thought.

"Okay, we're rolling now," Sanderson said cheerfully. "You're Charles Edmund Reece?"

"Yo."

"Okay, Charlie, listen. You know who I am?"

"Cop." It was so faint, so muted and distant, that

Fraser leaned to catch it, along with the two deputy sheriffs who sat with Sanderson at the table.

"I'm Mel Sanderson. I'm a detective. I'm a sheriff. The guys who arrested you were city policemen. Do you understand that?"

"Yo."

"That guy over there," he pointed to Fraser, against the wall, "is a D.A. He's here to watch and maybe ask you some questions if you say it's okay. You understand?"

"Can you get this off?" Reece anxiously jangled the handcuffs on his wrist. "It's hurting my circulation. I've got real bad circulation from the viruses, so can you take it off?"

Sanderson nodded. "Sure, I think so. You know there are a lot of guys outside the door, don't you? You know you're not going anywhere?"

"Can you get me a doctor right now? I've got blood poisoning from the viruses." His voice went up in pitch suddenly, flutey and reedlike. "It's in my blood. I need to have a doctor give me a transfusion right away."

"You're okay, Charlie, just sit still. We'll take the handcuffs off and you'll be a lot better." Sanderson motioned to a deputy, who carefully removed the handcuffs. Fraser listened intently to each word and how it was spoken, noting minutely how Reece sat and how he moved, hoping that somewhere there was a clue to why this man had done these things.

"My blood is full of viruses, a lot of bad blood gets into my head."

"It's cold season, Charlie."

"No, these are special viruses. They gave them to me on purpose so I'd get sick. That's why I need a doctor."

"You can see a doctor as soon as we're finished, Charlie. We've got to do some things first. Like, we're recording everything that's said in this room. You mind that?"

"It's okay with me," he said, twisting his head from side to side. "They always record me. Everyplace I've been they record things about me."

"Okay, that's great. Now listen to me while I read you your constitutional rights, Charlie. You gotta give them up if you want to talk to us. You understand?"

Fraser saw the pale face flicker with interest. "I want to talk. I want you to hear all this stuff about me. You can get me a doctor. Then you can tell everyone how sick I am."

Tell everyone. A jury, perhaps? Was Reece thinking about turning them all into witnesses for an insanity plea? Fraser wondered what was going on behind the rubber-colored eyes.

Sanderson read each right from a printed card, in order to get the approved wording. Silence, self-incrimination, appointing a lawyer, all of it seemed of little interest to Reece. He sat listening to the plumbing of his own body. Each right was given up as briefly and blankly as the others. He wanted to talk, that was obvious. He wanted them to listen to him.

He doesn't look monstrous, Fraser thought, studying the restless mouth and eyes. He was neat and controlled, except for the gibberish about blood and viruses. He could walk by you on a street without making you turn your head or think twice about it. He was part of the scenery. But he didn't always look like this, if the witnesses at the killings were right. He changed, like mercury sliding in a glass dish, altering his appearance fluidly.

The voice changed too. Fraser heard it whine unexpectedly one moment, then ask quite naturally for a glass of water. What did I expect? he wondered. A monster doesn't have to look like one.

"What am I here for?"

"You killed a woman today," Fraser said.

Blank face. Blank stare. "Get me a doctor right away."

"Mr. Reece," Fraser said, "did you kill Eileen Tippetts this morning?"

Silence, the bony fingers twining in a ritual on the table. Sanderson looked inquiringly at Fraser.

"Mr. Reece," Fraser went on, "are you prepared to talk to us?"

"I don't remember anything." The voice was calm, the face without tremor. "I don't like all these guys here. I'll talk to you guys," he gestured at Fraser and Sanderson, "if you turn off the recorder."

Fraser nodded, and Sanderson told the deputies to stay

outside the door. They waited until the machine was shut off.

Reece sniffed casually, his fingers splaying, twisting, and arching like dancers in front of him.

"Now, did you kill a woman today?" Fraser repeated.

"I may have."

"Where's the little boy, Charlie?" Sanderson asked.

"I don't know. There wasn't any kid."

At each useless answer, teasingly offered with just a touch of information, Fraser saw Reece look at his questioners, as if to gauge his effect. He likes this, Fraser realized. He enjoys our impotence.

"We know you took that little boy." Sanderson stood over Reece. "And you can help yourself, Charlie, by giving us a hand finding him."

"How? Can I get out?"

"No, you can't. You'll just feel better. It looks good to cooperate, too."

Reece shook his head. "See, the virus mixes up my mind." He stopped playing with his fingers. "I don't remember stuff. I make up stuff. I hallucinate."

The word stuck Fraser like a small needle. "Have you been talking to psychiatrists, Mr. Reece?"

"Sure, a lot of them. They record me, write stuff down. I always get a doctor to talk to me."

"Would you talk to a psychiatrist now?"

"Sure I would. I'll tell him all my hallucinations. I'm sick. You'll find out. They all know I'm sick."

It was a taunt again, Fraser thought with disgust. He's got all the words and ideas from psychiatric theory already. He knows exactly how to protect himself from a charge of murder, even murder so horrible. Particularly murder so horrible.

Reece's face brightened. "You're going to get a big surprise."

For the second time that afternoon, Fraser was white with anger. The creature was laughing at him. He was making fun of the only weapons given by the law to destroy him.

Unlike the futility of his anger at Whalen, Fraser felt the stale tide of barrenness wash out of him as Reece continued grinning. Here was an opportunity to put everything right again, to bring it all back into flower once more. This was an enemy that could be vanquished.

He brought Sanderson out with him. Dr. Rudin, the small psychiatrist, was waiting at the interview room door. "I want you to find out anything you can about the missing boy," Fraser said to Rudin. "I want you to tell me what this guy's problems are."

"I won't be able to deal with any of them—" Rudin said, looking at Sanderson's quietly formidable bulk.

Fraser was short in reply. "I don't want you to treat him. He's a murderer. I want information from him. See what you can get."

FOUR

"Take your wife, Tony." A very tall, heavyset man used a manhattan as a pointer. "She's one of those springs that keeps a bunch like us wound. Does the spadework, goes the extra mile."

"Kate's a remarkable woman."

"Bar none, she's terrific. We'd be up the creek without her." He winked, and the manhattan sloshed dangerously. "Anytime you get tired of her, you just let me know."

"Oh, Angus," said the chunky woman at his side. "He's always like this at parties," she said apologetically to Fraser.

For the last half hour, he had been shunted from one small group of couples to another. The large living room, festooned with holly and blinking colored lights, exuded early Christmas cheer. He looked at the twenty or so couples, the elite of the Cities League, drinking and laughing. They made quite a contrast to the busy men and women at the Sheriff's Department.

He hadn't been able to stay with Kate for more than a few minutes before someone took his arm and he was being introduced to a new group of people.

"I hope you don't take offense," Angus's wife went on. "We all work together so hard that it's like a big family."

"Oh, sure," said Angus, draining the manhattan.

"I didn't take any offense. I assumed you were being complimentary."

He wanted to get back to Kate. She moved easily and comfortably among her friends. It was impossible not to admire, as the boob in front of him had, her poise and grace. That's what came from years of good schools, and the best upbringing a wealthy rose king could afford. She was perfectly at ease. He was not. These were the same people his father courted; many of them even recognized his name. Fraser had no real inkling of how people like this thought. They remained a strange breed, even though he had known their kind for years.

"Kate tells us you're a lawyer," Angus's wife was saying.

"Whose firm?" Angus asked.

"District Attorney's office. I'm head of Major Crimes."

"Oh, my," she said, "that sounds interesting."

"There enough money in it?"

"More than enough."

He saw Kate nearby and she waved to him. What struck him was how happy she looked. Her face was suffused with a brightness he rarely saw when she was alone with him these days. He was the cause of her sadness, her anger, her fear. At the heart of it he knew she was afraid. It pained him that he couldn't even give her the kind of simple pleasure she derived from mingling with these people.

She laughed, her slim neck and elegant features relaxed.

"Take this guy they caught today. Five murders? Makes me sick to think I've got to pay for a whole damn trial for this guy."

"It really does make him sick," his wife said seriously.

"I'm sorry. I can't talk about it," Fraser said, setting his gin and tonic down on a dainty table. "It's part of the rules. Excuse me." He sought Kate again.

"Rules," Angus grunted, a fresh manhattan magically appearing in his hand, "we're dying from rules."

Fraser sidled to Kate and drew her away from the people she was with. "Come with me for a second."

"We'll be back," she said. He took her to a darkened bedroom and switched on the light. He closed the door. The room was piled with stuffed toys, and a tawny giraffe as tall as his shoulders regarded them benignly.

"If I hear one more solution to the 'crime problem,' I'm going to start laughing, Kate."

"They can get intense sometimes. They're good people, mostly."

"I know. It's me. I'm bone tired. I don't think I can stick it out much longer."

"Try to for just a little while, please?"

"All right," he said. "They all seem to love you here."

Kate laughed. "There are a few who don't. They stayed away. These are my friends."

"Then I don't mind staying." She only wanted very small things from him. He felt a guilty pang. He might not be able to provide even them much longer.

"It reminds me of that first Christmas after we were married." She put her arms around his neck, and he pulled her against him. "I don't think I ever had such a wonderful time, Tony. You remember how my parents fixed up the house? All the lights and the holly, the people. You were wonderful. I couldn't take my eyes off you." She kissed him again. "I kept looking at you, when you were talking, when you and my dad got into that discussion—"

"More like an argument."

She had her cheek near his and moved him slowly, one step, then another, to distant and remembered music. "I kept thinking that I'd gotten everything I ever wanted. That's what I thought when I looked at you. I never wanted anything else."

Fraser kissed her, his mouth covering hers. They stopped moving and stood together in the room. "I want to go home," he said. His hands moved down her strong, supple back.

"Yes," she said, looking at him with an urgent delight he had not seen for months.

Their exit was made hastily, amid loud good cheer and wishes for the holidays. They barely spoke on the ride home, but Fraser drove with one hand, the other holding Kate's, as if they both needed the continuous contact for reassurance.

In their bedroom, Fraser's sensations of sight and sound were magnified as clothes were pulled off and unbuttoned quickly. Kate left her skirt and stockings hanging over a chair as she undressed. The times of longing and loneliness fell away when Fraser got into bed, first thigh-to-thigh over her as they kissed again, then swiftly rolling to the side, their arms drawing them together with a newness of sensation they had felt in their lovemaking in the first year they were married.

It was that strange dissolution of time that caught both of them in an intensity of feeling. His leg slid between hers as she kissed his throat. There was nothing else after this timelessness. Kate's breathing quickened as his hands moved along her breasts and belly and then he was inside her. She moved undulantly, and suddenly Fraser thought, this is what Reece saw.

Her body arched and she pulled at his wrists, her eyes staring at him with a frantic desperation. Stop time, stop life at this moment, she was thinking, I don't want anything else. I promise. Nothing else. I promise.

When they were finished, she lay against him. One hand held the sheet covering them in a bunched knot, like a white rose.

Fraser opened his eyes. Kate lay on her back with only a sheet pulled halfway up to her navel.

He trailed his hand over her belly. He traced her vertical cesarean scar lightly downward, feeling its ridges. Molly's birth engraved in flesh, confirming every fear Kate had about giving birth in the first place, or ever again.

She stirred under his hand and looked at him. "What are you thinking about?" she asked.

"We could have children, Kate." He kissed her. "We could have more."

"I can't think about it. I don't know, Tony."

"I don't have everything," he said softly. "I love you too much for us not to have a family."

The contraction under his hand told him he had reached the edge. Time had begun again for them both.

He lay back beside her and put his arm behind her head. "We caught the killer today. He's in custody. I've talked to him. It's going to be a damn hard trial, but I think I'll win."

She cringed slightly, as if suddenly feeling her body's nakedness. "I'm glad you caught this man," she finally said.

"It's just the beginning."

She moved closer, her body opening itself up to him

tentatively so that she nestled along his side, one arm across his chest. "I thought about so many things today. I don't know why. I just felt I had to make some decisions. I couldn't let things go on just getting worse. I had to do something."

"All right," he said, waiting.

"I'm going to try to live with the way you have to be."

"I'm going to make an effort, too," he said, without telling her that even as he tried to fill his mind with Kate and keeping the two of them together, another bedroom, speckled with gore, rose before him; and a grinning, jesting face loomed enormously. He would have to protect her from the knowledge.

In the languorous, charged darkness, she unwittingly found the most wounding thing to say. And she said it sincerely.

"I know you'll try. I trust you, Tony."

CHAPTER VII

ONE

The three of them sat in Judge Donelli's chambers—Fraser, the judge, and Albert Starkey, who represented Reece. They only had two simple tasks to complete, and yet Fraser marveled at how difficult Starkey was making each one.

"Are we finally going to arraign this guy today?" the judge asked. He sat slouched in his chair so his large body bulked upward. He steepled his hands together.

"I'd love to do that," Fraser answered. He waited for Starkey.

"Fine by me."

"At last, some light," the judge said. "You know, Al, there's a courtroom full of reporters out there. They're disappointed when nothing happens."

Starkey had niggled and nagged and twice postponed

Reece's arraignment, the reading of the charges against him. Starkey was a slim, short man with a pronounced chin, who favored dark suits and wore black-rimmed glasses. He was the senior assistant public defender, and Fraser believed he had achieved the position largely due to a mindless tenacity, a willingness to argue a point until either it or its defender dropped from exhaustion.

"I needed the time, judge."

Donelli heaved himself upright and took a great gulp of coffee from his mug. "All we've got to do is get through the arraignment and set a date for a prelim."

Starkey gazed over at Fraser.

Something unpleasant about the preliminary hearing date was in the air.

"You two have any dates in mind?" asked the judge, pleased that the bickering about the arraignment was over. "I assume there will be a time waiver." He spoke to Starkey while watching Fraser.

Fraser knew Starkey had been thinking about the prelim. It was the first major hurdle, the initial step in an intricate choreography taking Reece from jail to the gas chamber. Fraser wanted to bring Reece into Superior Court to stand trial as quickly, painlessly, and deliberately as possible. There were only two ways into Superior Court for trial. The first was traditional, the preliminary hearing held in Municipal Court. Fraser would be forced to call his witnesses, who numbered sixty and growing, and see them cross-examined by Starkey while Reece was present. Starkey would draw that process out for weeks, fouling the record, posturing and shouting, turning what was a simple first step into a roadblock.

Moreover, the preliminary hearing would give Starkey two chances to litigate his motions. There would be a shower of them, Fraser knew. The first ones he guessed already, motions to suppress evidence, to set aside the search warrant, to contest the validity of statements, identifications, lab results. Any others were whatever Starkey had the ingenuity to concoct. In a truly notorious death-penalty case like this one, fancy drove the defense, because there existed a chance—small, remote, even bizarre—that one imaginative motion might find a receptive judge. When the case was eventually certified for trial in

Superior Court, Starkey could redo any motions he had lost in Municipal Court. The preliminary hearing route gave every advantage to the defense and savaged his own case.

The second route into Superior Court was by way of grand jury indictment. Starkey wouldn't be present when witnesses testified, nor would Reece. No motions to litigate, nothing to contest until the case was in Superior Court. Its speed and purity appealed to Fraser.

He waited for Starkey's answer to Donelli's question. To waive time for the preliminary hearing meant Starkey conceded the grand jury to Fraser. I need that time, he thought, and there isn't any if I've got to put on a prelim.

Starkey shook his head decisively. "Nope. We're not waiving time."

That was it. Fraser tried to move Donelli. "We all know that is an unreasonable posture, given the complexity of this case, your honor. Just to get a holding order at the prelim will require a great number of witnesses. I need more than the statutory ten days to prepare them."

"Are you in cement about not waiving time?" Donelli asked Starkey.

"No waiver. We want our hearing in ten days."

Fraser had a sinking sensation. The tactic was obvious but still dismaying. To prepare a case like this in so short a time meant there was no margin for error, and no mercy for missing witnesses or evidence.

"Okay, champ," the judge said, "we'll have it in ten days. We'll be right up against Christmas. I don't think it helps your client, but it's your right to insist on it."

Fraser reached into his briefcase. "I've got a motion prepared requesting a continuance of seven days, your honor." He gave copies to Donelli and Starkey.

The judge's plump face wrinkled at this annoyance. "Make your pitch in open court, but I'm going to deny it, Tony. This is a death-penalty case, and I'm not going to grant prosecution continuances because you've got a tough job." He smacked his lips. "What it seems to me is that you two should reach an accommodation. You want time. Al wants a prelim. I think there's room to talk," he dropped the papers on his desk, "but you can kiss off the motion."

"This case deserves more time and care," Fraser said, turning to Starkey, "from both of us."

"And my man deserves his right to cross-examine your witnesses."

Fraser held up his hands. "I'm not going to debate the question of speedy trial and confrontation with you, Al."

"How about the shrink's notes? You had him in there going at my guy for forty-five minutes. I think I'm entitled to his notes."

Fraser shook his head. "Dr. Rudin only talked to Reece for the purpose of locating the Tippetts child. Reece didn't talk about it. I haven't seen any notes, and Dr. Rudin says his report of the interview will be ready in a couple of days."

"I can have the report?"

"Of course. I'll give you the notes if the court orders me to."

Starkey sniffed and stretched casually on the judge's couch. He was a plastic man, with features that shifted in a trial from extreme rage to twinkling merriment in an instant. His righteous anger now melted into conciliation. "I've got a proposal," he said.

Donelli's ears cocked at the prospect of hurrying the session along. Fraser waited for the other shoe to drop.

"I'll waive prelim to get the case into Superior Court," Starkey said. "When we get upstairs, I want two shrinks to look at my guy to see if he's crazy or not."

"Do you mean competent to stand trial, or completely nuts?" the judge asked.

"Both. I know when we do get into Superior Court Mr. Fraser wants shrinks to look at him. Fine. I'll go along with it." Studied indifference colored his argument. Played well, Fraser thought.

He saw the trap immediately. It was, though, a plausible deal on its face. "What happens if the psychiatrists say he is crazy?"

Starkey shrugged, conveying that this was minor, unimportant. "Then we send him off to a state hospital until he's able to stand trial."

"If the psychiatrists agree he's competent to stand trial," Fraser said, "I assume you'd want to go back to Municipal Court for a prelim?"

"Sure. That's only fair if he can stand trial."

The ploy was clever. It played on the linchpin of his case, which was that Reece must be sane, despite the horrific evidence to the contrary. An insane man can't be executed. An insane man might never even go to trial. Starkey counted on Fraser's absolute and necessary belief in Reece's sanity. From the first, Fraser realized, Reece hadn't struck him as crazy. The pattern that still tantalized and eluded him was there, and it wasn't the random eruption of a madman but a set of acts planned and carried out with deliberation. Starkey reckoned that he would agree to waive prelim into Superior Court for that reason. Starkey thinks I'm certain the psychiatrists will declare Reece legally sane. And Starkey thinks I'm wrong.

On the other hand, if Reece *is* found insane, it puts us back to square one. Starkey will demand a preliminary hearing whenever Reece is discharged from treatment. In the meantime, witnesses move, they forget events, and evidence is always lost or misplaced. It might become impossible to put Reece on trial. If, though, the psychiatrists decided he could go to trial now, Starkey would have the whole case returned to Municipal Court at once and get his hearing that way. He would be grinning from ear to ear at the idea of all those witnesses.

Tails he wins, heads he wins. I can't go to the grand jury either way.

The worst part, Fraser realized, was the obscenity of Reece in a state hospital, his trial delayed forever. There was no justice in that.

Donelli watched to see who flinched. He was ready to badger whoever did.

"No, Al, I can't do it," Fraser said. "I don't gain anything."

"Sure you do," Starkey said earnestly. "You get into Superior Court without any trouble. We fight it out there. You know I'm going to enter an NGI plea and have Reece thirteen-sixty-eighted as soon as we're in Superior Court anyway."

Not Guilty by Reason of Insanity. Not responsible. Not accountable. Not punishable. NGI. It was a curse that galled Fraser. Section 1368 of the Penal Code invoked it. Reece could be found legally insane at the time of the commission of the murders, even though competent to stand trial now. He would still go to a mental hospital. He would stay there until he was sane according to the law.

And then he would be released. A month, a year, two years, then he would be free forever. He would be abroad in the world again.

"What else do you want?" the judge asked snappishly. "Doesn't that sound good enough?" He pressed Fraser now.

Fraser fought back. "It gives every advantage to the defense, your honor, and leaves me high and dry."

"Well," Donelli wiggled his hands impatiently, "it might happen that way anyway, right? You can go to the grand jury, and then the psychiatrists can still say he's crazy. You can bet your boots when he gets out of the hospital he'll be entitled to a preliminary hearing. You don't win anything."

"I know it's a gamble. I'm going to take it. I'm not going to make deals in chambers."

Donelli went pink at the innuendo. "That was uncalled for."

"I apologize. I didn't mean it that way."

"You don't have to get on a high horse around me, Tony. I know what's a deal and what isn't. I know what compromises a case and what doesn't. All we're talking about is saving your time and the court's time. Al has a sensible suggestion."

He sounded like Kate, as if all around them was an ocean of reason and in it, swimming unreasonably, was Anthony Fraser. No. Kate was wrong and Donelli was wrong. For some purpose, only he had been given a clarity of vision about Reece and the case. Reece was a force of evil. That was how he had to be fought.

Donelli stood, the flush still on his jowled face. "Let's go arraign this lunatic if you guys aren't going to be reasonable. I did my part, didn't I?" He smiled murkily at Fraser.

Fraser looked from the judge to Starkey. They were not even talking about the same things. They were accustomed to dealing and fussing with cases, even ordinary murders, and when something appeared that precluded compromise or the usual dickering, they were annoyed.

"You did your part, judge," Fraser answered.

TWO

The courtroom was packed with people, other cases, other families, but the main attraction was Reece, and he drew friends of the victims, neighbors, curious characters, and reporters with their artists to sketch the scene, since cameras were not allowed inside. Fraser saw the man Tippetts sitting near the front of the crowded audience section, rigidly upright as though held in place with metal clamps. More marshals than usual milled around, glancing slowly from face to face, moving like dinosaurs. They hooked their thumbs solemnly into their leather belts.

Fraser found one and told him to watch Tippetts.

The racket of the crowd was incessant. He started to sit down near the jury box when Donelli's bailiff, a bald black man with thick glasses, marched out. "All rise. Department Three of the Municipal Court of the County of Santa Maria is now in session. The Honorable Gilbert Donelli, judge, presiding."

With a theatrical pause for a scornful perusal of the rabble, he added, "Be seated."

As he intoned, Donelli swirled out from behind the bench in a blur of black, mounted the three small steps to his chair, and thumped into it. He licked his lips. He looked as stern and magisterial as he could.

"Good morning," he said to no one. No one replied.

He made sure Fraser and Starkey were ready. "We'll take a case out of order on the calendar, Mr. Marshal, Complaint number two-three-two-five-seven-F, the People versus Charles Edmund Reece."

The courtroom stirred momentarily and Fraser went to his place at the counsel table. He tried to look impassive, but it was a facade. The case was about to begin, and it would not be over until either he or Reece had triumphed.

Starkey examined his short fingers. At the summer baseball games played between teams of assistant public defenders and deputy district attorneys, Starkey's short fingers threw aggressively aimed fast balls when he pitched. He had struck Fraser out several times. He darted around the diamond with a balletic ease, getting up on the balls of his feet so he seemed taller. He walked on the balls of his feet so he seemed taller. He walked on the balls of his feet in court, too. At every game, he brought his family, and from the makeshift stands both his teen-aged daughters and their mother rooted loudly and obscenely.

The court reporter waited. They all waited. From behind the heavy metal door of the tank came groanings, rhythmic clunks, the mechanical rumblings of a hidden engine about to spit something out.

But Reece wasn't brought out through the tank. He came from a rear hallway, inaccessible to the public, to the left of the bench in the front of the courtroom. He had on a belly chain, which linked his hands at the wrists to a belt worn around his waist. He wore a bright yellow sweat shirt. That meant he was in isolation, away from all other prisoners. It signified his uniqueness. He looked around the courtroom like a new boy at school. Marshals stood behind him and at his sides.

Starkey strolled over to him.

Donelli said, "Is your true and correct name Charles Edmund Reece?"

He coughed. "Yeah. Yo. I'm sick."

"Are you representing Mr. Reece, Mr. Starkey?"

Starkey nodded. "The Public Defender's office was appointed to represent the defendant, and I have been assigned that representation."

"Record will so reflect. I should also note for the record that Mr. Fraser of the District Attorney's office is present."

All the players were at hand.

"You are prepared, I understand, to go forward with the arraignment today, Mr. Starkey?"

"Yes, your honor. I've advised my client of that."

Fraser glanced at Reece, who was demonstrating his dejected expressions, a battery of sad, pitiful stares and sighs. They were evidently supposed to elicit compassion, or dilute anger. Fraser was unmoved by them. He had seen Reece turn them off and on each time he was brought into court. But how a jury would regard them, he didn't know.

"Very well," Donelli said with satisfaction. "Mr. Reece, the People of this state have filed charges against you. They are contained in the Complaint which I will read to you in its entirety. After each charge you will be asked whether you plead guilty or not guilty to it. Do you understand?''

Reece nodded slowly, as if his heart would break. ''I do. Can I please see a doctor today, judge? The jail won't let me see one.''

''If your client is ill, perhaps we'd better put this over until he's well,'' the judge said peevishly.

''No, your honor, I don't know of anything wrong with him at the moment. I talked with him prior to court and he's able to go ahead.''

''Then we'll proceed.''

Donelli cleared his throat. The courtroom, Fraser realized, was now utterly still. Even the assorted thieves and child-beaters, drug dealers and rapists sat in dumb regard of the man in the yellow sweat shirt who appeared so helpless. Ordinary criminals seemed to find Reece as incomprehensible as ordinary law-abiding people did.

With agonizing slowness, Donelli read the charges, five counts of first-degree murder, and the attendant special circumstances of torture, rape, sodomy, and burglary that followed. A conviction of one murder and one special circumstance would lead Reece to the gas chamber. A conviction of any one was going to be as hard as all five of them together.

Reece dramatized his weakness by slumping toward a marshal, who caught him adroitly. Whispered conferences with Starkey followed, the judge fidgeting impatiently, Fraser quietly furious at this manipulation of the court. From the very outset, Reece presented himself as a sick man.

When they resumed, Reece said he was not guilty of each of the first three killings and the special circumstances involved. He seemed to lose interest in them quickly, and his pathetic demeanor gave way to one of boredom.

Fraser caught the movement—sudden, startling, and completely ferocious—from the side. He had expected an outburst. He knew it might come during the arraignment, when the specifications of the charges were actually read and Reece stood up to deny them all.

There would be an explosion. He knew that a shrieking

figure would suddenly launch forward, hands bent into claws, the voice cutting through the courtroom's unnatural stillness. Now it was happening. Nothing could bind Eugene Tippetts, wildly springing over people; certainly Donelli's incantations could not. The audience split apart like a cloven tree trunk to get out of his way.

The shrieking voice was unintelligible, animal.

Fraser instinctively fell toward the protection of the jury box. The marshals were already moving toward the man rushing in with such terrifying force. Fraser saw more marshals immediately form a protective huddle around Reece, whose expression became one of great curiosity. No time. He was dragged rapidly backward, an apparition in bright yellow surrounded by burly uniformed men intent on his safety. In a second he was out of sight and on his way to a secure holding cell deep in the building.

But the man who continued rushing on, even as his tormentor disappeared, was overwhelmed by a wedge of marshals. They hid him completely in a great pile of bodies, and his muffled shouts went on from beneath that weight.

Starkey had thrust himself against the wall as his client was rushed away. The judge stood to see, then dipped down behind the bench.

A bell sounded loudly. More men, deputies from other courtrooms, ran in, shouting at the audience, dispersing the frightened mass of people to get at the struggling pile of men near the front railing.

Fraser glimpsed Tippetts, one arm around his throat, his own arms bent at odd angles, being frog-marched toward the same doorway through which Reece had just vanished.

Judge Donelli stood up as the commotion subsided. To a senior marshal he said, "Are we clear, Ed?"

"I think so, your honor. I think it was just the one."

Fraser went up to the bench. "He's the husband of one of the victims, judge."

"Clear the courtroom," Donelli said. "We're going to take a recess." The remaining marshals emptied the courtroom rapidly, hustling the crowd out.

Fraser, in spite of it all, felt calm in the chaos. He had a clear idea of what needed to be done, and a disruption in court was not going to unsettle him.

"Jesus . . . the husband," Donelli said, glancing hurriedly all around, as if there were others lurking in wait for him. "I should have had everybody searched before they got in here." He bent under the bench again and came up with a baseball bat. "I keep this here, right where I can grab it. They're not taking me without a fight."

Fraser heard Starkey whisper at his side: "What a circus." Starkey wiped his glasses carefully.

"Ed," the judge barked to the senior marshal, "I want you to get more guys in here. I want a search line set up outside, and I want everybody searched before they set foot in here." Donelli leaned on the baseball bat. "Jesus," he said again.

An hour and a half later the arraignment was finished. Each count and the name of each victim, read again. Each allegation of the weapon used and special circumstances, each lesser crime. To each of them, Reece—now trembling slightly and nervously casting his eyes through the courtroom—murmured denials.

It was upside down, Fraser thought, an inversion of the right order of things. The victim's husband was dragged away, while Reece was battened down and protected. Tippetts and his butchered family needed the protection.

Starkey, in his faintly clipped speech, listed the motions he intended to file, a paper blizzard designed to bury him, to take more time and argument, more postponements and appearances, until the whole voluminous enterprise collapsed from its own weight. That was the defense strategy. Delay, then delay again.

But his own burden was fixed. The preliminary hearing, as Starkey had threatened, was scheduled within ten days.

Fraser had no choice. He had to convene the grand jury before then.

The clock was running.

CHAPTER VIII

ONE

Two men sat alone in a room. One sat in a chair, at a bare wooden table, his legs crossed, a well-cut blue sport coat hung with care behind him. He scratched a pencil randomly on a pad. He was a chunky man, but his tailoring, the coat, his custom-made shirt, and his gray trousers concealed it.

A small tape machine noiselessly recorded the emptiness. Dr. Keddie stopped scratching with the pencil. He uncrossed his legs. At the other end of the room, Reece sat on his haunches, clutching his knees with his hands, motionless except for a slight rocking. He watched Dr. Keddie. The look was vague, the same arid glance he used each time the psychiatrist visited. Dr. Keddie sighed and rubbed his hand over his crew cut. He began again.

"Is it that you don't trust me, Charles? Is that it?"

"You haven't done anything for me."

"I'm trying, Charles."

"Then get me a transfusion, get something for my blood."

Dr. Keddie spoke, clasping his hands as if in prayer, his soft voice lulling. "I'm here to help you. You know I've got no other motive but to help you. I'm working for your lawyer, Mr. Starkey. You know that."

"They want me for those murders. They say I killed people. If I did, they were Nazis. They poisoned me."

The empty eyes and face regarded him like the stony side of a granite hill, immovable and impenetrable. Keddie wanted to convey his concern. He had to crack that blank facade. There was so much to understand, so much to do.

"Charles, you know there is only one way to save you. Your defense is insanity. They have the evidence. They know what you did."

"I didn't do anything. It's not my fault."

He was getting stubborn again. Keddie despaired of ever learning what Reece thought, how his mind worked.

If he didn't learn, then Reece would die. It was as simple as that.

"Charles, listen to me, you've got to cooperate with me. I need your help. Together we can save you. I must convince a jury of your illness. You've got to help me understand it, do you see?"

Silence. The rocking ceased.

At least he'd gotten Reece's attention. Of course, from the hospitals Reece had been in he had a rich amount of imagery at his command. Aside from the humanitarian effort to save him, Dr. Keddie was intrigued by Reece's almost instinctive survival skills. But there was more, too.

"Now," he said, "you drank the blood from those animals—the dogs and squirrels—because you've felt this way for a long time?"

"Yes."

Good. They were in rapport once again. "Don't you feel that Nazis have polluted your blood? They're responsible?"

"They poisoned me, my mother poisoned me. Those Nazi doctors at the hospitals gave me viruses so my brain is dying. I can't think."

Once started, Reece recited well, as he had before. Keddie didn't need to write this down. He knew the material intimately. Reece sucked his mouth loudly. He no longer fell over to one side, since Keddie had explained to him that this motion didn't improve his circulation. It marked the start of Reece's trust. He took the advice.

"I drove by this guy running. I shot at him a couple of times. He was a Nazi."

"You shot him because he was a Nazi and he was after you?"

"Yo." Hesitation and a surreptitious peek to see if it was noticed. Reece was hiding something.

"Did something tell you to do that?" Dr. Keddie asked. A little more information and he could categorize Reece as a paranoid schizophrenic. The clinical evidence fitted that judgment. It also made him legally insane.

"What do you mean?"

"Well, for example, did something tell you to go out and shoot people? Something you didn't recognize? A shape? A color?"

110

"Like what? Like a person?"

"It could be. Perhaps you saw an animal or some light. That's the kind of thing that would tell you to do things you wouldn't normally do."

"Yeah." He paused. "I don't know what it was. Could it be anything?"

"That's for you to tell me, Charles. You saw it, didn't you?"

Reece nodded tentatively. "Yeah, I did. It was . . . it had a lot of arms and legs?"

"A spider? What? Did it have a head? Wasn't that it? A spider with a human face?"

"Yeah. That's what it was, big spider. Told me to do these things, like I didn't want to, you're right. I was hallucinating."

"Think about it. Concentrate and remember exactly what this spider with a man's face told you to do. It's going to be very important."

Dr. Keddie scratched out his interview notes and then walked to the barred window to stretch his legs. Reece was always such a chore to work with. He was like an onion. Peel one layer away and another appeared. Yes, he had delusions about his body, yes he was fascinated by Nazis, but Reece would say almost anything to protect himself.

The afternoon drifted in through the window. Jails were dreary. How did they expect proper interviews, proper tests to be conducted in these surroundings? Reece ought to be saved so he could be probed in more appropriate settings. He has secrets, Dr. Keddie thought, looking back at him.

"Do you remember going into a woman's house just before you were arrested?"

Reece nodded. He remembered all right. "She was making trouble. She was a Nazi, and her dog was poisoned. I went in and shot her. Then I went to work."

"You just went to work?"

Snort. "Sure. If I hadn't gone to work, they'd think something was wrong. I cleaned up, washed myself, all the stuff like before."

"But, Charles, you cut this woman open. You drank her blood. I can't imagine why you'd do that."

111

"Because she was a Nazi. She made me sick."

There was, of course, something else. "What happened to the little boy?"

"I put the little boy in the trash can with the lid, in the garbage someplace."

"Was the little boy alive?"

"I don't know." The head rose slowly from where it had hung motionless over the linoleum floor. "I shot him a couple of times."

"Was that all? You killed him?"

"I sucked some blood, then I got rid of it."

"Do you remember, can you see yourself shooting the woman?"

"No."

"Do you remember removing her clothing?"

"No."

"How do you know you shot her if you don't remember it?"

"I know I did it. I know that."

Why? Because the secret memory was pleasurable? Keddie couldn't tell yet. Then, as often happened without warning, Reece became balky. He refused to speak further. Typical paranoid with a prickly temperament. Dr. Keddie deliberately turned off the tape recorder. He put his pad and pencil away. Reece saw. He uncoiled himself, slowly standing up. He walked to the table and sat down with his hands before him. He laughed.

"What's funny?" Dr. Keddie asked. He smiled, too.

"I don't know."

"Something is making you happy. Please tell me."

"I don't know." The smile froze and drifted off.

He's guarding again, Keddie thought, hiding things from me. "I'm confused, Charles, how you could hurt people, a small child who never did you any harm. Can you explain this to me?"

"It was me or them. They were after me. He'd be just like them someday."

"You had no feelings of remorse or conscience?"

Reece mulled it over. "I feel bad about it now, I guess."

"But not then? Is that the truth?"

"Yo. I didn't feel bad then."

112

There was that flicker again. Keddie stirred vigilantly. What was going on underneath that blank surface? "The police say you sexually molested these women. Did you do that because they were Nazis?"

The eyes drooped. "I don't remember."

"You've got to tell me these things, Charles. When I ask you about the women and the little boy, I'm trying to help you, believe me. I just want to understand so you can be protected."

He waited and the room was silent. He sat back and Reece sniffed again, watching to see what he did. He's quite alert, Dr. Keddie noted, he isn't missing anything. "Just tell me why you molested the women, Charles. That's all."

The face turned to him. The eyes were clear and the voice was confident and full. There was no whining or hesitation. "Because I wanted them," Reece said firmly. "All of them. I wanted the women and the little boy."

Keddie was momentarily hobbled by the gloating defiance. He hadn't seen that before. Was this some kind of trick? Was Reece revealing a false trail in order to conceal a deeper mystery? No. Not possible, Keddie reasoned quickly, the delusions of persecution were consistent. This was the truth, then. It was the simple, consuming reason for the acts. He wanted them. He must have them if he wanted them.

"Why? Why did you want them?"

"I don't know. I was sick. They were poisoning me. I need a doctor." The voice was flat again, the eyes empty and curdled. The surface was calm once more; nothing moved beneath it.

"Fine," Keddie conceded. "We'll leave that for a moment. We'll go back. Tell me about Sunnyslope Hospital."

Silence. Empty, blank whiteness, nothing. Reece shuffled back to the other end of the room and sat on the floor. He bathed his white face in the sunlight.

"Charles?"

Nothing.

"Is it that you don't want to talk to me anymore?"

"I don't want to talk," Reece answered finally, "I want you to save me."

113

End of interview. Keddie had learned that Reece determined the moment the interview began and the moment it ended. But today, Keddie thought excitedly, I've seen something. Reece didn't care about what he'd done. He was a model of inhuman selfishness. He was moved by nothing other than a radical freedom, the kind most people only dream about. What he wanted alone decided his actions. That was worth pondering. Keddie nodded. That was worth saving and studying.

The important thing now was to maintain Reece's trust. For now and later, when he could be studied and treated. Without that trust, Reece wouldn't provide the information needed to help his case. Keddie decided that there was nothing to be done for the Tippetts child. There was no record of Reece's admission of killing him. And Keddie wasn't going to destroy Reece's trust by revealing information that would serve no purpose and do a great deal of harm.

If Reece wouldn't talk to him anymore, there was little chance of building a credible insanity defense. And then they would execute Reece. They would kill a very disturbed human being. That was the crime Keddie could prevent.

Dr. Keddie went to the door so he could be let out. He rapped on it. "I'll see you again soon, Charles."

Reece had closed his eyes.

TWO

"Please slow down, Mrs. Reece, I can't follow everything you're saying." Starkey had a clipboard on his knees, and he tried to write as quickly as the words spilled from the woman sitting across the living room.

Naomi Reece nodded and took another drink from the glass of grape juice beside her. When she put the glass down, the bluish crescent above her upper lip was thicker.

"I just can't help it, Mr. Starkey. When I tell you how they treated me, what they did to my home . . . And I think about what they must be doing to Charlie." Her voice was hoarse and singsong.

"Well, he's all right. Jail isn't a pleasant place . . ."

"Poor Charlie," she said, her head shaking, "my poor, poor Charlie."

Starkey had difficulty recalling a more tortured interview. The woman would talk along the lines he wanted for a few moments, then the voice rushed forward, her breathlessness increased, and she went into a monologue compounded of self-pity, pride, and bitterness.

"I know you've told these things to my investigators and Dr. Keddie, but I want to hear them from you myself. That's how I work in a case like this. I want to see and hear all the people personally."

"You're doing everything to help him. I know you are. I know Charlie would thank you."

"He still won't see you?"

She shook her head. Even though he was not a tall man, he seemed to loom over Naomi Reece when they met at the door. She sat tensely in a wing chair across from him. "That's why I think they're doing something to him. When he was with me, at least he'd listen. I could say, Charlie, Charlie you've got to stop this. You've got to be a man. I could make him clean up. He'd eat his food. But now, they're telling me he won't see me at all. Would they trick me? Would they do that?"

Starkey wished he hadn't decided to see the Reece house for himself. It wasn't worth it to have come here just because this woman said she couldn't breathe most other places. Keddie said she was a hysterical asthmatic. She had started snapping questions at Starkey the minute he arrived—whether he smoked, complaining about her poor breathing, the polluted air, the dirty things that could get into your lungs. She even sniffed at him suspiciously when he said, untruthfully, that he didn't smoke. Starkey thought she was simply hysterical.

The house was perfectly in order, except for those holes left by things missing, taken when the police marched through the place. She insisted on showing him every bit of damage, each nick and smudge.

"They're not lying to you," he said. "Charlie says that you poisoned him. He told that to me. He told that to Dr. Keddie."

"That's how much he's changed," she cried. "He's so

helpless now. He's like a baby. You can't put a baby in jail, can you? That isn't fair. He'll only get more confused and frightened.''

She was about to go off again. He knew the signs now. Talking to this woman was like tossing a stone into the air. Normal laws said the stone would fall back to earth, but this one took the momentum as an excuse to go soaring away.

"I've got a lot more ground to cover, Mrs. Reece," he said to her. "Bear with me if you've already gone over this information before.''

She heaved to one side in the chair and nodded. The inhaler came out and she squirted it into her mouth.

"Let's start at the beginning. When did your husband die?"

Naomi Reece breathed heavily for a moment. Her mouth was partly open, fishlike, her eyes obsidian. "He died when Charlie was six and one half years old.''

Starkey asked, "How long had you been married?"

"Eight years. Six months of heaven and seven and a half years of hell, that's what it was, Mr. Starkey. I won't varnish the truth.''

"You told my investigators he hit you. When did that start?"

She laughed, a short, hiccupping noise. "Listen to the innocent. He didn't hit me. He punched me in the face. He kicked me. I was lying down in the kitchen, on the floor, with pans and broken dishes all around me. I cut my arm . . .'' She fumbled the sleeve of her blouse up before Starkey could stop her, and exposed a thin mouthlike compressed ridge of white flesh. ''. . . and got eighty-two stitches. And he started kicking me. He'd punched me for a while because he was mad about what somebody had said to him at work.''

"So he hit you?"

"He hit me, he kicked me, he swore at me. That was Charlie's father. He wasn't a man. He was a man once, do you understand? Charlie was the result, but after that . . .'' She drank quickly, the blue glass in her pale hand, her red hair stiffly pressed to her head. "I was pleading with him. I had blood in my mouth, I was cut, and I was begging him to stop.''

"When you left him how long was that separation?"

"Two months. Something like that. He came to the place I was staying and he actually cried. That's what he did. He was so sorry, he was so sick at what he'd done, he apologized. I went back with him. I thought I loved him. I also wanted to be with Charlie."

"Your husband kept the boy?"

She nodded.

"Never reported him to the police?"

She shook her head.

"Why was that?"

Her voice was lower. The generator could be heard, as if very far away, droning outside. "I don't know, to tell you the honest truth."

"Did he ever hit Charlie?"

"Charlie was his darling. He never touched that child."

"But Charlie saw him hit you?"

"He was standing there, right there," her small arm pointed into the air between the two of them, "in the kitchen doorway in his peejays watching his daddy kick me and listen to me begging. I covered my eyes, Mr. Starkey, so I wouldn't see that child staring."

Starkey wrote easily now, his hand sliding across the pages. He had heard this one before. This was exactly the kind of thing a jury would take to its heart.

Unbidden, she went on. The years were indistinguishable from each other. Beatings, tearful apologies, interludes of tranquility. And Charlie grew up. When he was six and a half his father died suddenly in the night. Naomi Reece said she heard him making odd sounds after midnight, sounds that suggested he was choking or in pain. She listened for a time, then quietly gathered up the topmost cover from the bed and went downstairs and slept on the couch. In the daylight when he hadn't come down to go to work, she went upstairs as quietly as the night before and found him.

Naomi was then, she said, very calm, very at peace. There was, though, something tugging at her mind, something she had to do. She went to Charlie's little room and took the still half-asleep boy back to the bedroom.

She drew him to the edge of the bed. His father was tangled in the sheet and blanket, as if his legs and arms had spasmodically thrashed about. Holding Charlie by the waist, she pushed him toward the body. The boy was wide awake now, his eyes great, his body as hard in her hands as stone, his neck rigid. "Kiss him good-bye, Charlie," she whispered. "Kiss him good-bye forever."

The little body touched the other cold one and she then pulled Charlie to her, stroking him.

"That's all he's ever needed," she said to Starkey. "He needs love. He doesn't need these doctors, they can't give him anything. He needs love. I give it to him."

Starkey glanced up at the emphatic declaration. *I give it to him.* He underlined the words.

Naomi had then sold the house, thus beginning the first of many journeys that took them from Merced to Manteca and Stockton, smaller towns, and finally to Santa Maria.

Naomi had skills as a typist, she was quick and could be courteous; she worked for various businesses as a receptionist and secretary. There were one or two suitors, too, but she never remarried.

Charlie was put in a sort of babysitting care. It was run from the home of one of several older women who watched a dozen or so children. One day, Charlie ran away. In the bare outer room where the children were put to play were two cages of hamsters. In front of the other children, who watched unbelieving, Charlie cut four hamsters to pieces with blunt scissors.

Charlie was found a few hours later. Counseling was suggested, but Naomi prevailed. "I just loved him more than ever," she said, "I gave him as much love as I could stand."

He was about seven years old.

Why hadn't he been in school?

Naomi didn't want him with so many other people. He was afraid of people. It had been hard enough to keep him with the children and the babysitters.

But finally he did start school, well behind his peers, yet displaying a lively mentality, so he soon caught up. These were good years, by and large. "He was the best boy," she said. "You ask our neighbors. He mowed lawns. He was always helping people. He collected food and clothes, he went door to door when he found some people down on their luck. One time he had a lawn sale of some old stuff in our garage. He sold it all. He gave that money to poor folks, or what he thought were poor folks. It was all his idea. Everyone liked him.''

She had even kept a cat for a while. Coming home late one day, she discovered the cat and the bloody steak knife he had used on it. The cat was put to sleep and there were no more pets.

Starkey paused in his writing and massaged his hand. Naomi Reece went on talking.

''He was on the football team and the baseball team at Mount Washington High. He worked and got good grades. He went to college, it was Santa Maria Community College, for a year. He had a hard time. There was just the two of us, but Charlie kept up. He was the best.''

''When did he change?''

She was silent. Then: ''What do you mean?''

''Well, you moved about six times in the last three years. That wasn't because of new jobs. I want to find out what happened to him. I want to know why you moved.''

''People are vicious. They are liars and they are vicious. They would say things about Charlie to his face. To me. To the police. They accused him of things.''

''Were any of these accusations true?''

''Even if they were true, do you go around trying to upset and frighten a child?''

''Charlie wasn't a child at that point.''

''He was my boy. He was always a child, a wonderful, little boy who got scared. Sometimes, yes, he did things— not everything they blamed on him—but sometimes there were things I found out about.''

''With animals?''

She nodded reluctantly.

''Well, I know about what he had in the bedroom here.'' Starkey half-pointed toward the room that had been stripped of most of its contents by the police. ''That was pretty gruesome. Tell me about what you knew. I need to know so I can help him in court.''

''That's the crime, putting him in jail, taking him away from me.''

''Did you know about what he was doing back there?''

She drank again, emptying the glass. Starkey sensed her

antagonism. She was angry that even he, her son's champion, had to intrude into the hermetic world they shared.

"I do not, to this very moment, honestly know what he was doing. I do not believe what they're saying, and if I could just see him, I know Charlie would tell me the real facts. I do know," she swallowed with an effort, "if you love something, as I do, you take the good with the bad. I know there is a great deal of good in him. Maybe I closed my eyes for too long. But I have never stopped giving him my love."

Starkey underlined the word again.

"He's been hospitalized three times? The last time was this year, at Sunnyslope. Did Charlie threaten anybody you know about? The staff said he was always threatening them."

"I never heard him say anything."

"Who put him in the hospitals, Mrs. Reece? Was that your idea?"

"They were all voluntary commitments."

"Well, Sunnyslope was ordered by a psychiatrist," Starkey said gently. "Even if your son didn't spend much time there, he wasn't at the place voluntarily."

She didn't seem to hear what he said. Starkey was forming a notion in the back of his head as he waited for her to say something.

"I told Charlie that he ought to see professionals. He threw a chair at me. It was a small metal chair. But he was very bad then, very poorly. That was the first time he went to the hospital. Then a year later he went again. This was right after he left college. He stopped seeing his friends. He had a lot of them. He had a lot of girlfriends, too. Everybody liked him. He was good with cars. He could build anything. Then he would get very bad and I couldn't get him to get better."

"So he agreed to admit himself to the hospitals?"

"Twice. Then they made him go, the last time."

"And that was because of this incident with the Torres's dog in your last neighborhood." Starkey flipped through his notes. Charlie had tried to steal the dog at knifepoint.

She nodded. "But he got better. They let him out. He can get better, Mr. Starkey. I hope you tell everyone that

120

my son isn't some creature. He's a good person who needs all the love I've got.''

"I'm going to try to do everything to save him."

"They can't hurt him. They can't be allowed to do that."

"Everything's going to be done, Mrs. Reece." Starkey had formed that notion now.

After seeing Naomi Reece for himself, if Charlie's only defense was insanity, here was a witness who could make it almost an ironclad winner.

"That's what you must do," she said to him, pouring two glasses for them, "everything must be done to help Charlie. There isn't anything more important in the world."

CHAPTER IX

ONE

"I've got witness problems, Harry," Fraser said.

Ballenger lay asprawl in a chair. The office was bright and the night dark.

"The jury commissioner is working on the grand jury meeting for two days this week if I need it," he said wearily, "but I'm not sure if I'm going to have all my people."

"You've got to go, even if you're short."

Fraser slammed his hand down on the desk top with a wallop that resounded down the empty corridors. "I've got to treat this case like it was a damn malicious-mischief trial. Rush it, push it, throw it into court without preparation. You read the whole damn file on your way into the courtroom, and you pick the jury without knowing if you've got the evidence, or the witnesses, or any damn case at all."

His frustration came in part from the plague of all trials,

the witnesses, witnesses who couldn't be found, travel schedules that couldn't be arranged, people who denied seeing or hearing anything, the slippery quarry always running ahead.

But it was also because Ballenger was sitting across from him, and even though he saw Harry every day, he hadn't told him that Whalen was using him as bait, or that his last major assignment hung in the balance. Fraser knew it was cowardly, but he had enough troubles right at the moment without involving Harry.

Calmly, Ballenger asked, "Who's missing?"

He ticked them off. "I've got two cops off on vacations where there aren't any phones, one civilian who won't call in and is apparently evading the process servers. I haven't heard from a half dozen others."

"How important are they?"

"Well, they add up. I'll start losing counts when the grand jury indicts. I don't want to lose any of them. I want him indicted on all counts."

"Can you work around them?"

Fraser shook his head. "The cops found evidence at the Tippetts's house and Reece's place. The civilian puts Reece near the Ellis home at the time of the murders. No. I need them."

"I guess you do." Ballenger yawned.

"I thought you might have something more constructive."

"Not me. I'm strictly nine to five, and it's past my bedtime." He yawned again. "Besides, these things always work out in the wash."

Fraser didn't know if Ballenger had heard about his own troubles. But the nonchalance seemed genuine. Ballenger, who could be sly in trial, lacked guile in his friendships. Fraser turned to the other nagging problem to avoid tackling Ballenger's difficulty.

"Starkey has a psychiatrist in with Reece. He's seen him three times now. I can't get a psychiatrist to look at him until after the indictment is handed down and we're in Superior Court."

"What about that guy Rudin?"

"Rudin doesn't count. He only went in to give me a general idea of what we had. He isn't a forensic psychiatrist, so I can't use him in court. He hasn't even given me his report yet.''

''Who's Starkey got?''

''Ben Keddie.''

The name made Ballenger chuckle derisively. ''The good doctor. Fair and square and never testified for the defense. It's pure chance that his diagnoses come out that way every time. It's fate.''

''He's a whore, and he's going to lead the defense charge up the hill. Right now he's getting his testimony worked out while I go crazy hunting up witnesses.''

His frustration brought Ballenger into action. He went into his song and dance. My jester, Fraser thought gently, always ready. ''They have their experts. Okay. We'll get our experts. We'll get what's-his-name from San Diego. Gables.''

''Why Gables?''

''He's absolutely terrific,'' Ballenger said enthusiastically, flapping his arms. ''He'd say anyone was sane. He'd look at a guy wearing an airplane-propeller hat with two muffins stuck to his cheeks and a sign that said 'I'm Radioactive' across his chest and tell you the guy's perfectly okay. I'll admit he's eccentric, that's Gables talking, but mere eccentricity is no indicator of insanity. He'll look the jury right in the eye and say that stuff.''

''I'll need more than one shrink.''

''Hire more. Hire a dozen of them.''

Fraser was melancholic. ''So it comes down to a numbers game. You know—two for sanity, two for insanity, and one oddball for maybe thrown in. The jury might decide to flip a coin after that.''

Ballenger gripped the edge of the desk. ''Gables will talk you right out. He's on the stand looking in the air, going on about how crazy ideas don't necessarily mean you're crazy,'' Ballenger flexed his arms and flicked his shirt sleeves, ''and all this time he's backing up against the stand, getting this wild gleam in his eye. He braces himself,'' Ballenger froze, ''he starts snorting,'' Ballenger snorted, ''and then he tells you about his last astral trip to Jupiter.''

''Why do I want this man, Harry?''

Ballenger dusted himself off. ''Well, Tony, you can't

keep a shrink on the witness stand too long, you know. Unless he's on the other side. Sooner or later they spill the beans."

It was a slapstick performance designed to lighten his mood, and it worked well enough that Fraser smiled. "You're crazy."

"You want a drink on that?"

"Who buys?"

"Hell buying," Ballenger swore with gusto, "we'll dig some up. I bet Spence has a whole stock upstairs. You want to look?"

Fraser surveyed the work waiting for him, reports, witness lists, investigation requests, all needing immediate attention. "Sure. Why not?"

Ballenger was delighted. "I'll have to restrain myself if we strike pay dirt, so you better enjoy whatever we find."

"Lead the way."

A finger in the air: "Don't overlook any possibilities. I have an idea where to start down here."

They began by making a detour to an office where a Highway Patrol investigator was temporarily housed. Ballenger suspected him of hiding liquor, and he rooted happily in the man's desk and cabinet without success. During it all, Ballenger kept up a nonstop patter, obscene and ridiculous, and gradually Fraser joined in. Ballenger had the ability to make him laugh. It all receded for a while—Kate, and the rush to get the grand jury, even Ballenger's own peril. No, not that. He would have to be told tonight about Whalen's threat.

They grew almost carefree, going into two more offices where Ballenger said he detected the unmistakable odor of spirits. They pulled open drawers and upended wastebaskets without finding anything but two old issues of *Hustler* and three stale cupcakes.

Then it was on to the fifth floor. They approached Whalen's door. The lights were on throughout the floor for the cleaning crew and security. Ballenger paused reverently at the door. "He dwells inside."

Fraser pushed the door open. "Don't you feel like you're breaking into the principal's office?"

"School days, school days," Ballenger muttered nostalgically, disappearing under the conference table to check the boxes stored there. Nothing of substance was found. "I know it's here," he said with conviction.

Then he tapped on a large cabinet to get Fraser's attention. He tapped it again, as if sounding for imperfections. "Spence brought this monster from his old office at the Water Commission. It's oak. Weighs a ton, gave three moving men hernias."

"He went to a lot of trouble to get it up here," Fraser said. "You think he's sentimental?"

"He's thirsty." Ballenger tugged at the twin wooden doors, latticed with rattan, that secured the cabinet. "He's got it locked."

Fraser saw the game was over. "I'll spring for drinks someplace. We'll make it an early night."

"You won't spring for anything. I wasn't the wonder of my high school for nothing." Ballenger produced a pocketknife and deftly inserted its thin blade into the simple lock. He turned the blade delicately, sighing and muttering, until it caught with a faint click and the doors swung open.

"Very professional, Harry. I'm going to have my locks changed."

Ballenger was in transports. "I grovel in joy." He assumed the attitude of a Hindu supplicant.

Fraser cataloged the large selection of wines and liquors in Whalen's cabinet. It was filled with bottles. A definite preference for scotch was apparent. He picked out a full bottle of red label and two glasses, and found some soda. He brought the load to the coffee table by the sofa and mixed a scotch and soda for himself and a soda for Ballenger. They toasted each other ceremoniously.

Wistfully, Ballenger watched as Fraser sipped. "Jesus Christ, I miss that," he said.

Fraser told Ballenger what Whalen had threatened. There wouldn't be a better moment.

Ballenger listened, drank, and said nothing. He chuckled grimly at the news. "I'm not very popular, am I? It's no big secret I didn't support the son of a bitch in the election."

"None of that makes any difference. He wanted a hostage for my good behavior, and you were convenient. I'm sorry I didn't tell you sooner."

"Doesn't break my heart that you waited."

Fraser balanced his glass in the palm of his hand. The glass was cool and heavy. Whalen liked thick glasses he could grab hold of. "I've got a notion," he said.

"Give."

"I can get a leg up on Whalen if you work on this case with me." He waited for Ballenger's reaction. "Do you want to work on this case?"

A thoughtful tilt of his head, then Ballenger replied, "I'd like that. It'd be like the old days."

Fraser warmed to it. "You can't be transferred if you're working with me. Whalen can't move either of us. You can do a lot of the legwork for me, too. I won't have to explain everything to you."

"Don't count on it," Ballenger said.

They toasted once more.

"I'll break it to Spence tomorrow," Fraser said.

"Don't be too cruel."

Fraser proposed a third toast. "Here's to Gables and all the other shrinks. Here's to winning."

"Here, here."

Ballenger downed his soda. They talked about the old days for a while. Fraser vividly described the nearly identical expressions of horror from his father and Kate when he'd told them where he would be working.

"Why did you take Gleason up on his offer?" Ballenger asked. "You had another place to go. I ended up here by default."

"I'm not really sure. The idea of making things right appealed to me, I suppose."

"Oh, dear."

"I wanted to do something my father never had."

"Handle a mass-murder trial, or go broke?"

"Well, I'm not getting rich. I'm not going broke. When you're the only one of three kids who goes to law school, you want to strike out in a different direction."

Ballenger nodded and sighed at the red-label bottle standing so close. "I joined up to nail the bad guys."

"Oh, dear," Fraser mimicked, and they both laughed.

They got ready to leave. "I've got work to do, and I don't want Whalen hanging a trespass on us."

Reluctantly, Ballenger helped him push the bottles and

glasses roughly back into the cabinet and lock it again. Ballenger accidentally knocked over a vase on Whalen's desk as they went out.

In the stairwell they met Earl Campion, an odd blond kid who was the night security man for the office. He looked as if his eyes had been sewn in too tightly.

"You'd better check Mr. Whalen's office, Earl," Fraser said, "I think there's someone up there. I heard some noise."

"More than one, do you think?" Campion asked worriedly.

"A small army," Ballenger reported, "knocking stuff over. You better get up there quick."

Campion skipped past them, panting suddenly and muttering to himself.

"Nice boy, Earl," Ballenger offered in an imitation of Sally Ann, "but kind of a pinhead."

TWO

It was after two when Fraser got home, very tired, still buoyed by Ballenger's tricks. The first of the grand-jury witness interviews was that morning. Or rather, in just a few hours. In a moment, he lost any lightheartedness.

Kate was on her side in bed when he slipped into the bedroom, his shoes left in the hall. He undressed at the closet in the dark with as little sound as possible. She heard him anyway.

"Sorry I woke you," he said, stepping to the bathroom, splashing water on his face.

"Are you just getting in?"

"There was a lot to do."

He came out of the bathroom, drying his face. "Well, at least you're not prowling the house anymore," Kate yawned. "Turn on the light if you want."

"I'm coming right to bed." He held the towel to his face, then lowered it, all pretense falling away with it. "I'm afraid, Kate."

"Of what?"

Fraser could make her out in the dimness as she lay waiting for him. "I'm afraid of losing it all. It's all there,

127

in my hands. I only have to drop it once. That's what scares me."

"You're very good at what you do, Tony," Kate answered after a moment's pause. "Sometimes I wish you weren't. You don't have to worry about it, I'm sure."

He sat down on the bed near her. "You don't know what goes into a thing like this, the kind of mistakes I can make, the consequences."

"I don't want to know. I know you. I know all about you." She drew him closer, and he let himself be comforted.

"I'm so afraid."

She put a hand to his lips to quiet him. He didn't wonder at the irony of Reece, who threatened to drive them apart, drawing them closer at that moment than they had been for some time, or might be for some time to come.

He rested in the temporary haven Kate offered.

CHAPTER X

ONE

Dr. Mahon was the first witness in his office in the morning. The lanky pathologist cordially chided Fraser for neglecting their promised dinner.

Mahon examined several of the exhibits lying around the office as he talked, analytically fingering a rifle and butcher knife. He had to actually touch whatever caught his interest.

The grand jury met in two days, and Fraser wanted to interview as many of the witnesses as he could early in order to expedite the testimony and also allay the fears of those who had never before been within the secret precincts of a grand jury.

He also wanted to find out how far a witness like Mahon would go.

The meeting became less pleasant at that point.

"I'm sorry, Tony," Mahon said, shaking his head, "I can't say that. I don't know if the Ellis woman was alive when this man started to work on her."

Fraser had the pathologist's report. He flipped through it. "It is possible. I mean, you say here yourself that there was vascular pressure. That means she was alive."

"You want me to state, with certainty, that this woman was living when your killer started cutting her. She may have been. But it's by no means certain. I can only say it's a possibility. Not a good one, either."

Fraser's patience ended. He assumed Mahon would understand the significance of his testimony and act accordingly. He wasn't being asked to lie or fabricate evidence. Fraser only wanted him to tell the grand jury what he'd found at the autopsy. But Mahon was querulous. He wouldn't say anything that hadn't been verified, quantified, or measured completely. He wouldn't speculate.

And he didn't really see why it was so important.

"George," Fraser closed the report, "you can state an opinion if I ask you in court. That's all I want you to do. You simply say the Ellis woman was alive."

"I can't do that." Mahon had a puzzled smile on his face, as if Fraser's insistence struck him as very strange. He pulled out his pipe. "May I?"

"Go ahead."

"The old hands said a pipe or a strong cigar made the job a little easier. I thought they meant it kept your mind a trifle distracted. They meant the smell."

Fraser smiled automatically. He watched Mahon go through his routine of filling and tamping the pipe, striking a match, drawing until the aromatic smoke appeared. Mahon might nod during the process, but he wasn't listening to what you were saying. Not until the pipe was lit was his attention focused. When Fraser saw he was settled comfortably, he said, "One of the special circumstances I've alleged is that Reece killed Mrs. Ellis by means of torture. That means she was alive and capable of feeling pain."

"Oh, well, saying she was alive and able to feel pain, Tony," Mahon puffed thoughtfully, "no, that's really too much for me."

"The grand jury is going to be listening very carefully, George. They will take an expert's testimony very seriously."

Mahon puffed at his pipe.

"If you don't say this woman could have suffered, as I know she did, they might not indict Reece on that special circumstance."

"Well, that's only one down. There are many others. I can't say what I don't know for a fact."

"It isn't just one allegation," Fraser said bluntly. "I'm talking about the whole idea here. My job," he looked at Mahon, "our job is to hold Reece to answer for what he did. That means evrything he did."

"Well, you've got some higher source of knowledge than I do, because my findings do not support a conclusion like yours."

"Does it bother you that he might escape responsibility for his acts?"

"I imagine if I thought he'd get away from the other charges, yes, but this is one of many, isn't it? I hope he's found guilty. It strikes me that it makes very little difference which of these legal roads gets him there."

Mahon puffed placidly and waited for Fraser to say something. Fraser rubbed his forehead. He had to increase the pressure. "I don't know how much of my case is going to hold together," he said. "I've got missing witnesses to worry about. I don't want to worry about your testimony."

The pathologist smiled. "Tony, I told you this case was not for you. You won't give it a rest. You won't give yourself a rest, I'm sure. I'm sorry about your problems. But you understand what I can say and what I can't."

Fraser had hoped Mahon, as a friend and colleague, would have more insight into the nature of Reece's crimes. He did not. He was hardly better than Kate. "I can keep you on the witness stand," Fraser said, "and ask you enough questions to make it sound as though you reached these conclusions."

"Well," Mahon answered, with a look of friendly concern, "you can try."

"I don't want to do that, George."

"No, I understand."

"I'd much rather leave it up to your conscience."

"Yes, I see that."

"Will you at least give it some thought?"

Mahon nodded. His pipe had gone out and he hadn't relit it. "I'm going to give a great deal of thought to what you said."

It was a small concession, and Fraser hoped it would bear fruit. "That's all I'm really asking, George."

TWO

More witnesses followed. His mood had been soured by Mahon. Wringing the details needed even for the quick brush strokes of a grand jury grew more and more burdensome.

The phone rang incessantly. Sally Ann blocked most of the calls, but some had to go through. He spoke to half a dozen reporters.

"Channel Eight Newsteam, Mr. Fraser. We understand that the grand jury is meeting this week on the mutilation murder case. Is that true?"

"I can't comment on that."

"So it is meeting?"

"I'd like to help you out, but it's not something I can talk about."

"Sounds like you're all set."

"Nothing's all set."

"Starkey says you've got to go to the grand jury this week."

"Then you'll probably get more from him . . ."

He finally told Sally Ann to hold all the calls and to keep people out. Sanderson popped in a few moments later, looking satisfied. He wore a bluish leisure suit and carried a file folder.

"Not now, Mel," Fraser said.

"It'll make your day." Sanderson shoved the folder in front of him.

Fraser read it. "The Crime Lab's finished with these comparisons?"

"Bottom of the fourth page. I waited until I got the results, in case it was a dry hole."

He had read too hastily. The news was too good, too strange. He read again. "Is the gun still out at the lab?"

"No, I got it booked back into property this morning."

"Are these witnesses available? I'm going to have to

add this to the indictment and get it over to the grand jury.''

"They're handy."

Fraser put the folder down. "This is the damndest thing."

Sanderson took a chair. "This officer remembered the jogger getting shot. Who knows why? Maybe because it was one of those wild ones, joggers normally don't get dinged. Maybe the white Chevy at the scene clicked. I don't know. Anyway, he figured this one and the later murder might be connected.''

So he had ballistics tests done, and the results demonstrated that the gun Reece had at the time of his arrest—the gun from which all the other bullets had been fired— also killed a man named Vale who was out for an evening run. It was another of the mysteries of murder, like witnesses who couldn't be bothered to testify even against a killer. Why an isolated police officer, for some unknown reason, recalled an isolated fact out of a random, cartwheeling array of facts, and matched it to a particular crime, was unfathomable.

"Thanks very much, Mel," Fraser said. "This does help. I wonder what he was doing that night? Shooting a jogger doesn't fit at all with the others."

"Who knows."

"Maybe all he wanted was to see what it felt like."

"What?"

"Killing a human being."

Sanderson stood, but seemed hesitant about leaving even as he headed for the door. He paused. "Good. Great. Well. Look, if there's anything I can do, just tell me."

"I will."

"Could be anything." He smiled awkwardly in the doorway. "Something special even. I'm your man."

He half waved and ducked out before Fraser could reply to the invitation. It was hard to tell what Sanderson was proffering beyond a welcome desire to be useful. How unlike Mahon, Fraser thought.

He quickly redrafted the indictment package. It consisted of all the charges against Reece, identical to the complaint in Municipal Court once the grand jury was finished. He added the Vale shooting as the last count.

Sally Ann scowled at the idea of doing the work over again.

"Only for you, darlin'."

She shouted at him from her typewriter an hour later. "They've got Mr. Tippetts down at reception. He's a little funny."

"Tell him to come up," he said. "No. Wait. I'll go get him."

Tippetts. Fraser braced himself for an interview with the man. Victims' relatives were never easy to talk to, and Tippetts had *seen*.

He went down to the first-floor reception area. Squeezed together on the arsenical green plastic couch was a Vietnamese family, waiting for someone. Tippetts leaned against a wall. He had on a tie, but it had been loosened and he wore no belt. His hair was only partly combed.

"Mr. Tippetts?" Fraser said. He didn't like the man's appearance.

Tippetts stirred and pushed forward. "Reporting in." He stuck out his hand.

Fraser shook it; it was damp, doughy to the touch. "Come on to my office. I'll go over the whole grand jury procedure with you so there won't be any surprises."

Tippetts gave out a wet giggle. "You better be a hell of a salesman."

"Why?" he asked as they walked. Tippetts moved with sluggish carelessness, stepping on his own shoes or rolling into a wall. He kept quiet until they were in the office and he fell into a chair.

"How about coffee?" Fraser asked. "I'm having some." He motioned to Sally Ann.

"I don't want any coffee, thanks. I don't want anything."

"Bring us some, will you?" he asked Sally Ann. "You might want it later."

Unseen by Tippetts, Sally Ann gave a small shudder of sympathy in Fraser's direction. Soused witnesses could be bogeymen. They required coaxing and threatening in judicious measure, and often didn't appear to testify anyway.

Fraser sat down opposite Tippetts, who reclined fluidly in the chair, taking in the office, finally swinging around

133

to him. He had a bland, casual expression that Fraser distrusted.

"Thanks for taking care of that assault thing in court," Tippetts offered.

"We were lucky. No damage, nobody was hurt."

"I lost my head for a while." Tippetts laughed. "I went off the deep end." He wiggled his head comically. "But I'm okay now. I'm great now."

Studying Tippetts's disintegrating self-control, Fraser steeled himself for what he might have to do to him. "Tell me why you're not going to appear before the grand jury."

Tippetts's gaze stayed unfocused. "He's going to get off. That's what's going to happen. Everybody knows it."

"He is not. I promise you that. I need your testimony."

Tippetts snickered. It was unclean and terrible.

All right, that was how Tippetts saw the thing. Fraser realized he had no comfort for the man. He had very little for himself, or for his own wife, much less this stranger who was in so much pain. But, at least, unlike Kate, he could make Tippetts see what must be done and why. "I'll lay it out very basically for you, Mr. Tippetts. If you don't appear to testify Thursday night, you make it that much harder for me to convict this man. Your testimony is important. It's difficult to say this . . . but you were the first person to find your wife. I need to have the grand jurors hear you. I need to have them *see* you."

Tippetts rubbed his nose with his whole hand, like a child. "You're not going to convict him. They say he's nuts. I bet you think he's nuts."

"No. I don't think Reece is crazy. He knew exactly, precisely what he was doing when he killed your wife and the others."

"So what? Everybody else thinks he's nuts." He waved his hand in dismissal. "Waste. Waste of time."

"It isn't—"

"I don't *have* the time. I stay home and watch my boy. That's what I do. I watch him. I don't let him go outside. He doesn't go anyplace. I got him outside now, locked in the car. I watch him all the time."

"Look," Fraser said, blocking out squares with his hands to make Tippetts see and understand, "this case is like Chinese puzzle boxes. Each part has to fit exactly into the others. If we start leaving out testimony or witnesses won't cooperate, the boxes don't fit, the whole thing gets off center and may not come together at all.''

Tippetts licked his lips. His face was rigid, the way it had been in court.

''We're preparing to meet Reece's insanity defense. I'm asking for the death penalty. I believe a jury will vote for it. But I've got to start as strongly as I can. Imagine what happens if he's acquitted or found not guilty by reason of insanity. He'll get out of prison or a hospital some day. He'll be on the streets again.''

No idea could be calculated to stir Tippetts more, and Fraser applied it with distaste.

''No.''

''I'm telling you what will happen. It has happened before.''

''No,'' Tippetts said again, ''I'll kill him. You can do whatever you want to. But I'll kill him.''

He wouldn't let that go for a while. Fraser saw that he'd broken through Tippetts's stupor, at least. Now was the time to play the last, cheapest card.

''You've got your son outside. Andrew, right?'' Fraser said, and the hardness of what he was going to say stung him even before he said it. ''We still don't know what happened to Aaron. He's still missing.''

Tippetts breathed deeply, and a steady pulse showed in his jaw as he clenched it tightly.

''It's a terrible thing when you lose a child.''

''You don't know.''

''I do know, Mr. Tippetts. I had a daughter, younger than Aaron. I lost her about six months ago.''

''Little different, wasn't it?'' Tippetts laughed bitterly. ''Lost? What does that mean? You don't know what it means.''

''She died,'' Fraser said, and then saw that Tippetts wasn't going to allow him the luxury of stopping there. ''She had pneumonia, and it seemed to be getting better. We had her in the hospital, she had good care. I spent a lot of time with her. My wife and I did. When it seemed to be past the dangerous stage, I went to work. I had a trial to finish. My wife stayed there at the hospital.''

Sweet Molly. Asleep in a bed of mist, floating away on a cloud. "The last time I saw my daughter, Mr. Tippetts, she was in an oxygen tent. I thought she was safe. So I went to court," he took a breath, "and the next day at a recess I got word that something sudden had happened. Cardiac arrest, a fumble with the air tube they tried to insert . . ." He saw that Tippetts had turned away. He couldn't tell if Tippetts was crying. "She died. My daughter died and I wasn't there. My wife had to bear that particular pain alone."

Fraser lost track of the point suddenly as Kate's exhausted, tearstained face loomed before him, as it had when he got to her at the hospital. "It's very hard to forgive that kind of desertion," he said absently.

"I'm sorry," Tippetts said.

Fraser fought to get back. "So . . . so I think I have some idea what it feels like to lose—" he corrected himself, "to have a child die. I don't think you ever really get over that."

"No. No." Tippetts's head shook slowly, still turned from him.

Grave little Molly, waiting in the dark for him to finish a bedtime story, her eyes intent on him as he told whatever fantasy came into his head. A story each night before sleep. Not very good stories, because he had little talent for imaginative fancies, so Molly heard a rehashing of the day's events with animals and funny names. And each night she was a little different, more a full human being when she went to sleep, changing and growing magically in the dark. Then she was gone.

"I want you to think for a moment." Fraser struggled to drag himself away from the beautiful, draining memory. "About your wife and your dead son. You have an obligation to appear before the grand jury. You have incurred a debt to your wife and son. Think of what they suffered, and ask yourself if you have the right to obstruct the prosecution of their killer."

Tippetts turned rapidly, caught between the urge to lash out at Fraser and the start of another weeping jag. Fraser didn't flinch from the fury he'd tapped, expecting a blow from the sweating man only a foot from him. There was a little expiation in a blow like that. He wouldn't turn from it.

But Tippetts hung there, agonizingly, and then something broke. He slowly caved inward, his eyes full of tears.

"You know the worst part," he said slowly, "is not knowing what happened to Aaron. I mean, like you said, he's dead. I think I know, but I don't know for sure. That's the worst part. I guess it's worse than what I saw." He wiped under his eyes with his palms. "Sometimes at night I start thinking, hey, he might be okay, he's hiding somewhere, he might have gotten away. Someone took him in, maybe his name's changed and that's why he hasn't come back. It could've happened." He daubed again at his eyes. "I've been thinking a lot like that." He looked bashfully at Fraser, as though they shared a tiny, shameful secret.

"I'm sorry I put it to you so strongly. I have to make you see the importance of testifying on Thursday."

"It's your job, right? You do your job. I'm not mad." He squeezed his nose. "You make a lot of deals, right? That's the way you do things?"

"There won't be any plea bargaining."

Sally Ann rapped and appeared with two cups of coffee. "I take no blame for this. The machine is busted, so I had to go down to the county recorder before I found any." She looked at Fraser for a sign.

"We're fine," he said. "Thanks."

She smiled and left.

"It's up to you, Mr. Tippetts. I'm leaving it to your conscience."

Tippetts drank several large mouthfuls, breathing thickly, then he set the cup down. "We didn't go to church when Eileen . . ." He stopped, then started jerkily, "was alive. I didn't have any religion and she didn't, so we didn't go." He smiled awkwardly. "No reason we couldn't. I've been thinking about that since all of this. About him. What he did."

Fraser watched him. Tippetts's face grew sly, odd and crafty. "I mean not going to church, I don't know the ins and outs of this stuff. I thought about what happened . . ." He drank, smiled, waited. "I think it was God's idea."

"I don't know, Mr. Tippetts. I'm only interested in the grand jury."

"That's it," Tippetts insisted. "I don't know why, see, but God made a judgment against us."

Fraser was heartily ashamed for bullying Tippetts, who was ready to pull some monstrous unknown sin over himself to explain Reece. He was willing to go into the depths so that the terror would make sense. "No," Fraser said, "I'm sure you're wrong about that. What Reece did, he did for his own reasons."

Tippetts nodded, but he had seen the purpose behind his suffering and wasn't about to be dissuaded by a lawyer. "What happens if I don't show up?" He lay back in the chair, empty and red-eyed.

"You're under subpoena now. The worst thing I could do is have the sheriff arrest you."

Tippetts giggled mirthlessly. The worst thing. Fraser knew that's what he was thinking. That's the worst thing this guy can do to me. "Suppose I left? What if I went to another city, another state maybe?"

"Then I could have a warrant issued for you, Mr. Tippetts, those are the powers the law gives me. I can use them if I choose to. Believe me, I'd rather not."

"You'd do that?"

"Yes," Fraser said, "if it was necessary."

Tippetts wiped his eyes again. "I guess there isn't any other way, is there?"

"No, there isn't. Help me convict him."

"I'll be there," Tippetts said with a great weariness. "I'll do anything you want."

"You've made the best decision, even if it's the most difficult one." Fraser put out his hand and Tippett shook it heavily. "Meet me here Thursday night at seven-thirty. We'll walk over to the courthouse together."

"Okay. If that's what has to be done, okay." Tippetts got up and bumped his way out. "I'll be there," he repeated.

Fraser watched him stumble down the corridor until he turned toward the elevators and was lost from sight.

Fraser's stomach was knotty. Sweat cooled down his sides. The ruin of Tippetts lay soddenly over his office.

THREE

If he wasn't a good man, good on the line, a good worker, nice guy all around with a pleasant family, it might be a little different, or so Cerrutti reckoned as he tried to figure Gene Tippetts out. Not that anyone would feel less broken up about what happened to his wife and kid. It would just be easier to handle things businesslike, efficiently, without wondering if you were being too hard or too soft or if you were saying the right things.

It was, Cerrutti decided, a damned confusing situation because Tippetts happened to be a good man.

He sat there on the other side of Leo Cerrutti's spanking new office—a new office for the new personnel manager—not seeming to listen very much. He just wanted to disagree about everything.

"I'm not 'making' you do anything, Gene," he said. "I'm saying you can take a week or two, or three if you want. You don't have to make any decisions now. You've got a lot . . ." Cerrutti was embarrassed again. "Well, I know you're not in your usual frame of mind, so to speak."

"I'm quitting."

"Now, Gene take my advice, take some time off. I've got it cleared upstairs. Everybody's on your side. We're all pitching for you. Don't walk away from us."

Tippetts stirred at last. He didn't look drunk, but then he didn't look sober, either. He looked funny—bleary and taut at the same time. He looked like he was coming from three or four different directions at once. Damn, if he'd only listen.

"Thanks, Leo. I know what you're saying."

"Good. Settled. I'll say three weeks. We'll go on after that."

"No, I'm quitting. I'll come back tomorrow and get my stuff."

Cerrutti went to Tippetts. He was only a little older than Gene. They'd started at the plant together. How would he act if he was going through what this poor bastard was feeling? He said gently, "Now, Gene, nobody squawked when you were out a couple of days. We all covered for you. Hell, there wasn't a man who wasn't glad to do anything. We want to help. That's why I'm saying, take the time, straighten yourself out."

"The D.A. wants to help. Everyone wants to help," Tippetts said, already leaving. "Nothing's going to change. I've made up my mind."

Cerrutti followed, still trying to say something that would work. But it was like Tippetts was ice inside. He couldn't make any sudden moves or he'd crack. As they went down to the bursar's office at the far end of the floor, the men working on the assembly line—Tippetts's pals, guys who'd heard he was leaving—all watched him, called to him. He barely let them know he heard.

Tippetts's kid was in with Delores, sitting in a chair far too big for him. She was trying to play with him, without much luck. When they came in, her smile faded. "We've had a good time," she told Tippetts.

He held out a hand for his son, who hopped off and fastened his hand around his father's. He's a quiet little kid, Cerrutti thought, he doesn't talk much.

"Thanks for watching, Del," Tippetts said, "and tell the other guys and everybody, thanks for the money and the cards." He said to Cerrutti, "I don't know when I'll write or anything. You tell them thanks for me."

"I sure will. And I'm not going to fill your slot, Gene. I'll hold it. You want to come back in a couple of weeks, why you just come back."

"I'm not coming back."

"What are you going to do?"

"I don't know. I don't know what we're going to do. I've got to think about a couple of things first."

Delores stood there very misty-eyed, a gray-haired lady with big glasses. She waved at the kid. "Bye, bye Andy. Come back soon."

Tippetts walked out of the office. Big man and little man; Cerrutti watched them go. He felt lousy: helpless and plain lousy.

"I couldn't make him change his mind," he said to Delores, who was about to bawl. "Maybe you better pull his records and tote up the salary and pension figures. I don't think he's coming back after he gets his gear."

Delores went slowly to her infallible records to find Tippetts's personnel sheet.

Outside, Tippetts and his son got into the car. Was he hungry, Gene wanted to know, did he want to take a nap?

Andy answered, not hungry, not sleepy.

Gene drove them back to the motel. He unlocked the room door. It was like they were on a long vacation, new smells, new places. They ate in the coffee shop. But it wasn't a vacation, because they didn't go anywhere and they didn't do anything.

The room itself was nearly pitch-black with the drapes drawn. The heater hummed. The maid had been in.

Gene had to do a few things. He tried to zero in on them, but it was an awful exercise of willpower. So much coming at him that morning, from the D.A., from Cerrutti, too much to digest all at once. Just going to the plant was bad enough.

There was also the constant terror of seeing a newspaper or hearing something on the radio, the burden of keeping his eyes and ears open to hide things from Andy. The funeral had been bad. Lying to him so he still didn't fully understand the horror of what had happened. But the fear that he would see something before Gene could shield him from it—that was almost too much.

He tried again to think. What had to be done right away? Call the real estate agent again, make sure the listings on the house were ready. Ask again how long a sale might take. Even without a new paint job, the place wasn't in bad shape.

Andy lay on the bed, on top of the covers.

"Want to watch some TV?" Gene asked him.

"No."

That was all. He's turned into a quiet kid. He hardly talks now.

Call the real estate agent. He sat down in one of the two chairs in the room. The phone lay between them on a mock-teak table, along with a dog-eared Gideon Bible.

He sat there, and suddenly, without knowing why, he called Andy to him, cradled him almost like he was a baby, the two of them sitting alone in the strange room, hearing new sounds, unknown voices outside.

Gene had one prayer, a short and quite simple one. He held his son and fervently made his prayer. No questions today, please, don't let him ask anything. And please, he whispered to himself, if he does ask, don't let him ask that one. Please not that one.

CHAPTER XI

ONE

"Ladies and gentlemen," read Engstrom, the foreman of the grand jury, "we are about to consider the charges of violation of sections one eighty-seven, six counts, and two eleven, two counts, of the Penal Code of the State of California, against Charles Edmund Reece."

Fraser looked over at the Grand Jury of Santa Maria County, all of them assembled in the cavernous Department 11 of the Superior Court. He knew them all. He had appeared before them several times. He smiled. This was an older grand jury, in its ninth month, and nearing the end of its term. The successful men and women of the community who sat here had heard a great deal during that time; until now even the most compassionate among them found it hard to combat a sense of boredom at the sobbed-out stories of child molestation or corruption.

They were critical, these jurors. They had added an overlay of legalism to a layman's ignorance of the law. And he was missing witnesses. Tippetts was not among the harried people milling back at the office, waiting to be shepherded over by Ballenger in batches of ten. This jury would treat his evidence even more strictly than necessary.

While Engstrom went through the opening rituals, Fraser tried to rearrange his evidence indexes to take account of the missing witnesses. There was always hope that Tippetts and the others might show up late. But he had to contend with the gaps that existed and hide them from this too-observant, too-wise grand jury.

Besides, there were only a few days left until Christmas, and this cut into all the preparations that had to be made. The jurors were subtly impatient.

Engstrom was reading from his prepared card. The roll had been called. The court reporter was taking everything down on her machine. The empty bench signified to Fraser his own isolation and dread. He held the case in his own hands completely.

". . . In connection herewith, it is my duty to state to you if any member of this grand jury present has a state of mind in reference to the above-stated matter, or to any party interested therein, which will prevent him from acting impartially and without prejudice to the substantial rights of any party charged, he is directed to retire from the jury room at this time."

Engstrom cleared his throat. "Does any juror have such a state of mind?" They sat quietly. "Let the record reflect that all the jurors have remained."

Fraser had planned his attack. The smug jurors thought they were on home ground, but the announcement of the defendant's name had stirred them so they rustled anxiously like children. From the first moments Fraser was going to unnerve them. He would shock them to the point that they might overlook the evidentiary deficiencies.

The foreman turned to him. "Mr. Fraser, do you want to say anything to the grand jury before you call your witnesses?"

"Yes, Mr. Foreman, I do."

Engstrom settled back. He was casually dressed, as were almost all the jurors. This was their after-hours employment, and they changed from their workday clothes into the same comfortable things they would wear to lounge around the house or tinker in the garage.

Fraser stood, automatically fastening the middle button of his coat. It was a habit he had picked up from making closing jury speeches. He stood close enough so that he could see everyone, but not so close that the people in the front row felt pressed.

"Good evening, ladies and gentlemen . . ." In short, direct statements, he recited the facts they would hear. He

143

promised them that he would prove Barbara Ellis did not die immediately after Reece shot her. This was quite a gamble. Mahon had avoided him at the office and had come over to the courthouse alone. Fraser was concerned about what he would say when he finally faced the jury.

As he spoke, however, his own fears ebbed. The jurors would see Reece as he saw him.

"I've prepared a chart for your convenience, listing the charges in the proposed indictment, the elements needed to prove each charge, and the date of each incident."

In neat script on the chart at the side of the jury box was the definition of torture as a special circumstance. "The murder must be intentional and involve the infliction of torture. Torture requires proof of the infliction of extreme physical pain no matter how long its duration." That was Mahon's task. Fraser didn't know whether Barbara Ellis had been alive or dead when Reece began cutting her open. He did need a plausible theory to support convicting Reece of that special circumstance. Like all prosecution theories about crimes, it depended less on being accurate in all details than it did on satisfactorily taking account of the facts in the case. And one fact Fraser couldn't ignore, personally or professionally, was the vascular pressure that still existed as Reece's mutilations began.

Finally he came to the one great chasm that could swallow his entire case even before he finished presenting the evidence.

"You may be tempted," he said, "to speculate on the mental state of Charles Reece in your deliberations. You may believe he was insane at the time he committed these crimes. But let me warn you strongly. This is not the time or place for such speculations. Whether he is sane or insane is a question to be decided at trial, and not here tonight."

He went back to his seat. Engstrom looked up. "I guess you can call your first witness."

"The People call Dr. George Mahon," Fraser said.

Engstrom started to get up, but Fraser waved him down. "I'll bring him," he said under his breath.

He strode back to the courtroom's blinkered doors and opened them. "Come in, George," he said to Mahon. The pathologist was puffing serenely on his pipe. Wordlessly, he tapped it out and put it in his pocket, then walked past Fraser.

The rest of Fraser's first batch of witnesses waited on the badly padded benches in the corridor. Ballenger gestured broadly at them when he saw Fraser. He shook his head. "I'm hoping." He crossed his fingers. No sign of Tippetts or the other missing witnesses.

Fraser smiled thinly. He cleared his mind and followed Mahon inside.

"Just a second, doctor," Engstrom said, standing up. He raised his hand. "Would you raise your right hand, please? Do you solemnly swear that the testimony you are about to give before this grand jury shall be the truth, the whole truth, and nothing but the truth, so help you God?"

"Yes," Mahon answered. He sat, crossing his legs. His hands rested loosely on his knee.

Fraser couldn't decipher Mahon's placid expression, but his silence and chilliness were fair indicators that he was going to be a hard witness. With dispatch then, Fraser established Mahon's credentials for the record. Pathologist, Santa Maria County. He outlined his schooling and training.

Now it was time to unnerve the jurors a little. They would hear things that had not been printed in the papers.

"Dr. Mahon, I'm going to hand you several photographs that have been previously marked by me as grand jury exhibits. Would you look at them and tell me if you recognize them?"

Fraser gave Mahon a packet of color photographs. On the back of each, Fraser had placed an exhibit sticker and numbered it. Mahon laid the pictures in front of him on the witness stand, appearing to study them closely.

"Yes, I do recognize them."

"What are these photographs?"

"These are the photographs I take before performing an autopsy on the individual in the photo."

Fraser began with the picture of Barbara Ellis. He led Mahon through a detailed description of the wounds and abominations committed on her. He was soon at the threshold of Mahon's certainties, and it was time to see how far he'd go. The jurors listened intently.

"Dr. Mahon, based on your external examination and

the autopsy itself, do you have an opinion as to the cause of death of Barbara Ellis?''

"Yes, I do.''

"What is that opinion?''

"I believe death was due to the two gunshot wounds to the head that I described.''

Mahon watched Fraser without concern. He answered easily.

"Was the other gunshot wound, the chest wound, a fatal one?''

"I think not. I think it was serious, but the bullet did not penetrate any major vessels or damage any vital organs.''

"Doctor, based on your medical examination and with a reasonable degree of medical certainty, do you have an opinion whether or not this woman was alive at the time the massive abdominal wound was made?''

Mahon frowned, his black eyebrows coming together. "It would be speculative at best. I'm not one hundred percent certain. I do not like to speculate.''

"Do you have an opinion or not?''

"I do have an opinion,'' Mahon said coolly.

"And what is it?''

"I believe this woman could have been alive at the time the wound in her abdomen was made. In other words, I can't say for certain when she was shot in the head, whether before the chest wound or before the abdominal wound, or after the abdominal wound for that matter. It's fairly apparent to me that she was either dead or unconscious at the time of the abdominal wound.''

"Why do you say that?''

"Because of the nature of the wound. It isn't the kind of wound you can inflict unless someone is completely unable to do anything about it.''

Mahon had to be drawn out, like a filament, and in the process Fraser knew he was straining their friendship. It wasn't a pleasant task.

And knowing that, he didn't pause in his questioning.

"Dr. Mahon, when you examined the abdominal wound, was there any evidence of vascular pressure at the time the wound was made?''

"Yes. There was.''

"What significance does that have?"

"It could mean that the woman was still alive. Vascular pressure indicates blood flow, which ceases after death, obviously. I found signs that there was a small amount of vascular pressure when she received this injury."

"Would you say that increases the likelihood she was alive at the time of the injury?"

"I can't say absolutely—"

"None of your findings are based on absolutes, I assume."

"If you mean without any qualification or possibility of error—"

"Yes, that's exactly what I mean."

"No. None of my findings, or the findings of any honest scientist, particularly in pathology, are based on absolute, ironclad certainty. We make very educated guesses based on experience, tests . . . hunches, I suppose."

"And by the same token, you don't discount your opinion as to the cause of death in this case because of a lack of complete certainty, do you?"

Mahon sighed quietly. He could see where Fraser had taken him without much difficulty. "No, I don't. I would say my confidence in an opinion in the cause of death in this case is greater than my confidence whether this woman was alive."

He had taken out his pipe. He held it in his hand. It was the only sign of his agitation.

"If she was alive, Dr. Mahon, do you have an opinion whether she was aware of the wound when it was inflicted?"

"We're growing more speculative, but I'd suppose she was unconscious, for the reasons I've already noted."

Fraser waited. "Doctor, would an unconscious person feel such a wound?"

"Be aware of it?"

"Yes."

"Possibly."

"Would that awareness be of pain?"

"Yes, but given the other injuries, I can't say exactly what this woman felt. She was fairly insensible no matter how you look at it."

Fraser had not raised his voice, but he pressed firmly and briskly forward.

"Given the other assumptions, though, this type of wound would cause extreme pain?"

"I imagine so." Mahon pressed his lips together, and Fraser didn't think he would say more. There was enough for the jurors to find the special circumstance and it would take a great effort on their part to reject it. The point was made.

"Do these photographs accurately depict the injuries you've described?"

Mahon didn't look at them again. "Absolutely, Mr. Fraser. You can see what this woman looked like without any trouble."

Fraser took the pictures and handed them to the juror nearest him, an angular, middle-aged woman, Celia Mandeville. She was an office manager and one of the stronger voices on the jury. She took the pictures, her mouth set, her eyes pinned to the topmost flat color image. She closed her eyes briefly, only once, and then studied the first picture as if to memorize it. She looked at him and her head moved slightly. She understood now.

The pictures would circulate among the jurors while Mahon continued testifying. The relatively toughened men and women reacted as would any trial jurors or average people. They froze, appalled; they blinked; or they roughly shoved the pictures along. They were interested only in the atrociousness of the deaths, and he felt there was a good chance to direct them away from any gaps in his case.

It was hard to argue against the woman grotesquely laid out on the white table in the first picture.

He took Mahon through the other autopsies, five more causes of death. The examination lasted almost thirty minutes, long by grand jury standards. He and the pathologist were professional and controlled. But he had no illusions about Mahon's distaste at being forced along this way. Mahon would never quite trust him as fully again. The breach opened between them.

Engstrom picked up the pictures and reverently laid them in front of Fraser without saying anything. He had not looked at them.

"Are there any questions from the grand jury for this witness?" Engstrom asked.

The jurors looked at each other, and several began scribbling quickly on scraps of paper. Like petitioners, the jurors passed the white notes forward, and Engstrom gathered them up, placing them before Fraser.

He took the first scrap, torn from a notepad.

For the record he announced, "Dr. Mahon, I have a question from a grand juror that I will ask you. How long could Barbara Ellis live after the abdominal would was inflicted?"

He noticed Clay Axman leaning forward, listening. He folded the scrap. Axman's question, then. A very interested juror.

Mahon answered, "I think a very, very short space of time."

Another slip of paper said "Why would someone steal a heart, liver, etc.?"

Fraser said, "I have another question from a grand juror. I will not ask this question because it is irrelevant and asks the witness to speculate beyond his competence." He put the paper in his pocket and continued until all the questions had been asked or rejected. He saw Axman rereading the boldface definition of torture near the top of the chart.

"There are no further questions from the grand jurors," Fraser said, "and I have no additional questions." He wished there was a way to say something conciliatory to Mahon in private, but there was no time.

"Dr. Mahon," Engstrom read from another card, "you are admonished not to discuss or repeat at any time outside of this jury room the questions that have been asked of you in regard to this matter or your answers, with the understanding that such disclosures on your part could be the basis for a charge against you of contempt of court. You are excused, doctor."

The pathologist stowed his pipe again and walked out without a glance at anyone in the room.

Fraser spent no more time on Mahon. He had over two dozen witnesses to hurry through the jury room, whether the missing ones appeared or not. He called another name.

CHAPTER XII

ONE

It rained the next day, sullen, dark rain with a forlorn persistence, until everything was sodden and glazed with moisture.

Dr. Rudin hated to think he cringed, but the feeling grew that he did as he talked to Keddie. He was foolish to have come to Keddie's office, giving away that advantage, leaving himself more open to the persuasive arguments now beating him down. It was not that Keddie threatened or shouted; he didn't. It was the adamantine logic of what he said that made Rudin weak. Keddie was his friend and adviser, which made everything he said more devastating. At this point, Rudin didn't even have the will to push himself out of the soft, plush chair as Keddie circled him, making him constantly twist his head to keep the other man in view.

"We have to think of our survival," Keddie said to him, "and I've got to think of my patient. Those are the only two fixed points I see."

"I understand, Ben." Rudin rebelled at the suggestions Keddie had made obliquely for the last hour, and would have left earlier, but he was frightened now. Still, Rudin felt compelled to voice his opposition as a matter of principle, even if Keddie was right. "I just can't agree with your method."

"Paul, your attitude is admirable. If the situation were slightly different, I'd have kicked someone like me in the pants and thrown him out." Keddie looked saddened. "But we don't have much choice. I need your help."

"There must be another way of approaching this," Rudin said, hating the tentative, diminished sound of his words.

Keddie shook his head. "It's only a matter of time before the D.A. finds out you examined Reece at Sunnyslope."

"Only for an hour."

"Then again, less than two months before the first killing. You agreed he was well enough to be released."

"But I didn't have all the facts," Rudin protested feebly, "I didn't have all the information they have now."

Keddie sympathized; it showed clearly on his rough features. He sat down behind his desk of plexiglass and steel tubing. "Do you really want to rely on that when you get on the witness stand?"

"No. No, I don't want to be the scapegoat."

"My point," Keddie said gently, "is that you will be exactly that, once the D.A. discovers you saw Reece before the killings started. You'll be destroyed. You'll be nothing afterward."

It was intriguing, Rudin thought, to feel angry at Keddie and not Fraser, the D.A. It ought to be the other way around. Fraser, after all, was the one who threatened him. But Keddie exerted the pressure, subtle, inexorable, unavoidable. He sat enthroned in his office among his monographs and diplomas and plaques and the damn pictures of half the prisons in the country where he'd been the staff psychiatrist. Keddie knew he was important. He knew he'd done good works everywhere. He displayed the evidence of them for all to see.

If I do this for him, Rudin realized with real fear, I'll be trapped forever. I'll never be free.

"I can't falsify the interview," he said.

Keddie looked horrified. "I didn't say falsify, Paul, good God. We don't need to falsify anything in this case. We only need to form a common front."

"I'm sorry," remorse washed over him, "I thought that's what you were saying I had to do."

"Let me try again. I think you ought to misplace the interview notes from your jail talk with him. Misfile them."

"That doesn't sound much better. I haven't given the D.A. my report yet. He's been asking about it. How can I keep it from him? What do I do when he asks me about it at the trial?" Rudin dragged out a cigarette, the one he allowed himself for the whole damn day, which he'd looked forward with pleasure to smoking that afternoon after his last patient. He needed it now.

"Well, you're under no legal or ethical obligation to give him any report, Paul, much less the notes of the interview. I think you can legitimately claim a doctor-patient relationship exists between you and Charles Reece. The D.A. can't force you to produce the notes."

"But should I give him a report?"

"Oh, I think so. One you honestly feel comfortable with. Recount the report from your dictated interview. You won't have a recollection of the actual words, the things Reece said exactly, and you can't find your notes now. All you'll have will be the dictated interview."

"It's the same as falsifying."

"Believe me, it's not. I am not asking you to do anything like that."

"Assume I did that, Ben. What about the rest of it? What do I say?"

Keddie drummed his fingers, locked together like marching soldiers, on the clear plexiglass. He seemed to want to help so much; Rudin felt guilty for these accusations.

"I can describe the whole situation for you. It's very simple. As soon as it becomes common knowledge that you examined Reece, certified him, and let him go, you will be sued. You will be sued by the dead victims' families, their relatives, I don't know who else. You will be found guilty of negligence or some neglect of duty. It's a matter of logic. There is no question Reece killed those people. The only question is why. That won't help you, though. If he's guilty of those crimes, any jury will persecute you, too, Paul."

"I've got to find him insane? In my testimony?"

"Isn't he?"

"I haven't finished my report," Rudin said stubbornly. "I don't know. I have strong suspicions."

"Of course you do. I'm sure you'll arrive at the same diagnosis I did. He's a paranoid schizophrenic. The rage, hallucinations, the global psychosis all fit. You simply have to say what you truly know to be right. Just as I will."

Rudin had smoked only half his cigarette and then ground it out. Looking to Keddie, he asked for another. Keddie knew he was trying to quit.

"I've never prejudged a diagnosis," Rudin said. "I've never made up my mind before I had all the facts."

"I'll back you up completely in that diagnosis."

"Before you've finished your examination?"

"I've seen enough to convince me. I know a condition that could easily describe his behavior. I also know that condition will save his life."

"What about the other psychiatrists?"

"They aren't as important as we are," Keddie said, looking at him intently. "You saw Reece immediately after the crimes. I've spent the most time with him. We've had access to more information and records than the ones who'll come later. It will be our opinions that matter, not anybody else's."

"I don't know, Ben. I'm not sure."

"Look at it this way," Keddie said helpfully. "Reece is a creature who has killed defenseless men and women, and taken an innocent child. He's shot at people. The law will take his life for those things unless," he paused, "unless those things demonstrate his inability to choose right from wrong. We're merely saying what everyone believes to be the case. Reece is insane."

"If I came to the conclusion he was sane?"

"I would try to persuade the jury otherwise. You, though, Paul, would be alone. None of the other doctors face the same unfair treatment you do if Reece is found guilty."

Rudin was irritated to discover that he'd been gripping the hard edge of the armrests, and his hands were moist. Keddie was suggesting he commit professional mayhem, lose notes, concoct a diagnosis whether or not it was true. Why couldn't he tell Keddie it was wrong and sound as if he meant it?

Because Keddie had the only way out.

He slumped defeatedly in his chair.

Keddie asked, "Did Reece mention anything to you about Nazis when you first saw him?"

"No," Rudin said in a low voice, "I don't think so. I don't recall. He might have said something."

"About Nazis persecuting him?"

"No, no Nazi persecutions. I would have recalled that."

Keddie coughed very slightly. "You might want to add something small, a few comments in your dictated interview would be enough, about his fears of Nazi persecution. A persecution delusion, that's all. It's part of his paranoia."

"He has that delusion?"

"I had to draw it out of him," Keddie said with some pride, "but it's quite consistent with his interest in Nazis. If you make those small adjustments, I think it will help coordinate our presentation of his symptoms."

A black thought suddenly welled up in Rudin. "I may have records," he murmured, "back in the office."

"I couldn't hear you. What did you say?"

"I just thought there may be entries in my old appointment books, dates and personal information about when I saw Reece. There may be other records."

"I'm sure you can take care of that," Keddie said dismissively.

"What? What should I do?"

"Paul, I know you'll do whatever you can to help this man. He needs our help. We're the only ones who stand between him and death."

Rudin wanted to say more, but somehow the words deserted him. There was nothing more to say. Spatters of rain pummeled the windows. It was time to go. "Thank you for your time, Ben. Thank you for calling me."

"Keep up the good fight."

Rudin dashed to his car through the parking lot, along with several other black, fleeing figures in the shimmering gray wetness, covering his head with his arms because he'd forgotten to bring an umbrella. The rain soaked him. He clambered awkwardly into his car, getting water inside as he did so, his hair sticking wetly to his forehead, his breath husking in and out from the running, and a chill settling onto him.

TWO

"Tippetts skipped," Ballenger said.

Fraser looked up. "Definitely?"

"The investigators got back ten minutes ago. He moved

154

out yesterday with the kid, left the motel, no new address. He's gone into thin air."

Fraser leaned back in his chair and rubbed his eyes. He knew somewhere it was raining very hard and it was very cold. But back here in the law library, without windows, buried deep inside the building, there was no day or night or wind or rain. He pushed the books away. There was only the law here. Nothing in the books about Tippetts or his suffering. You couldn't press that between covers or tie it neatly down with precedents and citations.

Fraser thought about it. The man wanted to run. His testimony was valuable, it added to the case, and Fraser was very uncertain about the grand jurors. Axman's gruff exterior symbolized his uncertainty about all of them. It was worth the effort to try to drag Tippetts back from whatever hole he had run to. Now he could join all the others, the fleeing felons who jumped bail, frightened and hostile witnesses who didn't want to be found, and fathers who didn't pay child support. There would be a warrant out to arrest Eugene Tippetts because he couldn't see the point of coming to court.

"Let's get a warrant out for him, Harry," he said.

Ballenger nodded. "I've got another rocket for you."

"I can't wait."

"That shrink you sent in to see Reece? Rudin? I tried to get him to talk to me about what Reece told him."

"I don't care about that information as much as the Tippetts kid."

"I know. I was tickling Rudin to see if there was anything. Well, he isn't talking at all. He's shut up completely, about anything and everything Reece said. Mental state at the time of the interview, whether he wet his pants or picked his nose or cried like a baby. Your shrink won't say a fucking thing."

Fraser let out his breath. "Oh, boy."

A ruddy face appeared over Ballenger's shoulder. Whalen hailed them both and clapped a meaty hand on Ballenger.

"They said I could find you two hiding out down here." He surveyed the library with the empty curiosity of a visitor. "What's the good word?"

The last man Fraser had either the time or the inclination to deal with was Whalen. "Harry tells me our shrink won't say anything now."

Whalen, dressed in his office sweater, buttoned two buttons up, with an ivory shirt and regimental tie that belied his crudeness, seemed to have been struck dumb by this intelligence. He peered first at Fraser, then at Ballenger. Finally, he said, "Ah, yes."

"It could mean," Fraser explained, "that Dr. Rudin has decided to say Reece is insane. He doesn't want to talk to us, even though, of course, he has no legal right to refuse. He's nervous, I guess."

"Well, you've got other shrinks?" Whalen asked.

"Sure, but the real bombshell could come from Rudin. He's a prosecution witness, or that's how Starkey will characterize him. I asked him to talk to Reece. If he then comes in and says Reece is insane, it has a lot more weight than if he was a defense psychiatrist."

"Damn," Whalen cursed with forced intensity.

"Our ace is that Rudin isn't a forensic psychiatrist."

Ballenger watched Fraser. Ballenger hadn't moved an inch to let Whalen pass into the library.

Whalen nodded sagely. "Ah, yes," he said again.

"Only a forensic psychiatrist," Fraser explained, "is qualified to state in court whether a man is sane or not. Rudin can try to sneak in an opinion, but I'll go after him."

Whalen smiled broadly, pleased that the exigencies had been foreseen, and that all was well. He then assumed a more serious cast. "Tony, do you have a minute?"

"Just barely."

Whalen turned to Ballenger. "This is something I have to talk to Tony about privately."

"I'll stay," Ballenger replied. "I've got a small bone to pick with you."

Whalen was going to argue, but something restrained him. He turned back to Fraser. "Tony," a deep breath, "I like to think I'm big enough to say, buddy, you made a big, big mistake."

He waited for Fraser to answer. Fraser watched him silently.

"So," he went on a little less surely, "I'm sorry we got

156

off on the wrong foot the other day. I was out of line. There was no call for it. I had a lot of things coming at me all at once and I took it out on you." He smiled again, his great red face splitting. "So, I'd like to clear the decks. How's that?"

Fraser had put his hands behind his head and closed his eyes. Get it over with quickly and get him out. Speed was the only consideration. "I'm happy, Spence. We'll forget it."

"Well, great, great." Whalen smiled from Fraser to Ballenger and back again. "Great," he said.

Ballenger was the epitome of ease, lounging against the door, watching Whalen the way a sated animal might let a small rodent walk by. "Spence," he said, "you having me followed?"

Whalen was surprised. Unease flooded over him. "What? Following you?"

"I thought I saw Huey or Sid trailing me the other night. I hear you and Infeld are trailing some of us."

"Who said that?" Whalen demanded.

"Some guys in Investigations, a couple of old-timers who didn't like the idea."

"Who said so?"

"Spence." Ballenger shook his head.

"It's crazy," Whalen exclaimed, looking to his new friend Fraser for confirmation of the verdict. "That's a crazy rumor." He tried a short, barking laugh. "Nobody's following anybody."

"It occurred to me that you might want something for a civil service hearing in case you decided to chuck me out. I had a silly idea like that."

Whalen grew more heated and perplexed. "Harry, I tell you there is no thought whatsoever of anything like that, and I'm certainly not detailing the staff of this office to follow you."

Fraser put his hands down. "I've got to finish here and I need a little quiet."

Whalen stopped in midprotest. "You're right. Yes. Harry, come to my office. Have some coffee. We'll settle it right now."

Ballenger indicated his gut. "No coffee, boss."

Slightly flummoxed, Whalen said, "Forgot. Tea? No? I'll get something. Maybe there's some apple juice."

Fraser heard the door close after them, and the stillness, shut off from the world, settled on him again in the deserted law library. A clock reminded him how fast the afternoon was grinding down. The grand jury would meet again at eight that evening.

He tried calling Rudin's office three times. The doctor was busy, the doctor was on the phone, the doctor had gone home, until it became abundantly clear that Dr. Rudin really wasn't going to talk to him. He left his name and number anyway.

At least the question was resolved. Rudin was no longer safe.

He held back his worries as he worked until after six and ate alone in his office. It grew black, and the rain drummed ceaselessly, blown by a hard wind. The lights in the office, bitter bright, gave everything the sheen and unsteadiness of a fever.

At eight, the grand jury assembled and he presented the final witnesses. The jury by now was bloated with horrors, stuffed full of them, enough that they might overlook missing bits and pieces like Eugene Tippetts. He argued his theory of the case, why they should indict Reece for first-degree murder, and almost as soon as he finished, the hands started going up. He was ready for them.

"Why didn't you bring in the husband?" Axman called out.

"I'm sorry, what do you mean?"

"You had all the other witnesses who found these people," Axman gestured at the counsel table on which the exhibits were laid out, "and all that evidence. Why not this guy Tippetts?"

A left-fielder, Fraser thought nervously, a wild card. Axman, Axman, he tried to recall the data on the man, but came up almost blank. There was nothing but his truculence. "I can't comment on the absence of witnesses beyond saying that you were presented with evidence of Eileen Tippetts's condition when she was found by the police officers who went to the home."

"But they weren't the first to see her."

"No, they weren't."

"So why didn't we get to hear from the first person?"

"I can only urge you to examine the testimony of those officers. If you decide it provides enough evidence, taken with all the other evidence, to indict the defendant, then that should be your decision."

Axman was nettled. "Hold on, I'm not asking much, Mr. Fraser. Won't you tell me where this guy is? Why he wasn't here? Is there some problem?"

"I can't discuss anything relating to that matter," Fraser said, knowing how much Starkey would like to find just such a discussion on the record. Out would go the indictment, out would go sixty-eight witnesses, out would go the grand jury. It was like pushing taffy, trying to show Axman the situation when he so obviously didn't want to see it and Fraser couldn't fully explain it.

"Okay," Axman said irritably, "if you don't want to talk about it."

Celia Mandeville raised her hand. Gratefully, Fraser called on her.

"You said we can't consider this man's problems—it's plain he's got mental problems—if we want to find him guilty of first-degree murder?"

Safe ground. "No, you may not. You have no evidence on which to base any such speculations."

"But he does have mental problems?"

"It's not a subject for us tonight."

The questions went on, a few allowing him to expand on the ways they could indict Reece for murder. And, of course, he knew they would talk about Reece's craziness. It drew them on; they would feel it as they touched the exhibits. How else could they come to terms with what Reece had done, unless they talked about madness?

It was nearly eleven, late, and the acid taste of fatigue and worry clung to him. The questions mercifully ran out.

Engstrom made ruminating noises. "Very well. We'll excuse the court reporter and the People's representative while we deliberate."

He escorted Fraser and the reporter to the doors and closed them after both were outside. The lock turned.

"I'm going to the lounge for a smoke," the court reporter told Fraser, "in case they need anything reread."

"I'll tell them."

He sat down on the bench. Ballenger strolled over from the other end of the corridor. The witnesses had gone home for the night. It was very quiet. No sound seeped from inside the shuttered courtroom.

"They started?" Ballenger asked.

Fraser nodded.

"Well, we didn't do too badly. Almost had everyone here. Both cops, most of the civilian jackasses."

He and Ballenger talked in two different ways about this case. Ballenger rose or fell as the mechanical aspects worked or not. They were, of course, vitally important, and yet Harry saw no more. He hadn't experienced two days and nights when an appalling crime became a chance to fight something wicked, and win. It was an unbearable gulf.

"You didn't hear their questions," Fraser said as Ballenger started a clumsy hopscotch on the large square tiles of the courthouse floor. "I don't think I've got anything going for me there."

Ballenger blew a raspberry.

"Harry, this is the first test of the evidence in this case. I went in hoping they'd come with me. If it doesn't fly now, with all the breaks on our side," he checked himself, "with a few anyway, it isn't going upstairs."

"I have more faith in you."

Close to what Kate had said. The two of them were more alike in their guileless feeling for him than either realized.

Ballenger stopped. "No, no, look at this objectively. You got a bunch of citizens scared out of their brains by this man. Do you really think they're going to screw up on this guy?" He went back to his hopping. "Nope. Not this one."

Fraser nodded, tiredness taking the place of the tension that had driven him for almost a week. And there was Kate at home to think about.

"I didn't tell you about this afternoon." Ballenger scooted onto the bench, grinning as he sat. "When I went over to SMSD to get the cops you needed, I hung around, and then my pal over there drove us to a taco place for lunch, his car, we went out the back way. I left my car sitting in front of the Department in a ten-minute zone, so if old Huey was tailing me, he'd stay put, thinking I'd be out in a minute. I liked the idea of him sitting out in the rain through lunch waiting for me to come out. I didn't get back for an hour," he stamped his foot in merriment, "so if old Huey gets the sniffles tomorrow or if his shoes are full of water, you know where he was."

"Christ, I hope Whalen's not doing that."

"I don't give a shit if he is."

Fraser listened, answered, and somewhere along the way as they rambled on, he must have dozed off because Ballenger roused him after one. Engstrom peeked out of the courtroom. The reporter darted back in.

"Knock 'em dead," Ballenger said.

The courtroom was whitely lit, and on the bench in a circle of light sat Judge Ira Zucker, an ascetically thin man who meticulously arranged his pens and papers and water carafe while Fraser walked to the counsel table.

The judge asked the jurors if they had completed their deliberations.

"We have," Engstrom said.

Fraser couldn't bear to look at them, but when he did, embarrassed for doing it, the jurors were icily stiff and silent. They waited for the judge.

Behind him, Fraser heard the doors close again that night, sighing softly shut, irrevocable and final.

THREE

As Kate slid into the booth, her face pink from the night cold, Fraser half stood for her.

"You don't have to be ceremonial for me, Tony," she said, shrugging off her coat. She smiled at him.

"I didn't know if you'd have any trouble spotting me."

She glanced around the all-night restaurant, where a few people were absorbed in newspapers and others drowsed over plates of partly eaten sandwiches. "I don't think I'd have too much trouble," Kate replied. "But if you want to go somewhere, I can think of almost half a dozen places."

"I kind of like it here. It's only a few blocks from the courthouse." He leaned over the mustard and ketchup bottles between them. "It reminds me of the places we ended up in when we were going out."

"That was a lifetime ago," Kate said, mixing happiness with regret. "This is almost creepy though. Look at these people." Her voice dropped to a whisper. "I mean, what are they doing here at this time of the morning?"

"Eating. Among other things."

Kate settled back, the smile still indicating she thought of the excursion as an adventure, a tour of intriguing forms of life. "I'm glad you called, though," she said with enthusiasm. "It's almost like we were thinking the same way. I've got some news, too, and yours will just have to wait."

"Okay. You go first." His third cup of coffee was nearly empty. His legs, he discovered, were trembling beneath the table.

"The Cities League is having a special meeting in Baja next weekend. Baja? Sun and Sea? It's a four-day conference. The hotel is terrific, the beach is terrific. They want me to go. I'm going to represent Santa Maria."

"It sounds great." He put a hand on his left thigh to steady it.

"Of course it's great. So I told them I wasn't going." Kate looked at him mischievously. "I said let someone else go."

"Why on earth did you do that, Kate?"

"Well, I knew you wouldn't come with me. Not for four days, not right now, with all this." She tilted her head in the direction of the courthouse, but it seemed she included the faded, oily restaurant in the conception. "Not with everything that's going on."

"That's true. I couldn't go."

"But I thought that if I wasn't going to get to go to Baja this weekend, we could at least go away for just Saturday and part of Sunday week after next. We could drive to the very same hotel and have the very same beach. You'd be back here Sunday night."

A waitress, looking wary, came over to them. "Order?" she asked sharply.

"No. No," Fraser stammered. His leg would not stop. His hand fluttered uselessly over his jittering left knee.

"Some tea. And a blueberry muffin. If it's fresh," Kate said.

162

"They're all fresh," the waitress muttered, walking off as quickly as she had come.

"Kate—" he began.

"That's not all," Kate said. A discordant edge clipped her words. She patted his arm. "I planned it so we would just miss all the people after Christmas. I mean, there'll still be tourists, but the crowds will be gone. I've got a room already. I've got plane reservations."

He forced his legs together to quiet the spasms. He took her hand. "There's no possible way I can get away. The case is moving now. I have to be here."

"I know you've got obligations. But I'm only talking about part of a weekend. Only part."

"Maybe in a little while, after the first of the year. I can't now. There are too many things to investigate. I've got too much to watch. Oh, hell."

Kate's animation dimmed noticeably. The light of the early morning always makes things harder, the shadows darker. He noticed in that light a porcelain hardness in the smoothness of her face. He wished he could dissolve that unnatural shell. He wanted to make her a present of something that would matter to her very much.

But he couldn't.

"Kate, listen to me. I'll tell you why I can't go away now."

He gathered her hands and leaned forward so that the table edge cut into his ribs. He told her about the grand jury. He described the evidence. For the first time in their marriage, he laid before her all the terrors of a case and the watchmaker's patience required to subdue them. He spared her no detail.

When he was finished, he let go of her hands. She didn't say anything for a while, and he made no attempt to fill the silence between them. The waitress brought Kate's order. He could hear a man snoring somewhere in the harshly lit room.

Kate shook her head several times. She studied him. She said, "What an ugly place. What a disgusting, ugly place the world is. If things like that happen . . ."

"They do."

She quietly spoke again. "I must seem awfully trivial to

you. Here I am spending my time worrying about parks and charities. How many benches, how many couples, how much civic improvement . . ." She pushed the teacup gently. "I'm not saving the world. I never said I was trying to save the world. I just want to make it a little more beautiful. It should be, shouldn't it?"

"Kate, I think you run yourself ragged because of very important things."

"They are important. Parks matter. Having a city to be proud of is important. Maybe it is just saving a small part of the world. I think that's better than nothing. I don't have to know about the rest of it, all the evil and disgusting rest of it."

"No, you don't. I do."

"I think people are to be treasured," she said adamantly. "They need to be shown good things."

The trembling had traveled upward along his right side, too. Kate sat back watching him.

"Well, you made your point," she said. "We won't go. I won't bring it up again."

"I'm not trading us for this case, Kate. It's not like that. You see that, don't you?"

She nodded without agreement. "I just wonder how we're going to get through the next two weeks. And the two weeks after that. And after that. That's all I see."

Fraser leaned back against the hardness of the plastic booth. Not long ago, he had listened while Judge Zucker called for the indictment to be read into the record. He had scanned the faces, Axman, Mandeville, all of them watching him. Engstrom read sonorously. Pages flipped, and Fraser thought there must have been a mistake, some error in the indictment that the judge or Engstrom would spot.

There was no mistake.

A fierce exultation had filled him as he realized what the grand jury had done. And more than that, he wanted Kate to know how he felt. There was no earthly way he could communicate it to her. He had just tried and failed.

The grand jury had indicted Reece on all counts.

CHAPTER XIII

ONE

Television mobile units ringed the courthouse plaza like a wagon train wound tightly in preparation for an attack. Fraser passed through them and to the third-floor courtroom, Department 4, where the honorable Peter Strevel held forth. The corridor near the courtroom was thick with cables and wires, and when he got close enough, cameras and lights switched on. Microphones and shouted questions were pressed on him, and he had to push politely through the reporters and oddballs waiting to get inside. He wasn't going to say much to any reporter now. Anything he said would simply add fuel to Starkey's request to have the trial moved to another city because of the amount of publicity.

The two deputy sheriffs guarding the roped-off courtroom doorway recognized him and made small talk while they passed a metal detector over him and, with a little embarrassment, asked to see his badge.

Behind them the waiting line of oddballs, strung out for the entire one-block length of the corridor, watched with thinly veiled anger as Fraser was specially treated and admitted to the secure courtroom. The camera crews, for lack of anything better, now moved down the line of people, bathing them in the vivifying light, turning sullenness into abrupt perky grins and giggles. People waved now, like contestants at a game show.

"Freak time," grumbled one of the deputies as Fraser slipped inside.

The courtroom was almost empty. Another deputy was peering under all the seats and the counsel table with canine enthusiasm, rummaging for anything strange. "Better hustle," he told Fraser, "the opposition's been back with the judge for fifteen minutes."

Fraser went back to the judge's chambers. The morning was not as bad as he had expected. He and Kate were still caught up in the odd calm that renewed itself each day, even on the day Reece was to be arraigned in Superior Court and

165

his trial date set. What bothered him was the calm itself. It couldn't possibly last, and its dissolution would be violent.

He knocked on the door to the judge's chambers.

Starkey sat looking sad. Strevel, his glasses halfway down his fleshy nose, stood at his desk, his imitation silk shirt stained with sweat at the armpits and his eyes heavy lidded. He was smoking a long brown cigarette, and its acrid vapors clung to him. On the back of a chair in his chambers was a saddle, setting off his modest display of riding pictures and awards.

"Goodman Fraser," the judge boomed out without looking up, "you've finally joined us."

"I didn't know we were convening early," he said, but Starkey ignored his chiding.

"Well, your honorable opponent has done us a turn this morning so perhaps you don't have to get upset about our ex parte chat." The judge grinned humorlessly at Starkey. "Now, Al, why don't you run that by me again with Mr. Fraser here."

To Fraser, Starkey appeared subdued. He lacked his usual bite.

"Judge, I've advised my client that you would be hearing all the motions in the case and the trial itself under the agreement Tony and I worked out to save court time and resources. One judge, familiar with the facts, does all the pretrial hearings and, assuming a change of venue fails, hears the trial."

"I'm with you so far." Strevel looked to Fraser with a sarcastic glint.

"When I explained this to my client, and your background . . . well, it's my client's wish that another judge hear the case."

"You're papering me?" Strevel asked.

"I've got the affidavit, judge. I have no choice, that's what my client wants."

Fine and dandy. Fraser understood Starkey's discomfort. If it was possible to avoid, a lawyer did not want to figuratively slap a judge in the face by kicking him off a case.

"I buy that," Strevel said. "It's your privilege, one bite at the apple if you want another judge. I guess your guy isn't so crazy. He knows what kind of judge he wants to hear his case, anyway."

166

"I'm not sure what his reasons are, judge."

"I can tell you, Al, I'm absolutely capable of hearing this case dispassionately and giving your man a fair shot."

"I explained that to him. I laid the whole thing out for him. I told him we have only one challenge and this uses it up, but he was insistent."

Or someone persuaded him to bounce a former U.S. attorney like Strevel. Fraser doubted Starkey would have done so. Perhaps someone else on the defense side who had access to Reece? Or it might have been, as Strevel said, Reece himself, quite cognizant of the risks Strevel posed.

"Well, go ahead, file your papers, affidavit me. I'll only criticize you for giving us so little time, Al. You should have told us, probably."

Starkey turned to Fraser. "Since the grand jury indictment was only thirty-six hours ago, judge, and we have to meet on Christmas Eve, I don't think I had all the time in the world."

"Sure, sure. Okay, well, let's go out and take care of this."

"In open court?" Starkey asked.

Strevel sucked deeply, for perhaps ten seconds, on his cigarette, and then expelled a cloud of smoke around himself. His watery eyes blinked behind the half-cocked glasses. "Even though you're papering me, I want the record to clearly reflect a time waiver for arraignment in case we can't get another judge today. It is a holiday. I'm sure your man didn't forget that."

"Whatever you want, judge," Starkey said. He was very out of sorts.

Fraser simply stood there and listened. Starkey's problem wasn't immediately useful, but it had possibilities. At the very least, it threw light on Reece's dilatory abilities.

"I think I deserve a little publicity out of this circus if I can't hear the case," Strevel said gaily. "Bailiff tells me the place is crawling with reporters. We've got someone from New York, and some guy from Manchester, England." He strode back to the closet and plucked out a rumpled robe, pulling it on, smashing the cigarette out hurriedly.

When Strevel felt the impulse to move, he moved quickly. Fraser wouldn't have minded him as the trial judge. He was eccentric and touchy, but he had the good instincts, and they counted for a great deal more than either scholarship or sympathy.

They straggled into the courtroom behind the judge, the bailiff shouted Strevel's presence, and the courtroom rose. It was a circus, a capacity crowd. The judge, out of character, preened at the bench; artists sketched in the jury box; the goggle-eyed crowd crushed into the audience section waited for the arrival of the main attraction.

"Bring in Reece," Strevel said curtly to his bailiff.

Fraser studied Reece again, held between two marshals, dressed in his yellow sweat shirt. Reece acted bewildered and annoyed, glaring at the judge and Starkey. He was as unhappy as Starkey. Fraser hoped there was friction between them.

"Record reflect the defendant is present along with both counsel," the judge spat out. "We've got the case down for arraignment on a grand jury indictment, but I understand, Mr. Starkey, that you've got a matter you want to bring up first."

Starkey held his arms over his small chest like armor. "Yes, judge. At this time I want to file an affidavit with the court exercising my client's right to appear before another judge."

"I understand, I understand," Strevel boomed, a little sadly, Fraser thought, because he really would have liked this one. He leaned over toward Starkey so he was hunched awkwardly on the bench. "Now I've got to ask your client if he does."

"That's fine, judge."

"Mr. Reece, do you hear what your attorney is saying now? You want another judge to hear your case?"

Reece shuffled and his eyes swept the room. Fraser wondered at the restless, searching gaze. What was he looking for? What was he thinking? How can I penetrate him? Fraser thought.

Reece twisted to scratch his neck and the marshals tensed. "Yeah, I want another judge," he said.

"So be it. We'll get hold of Master Calendar now and see if we can't scare up another member of the bench to hear your case."

"Can I say something?" Reece called out, eyes locked on the judge.

"Maybe you should talk to your attorney first."

Starkey stood, arms still resolutely folded.

"I want another lawyer. I've had trouble with this man and I want another lawyer. I don't have confidence in this man."

"Mr. Starkey?"

"Your honor, Mr. Reece is expressing a sentiment he told me about this morning. I can't add anything."

"Well, I can't do anything," Strevel smirked, pushing his glasses up again, "because I've just been challenged and I have no jurisdiction to hear this case now. So, off you go."

The marshals pulled Reece back into the open steel doorway of the holding cell. Reece was hollering, but his words were muffled in the cell, then cut off entirely when the door slid shut.

"Doesn't sound like he expected that," Strevel said. "Okay, take a ten-minute recess before we start the rest of the morning calendar." He was heading off the bench. "And it was a pleasure seeing both of you gentlemen again, if only briefly. A merry Christmas to you." He threw a jaunty wave to Fraser.

Fraser had to move quickly. Starkey's problems presented an opportunity. While Starkey went back to console or yell at Reece, he would be out of action for the next half hour. There was time for Fraser to find another judge. One *he* wanted.

The crowd was stirring, disappointed at such a poor show. Deputies and marshals held the doors as the crowd pushed out. Fraser trailed unnoticed, trying to hurry the sluggish stream along. He was at the stairway when the voice called.

At first he didn't know if the voice was calling to him.

A large black woman in a scarlet caftan began gibbering loudly, crying with her eyes closed, her hands upraised, jiggling wildly back and forth. The lights and cameras turned to her as reporters with no story thus far pressed around her. The sullen crowd reformed. Here was some excitement.

Someone was clapping for her, like the caller at a square dance, while the cameras recorded and she flailed about.

Standing near the courtroom doorway was a stocky man with a crew cut and a lined face, like a crushed piece of paper unfolded. He was wearing a precisely tailored suit, herringbone, and a peep of blue silk handkerchief emerged from his coat pocket.

Fraser felt the man watching him, not the woman. Was he the one who had called his name? Fraser recognized him then. It was Dr. Keddie. In the courtroom. He must have been in the courtroom, too, watching, listening, watching.

Fraser was uneasy. He had to talk to Keddie.

"I'm sorry I didn't answer you," he said, "I couldn't hear very well over the noise."

Keddie nodded. "It is loud. I don't think I said anything, though."

"Didn't you call my name?"

"No, Mr. Fraser, I didn't." Keddie shook his head as marshals cleared a space around the woman and began checking to see if she was ill. "But I'm glad we have a chance to meet."

"So am I, Dr. Keddie. We haven't worked on a case together before. I've got some materials relevant to Reece's condition. I'd like you to read them."

"I'd be delighted. The more information the better."

"You're still in the process of formulating a diagnosis?"

Keddie nodded again. "I've reached a tentative conclusion, Mr. Fraser, but I'm willing to examine any material you have."

"I hope you keep an open mind until you've gone through all the material," Fraser said.

"Of course. Send it over. We're going to have an interesting time on this one. The issues are very clear for you lawyers," Keddie shrugged in self-deprecation, "but psychiatrists have to slog through the swamps."

Fraser tightened as Keddie talked. There was something arrogant about the man, his stance, his speech. Was Keddie the adviser to Reece, mapping out what he did in court, or was it Reece himself? Fraser couldn't tell. "The law has to be simple, Dr. Keddie," he said too coldly. "The law assumes a man knows right from wrong. Even a man who does something as berserk as Reece can still know it's wrong."

Keddie's lined face was intent. He watched Fraser very closely. "You call it free will. The ability to choose one alternative from another." He said it in clipped little declarations. "Very few people have free will. It's a rare luxury, not a common attribute. My experience is that the law generally punishes those who don't have free will."

The black woman was groaning. She pressed a large hand to her breast. "You're wrong," Fraser said, again with undue coldness. "We punish people who know what they do is wrong and still do it."

"An arguable point. We'll have an opportunity to discuss it later. It's a world of appearances, Mr. Fraser. Our job, both yours and mine, is not be deceived by what we think we see in front of us."

"I'm glad you're interested in truth, Dr. Keddie."

He had to hurry. Starkey wouldn't be tied up with Reece much longer. He turned from Keddie. "I'll have those articles and materials sent over to you today."

The psychiatrist was watching the woman. "Fine. Isn't this remarkable? People are taken into court every day. Look at all these seekers here. Why is this any different? What do they think they'll find?" He chuckled. "I'll never understand people."

TWO

He went to the offices where Master Calendar held sway. Secretaries scurried with papers from ringing phone to ringing phone, and clerks with bundles of documents vanished into open office doors, came out empty-handed, and returned with more bundles, as though feeding some beast.

Fraser found the head clerk in his office. He was busily scratching on a pad, trying to match the grossly overcrowded civil court calendar with the few available courtrooms not already given over to the priority of trying criminal cases. Fraser caught his eye and then slipped inside, closing the door.

171

The head clerk, Augustino Maldanado, spoke with a heavy accent. He dressed in flamboyant severity, white shirts starched too much, with buttons too large, flowered ties knotted with mechanical exactitude, and sparkling and gleaming cuff links. He was nearly fifty and slender.

He hung up the phone.

Fraser said quickly, "Before you get involved again, Gus, Starkey just papered Judge Strevel. We're out of his courtroom."

"I know. His clerk called right now. That guy. He could have let me know. I'm nuts with things to do now."

Augustino had his finger depressing the phone button while he held the receiver and waved it in the air.

"Tell me who's available to hear this case, Gus."

Fraser watched while the clerk muttered and read down the master calendar, showing which judges had been assigned cases that morning and which had not.

"I got Clausen, McKinsey, maybe Hintz if his case folds up. He's supposed to plead in there. Why do they wait?" he said to Fraser impatiently. "Making me do all these things now when I could have made a nice assignment, now I've got gummed up works and we're on half-day before a holiday."

"How about sending this one to McKinsey?" Fraser said. McKinsey was old enough, hard enough, and smart enough to handle the complexities and pressures of the case.

"You want him?" Augustino asked thoughtfully.

"He'd be very good."

"Yah, he's good. Okay. I send you to McKinsey. I get the file over there from Judge Strevel. You go up now and it's okay." Augustino red-penciled *Department 7* beside the box on the long court-case calendar that bore the title PEOPLE *VS.* CHARLES EDMUND REECE.

"Thanks, Gus." Score one.

"You think Starkey wants McKinsey?"

"I think he'd rather have Clausen."

"Yah," Augustino swore, letting up the phone and dialing furiously, "he had his chance and he didn't let me know before he papered the judge. So that's to him, boy." He shot a conspiratorial grin at Fraser. "He gets who he gets."

THREE

Two men in a cold cell. Starkey asked again, "Who's your friend, Charlie? I'm your friend. I'm your lawyer. I'm doing everything possible."

Reece rocked on a greenish chair. "No. I'm sick. You don't get a doctor or anything."

"I'm your friend, Charlie," Starkey repeated.

Reece was silent.

"What's he telling you? Tell me. What's he telling you?"

"Nothing. We talk about my being sick and all."

"What's he saying about me?"

Reece was silent again. He made a splattering, baby sound with his lips pouted out, spittle flying. Starkey kept clear.

"He must be saying something about me. You'd talk to me if he wasn't, wouldn't you? What's he telling you?"

"I'm sick. You make them understand. I'm full of viruses they give me."

Starkey tried again. First he'd had to deal with Keddie, who insisted on showing up in court so he could see Reece, then Reece, then Strevel, now Reece again. It was a very trying morning. "You can't keep secrets from me, Charlie. That's not a good idea. I'm your friend."

Zip. Blank.

"Does he tell you to hide things from me?"

Groans, grunts; more spittle.

"He's a psychiatrist. I'm your lawyer. I'm the one in court all the time, not him. I know what's going on."

"I know what's going on," Reece answered slowly. "I know who's helping me."

It was icy in the cell. Starkey felt it, but Reece, dressed less warmly, apparently did not.

On impulse, Starkey looked at his watch. He'd forgotten about the time. He'd gotten caught up with Reece and forgotten.

He pushed a button to call the deputies to let him out. He pushed it again.

"Shit," he said. "Goddamnit."

"What's the matter?" Reece said. "Something wrong?"

Another futile check of his watch. You can't recall time. Fraser was out there and he was stuck in here and that was it. He pushed again, then again. He tapped the cell bars. Behind him, Reece asked, "What's wrong?"

He kept pushing continuously, hoping the little bell was ringing madly in the control booth. "I said shit. Just shit."

"Why?"

"Because I felt like saying shit," Starkey snapped.

FOUR

Two floors above Strevel's courtroom was Department 7. When Fraser got there it was in session, with McKinsey presiding rapid-fire over the arraignment and sentencing of the defendants on his morning calendar. He gave one car thief four months in county jail, and a business burglar two years in state prison. Done with dispatch, no wasted motion or false sentiment. He was a master.

He noticed Fraser sitting near the jury box. Before calling another case he said, "You want to approach the bench, counsel?"

Fraser went to the side of the bench where he couldn't be easily overheard. McKinsey smiled at him. There was a bowl of mints on the bench and the judge stuffed a handful into his mouth. "What are you up to?" he mumbled.

"I want to warn you, judge. Gus is assigning the Reece case to you. Starkey challenged Judge Strevel, so the case is coming here. The file is on its way. It's on for arraignment on the grand jury indictment."

McKinsey swallowed the mints. "Mother Mary and all the little saints, you bastard," he whispered. "Why the hell do I get that can of worms?"

"Your name came up."

"Mother Mary, that's exactly what I needed. Okay, sit tight until your little pal gets over here, and then we'll go into chambers and I'm calling Gus to get his butt in gear and find another judge."

Coolly, Fraser said, "There isn't anyone else, judge. I don't want to wait on the arraignment, either. I think Reece is going to try to relieve Starkey. I think he's hoping to make us drop the ball on the arraignment so he has an appealable issue. I'd hate to lose a death penalty case like this on something that petty."

In a throaty whisper, McKinsey agreed, popping mints into his mouth, then straightening to look out at the impatient courtroom. "The sons of bitches would do that, too. Okay, park yourself over there. We'll take care of this as soon as everyone gets together." He wagged his head in annoyance.

He called out the name of a case and a group of four fat men and women lumbered up from their seats to the railing, their attorney herding them like a pack of goats.

"Good morning, your honorable," the attorney said with a toothy smile at McKinsey.

Fraser raised his eyebrows sympathetically at McKinsey and sat down. When McKinsey realized there was no one else, he'd get over his distaste for the case. He was the right choice.

Twenty minutes later Starkey hurried in, even more put out than in Strevel's court, sourly taking his assigned part as Reece was arraigned on the indictment. As he had in the lower court, Reece gabbled and denied each charge McKinsey read to him.

The remainder, Fraser thought, was predictable. Starkey got a two-week continuance to file his first motions, then he declared a doubt as to Reece's competence to stand trial. Two psychiatrists were appointed to examine him. Fraser made Dr. Gables his choice.

"I want another lawyer," Reece suddenly complained again.

"You have the money to hire one?" McKinsey asked testily.

"Nope."

"What don't you like about Mr. Starkey? He's a darn good attorney, my friend, and I'm talking from thirty-seven years experience in this town. So tell me what's wrong with him."

"He won't call the people I need for my defense. He won't help me defend myself." Reece was downcast, put upon, as McKinsey eyed him frostily.

Starkey said, "I've determined who would be of assistance in Mr. Reece's defense. Mr. Reece doesn't completely agree with my choices, your honor."

"Well, then, that's no good, my friend. You've got a good lawyer already." He looked at Fraser, then quickly at Reece as a thought struck him. "You want to represent yourself, is that what you're asking?"

"Nope. I want another lawyer, a street lawyer."

McKinsey pounced. "I've heard that one each and every day I've sat up here, Mr. Reece, and not one person who's been where you are right now knows the slightest thing about what makes a good lawyer. I wouldn't give you ten cents for the abilities of the so-called street lawyers running around town. You sit back there and you hear from some jerk that so and so is a great lawyer. Did you ever stop to ask yourself how much your pal knows if he's sitting back in the same cell with you and he's got such a hotshot lawyer? Did you?"

Reece twisted part of his sweat shirt into a knot.

"I'm not going to relieve Mr. Starkey on those grounds. He knows how to take care of your defense and how to do a damn fine job at it, so let him do his job. Motion denied."

"Thank you, your honor," Starkey said, glancing at Reece.

Reece's frustration was apparent. You struck out, Fraser thought. You thought you'd get a delay, and McKinsey just walked over you.

"Both counsel approach the bench."

Fraser and Starkey came up to the bench, which rose to the height of their faces so they peeped over its top like children at a teacher's high desk.

"I don't know which of you smart alecks I ought to sock for dropping this little goose egg on me. You dumped Strevel," the judge scolded Starkey, "and you aced me," he said to Fraser, "so let's try to make life easy for ourselves if we can. Is that fair enough?"

"I'm going to play straight," Starkey said. He shook his head at Reece who was gesturing to him.

"I'm agreeable," Fraser said, feeling better for once that morning.

McKinsey grumpily eyed them both. "Bastards," he said in resignation.

FIVE

Gene felt Andy's solemn eyes on him as he plugged the gas tank, wiped his hands, and paid the attendant. Cars sang past them on the nearby highway, and a few suddenly turned off toward this little oasis of gas stations and fast-food stands. A shiny-headed bald man behind Gene honked his horn twice. "You gonna sit there all day?" he shouted.

Gene got back into the car beside Andy.

He could barely see over the bundles of clothes and toys and the few household items piled in the back of the car. They filled his vision, all that jumble, in a dark mound. Andy, snugly fastened in, turned to see the bald man, still making impatient noises to someone in his car.

Firmly, Gene pointed him forward. "Don't look back there. There's nothing to see."

Andy looked up at his father and folded his small hands in his lap.

"I'm starved," Gene said. "We're going to eat. You hungry now?"

"I guess so."

"All right. We'll eat."

Gene carefully eased back into the rushing traffic that hummed angelically around them. He drove a short distance to a dusty picnic ground and pulled in. It was after one on a weekday—the day before Christmas—and very few cars stood in the parking lot. The ones there were old cars, sad and beaten.

I need a shower soon, Gene decided ruefully. Maybe there's a motel up ahead. He stopped. What was up ahead? What was the next town? He'd lost track of the last dozen or more, driving by sign after sign without reading them. Only the black ribbon unwinding endlessly in front of him mattered.

He dug into the backseat mound and found a can of roast beef hash. He took Andy to one of the picnic tables, scored with a bewildering tangle of initials and symbols.

He could see the car needed a good hosing. It was as dusty as any other in the parking lot. There were long streaks of dried mud on it, and the whole car looked roughly used.

Gene checked around them. There was an old couple sitting about twenty feet away in the gathering sun, as still and passive as commuters waiting at a train station. He didn't worry about them. They were too old and far away to cause trouble. He made this a habit now, taking a quick look for possible trouble. Only when it seemed really safe did he relax, take out a small butane burner, and light it. After opening the can, he set it on the ring of blue flame.

He smiled at Andy. How peaceful it was out here. How distant and strange and peaceful. Blissful to know no one.

"Did I tell you what I decided this morning, champ?"

Andy shook his head.

"Well," Gene took a deep, satisfied breath, "I think you and me are going to stay on the road. We're going to drive and drive. We're going to drive maybe forever."

Andy squinted at the sun, glanced at the hash to see if it was ready. "Aren't we ever going to stop?"

"Oh, sure. We'll stop like this to eat and stuff. Maybe we'll stay in a motel for a while, too. But, mostly we'll drive and see places. You like that idea?"

"I don't know. Is there anybody to play with?"

"Sure. We'll find kids to play with. We'll play together, you and me." He hugged Andy tight. The little boy accepted it quietly. It had come to Gene that he was not to stop anywhere for very long, but to keep moving constantly. There was safety in that motion. A future of dark asphalt and concrete stretched comfortingly before him.

He loved to watch Andy eat, the tiny bites, the slow thoughtful chewing, sometimes the careless way his son ate, as if he didn't have the slightest interest in the food. At such moments he would think: That's how Aaron would eat. That's what Aaron would say.

Gene banished these thoughts almost as swiftly as they rose up. No, it was all clear to him. The house would be sold in fairly short order, the real estate agent was confident of that. All the money would be sent to his sister in Albany, and he could get hold of it from her.

Then he could drive forever with Andy.

Forever and ever.

When they were finished eating, they were alone in the picnic ground. Today was Christmas Eve. He decided that the next motel on the road would be their stop for the night. He'd give Andy his present, a flashlight with a compass in it.

He took out the Gideon Bible. Ever since they had left Santa Maria he'd read to Andy from the book. He'd never read it before, particularly. Now he had the time. He sought passages at random, reading them without any pattern, finding the most satisfaction in the verses where the enemies of God were smitten and rendered to dust.

SIX

The choir, in blue cassocks and white surplices, was singing a second hymn, their faces illuminated by the myriad of tall white candles wound with holly at each pew, when Fraser realized that Kate was crying. The shaking of her body in the crowded pew was almost undetectable, except that he'd known somehow it would come.

"Kate?"

"I'm sorry. I promised myself I wouldn't. I tried. I just can't help it."

"It's all right," he said, putting his arm around her. The other people sitting to either side of them hadn't noticed. The choir sang gently, entreatingly, and it washed out suffering so close at hand.

Kate had been talkative all afternoon, with the forced cheeriness that Fraser had seen often of late. Sooner or later it would run out, almost the way a well-played song of a certain length and quality comes to an end, leaving whatever feelings it briefly concealed free once more.

He felt the shaking subside as she controlled herself again. A paralytic helplessness compounded of rage and pity seized him. Rage because he was certain she would never absolve him of the guilt of one imbecilic moment's selfishness, and pity because she was terrified of loneliness. It wasn't my fault, he wanted to say to her. Yet he felt he had caused her suffering.

"Do you feel better?" he whispered. She faced toward the choir and the altar, dominated by a self-consciously rude wooden cross.

"I just couldn't help it, Tony. I'm all right now." She held his hand for a moment.

"We could go . . ."

"No. Please. I'm fine now."

He nodded and faced the choir with her. How were they to cling to each other when neither of them, even at moments like this, could bear to speak of what haunted them most? He could feel the warmth of her thigh pressed against his, yet they were distinct, separate, united only in their conspiracy of silence.

When they had come in, Kate had bowed at the pew and sat down. Already the church was full, a half hour before the Christmas hymns began. Fraser, reminded of the crowded courtroom that morning, thought: This is a crowd with a different purpose.

Kate knelt briefly while he sat and perused the program. She still followed the rituals of faith, even though they rarely went to church. The last time had been the previous Christmas Eve, at a different church, with Molly, who fell asleep before the last gentle hymn was sung.

Here was one kind of mystery, Reece another. There was one God in heaven, and many on earth. He looked at Kate, now composed and relaxed. She was a good woman. Everyone thought so, Fraser knew she was. But Kate could kill. Anyone could. Even he could kill, he was certain, at the right time and place.

Most people, at most times, do not kill. They restrain that desire, master the abominable suggestion. But others, like Reece, choose to obey the savage commandment of their private deity and kill whenever and however they wished. It was against that violent anarchy that Fraser rebelled so strongly. It was what he had sensed the first morning in the blue bedroom.

"Don't frown," Kate said, touching his mouth. "Listen to the music."

"I was thinking."

"Just listen," she said.

In a few minutes the lights blazed up, the organ sounded a tocsin, and the congregation rose. The service was about to begin. He and Kate slipped out.

When they got home, they exchanged gifts. She shyly brought out a gold fountain pen engraved with his initials. Like the shirts she bought for him, always monogrammed.

He gave her a watch. She kissed him on the forehead. "I'll never be late for a meeting," she said.

It seemed so insignificant a token. The desire he had felt in church welled up in him again. There was a gift he could give her. He said with conviction, "Kate, I promise you this will be my last case in the D.A.'s office. If I win this one, I'm going to quit."

"What are you going to do?" she asked, startled.

"Get another job. Someone can use a trial hack."

"You have no idea what this means." Her eyes were tearing as she looked at his face. "You don't know how this makes me feel."

He did, though. All the old dreams that had grown pale while he worked in the D.A.'s office were flickering to life once more. Perhaps she was thinking of a family again, too. But Fraser really had no other choice. The promise had been driven from him by the months of pain after Molly's death.

She said her father could help him with clients and business; already she saw a new future.

"We can talk about that," he said. "I don't want to work with your father. But that's my present to you."

Kate held him. "You couldn't have given me anything more lovely." She closed her eyes. "I hope for both of us you do win. I hope with all my heart you do."

PART TWO

CHAPTER XIV

ONE

Starkey had saved the most dangerous for last.

Fraser had no doubt of it when he sat down in Department 7 for the last hearing on Starkey's seemingly endless series of motions. The trial was now less than a week away. Although the previous motions had been important, this final one posed the greatest danger to the case. If the earlier ones harassed and delayed, swarming like wasps but leaving the case itself untouched, this was a rifle bullet aimed at the vitals of his prosecution of Reece.

The purpose was to suppress evidence because it had been seized illegally. It would deny Fraser the use of that evidence in the trial. Starkey had saved this most devastating assault for the end, when Fraser would have no time to recoup and the damage to his case would be gravest.

It was nice strategy.

As much as he could, Fraser had prepared himself and his witnesses. He knew by now how Starkey acted, what he might try to do. Starkey was generally a plodder, but he had the dangerous capacity to lunge at a witness's most vulnerable words.

McKinsey had been on the bench for some minutes, wan and nearly immobile, munching mints, occasionally coughing loudly, while rereading the motions and responses filed by Starkey and Fraser. They sat virtually alone in the courtroom which, except for the area closest to the bench and counsel table, lay quiet and sunk in twilight.

Starkey and Reece sat at the other end of the counsel table. Behind Reece were his two faithful guards, rocking like sedate grandmothers in the county's blue plastic chairs. They now watched Reece with almost benign interest after so much time carting him in and out of court-rooms, in and out of cells, in and out of the jail and the sheriff's buses. Starkey and Reece sat like an estranged couple forced by circumstances to be close to each other.

Fraser waited for McKinsey to finish reading.

He knew all the evidence found in Reece's home was in grave jeopardy at this hearing. The essential parts of the puzzle hung exposed.

He had to keep the evidence together and intact. It was that simple.

He glanced down the counsel table. Starkey was busy making notes. The guards were looking elsewhere. Fraser's eyes found Reece, who wasn't smiling. He looked at Fraser. And he winked.

The judge rustled on the bench. Fraser abruptly looked away, shocked at Reece's unsettling confidence. He looked again quickly. But Reece was whispering to Starkey. No one else, apparently, had seen it; all eyes had been somewhere else.

Reece had known that. It was meant solely for Fraser's benefit.

After all this time, Fraser's next impulse was to doubt that it had even happened. It was over in the briefest moment.

"All right, Mr. Starkey, Mr. Fraser," the judge said finally, "I've read your motions, documents filed in support thereof, responses from the People, and additional documents filed by Mr. Starkey. Do I have everything you want me to consider before we start taking testimony?"

"That's all I'm submitting," Starkey said lightly.

McKinsey thumbed the thick stack dubiously. "Are you sure? I don't want to go through another thing where you say you've given it all to me, then you want to file some papers afterward, and he"—the judge jerked his head at Fraser—"objects, and we have to go to the Court of Appeals again to straighten the mess out and then I've got to rule. So are you absolutely sure I've got the whole ball of wax up here?"

"You have it all," Starkey assured him.

"Mr. Fraser?"

"The court has all the responsive pleadings from the People."

"Fine, just so we're talking on the same wavelength. Anything else before we start taking testimony?"

Reece sometimes grew physically ill at this juncture, Fraser knew, groaning and clutching his head or stomach, and they would recess for an hour, or a day, or a week, until he was calmed down enough to go on. Sometimes he argued violently with Starkey. Sometimes Starkey wanted to use the court to locate a distant, unapproachable witness on a point so minute it strained the intellect. Fraser counted to twelve. Starkey had said nothing. Reece stayed quietly in his seat.

"One thing, judge," Starkey said. "I move that all potential witnesses be excluded from the courtroom until called."

The judge looked out into the empty seats. The guards sniffed in amusement. Starkey always made this request. "If there are any witnesses here, you are directed to wait outside in the hallway until called," McKinsey said wearily, "although I don't see anybody hanging from the rafters, counsel."

"No, judge," Starkey said.

"I expect respective counsel to police the court's ruling since I don't know what your witnesses look like."

"For the record," Starkey asked, "you granted the motion?"

"Yes, counsel, I granted the motion. It's on the record now, plain as day." McKinsey picked up the first page from the stack in front of him and peered at it. "All right, we're here today on two items of business filed by the assistant public defender, Mr. Starkey, on behalf of his client. The first is a motion under section fifteen-thirty-eight-point-five of the Penal Code to suppress evidence seized by the police in a search of the defendant's home. The second is a motion to traverse the search warrant itself. Is that right?"

Starkey said, "Yes, sir, judge."

"Do both counsel agree that these two matters can be heard at the same time, since it looks to me as though the witnesses for one will be witnesses for the other, too?"

"So stipulated," Fraser said. He was anxious to deal with whatever Starkey had in mind. The wink bothered him.

187

"Yes, stipulated," said Starkey. Usually he tried to beat Fraser to the punch getting his agreement on the record. It was part of their constant warfare. He was slow today.

McKinsey rubbed his eyes. He looked quite tired. Some days it was less obvious, but Fraser thought he looked tired all the time now. "You can call your first witness, Mr. Fraser."

"Is the D.A. stipulating there was no warrant when the police first went into Mr. Reece's home?" Starkey said in a needling tone.

"Of course he is," the judge said. "Let's get going."

"Yes. So stipulated," Fraser said. "The People call Detective Mel Sanderson."

McKinsey noticed that his bailiff was missing. He pointed at one of Reece's guards. "Will you step out into the hallway and get the witness?"

"We're not supposed to leave him, judge." The guard indicated Reece. "That's orders."

"We'll keep an eye on him," McKinsey said.

Reluctantly, the guard got up and brought Sanderson into court. Sanderson strode in without looking at Fraser, went to the clerk, and took the oath. He held his reports in one hand. He was fragrant with after-shave, and very formal.

Fraser had to treat Sanderson carefully. In the interview before court, Sanderson had kept yawning from a long late shift. He told Fraser he didn't want to say anything to hurt the case, or himself. He had made a mistake long ago, at the beginning, and it struck him as stupid for it to cause any trouble. Fraser had told him to simply tell the truth. No more, no less.

Now Fraser led Sanderson through the important events of that morning months before. He described why he went into the house without a warrant, the fears for Aaron Tippetts, and how Reece closely matched the appearance of a suspect seen near the murder scene.

Sanderson read from his reports without inflection or emphasis. It was made to sound routine, normal. He listed all the things he could see with his naked eye in Reece's bedroom. This was significant. If Sanderson could see it, it wasn't a search, as long as McKinsey ruled that entering the house was lawful. He listed the charts, the books, the rotting food, the crates, the piles of clothes, the organic tissue in the shower stall.

He left out finding the bullets.

Fraser heard the omission in his mind. He couldn't ask about it without arousing Starkey's suspicions, so he passed over it. "Detective Sanderson, did you physically seize any of these items prior to obtaining a search warrant?"

"No. They were seized after we had the warrant," he replied levelly.

Starkey waited for his turn, thumbing the police reports he'd so meticulously indexed. He jotted notes and sucked on the end of his pencil, peeping at Fraser, listening closely.

The lie was part of the record now. Fraser knew Sanderson had lied. He rose. "I have no further questions of this witness now, your honor. I do have a final stipulation Mr. Starkey and I would like to offer to the court."

"Okay. What is it?"

"That the items listed in the search warrant return constitute all the evidence seized, and therefore what Mr. Starkey seeks to suppress."

"That it, Mr. Starkey?"

"Yes, judge. That's the stipulation."

McKinsey coughed harshly, covering this mouth, then said, "Accepted. Cross-examine." He sank into his chair.

"Thank you." Starkey smiled, appraising Sanderson. The detective had told Fraser that he and Starkey had tangled before, always unpleasantly.

It was uncanny when, a moment later, Starkey went right for the lie. Fraser watched him with an acid taste in his mouth.

"Officer," Starkey instantly demoted Sanderson, "what time was it when you first broke into my client's home?"

"About two, two-fifteen."

"And what time was it when you went back with your search warrant?"

"Nearly five. After five, maybe."

"You got the warrant with Mr. Fraser here? The two of you were both at the house and then you went and got this warrant?"

"That's right."

Starkey, with an affable smile, flipped through his reports. He stopped at one. "Now, it says here in your search warrant return, officer, that you found some twenty-two caliber shells in the rear bedroom. You found them after you got this warrant?"

"I didn't personally," Sanderson said calmly, "but they were found after I had the warrant."

"You were in the room when they were found?"

"Yes."

"Those shells are pretty important to the case, aren't they?"

Fraser objected. He didn't like Starkey's gentle opening. It suggested worse to come.

"I'll withdraw the question for now," Starkey said. McKinsey sighed.

Apparently Starkey had enough to hammer at that he could afford generosity.

"In your first search of my client's bedroom, didn't you open drawers or look in closets for clues? Weren't you trying as hard as you could to find something that might tell you where this little boy was?"

"We were looking carefully," Sanderson admitted.

"You didn't just walk into this room, peek around, and then walk out again, did you?"

"No, we looked. I looked." Sanderson smoothed a crease in the corner of his mouth.

Fraser heard the thudding tread coming nearer. He ached to leave the courtroom, but he was bound to his chair as if strapped in. There was no escape.

"You even looked closely enough to see this frying pan, didn't you?"

"Yes, I did."

"You saw what you thought was blood in it?"

"It was blood."

"So you were being quite thorough, very detailed in your examination of my client's bedroom?"

"I made observations of whatever was in plain view," Sanderson said, "and seized items I thought were evidence later."

Starkey's smile hadn't wavered, and the detective remained studiously at ease. Sanderson had adopted the course Fraser suspected he would. It meant lying, but it was the safest way to save the evidence. Starkey sensed it, obviously, without being certain.

"Were you in a hurry to find the boy?"

"I was anxious to do whatever I could to locate him. I thought the situation very dangerous after I saw what happened to his mother."

"You thought it was an emergency?" Starkey's small face thrust at Sanderson.

"It appeared to be."

"And you'd do whatever you could to find him?"

"I would do whatever I could," Sanderson responded with brittle shortness.

"And you didn't care what the law said, is that what you mean?" Starkey said accusingly. "You'd do whatever you had to, come hell or high water?"

Sanderson was ready for the question, and now he smiled at Starkey. "No," he said slowly and deliberately, "I kept in mind what the law was at all times. I didn't forget that."

The exchange netted Starkey some interesting material, but he had failed to wrest any concessions from Sanderson, nor did he as the cross-examination went on until midafternoon. The worst he developed was an apparent contradiction between the urgency of finding Aaron Tippetts and Sanderson's punctilious initial check of Reece's bedroom. It was clearly less than Starkey wanted.

He did take Sanderson through every bit of evidence, tagged its time of discovery exactly, pinned down who found it and where Sanderson was, questioning the methodical restraint Sanderson claimed.

Detail by detail, it forced all of them, Fraser knew, to hold fast to the story Sanderson set out. Fraser knew he wasn't exempt, either. Sanderson had wound him in the same snare.

Everything was seized after the warrant. Everything.

"You can call your next witness, Mr. Fraser," the judge said.

He considered it. Sanderson had supplied all the required support for the warrant. There was no point in feeding another witness to Starkey.

"The People rest, your honor. I have no more witnesses."

"Defense then. You wish to call any witnesses, Mr. Starkey?"

Starkey nodded agreeably. "I most certainly do." His black glasses bobbed up and down. "I'd like to call Mr. Fraser as my first witness."

The request startled Fraser. He hadn't anticipated Starkey striking at him personally. It was like Reece's hideous wink. But it was his own fault for being so hasty and going to the Reece house. He had made himself a witness, and now Starkey was taking advantage of his stupidity.

"Mr. Fraser is a precipient witness to everything the officer said, judge. He advised the officer on obtaining the search warrant. I'm entitled to call him as a witness to find out what he has to say."

"I know you are," McKinsey said quickly, "but do you really want to?"

"Yes," Starkey replied obstinately, "I do."

Fraser ran a hand over his face. Starkey was more than just technically right. He was trapped. He looked up at the judge. "I object to being called as a witness, your honor. There are a number of other witnesses who can testify to precisely the same facts as I can. Calling them does not require putting opposing counsel on the witness stand. Mr. Starkey is merely showboating. I object to it."

"Objection noted. And I overrule it. Mr. Starkey can call you as a witness."

"As a hostile witness?" Starkey inquired hopefully. It would permit him greater leeway in grilling Fraser.

"Don't push it, counsel," McKinsey said. "He hasn't shown any hostility yet. No, you treat him like any witness. Mr. Fraser, do you want to call someone from your office to come over and lodge objections and handle the cross-examination?"

He thought of Ballenger. Then he dismissed the idea. This was his tangle and he had to get clear of it in his own way, without pulling Ballenger in, too. "No, your honor."

McKinsey brightened with a notion. "I tell you what we'll do to save time. I'll permit you to answer Mr. Starkey's questions as fully as you'd like. That will save us any cross-examination."

Starkey started to protest but thought better of it. He was getting most of his cake.

Fraser walked the short distance from the counsel table to the witness stand. He had testified before, sometimes in cases he was handling, and there was always a peculiar fear as he mounted the short steps and sat down. It was the fear that he would blurt out some awful fact, or that his mouth wouldn't obey him. In front of him was the barren plain of the large courtroom, and closer, the counsel table, his own vacant place at it, and Reece and Starkey measuring him with predatory glee.

He was going to have to lie, or compromise Sanderson and lose the evidence.

Curiously, the sight of Reece staring at him made him relax suddenly. The face shone at him against the black backdrop of the courtroom. There was even, he thought, the trace of a smile.

Starkey wasted no time, coming up to the witness stand rather than conducting the questioning from his seat. He leaned against the jury box. Fraser found himself saying that it was about two forty-five in the afternoon when he got to Reece's home.

"Where was Mr. Sanderson?"

"Detective Sanderson was in the living room. He was waiting for me."

"Were there other officers in the room, police officers that is, when you got there?"

"Yes. A number of them."

Starkey's sarcasm bloomed. "And were they all standing around, too? Waiting for you? Cleaning their fingernails?"

Fraser knew where Starkey was trying to lead him. If these police officers were so frantic to find the child, why were they calmly waiting? And if they weren't just waiting, then weren't they in fact ransacking the house? Either course was perilous. He chose one. "No, they were waiting, too. They'd made a search for Aaron Tippetts and hadn't found him. They were waiting for my advice on what to do next."

A grunt of disbelief came from Starkey. He strode to Fraser. What had all those men been doing while they waited for him? How long did it take to look around a house to see if a little boy was there? Didn't Sanderson show him the rear bedroom? Weren't the items of evidence already in bags and tagged? Didn't they try to find any evidence before the search warrant was issued? And then didn't Sanderson, with words supplied by Fraser, use this evidence found without a warrant to justify getting the warrant itself?

"No," Fraser answered simply. He couldn't see Sanderson sitting in court. The detective must have left after stepping down from the stand. Fraser was truly alone.

"Let's take a concrete example," Starkey said. "You heard Mr. Sanderson say the twenty-two caliber shells were found after the warrant was issued. Were any shells or bullets found while you were in the house?"

He could be truthful on that small point. "No," he said again.

"Well, were you told about or shown any shells they'd found before you arrived?"

Fraser, like all men, counted on some part of himself as an intrinsic kernel that was beyond daily temptations or even great temptations. It was an integral part of him that he had never misrepresented the law or the facts in any case he had handled over the years. He believed no case was worth that effacement of his ethics and training. It was reaching into himself and crushing that hidden, intimately held part. Holding to that ideal had cost him some cases, and made others more difficult. But the principle was ironclad. He had never compromised himself in order to win.

Now Starkey had asked the question. Fraser couldn't let Sanderson's dissembling pass by mere silence. He had to deny or support it. He saw Reece fiddling with Starkey's notepad; he thought of the blue room. There was no real choice in the face of that abomination.

He *wanted* to lie.

"No, there were no shells at that time," Fraser responded clearly. "I wasn't present when the shells were found later."

Done. Years erased. A new path broken. Something within him, generally unfelt, simply ceased to exist.

He had broken with himself.

From then on, Starkey had little to work with. All he had done was to memorialize Fraser's words in case other witnesses said different things. He was hoping to land inconsistencies and legal issues for appeal. He might even be hoping to show perjury, collusion, obstruction of justice. But Fraser was sure that the careful and ambitious Sanderson had worked it out with all the other officers who had been in the Reece house.

"I'm finished for now," Starkey said lamely, after an hour.

"Thank you, Mr. Fraser. Step down."

There was stiffness as he stood. What have I done, he thought in a flash of terror and sickness—but it passed as soon as he walked by Reece. He knew exactly what he had done, and why.

Starkey called more witnesses, wearing down the whole afternoon, and by five-fifty they all wanted it to end. Fraser declined to put on any rebuttal.

McKinsey sniffed loudly and pushed forward in his chair. "I'm going to rule on both motions now, Mr. Starkey, in case you have appeals you want to take up immediately. We've got a rapidly approaching trial date I'd like to keep, if at all possible. Of course, if you do file any appeals, I assume the trial date will be stayed." He almost added *again*.

Fraser listened as McKinsey quickly went back over the testimony. At the end of the counsel table, Starkey let his breath out in a slow, exasperated wheeze. Reece, for once, seemed not to mind, in contrast to his usual demeanor. He's saving himself for the trial, Fraser thought.

"The emergency nature of the situation justified a fairly extensive search for clues that might lead to this child," the judge said. "On that basis, the motion to suppress is denied."

"You're admitting all the evidence? The bullets, too?" Starkey asked.

"That's my ruling," McKinsey said. He passed with equal swiftness to the motion to set aside the search warrant. Denied on similar grounds. The warrant was properly issued.

The judge looked satisfied for the first time all afternoon. "Well, then, my friends, court stands adjourned. I'll see you next Tuesday morning bright and early so we can start jury selection. Unless Mr. Starkey files an appeal first. Are you going to do that in light of my rulings, Mr. Starkey?"

Starkey snatched the notepad from Reece. "I haven't decided yet, judge."

"Be my guest. Go ahead and take me up if you think you can get a better reading of the law, Mr. Starkey."

Starkey didn't answer, and began packing up his broken briefcase.

McKinsey bustled off the bench with a backhanded wave at them all. "I'm taking the weekend off. See you Tuesday," and he was gone.

Fraser slowly walked out. He felt light-headed and lightweight, as if all his substance had dissolved. In the corridor he found Sanderson and two reporters. Attention from the press had waxed and waned with various delays, and a hearing didn't create much interest. He talked with the reporters long enough to give them something to say.

Sanderson jumped off a bench when they were alone. "How'd it go?" he asked. Sanderson stretched his neck nervously. He wouldn't look directly at Fraser.

"I had to testify, but other than that, it went well. The judge denied both motions. We kept all the evidence."

Sanderson's freckled face split into a wide smile. "That's great." Then the smile shrank as he realized what Fraser had said. "You testified, too? About being with us at the house?"

"Yes."

Sanderson was somber at once. "Thanks for backing us up, Mr. Fraser. I know what that meant."

"Yes," he said again.

Sanderson stood awkwardly. "I had some good news. They're moving me up to lieutenant in a week. I got a promotion."

"Congratulations," Fraser said. He wanted to go home. He was very tired suddenly and he didn't want to see Sanderson anymore. "I'm beat, Mel. I've got to go."

"I won't forget this," Sanderson said. "I mean it."

"That's good," he said.

He walked away alone down the corridor.

CHAPTER XV

ONE

At first he thought the worst thing was regaining consciousness without any idea of what had happened. He remembered leaning over his sleeping father, whose black and toothless mouth had fallen open, one eye squeezed shut, a bald gnome who was his father not by appearance anymore or voice or even smell, but because a nurse outside had shown him in, as she did the first Sunday of every month and said loudly, "Your father is doing much better this time, Mr. McKinsey," and then left them. He wanted to wake the old man up, wrench him from the drug-enchanced slumber, so he bent low to the one good ear, tufted with hair like bits of moor heather, and called out, "Dad, dad, it's Sam, I'm here, dad."

But the drowsing old man snored on, a frail spidery creature wrapped in a heap of nursing-home blankets.

He straightened up after calling again, and looked at Iris, who stood as she always did at the foot of the bed. "I can't get him up," he remembered saying, and then a haze wrapped swiftly around him. That was the last thing he recalled. . . .

But now he heard voices and felt the cold, hard silver dollar of a stethoscope pressed against his naked chest. Even before he opened his eyes he heard Iris, her voice quavering and frightened. "Strain, he's had so much, he's the judge on this Reece trial, and he's been working so hard, so hard, I tell him what our doctor said, but he keeps working . . ." and after that, the professional murmur of a man, and the cold silver dollar slid malignantly across his chest.

He opened his eyes.

Iris hovered near him, and the nurse—that fat brown woman his father called The Loaf—was standing next to her while a man in white began feeling along his neck, all of them talking together, and in his first fear he thought he must have had a stroke because he hardly understood them.

But now, as he realized where he was—the shuffle from the hallway, carts and wheelchairs and slippered feet—he was scared that his father, disturbed by the commotion, had awakened to see his only living son collapse.

He looked around quickly. He was on the bed alongside the one where his father lay. The old man slept. His chest, under the oppressive weight of so many blankets, rose slightly, fell slightly.

He was immensely grateful for that.

"Sam, I'm so worried," Iris said.

"I fainted," he said. "I feel better now."

He started to sit upright. All these strangers and his shirt hastily torn open, no doubt by The Loaf in her zeal to treat the son just as she treated the father, bed to bed, invalid to invalid, the two McKinsey men. It was too shameful.

"Don't move," ordered the doctor, who pressed him back to the mattress. "Let me check you out first."

He lay back.

He saw his hands as they gripped the mattress to pull him up. The right one, with the twice-broken third finger. The first time, he'd driven drunkenly across the levee road at four in the morning, coming home from a high-school party, screeching and turning the car exuberantly, honking the horn, until he lost control and tumbled into the river, only managing to pull himself out and lie on the rocky side of the levee as his father's car sank to its taillights. And the second time, when he represented that son of a bitch Danker. Saved him from the gas chamber when the jury came back and said murder two, instead of the righteous murder one it was—and the hulking jackass got so infuriated he hauled off and sucker-punched him in the jaw while he was talking to the judge. Without thinking about the judge, or what the jurors might think, he had turned on his client and punched him into the courtroom wall.

It can't be a stroke, he reasoned. I can still remember.

Had he said anything? Had he disgraced himself any more after collapsing like that? His eyes roamed from Iris, pale, slim, worried, to The Loaf, and the curious old faces that peered in through the door.

The doctor was finally satisfied. "Well, you seem all right, Mr. McKinsey. Has this happened before?"

"Nope. Never. Is it going to happen again?"

"I can't tell. You are seeing a doctor now?"

"We've got a family man."

The doctor nodded and helped him sit up. "My suggestion is that you see him when you get back home. Let him check you over. It's a lot better to be safe than sorry."

Stiffly, he buttoned his wool shirt. Three buttons gone. What had they done? He was glad he had a heavy jacket to cover the thing.

His father lay stretched out beside him.

He had an impulse to shout triumphantly at the doctor, I'm sicker than hell, you bastard. I've got more things breaking down than holding together, and you can't tell the difference. He finished buttoning and stood. Iris gripped one arm, The Loaf his other arm.

"Let go," he demanded. "I came in on my own. I'm fine. I don't need any help."

"A wheelchair? Sam, you look tired. A wheelchair?" Iris looked inquiringly at The Loaf.

"He walks fine to me," she said. "He don't need no wheelchair."

"I sure as hell don't. I'm sorry for all this," he said perfunctorily to the nurse. She was the one who walked his father, fed him, cleaned him because he couldn't get to the bathroom, and bathed him. She shaved him every other day apparently, so his wrinkled jowls, hanging limply, were smooth and shiny.

He could barely bring himself to talk to her. She tended his father as if he was a baby. A McKinsey treated like that.

"Let me say good-bye," he told Iris, walking slowly to the other side of the bed. He kissed his father on the cheek. It was mildly warm. A tear from the irritated, open eye coursed through a furrow down his father's cheek, like a small stream seeking a channel to the open sea. He dabbed at it with the corner of his shirt sleeve.

"He's dead to the world."

"Well, he's been fussing the last two days, so the doctor had him get some more tranquilizers," The Loaf explained. Her glasses had a flinty gleam, one brown arm cocked onto a mountainous hip. "So he gets more rest. His heart is pretty weak."

They hovered over him on the way out, and at the nurses' station he paused, slipping twenty dollars into The Loaf's dry palm. "See you next month," he said. She nodded and folded the money into quarters, putting it into her skirt pocket. He had the faint hope that the money might buy a little special attention for his father.

Iris insisted on doing the driving back to Sarah's, and she told him they would have to spend another weekend with their grandchildren; he was obviously too worn out to stay any longer this time. He grunted noncommittally.

That was death, tapping lightly, when the haze gripped him. That was how it would come, suddenly, terribly, in the middle of something he was doing, without regard for his dignity or preference or hopes. He looked down at his legs in their corduroy pants. They had gotten flabby, thinner and unused over the years. His father's white limbs were mere reeds. The old man was eighty-three. He was sixty-four. He stole a glance at Iris as she drove and talked. What did she think? He didn't feel any differently than he had when he was thirty, twenty even, when he'd jumped from a plane over Germany and ended up in Aachen, shot in the ankle, wearing a dirty boot filling with blood. He had the same feelings. He knew Iris did. She still loved him without any idea that they had gotten older or changed. I am the same, he thought fiercely, my body just got old.

What about the old man lying in the nursing home? Did he dream, in that pampered, foggy sleep, of when he had been young? Did you stay that way, longing for what had gone by so cruelly in haste, until the haze grabbed you, even as you were dreaming and aching, feeling yourself, you inside, breaking apart?

"What's the use, Sam? What's the point if you kill yourself? You don't have to prove yourself with this trial," Iris said looking over at him as she drove precisely down the middle lane of the highway. "You don't have to make any friends."

"Not anymore," he replied.

"I want you to see Dr. Osling when we get back to town."

"Tuesday."

"Doesn't the trial start Tuesday?"

"Sure does."

"Then how can you see Dr. Osling?"

"Let it go, Eye, I'll see him when I can."

"I'm worried, that's all it is. I don't think you look well. I think you should have passed the trial over to someone else."

"I should have granted the change of venue and moved Reece to another county?" He patted her leg. "I want to hear this trial. The people of this county deserve to have it heard here." And I can't think of a better way to go out with a big beautiful bang, he thought.

"It's not the people of this county I'm worried about," Iris said. "You've got to take it easy. Take recesses. Lie down in your office. That's why I bought the pillows. You're not running a four-minute mile, Sam, and I know they'll try to make you run as hard as you can."

"I think it's going to be a little of the vice versa," he said with a grin.

"No, seriously, I know how you've worked on this trial . . ." She fell abruptly silent and concentrated on her fixed course down the highway.

He looked at her again. The auburn hair was paler now, shading into a lustrous gray. She had a good figure, and now her face was softer, the lines delineating rather than destroying. We've grown older together, he said to himself with a trace of wonderment.

"I'm a big boy now, Eye."

"And you've got to cut down on the smoking, too. Dr. Osling told you about it. Try to cut back even one or two cigarettes a day."

"I'll try."

"I mean it, Sam."

"I'll really try."

"I wish you'd retired last year," she said sadly. "I

wish we were living here with Sarah and Ron. We could even visit Susan if we lived here.''

''We will. Give me another couple of years and I'll be the first one to chuck the robe, close the doors, and get out of the courthouse.''

''I know you will.''

He looked at his watch. ''Shake a leg and we can have a drink before dinner.''

He knew she wouldn't increase her speed by one mile per hour. She was a steady hand that had come into his life and stayed. God knew where he'd have been by now, broken, battered, full of booze and half starved someplace. She'd saved him from that. He watched her with a longing that was almost a physical ache.

''What are you looking at?'' she asked.

''You, my love.''

The high desert flatness rolled relentlessly past them.

TWO

Six-thirty already. Fraser finished his breakfast, having no desire to linger over it. Kate sat opposite him. She had said little.

''Well, at long last your trial finally starts.'' She leaned over and took his plate, stacking it on hers.

''I don't need any sarcasm, Kate.''

''I didn't realize it was. I was just saying that you're going to trial. I didn't mean anything else.'' She took the plates to the kitchen.

''Then you can't hear yourself anymore.''

''I'm sorry.''

''You sound like I'm at fault for this thing dragging out.'' He pushed out of his chair. ''You know damn well I didn't have any control over it.''

Kate didn't answer as she set the plates in the sink. ''I can't even talk to you now. You always want to fight.''

''Because you won't give me any slack.'' He stood, hands in his bathrobe pockets, thinking there was something more he ought to say, either to vent his anger or apologize. The silence thickened. ''Thanks for breakfast,'' he said, turning from her.

''You're welcome.''

He showered, angry with her and himself, which was too often the case. Their quarrels and ill feelings jumped up like electric arcs, brightly, loudly, then subsided into a deceptive quiet as the charge built once more. Each change of the trial date had occasioned some spark; every delay strained them a little more. Fraser hoped he could finish the trial before they said or did something impossible to undo.

He washed carefully, standing for several minutes under the hard spray. He dressed for the jury to be chosen that day. A stiffly starched white shirt that pinched at his throat. Maroon and gold tie, small silver cuff links, freshly polished black wing-tip shoes. His hair, the graying streaks smoothed back, was parted neatly. When he slipped on his dark suit coat, Fraser saw himself in the bathroom mirror. He had changed. There was a disquieting tightness around his eyes and mouth. The face was somehow not quite his now.

He didn't kiss Kate on his way out, but as he stopped to get the car keys, she said, looking at him, "You're all set, killer."

THREE

The trial commenced sometime after ten in a courtroom filled with the pool of potential jurors. Fraser tried to put Kate out of his mind entirely and to think about nothing else but the delicate, hazardous task of choosing twelve people from that crowd behind him. One fool, one silly or mulish juror, and the whole trial could be wasted. It took only one to hang up the jury. He remembered, with particular distaste, the woman who had sat on a simple drunk driving case and refused to talk to her fellow jurors. She stayed in the closet and had them come to the door. The trial ended without a verdict and had to be redone.

That was an easy case. It took three days to try. There were only four witnesses.

He had over one hundred witnesses, and hundreds of exhibits. Starkey had some equally daunting number. One fouled-up juror and they would have to start all over again. He knew what that would mean to him, and not just for Kate's sake.

"We're going to conduct this trial in three parts." McKinsey sat under his halo of light on the bench, a pearly little man with a husky voice who drank often from a glass of water and sounded ill. "The first part is the guilt phase. The jurors will come to a verdict, if possible, on the defendant's guilt or innocence. Next, if the defendant is found guilty we'll have a sanity phase. Both counsel assure me this will be necessary. The same jury, in all probability, will determine whether the defendant was sane or not when he committed the crimes he's been found guilt of. Finally, if the defendant is found sane, we move to the last phase, the penalty. The jury will decide whether the defendant is to receive the death penalty, or life without possibility of parole. That should give you a general idea of how we will work."

Fraser looked to Reece. He was sallower from his time in jail, but neatly dressed in a coat and tie, somewhat like a junior salesman for a not very impressive line of appliances. His hair was slicked back. Jurors, Fraser knew, seldom had the pleasure of seeing a defendant as his victims had seen him. A jury simply saw a clean, presentable, often articulate person. Reece was on his best behavior. The antics, if needed, would come later. Fraser recalled McKinsey's "two charmers," the Rainier brothers who strangled without pity. A jury had found them insane and they had both survived.

Starkey rarely acknowledged Reece. He gave him a notepad to doodle on.

"Madam Clerk," McKinsey said thickly, "swear the potential jurors."

Marge, the judge's clerk of fifteen years, stood and raised a pale hand. "Will you please stand and raise your right hand for the oath?"

The crowd stood, reporters and Fraser and Starkey and Reece excepted. Fraser turned in his chair to watch these people, row after row of them, as Marge called on them, for the hundredth time he'd heard the words, to tell the truth. He watched their faces. Now they knew he was interested and his attention was on them.

A hundred and more voices rumbled "I do." The crowd sat again.

"The first job we've got this morning is to pick a jury to

hear this case. The lawyers will ask you some questions, and then we'll see who remains. Don't feel embarrassed or angry if a lawyer excuses you. Lawyers don't know why they excuse jurors.'' McKinsey rambled for a moment, and Fraser had the disquieting notion they might not even get past jury selection, much less the whole trial, if he was in this condition.

More business followed, reading the indictments, introducing everyone, and McKinsey finally saying sternly, "You may think this is like television or the movies, but it's not. They exist to entertain you. I don't want to entertain you. You've got to watch and listen to everything in this courtroom, because you'll have to go back and deliberate with your fellow jurors. This is serious business, my friends. A man's life is on the line in this trial, so don't get the idea we're running an amusement show for your benefit.''

That was the McKinsey of old, rapping their knuckles and making certain they understood the ground rules. Fraser felt less apprehensive.

"All right,'' the judge said, "we'll take a short recess and start jury selection. Ten minutes by the court's clock,'' and he left the bench. He hadn't even buttoned his robe; it swung breezily around him when he walked off.

Fraser and Starkey followed him back to chambers. Starkey was dressed quite casually. He hummed jauntily. It unsettled Fraser, still struggling with his inchoate anger at Kate and his fears at this crucial phase in the trial.

The judge's rumpled afghan lay in a bundle on one end of the couch in his chambers. Fraser wanted to fold it up, put it out of sight. It was a reminder of McKinsey's infirmity.

Starkey had gotten there a moment earlier.

"Where's the judge?'' Fraser asked him.

Starkey pointed at the closed door of the bathroom.

After a moment, Starkey said, "You still being unreasonable this morning?''

"I'm always reasonable, Al.''

Starkey was about to go into his routine again. Cut a deal for Reece. It's best for everyone.

A tightness constricted Fraser's chest.

"Okay,'' Starkey said, clapping his hands together,

"we haven't gone too far into the trial yet, so how about I plead him to all the counts, no promises, no deals, nothing, and you drop the special circumstances? I'll go along with a life commitment to a mental institution."

"I've heard it before, Al."

"You said you weren't unreasonable this morning," Starkey said. "It's a good deal. Come on. Let's go do it right now."

The judge flushed the toilet and hawked wrenchingly in the bathroom. The faucets ran. He came out wiping his face with a paper towel. "What are you bastards talking about?"

"Al wants to deal."

"Great. Always helps. You interested?"

"Not a bit. It's a very old, very discredited deal."

Crossly, McKinsey said, "Well, then, let's get this thing on the road. I don't want to waste time." He shrugged off his robe, lit a cigarette, and sat with his elbows propped up on his desk. "Do you gents have any better estimate for the length of this monster? How long are we talking about?"

Fraser pondered briefly. "I'd estimate three to four months, judge. My case-in-chief will take about a month and a half anyway." He hadn't even told Kate she would have another half year, in all likelihood, to endure.

"Four to five months," Starkey said.

"Mother Mary, you bastards are long-winded," the judge said, stabbing out his cigarette in circular jabs. "Can't we take care of this?"

"I'm willing," Starkey said. "I'll make any kind of reasonable deal." He took off his black-rimmed glasses and polished them with the end of his tie.

Fraser didn't like the direction of the chatter. "It comes down to this, your honor," he said simply, "Al wants his client to spend a little time in a state hospital for six horrible murders, and I want the death penalty."

"Five murders," Starkey said. "You can't prove the missing Tippetts kid."

"I think I can."

Settling his glasses firmly and making a show of sincerity, Starkey sat on the edge of the couch. "Judge, look at what we've got and tell me if what I'm saying isn't reasonable," he said. "We've got a manifestly sick man who committed several obviously sick murders. We can spend a half a year and God knows how much tax money proving he committed these crimes. So what? The psychiatrists are split. But any jury is going to come back with a dim-cap verdict, and the People aren't going to come close to what they want. Now if you follow *my* thinking, they get the guilty pleas, a shot at the joint for life if you don't buy our psychiatric evidence at sentencing, and a life term regardless for this guy, state prison or state hospital." He looked from McKinsey to Fraser with emphatic hope. "Hell, he's staying in a hospital till the cows come home, and we all know it. It's no big secret. Nobody's going to let him out."

"They did once before," Fraser said.

"You think any psychiatrist is going to certify him for release after all this publicity? Come on, Tony, that's nuts."

The judge yawned before he spoke. "I won't commit myself to you guys, but I'll tell you, Al, if he pleads in front of me today, you're not looking at any state hospital time."

"Okay, judge, I see your thinking. I'm willing to take the chance."

"We're talking life in prison," McKinsey said, "I mean, that's it. No end runs on me. He stays there."

They were dreaming and Fraser knew it. They persisted in haggling as if Reece was simply another murderer or burglar or coke dealer, and his crimes would be bleached away by the expedient chemicals of a plea bargain. "Ten years from now," Fraser said to McKinsey, "the parole board or whatever it's called then will look at his record and turn him loose. They haven't kept *anyone* for life, or even near it. The average stay on a life sentence, even with concurrent terms for multiple murders, is probably around twenty or thirty years. Charles Reece can plead his mental disabilities as a mitigating factor, too. He can say it's cruel to keep a man with severe mental problems in prison so long."

"It's still a chunk of time," Starkey said. "He'd be middle-aged by the time he got out. People change a lot."

"I don't care if he turned into the man on the moon."

"Simmer down," McKinsey warned, his lips moving only slightly, his head still propped up.

Fraser worried that McKinsey might start listening to Starkey's sophistries because they were built on truth. The defense, during the guilt phase of the trial, had to be either not guilty by reason of insanity, or diminished capacity, the aptly shortened dim cap. A dim cap defense would leave Reece guilty of lesser crimes than murder in the first degree and spare him from death. It was another risk Fraser had to cope with.

"You're talking about pleading Reece guilty without the special circumstances? That's what you offered?"

"Yeah," Starkey admitted.

Fraser turned to the judge. "You couldn't even sentence him to life without possibility of parole if he pled that way, judge. The best you could give him is life with parole, and that means sooner or later he'd be set free. No, it's completely unacceptable."

McKinsey lit another cigarette. His hands shook a little. He held the lighter tightly toward the cigarette. "I agree with you partway, my friend. I'd like to hang this gentleman up by his ears, but Al has a good point. I handled a couple of these cases myself, and juries don't like executing loonies. I'm sure Al's going to work on that angle."

"Damn right I am," Starkey said.

"So maybe a maximum sentence from me, some nasty letters from the community to the board, and you might get more out of this case than if you go to trial."

"I'm going to take that chance, judge."

"Come on," Starkey's patience ended explosively, "we're talking about realities here today, Tony. I feel sorry for the victims. Everyone does. But what are you going to tell the families when the jury comes back after we've been at it for six months and hands you a second-degree verdict? You can't keep him in the joint long with that, and you haven't gotten one damn thing you want."

Both McKinsey and Starkey were waiting for him to see the wisdom of their counsel. A deal was best for everyone, judge, jury, city, victims, the D.A.'s office, and of course, the defendant. How could he fly in the face of such overwhelmingly good advice?

Fraser was convinced that any deal was in no one's interest but Reece's, and that only a trial where the stakes were life and death could adequately vindicate him. Fraser knew Reece was sane because he knew Reece was terrified of discovery. He took all sorts of precautions to prevent his discovery. Now the great journey was to persuade the jury of Reece's fear, and the guilt that lay behind it.

"I'm not compromising the case," he said with quiet finality.

"I guess we go to trial," the judge said.

"I guess we do," Starkey said with disgust.

The recess ended. They went back into court, where a few hardier reporters were sitting among the prospective jurors. The process of jury selection could take a day or weeks. It was slow and without any particular attraction to those who looked for theatricality in the courtroom. Nothing much happened. Or so it looked. Jury selection, as Fraser knew, was perhaps the most significant part of a criminal trial.

They began with routine questions to the first twelve randomly chosen to sit in the jury box. First McKinsey asked his battery of general items, followed by Starkey's more intensive quizzing. Fraser was permitted to question each juror last.

Starkey excused the first two, and a third was excused by the judge because of undue inconvenience after she was told the probable length of the trial. The morning sped by; Fraser felt his tension ebb. He grew almost careless.

The fifth possible juror brought him up short.

She was a woman named Mrs. Milik, who sat in addled splendor. They had passed all the basic questions about her job, family, and habits, and arrived at the important issue.

"Do you have any reservations about the death penalty itself?" the judge asked her.

"I'm sure it's wrong to take a life," she replied. Her brown eyes looked back warmly at the judge.

"You are opposed to the death penalty on principle?"

"I think I am."

"You've got to answer more exactly, ma'am. Do you oppose the death penalty, the execution of a convicted person by the state?"

"Yes, I think that's wrong?"

"That sounds like a question. Did you mean it as a question or an answer?"

"I mean," she rubbed her temple, "I don't like the idea of killing someone."

It was a critical question. A juror who was unequivocally opposed to the death penalty could be excused by the court. This saved Fraser using one of his limited number of challenges. A juror who could apply the death penalty even once, even if only in the most extreme case, could not be excused by the court. Fraser would be forced to use a challenge, because a juror in that frame of mind could not be expected to vote the death penalty for Charles Reece.

Knowing this, Fraser posed a question to Mrs. Milik. "Would you oppose the use of the death penalty for Adolf Hiter?"

Mrs. Milik digested the idea very thoroughly. "Now you mean this as a suppose-type question, don't you? He's already dead, isn't he?"

Judge McKinsey snorted. "He's certainly dead, ma'am. We fought a little war about it. You recall that, I'm sure."

"I certainly do. Well, if I had to do it to him, I'm not sure what I'd do. I think all killing is wrong."

Warnings sounded for Fraser, but he ignored them. He was in control, he thought. "You'd vote against death for Adolf Hitler?"

"Perhaps not him," she conceded, "perhaps I'd make an exception in his case."

"How about the case of a man who committed several especially terrible murders? Could you vote death for that man, even if he wasn't as bad or didn't kill as many people as Hitler?"

"I don't believe so, no."

Fraser was about to ask another question. He'd seen immediately the danger carelessness had put him in. But Starkey interrupted. "Judge, I'm going to object. We can sit here all day asking this lady whether she'd vote to execute Attila the Hun or Stalin, and it's beside the point. The district attorney has gotten her to say she'd vote for the death penalty in one instance at least, and that's enough. Since he can't have her excused for cause, I don't think the district attorney can keep questioning her on this point.''

"I agree we're going off the mark now. Objection's sustained,'' the judge ruled. "Ask something else, Mr. Fraser.''

He was in a dilemma. Risk trying for a challenge by the court, which might give Starkey another issue for appeal? Or use one of his precious challenges and risk having someone else more to Starkey's taste end up on the jury because the prosecutor stupidly, stupidly wasted one at the very start of the trial?

He decided to risk removing her for cause. The appeal was far away.

"Imagine that a member of your family, your husband or one of your children, was brutally murdered.'' He rapidly formed a strategy. "The murderer was put on trial and convicted. Could you vote to execute the murderer?''

"I really don't think I could.'' She knew her answers were causing dissension and it bothered her. "I still wouldn't get my family back if I took a life.'' She looked at him unhappily.

"Why would you vote to execute Adolf Hitler?''

"Well, I guess everyone thinks that's right. They do think so, don't they?''

"You would vote the death penalty for Hitler because it is a popular opinion?''

Mrs. Milik nodded. "Yes, that's the main reason.''

He leaned back in his chair. Now to see if the judge agreed.

The time came for challenges and McKinsey was about to call for Fraser's when he broke in. "Your honor, I would ask the court to remove Mrs. Milik from this case for cause.''

"Oh, come on—" Starkey blurted.

"And admonish counsel, your honor.''

"Yes, let's take a deep breath, gentlemen,'' the judge said pointedly to Starkey. "Why should I excuse her for cause?''

Fraser hoped his strategy sounded plausible. "The prospective juror cannot apply the death penalty, your honor. She has said it might be appropriate in no other case but

211

that of Hitler, and only then because other people thought so. Given the example of a murder in her own family, she indicated an unwillingness to apply the death penalty. I submit this demonstrates her inability to ever impose it. I again request she be removed for cause.''

McKinsey smiled very slightly. ''Mr. Starkey?''

''We heard one example where she'd vote for the death penalty. Who knows how many others would pop up?''

Mrs. Milik listened in obvious dismay. Fraser had no sympathy for her.

Judge McKinsey said, ''Sounds to me like she doesn't want to vote for it, so we'll resolve this right now, ma'am. Give me a simple answer. Are you absolutely opposed to the death penalty?''

She was now desperate to get off this case. ''I am. After I've heard you all, I'd have to say I'm opposed to it.'' Her voice quavered as she answered.

''In every instance?''

''Any I can think of.''

''That settles it, Mr. Starkey. I find there is cause to excuse Mrs. Milik from service on this case, and you are excused, ma'am.'' He smiled at her to allay her nervousness, and she passed with relief along the first row of other jurors. They had watched with blank faces as she underwent the examination.

Reece pointed at another name on the list while Starkey shook his head. Good. Let them use up their challenges. Chastened, Fraser realized he had to be more cautious. Weigh every question, take nothing for granted. The cost of error was too high.

They broke for lunch with directions to return at two.

On the way to his office, he was stopped by three priests, formed in a jittery circle around an elderly priest wearing a gold cross. The old man moved slowly, but with an edgy alertness. The men asked directions and then headed for the office mentioned. They moved together like a black centipede.

Infeld was nearby. ''They're doing the prelim on that stabbing last week at St. Joseph's, the guy who ran in and stabbed Bishop Atwater. That's Atwater with the God squad.'' He pointed at the elderly man and his troop.

''Was it a robbery?''

212

"No. Guy ran past Atwater's secretary, pulled a knife, one of those double-bladed jobs, and took a couple of swings at him. Nicked the old guy in the gut and arm."

Fraser walked to this office. He had other worries.

"Like in your case," Infeld said, "he's making an insanity issue out of it." He turned toward the elevator. "It's a good shot," he said as the doors opened for him. "Who else stabs a bishop?"

CHAPTER XVI

ONE

Fraser ate very little lunch. Ballenger sat with him, doing most of the eating. "You've got egg salad on your face," he told Harry. "Next time we eat in my office, use a bib."

Ballenger swabbed his cheeks and chin with a paper napkin. Open bags of potato chips, coffee cups, and paper plates of cole slaw and pickle spears were scattered over the neat square of Fraser's desk. Placidly, Ballenger went on eating, taking the last pickle. "Mind?" he asked as he chewed.

"The damndest part of it," Fraser said, nudging his own half-eaten sandwich, "was that I knew the question was bad. I knew she'd say that. I wasn't thinking."

"You fixed it."

"I'm not going to be able to fix it all the time." Fraser closed his eyes. "What about the shrinks? Do I wait for the sanity phase?"

Ballenger swallowed and dabbed at his mouth again. "You've got to blow them out of the water the first thing. Don't hold back until later. Go for the throat now."

They had gone over Starkey's plea offer and the judge's warnings about what could happen at trial. It was a question now, they both agreed, of what Starkey would do to prepare the jury for an insanity defense, an issue really for the later phase, but one he would raise during the guilt phase by arguing that Reece committed the crimes in a diminished state of mind. This kind of tactical plotting was Ballenger's hobby. Fraser nudged him into it. "Starkey will bring on his big gun first. He'll open with Keddie and set the stage for an out-and-out insanity verdict. Keddie will start the ball rolling by telling everyone Reece has diminished capacity."

Ballenger wagged his finger in the air. "He might start slow, bring on a little guy, then put Keddie on, kind of lead up to him. You've got to take every one of them apart, the little ones or the big ones. When Keddie's through," he said, "the jury may not even come back with a murder second after he puts them through the hoops. He might get them to convict Reece of a voluntary, even. He's done some wicked things in cases I know about."

Fidgeting nervously, Fraser picked at the bags to see if there was something to chew on. He had no stomach for a sandwich. "Starkey wouldn't want a sanity hearing, would he? If he gets Reece down to a voluntary manslaughter, I'm sure he'll simply lie back and let McKinsey send him to prison."

"For six years? Ten maybe? You bet he'll lie back."

That was the tormenting paradox. The psychiatrists only helped Reece if their testimony enabled him to be found not guilty by reason of insanity or convicted of some lesser degree of murder. And he might be so convicted, if the psychiatrists persuaded twelve ordinary people that Reece had so little mental capacity that he couldn't form the intent necessary for first-degree murder. Bang. The jury comes in with second degree; voluntary manslaughter; even involuntary manslaughter.

But the psychiatrists could end up hurting Reece, too, once he was convicted of a lesser degree of murder, because in the sanity phase of the trial they might persuade the same ordinary people that Reece was truly crazy. Reece would then be sent to a state hospital, theoretically, for a longer time than he would do in prison.

Reece only wanted these psychiatrists to keep him out of the gas chamber or locked up for the shortest time possible. He had no other use for them.

"I've got to get Keddie as soon as he hits the stand,"

214

Fraser agreed. Ballenger had suddenly become unusually silent. "Funny thing this morning," Fraser said. "I looked in the mirror," he laughed slightly, "and I almost didn't recognize myself. That ever happen to you? Just a moment when you don't look the same?"

It was a strange thing for him to reveal, but he had been more bewildered by it than he had first realized.

"Not me." Ballenger hesitated. "Does Kate think you've changed?"

Odd for Ballenger to ask something like that. He rarely pried. Fraser wondered what was on his mind. "That's another story."

"Not too good?"

"No. Not good at all."

Ballenger crumpled his papers and pushed them into their paper bag. He didn't really want to talk about Fraser's troubles with his wife. "Tony, I heard something about that fifteen-thirty-eight last week."

"It was very dull."

"This was about something that happened there."

Fraser detected the gingerly, almost reluctant probing. He steeled himself. Subtly and suddenly, Ballenger looked different to him. "Like what?"

"It was about the testimony."

"What did you hear?"

Ballenger didn't like getting a question in reply. "There was some lying. Maybe perjury going on. Some of the cops maybe."

Fraser waited.

"Something about you." Ballenger looked away.

"Where did you hear this, Harry?"

Fraser saw the recrimination on his face. He had never seen it directed toward him before, not in all the years or all the cases they had worked on together.

"I heard it." Ballenger laughed with a short, expulsive breath. "It hasn't gotten around. I don't think it will. But I heard it. Did you lie?"

Fraser heard him, and knew what he meant, and who he was talking to. He met Ballenger's accusing look coldly.

"Yes," he said. "I did."

"Is that all?"

"Yes. That's it."

Slowly, Ballenger gathered his garbage and dropped it into Fraser's wastebasket. His heavy, slow movement, the softly made sighs were signs to Fraser that doors were imperceptibly and finally closing between them. Ballenger didn't understand about this trial, that was glaringly apparent; nor did he understand that more was demanded by this trial than any either of them had ever come in contact with before. The thing was insatiable, Fraser knew that now; it would crave more and more of him, finally consuming everything. It was consuming any hope he had for his marriage. It was now devouring his last, longest friendship.

"Jesus Christ, Tony," Ballenger suddenly flared to life, "what were you thinking of? What the hell was going through your mind in there? I just don't believe you'd lie. What the hell happened to you?"

He faced Fraser, solid, reproachful, and betrayed.

Fraser hadn't stirred since the first question. He knew he was losing Ballenger's friendship and admiration. It might be salvaged by another lie. But he didn't want Ballenger's accusations or narrow vision anymore.

"If you don't see the need for what I did, Harry, I don't really think there's any way I can justify it to you. Take my word for it, if I hadn't acted that way, we'd have lost some of the evidence. Sanderson made a mistake."

"Then let goddamn Sanderson ride his own beef," Ballenger said, lapsing into the language of convicts. "It didn't mean you had to jump in with him."

"It *did*. I'm sorry it had to be done, but I'm not giving up anything in this case, not because of stupid mistakes or deliberate lies or any other reason."

Ballenger shook his head, his mouth hard. "No case is worth your reputation. You don't lie for any case or anyone."

"You're wrong, Harry. I can't explain it to you so you'll understand, but you are dead wrong."

"Okay, Tony, okay." Ballenger nodded and turned away. "You're right. You can't explain it to me."

Fraser sat up. "Are you going to do anything about this?"

The question stung Ballenger more than Fraser's remorseless admissions. "Jesus Christ," he said under his breath. "No, I'm not going to do anything or say anything or write anything down, so rest easy." He looked like he was in pain. "Maybe that means I'm as bad as you. I'm doing it for a friend, though, not some goddamn maniac."

"Thank you, Harry."

Ballenger looked at him. "I don't know you. You have changed. You better be careful, boy. You better watch every step you make. You don't know what you're going to do next."

He left the room. Fraser heard Sally Ann toss a joke at him. There was no answer.

Fraser looked at his watch. It was a few minutes past one. A little more than an hour ago he had been sitting in Department 7 sweating out jury selection, and in a little less than an hour he would be back there doing it again. In the short time between, he had become a different man. He had severed the last human tie, other than Kate, that bound him to his life before Reece.

TWO

"Nobody thought we were going to get a jury this fast," Fraser said in the just-vacated living room. The clock chimed seven times and fell silent. He sat on the edge of the sofa and took off his shoes. He leaned back and touched his closed eyelids. They were dry and hot. "Eight days is some kind of record in a multiple-murder case. It's a good jury. Good-looking, anyway. Eight men and four women. We spent a couple of hours this afternoon picking four alternates in case anyone gets sick."

Slight jinglings, the sounds of drawers being opened and closed floated out to him from the bedroom. He went on talking.

"We got up to my opening statement," he said, "and right on cue Reece starts crying. A real weeping fit. So we had to recess until he composed himself." Fraser opened his eyes. "Kate? Are you listening?"

"Of course I'm listening," she said from the bedroom.

"Well, come out here. I don't like this long-distance conversation."

"I'll be out in a minute."

He put his hands behind his head. I won't say anything tonight, he thought, I won't start anything. "Reece has this routine down by now. He can turn his crying on and off. I don't know what the jury is making of it.''

Kate came into the living room buttoning her coat.

"Well, bully for them," she said, looking down at him.

"For who?"

"The jury. Bully for the jury. I heard everything you said."

Fraser hadn't moved on the sofa. He watched her checking herself in the mirror by the front door. "You're going out."

"Sorry. I have to."

"I thought we'd at least have dinner together before I started to work tonight."

"Well, I can't." She looked absentmindedly at the satisfactory aggregation of colors and lines she presented. "I've got to go out."

"With anybody?" No matter what, I won't start anything.

"Frank's offered to share a dinner with me. We may take care of some business. We may not. At least we'll talk, Tony. You know, say things to each other about the world and people."

"I ought to meet this guy sometime."

"I don't see why. I don't think you and Frank would hit it off at all."

Fraser stood up and tried to take her hand. She shook his off and reached over to the hall table for her purse. "No," she said. "Don't do that."

"I'd like you to stay with me. I haven't seen you all day."

"I'm not in the mood for another meal with the walking dead. I'd simply like a little companionship. I don't think I'll get much from you tonight, will I?"

"I have to work on the rest of my opening statement, but—"

"That's just why I'm leaving you in peace and quiet."

"I'll probably be up when you get back."

"I'll see you later, Tony." She opened the front door and left. Her scent, that mixture of lemon soap and perfume and the faint illusion of her skin, too, hung before him like cold smoke.

Fraser didn't even know which one Frank was among

the procession of friends, men and women, Kate had linked herself to with growing vehemence lately. Sometimes she was gone for entire weekends and he limited his gentle explorations to whether she had enjoyed herself. It was better not to know anything, he thought. It was imperative.

He ate a quick dinner and left the dishes in the sink. He took off his vest, tossing it in a chair in the study. He sat down behind the books and papers, siblings of the books and papers at the office, all of them his unshakable companions.

Everything witnesses had written, Fraser read. He had labored through texts on ballistics and chemical analysis, criminology, psychiatric articles and books written by Starkey's experts and his own. He studied the source books and authors Gables and Keddie cited particularly. This was the prelude to the great battle Keddie was going to lead.

Fraser picked up another book and found the notes he had made. It was an old battle, fought over the most ancient and insoluble questions of human experience: whether mankind was endowed with free will, capable of making choices and exercising moral judgment, or was fated from the start, guided along immovable tracks to a preordained destiny. The law said man had free will. He believed that himself. Otherwise nothing he did or thought made any sense. Besides, it was impossible to imagine a universe that demanded the monstrosity of Charles Reece.

Fraser had indexed, by subject and date, all the articles Keddie had written, the chapters he'd contributed to textbooks, the speeches he'd given. They all seemed tied together by a distaste for society as it was constituted, and a particular irritation with categorizations of mental illness. Keddie thought that mental illness revealed more about the society that labeled certain behavior than it did about the individual manifesting the behavior.

Crazy was in the mind of the beholder.

He actually believed it was all relative. The thought disgusted Fraser. Perhaps Keddie had reached this preposterous conclusion because he had spent so much time working with prisoners, or perhaps he truly longed for a word in which all human behavior was without standard, except that it be authentically itself. Either way, Keddie—who would not want to murder or torture—would defend someone who did.

It was this arrogance that Fraser had sensed at their first meeting outside McKinsey's courtroom. Keddie would be restless in his defense. He had no reservations about the rightness of his actions or the righteousness of his purpose.

Fraser had Dr. Rudin's report and Keddie's stacked together on his desk. He flipped through them again. Rudin had finally turned over his interview with Reece, just as the jury was about to start hearing evidence. It was impressive how the two reports dovetailed, how Rudin's questions laid foundations on which Keddie built his later interviews with Reece in jail. A perfect fit. Seamless, symmetrical, like the Chinese puzzle boxes he had told poor Tippetts about.

This defense puzzle, fitted together, pointed inexorably to a result Fraser detested. It said Reece was legally insane. In the simplest terms, that he lacked free will. He was impelled by his mental processes to commit murder. It was inevitable. It was fated.

Fraser put the reports down. He went to the window, which looked out onto a dark garden Kate had planted the year before, and which was now just beginning to flower in full. This was the surprise Reece had taunted him about. It wasn't enough to catch him, or to prove he committed these crimes. You had to show he was sane, and important voices were waiting to say he was not.

Silence was all around him. In pursuing Reece he had stripped himself of people and things of value. He had pushed deeper into the wilderness of the trial regardless of that cost. He had done things he'd once thought himself incapable of doing. He picked up Keddie's thick report again. What would Keddie do to save Reece?

Was there anything Keddie might not do? Looking to himself, Fraser admitted that there might not be an end, a point at which he said stop. If it was so for him, trying to destroy Reece, wouldn't it be so for the utterly confident and arrogant Keddie, trying to save him? Didn't Reece elicit that kind of devotion in receptive souls?

Wasn't it symmetrical, the two of them, he and Keddie, prepared to give up anything over Reece?

220

It's not fate, he thought defiantly in the iron silence. I will convict Reece. I will keep Kate. These things aren't chiseled in stone.

THREE

Yarborough put his face against the duct of the ventilation shaft and repeated in an urgent whisper, "Hey, Reece, let me turn on the TV. Let me watch some TV, you asshole."

From the other occupied cell in the three-cell isolation tier, Yarborough heard only the soft plupping sound of Reece's back hitting the far wall. For two hours that's all Reece had done; sit on his haunches rocking back against the wall, making that soft, sluglike noise. Jesus, Yarborough thought, this guy is a fucking psycho.

"Reece," Yarborough whispered again, "what the fuck is wrong with you? I want to watch the fucking TV."

A single television sat on a table. It was visible to all three cells. An hour ago, Yarborough had managed to get the thing turned on. It was prime time. It was a way to kill time. But no sooner had the show got going than Reece had started this yowling. He yowled and hollered until the fucking guards came running back, and he didn't stop his racket until the guards turned the TV off again. He was saying things like he couldn't hear with the TV on, he couldn't think, his mind was getting polluted when it was on.

Yarborough made a disgusted, sucking sound and sat down on his bunk. Plup. Plup. Plup. That was it. No talk. No distraction. It was seven-thirty in the evening. That was prime time on the tube.

By tomorrow he was out of isolation. They were taking him out to the correctional center at the other end of the county. Then his trial in a couple of months. Yarborough sat hunched over on the bunk. Reece killed five, six? And a kid? That was cold. At least he'd done it in a good cause. The fucking bartender threw him out for no reason. So he went to his pickup and came back with the shotgun. Their faces when he opened the bar door . . . Yarborough's sides moved as he remembered and chuckled. Both barrels right at the bar stools, wide bore. Took down

221

three of the motherfuckers. Only killed one, though, and it wasn't even the bartender.

He sighed. His hearing had gotten too good. That's how he could tell Reece wasn't on his bunk or standing up. Yarborough hadn't heard the gravelly crunch of Reece's sandals on the concrete floor, so that meant he wasn't walking around in there. Then the plupping started. Every two seconds. The guy was rocking back and forth. Thinking. That's what he was doing.

Yarborough decided to pick at Reece for a while. He went to the ventilation duct, which was how you conversed without the guards hearing you, and started talking. Just to Reece. For him alone. Yarborough ransacked his limited imagination for orgiastic splendors, anything to make Reece stop that rocking back and forth. Needling Reece was better than doing nothing.

"Oh, she's beautiful, she's fucking great, you should see her. She's got these legs and tits . . ."

From the other cell came the reply. Plup. Plup.

For several minutes he described women, his voice brutal. No matter what he said, he heard nothing from the other side except rocking.

Yarborough paused suddenly. The sandals were crunching along the concrete. "Reece," he said loudly, "what're you doing? Can I watch some TV now, you motherfucker? What're you doing?"

He heard the bunk in Reece's cell whine metallically as a body thumped onto it. Then nothing.

"Reece? Why don't you say something, man? What's your fucking problem?" Yarborough said into the unheeding silence.

Reece was finished. No more rocking tonight. He'd figured out whatever he wanted to figure out.

FOUR

It was ten minutes past ten in the morning. In exasperation, McKinsey had ordered them out into the courtroom. He sat on the bench, his face tightened into a mask of annoyance. Fraser and Starkey sat in the empty courtroom. They heard the milling, muted sounds from the jurors waiting outside in the hallway.

"Are we any closer to getting him here?" McKinsey snapped at his bailiff.

"The jail bus left twenty minutes ago, judge. He should be in the building now."

"Then I can't see why we don't have him up here in this courtroom. We've managed to produce him on time for a year. We're starting to take evidence and suddenly the defendant is late for the start of court."

McKinsey glared at the bailiff. Then he glared at Starkey and Fraser as if they were responsible. "I do not like keeping a jury waiting around in the hallway."

McKinsey waited only a minute more, then said sharply to his bailiff, "Call courthouse control and tell them Judge McKinsey wants to know right now where the defendant is. You call them now." The bailiff was dialing before the judge finished speaking.

"Well, it makes for an interesting little break in the routine," Starkey said with a smile at McKinsey, then at Fraser.

"Can it, Mr. Starkey," McKinsey said with a bluntness that was out of character when they were on the record. The court reporter stared straight ahead as she tapped out the rebuke.

Starkey cleared his throat and sat back.

"He's not in the building," the bailiff said to the judge.

"For Mother Mary's sake, where is he? Ask them where he is. Tell them I want to know."

Fraser was growing increasingly worried as the minutes lengthened without Reece's appearance. Something was wrong. Perhaps it was trivial, like a mechanical problem with the bus that brought Reece from the jail to the courthouse basement. It could be anything. But there was a problem.

A deputy sheriff briskly entered the courtroom from the rear, coming through the clerk's office and to McKinsey's side without asking permission. He was one of the control officers from downstairs who kept track of prisoners going from the jail to various courtrooms. Now he was leaning over and speaking to McKinsey. The judge's face was set angrily.

"Judge—" his bailiff began to say.

"Hold on," McKinsey said. "Thank you," he said to

the control officer, who retreated back down the rear hallway, down to the bunker of the control center on the first floor.

Fraser's body had tensed at the secret exchange carried on in front of him. Starkey's small face was pointed inquiringly at the bench.

"Forget the call," McKinsey said to his bailiff. The judge's voice was flat. He sat back in his high chair. "This is case number four-seven-nine-nine-five, People versus Charles Edmund Reece. He is not present, nor is the jury. Both counsel are present. I want the record to reflect that the time is now ten-eighteen A.M. We have been waiting for the defendant to be brought to court since a few minutes past ten. I have just been informed by courthouse control that he is not in the building."

Fraser looked at Starkey, who was leaning forward, listening.

"I have been informed that the defendant just attempted to escape from the custody of the Sheriff's Department."

FIVE

Sanderson held the small folding knife for Fraser to see. "This is what he used."

The knife was only five inches in length. The blade was small as well, perhaps three inches. Three inches of metal had almost bought freedom for Charles Reece. Fraser held the knife with revulsion.

"Where did he get it?"

Sanderson shrugged. Sweat had formed on his high forehead and he wiped his hand across it. "We don't know. He could have gotten it from her," he pointed at Naomi Reece, who was handcuffed to a chair, perhaps the same one her son had been handcuffed to. They were in the Detective Bureau at the Sheriff's Department. Half the Bureau stood and watched her, or pretended not to.

"I doubt it," Fraser said. "Everything that went to him was searched, wasn't it? She was searched when she saw him? She couldn't pass anything to him."

"It might have been gotten in because someone was careless."

"Could someone have given it to him inside the jail?"

Sanderson nodded.

"A guard?"

Sanderson nodded. "We're going to check it. She's got the money, you know. She sold that house."

"Find out how he got this," Fraser said, dropping the knife back onto the table. Sanderson tagged the knife and scratched his badge number on the handle. Someone inside the county jail, perhaps a guard, had either tried to help Charles Reece escape or been careless enough for him to nearly get away with it.

Fraser looked at Naomi. She was wheezing slightly with each breath, but her composure was complete. She blinked slowly.

"Where was she?"

Sanderson squinted over at a large wall map of the county. "About a block and a half from the courthouse. I guess she saw the jail bus turn around and head back to the jail. So she does a U-turn in the middle of the block and chases after the bus. She's got a full tank of gas in her car, clothes for him, some food. She was ready to pick him up and head for the hills."

Fraser pictured the events as Sanderson described them. At nine-thirty Reece had been brought down from isolation. He was dressed in his usual black suit and blue tie. He was handcuffed. He was the only prisoner transported in the small jail bus. It was a privilege of his rank. His two guards and the driver were the only other people on the bus.

They settled him into the front seat to the right of the driver. He had a guard to his left and behind him. They started downtown. It was only about four blocks.

Sometime during the transit, Reece had complained about the handcuffs. His guards, who had been with him for months, relented and removed them, because in that time Reece had done nothing but be led passively from place to place. Fraser knew they often talked with him, joked with him, even pitied him, in an odd, yet still pitying way.

Reece must have sat there rubbing his wrists, keeping up that incessant chatter about his illnesses, and then the knife was out. He lunged for the driver.

One of the guards was alert enough to catch the movement even before it registered on him that Reece had a knife. He grabbed at those thin, surprisingly strong arms. The other guard had to join in.

"The procedure is to head for the courthouse or back to the jail, whichever is closer, and you don't stop for anything. So back they went to the jail. Charlie has a few bruises."

Fraser went to Naomi Reece. She was going to be taken to the Women's Detention Facility, which was outside the city, and would be kept apart from her son.

"I'm not going to ask you any questions, Mrs. Reece. I understand you won't waive your right to remain silent." Fraser knew his voice was unpleasantly tight. "I want to tell you that I am disgusted by you. I can't even tell you how disgusted you make me."

Sanderson stood behind him.

Naomi made no sign that she heard him other than to turn her eyes deliberately toward the other side of the room. Her small body didn't move at all.

You were going to take him away, to another city, to hide him, save him, he thought. A strand of her stiff red hair had fallen across one eye.

"I'm going to convict him," Fraser said to her.

The wheezing breaths stopped. Naomi Reece looked at him with angry loathing. "You will not. I will not let you kill my son. I will not let you," and her angry shout became a long howl.

CHAPTER XVII

ONE

The page for Fraser had been repeated over the public address system. He excused himself from his meeting with Infeld, the twice-weekly briefing on the progress of the trial, and went back to his office.

He passed George Mahon on his way to court. It was

time for the preliminary hearings to be heard. Trials started in an hour.

"Hello, Tony," Mahon said. There was no warmth in his greeting.

"George. I haven't seen you for a while."

"Well, you know there's never any time." Mahon glanced at the nervous deputy D.A. anxiously waiting to leave for court. "I have to go. More testimony. I'm indispensable." He raised his eyebrows and went off with the deputy, who strode a few steps ahead of him. Fraser had not spoken to Mahon since the grand jury met. That apparently suited Mahon.

Sally Ann pointed to the office door. "He blew in here like they were after him," she said, chewing gum with gusto.

"Who did?"

"Mel. Mel. The big guy."

Fraser fought to tamp down his apprehension. He found Sanderson at the window.

"You're not testifying until next Friday, Mel," he said.

The detective turned from the window as the office door closed.

"It's not that. They can't find the gun. They've been looking for it since yesterday."

Fraser sat down at his desk. Two weeks into the trial, and he had already introduced sixty exhibits. The gun Reece used was to be presented that morning. Someone from the Property Section was to bring it over.

"I'll put off using the gun for a couple of days until they find it. It's somewhere in your department."

"They can't find it," Sanderson said again. His expression showed signs of early panic. "I had them turn things upside down. It's gone. The gun is not in Property anymore."

Fraser willed himself to stay calm. "I've got a very big hole in my evidence without Reece's gun. That is the only weapon we found that ties him to all the killings. Now I can still put him at the scenes, I might be able to show he bought such a gun, and the same caliber gun killed the victims. I could even convict him without that gun because we've got saliva and blood and hair and witnesses."

Sanderson relaxed a little.

"But what I can't do," Fraser's tone changed to cold fury, "is prevent Starkey from making a motion for a mistrial because evidence that is crucial to the defense has been lost. McKinsey has to grant that kind of motion, Mel. We've lost the evidence. We have a duty to preserve it."

"Jesus. A mistrial."

"We start all over again. More delays. Starkey can make a point of the missing gun. Why didn't we save it? What other sloppy things have we done? What other things have we done, period?" Fraser knew Sanderson would remember the hearing and the search of Reece's bedroom.

"Then I've gotta find the gun."

"That's right, Mel. You have to find it."

When Sanderson had gone, Fraser stayed in his chair until it was time to go to court. He would not let himself think of the implications of the missing gun. He would not think about McKinsey's ruling against any mention of the escape attempt. It was not probative on the question of guilt or innocence in the trial, the judge said, as Starkey wanted him to say. Who knew why Reece wanted to escape? Perhaps the jury would find out about it later, but until then he was prevented from mentioning it.

And now the gun.

Every case had some piece of evidence that was mislaid or improperly identified. But *this* piece of evidence . . . *now* . . . was as if the clumsiness of the legal system had gone into league with Reece.

Fraser met Sanderson at the lunch recess. They walked through a park near the courthouse. A few hardy winos, bundled against the winter's chill, bickered and snuffled on the concrete benches.

"I want to have a twenty-two caliber automatic to introduce into evidence day after tomorrow," Fraser said. They stood under an ancient oak. "Get one from the weapons you've got that aren't property in any pending case. You've got piles of guns. I want one of them."

The proposition didn't startle Sanderson. In fact, he looked relieved. "I'll find one. I'll get the right tags and ID on it. You don't think anybody's going to check it?"

Fraser shook his head. "Starkey has seen a twenty-two caliber gun half a dozen times now. He's expecting to see the same gun. He won't check it very carefully. I want it to look right and that's all.''

"Couple of reports have serial numbers in them.''

"Mel, all of the ballistics tests have been done, and Starkey's run over them. He's peered at this gun enough to be completely satisfied it is the one Reece used. I have to have a gun like it to show him in court. He won't look any further than that.''

"He might.''

"It's a risk,'' Fraser said, "against the certainty of a mistrial. There will be questions if there's a mistrial.''

Sanderson's eyes roamed upward through the branches of the oak. He lowered them to Fraser. "I'll take care of it,'' he said.

Two days later, Officer Edward Muñoz sat stiffly on the witness stand. His uniform was pressed, with the creases sharply defined. This was his first murder trial, and his whole family would be watching the evening news.

Fraser approached Muñoz.

"I'm handing you a nine-shot, twenty-two caliber automatic that has been marked People's number seventy-one for identification, Officer Muñoz. Do you recognize it?''

Fraser passed the gun to Muñoz. The officer looked at the butt and the barrel, as he had earlier in Fraser's office. He licked his lips. His voice remained dry, though. "Yes, sir, I do recognize it.''

"Is this the gun you removed from Charles Reece when you arrested him?''

"Yes, sir, it appears to be the same weapon.''

Fraser took the gun from Muñoz. "How do you recognize it, officer?''

Muñoz pointed at the barrel. "There's my badge number.'' He pointed to the butt. "I scratched my initials there. And the date.''

Fraser laid the gun Sanderson had given him on the clerk's desk. Amid the clothing and bloodstained bedsheets and photographs heaped there, it mingled easily.

CHAPTER XVIII

ONE

Three months later, Dr. Keddie sat under a catalpa tree, the remaining long brown leaves dropping onto him as though he were a stone monument. While Paul Rudin shivered in the brisk early spring air, a setter romped gregariously between his legs, nearly tripping him. He cursed, and Keddie called the tawny dog, growling at it, wagging his head in mock anger.

"You big bully," he shouted, "you big doggie bully." He grabbed a stick and threw it. The setter raced joyously away, barking ferociously.

"Can't we go in?" Rudin asked.

"The air is good for you. It's refreshing. You spend too much time cooped up indoors."

Rudin stomped his feet and shivered again. "I'm going to be called as a witness soon. Starkey thinks it may be in two weeks or less."

"I've told him your testimony is very important."

"That's the point," Rudin shivered. "I'm worried about it."

"Well, we can go over it so you feel completely at ease. You won't have any trouble."

"Can't we get started today? I'm nervous as hell."

The dog loped back, bearing the stick in triumph, and pranced before Keddie, growling. Keddie grabbed one end of the stick and growled back, shaking the dog's head from side to side. "No, I can't today, Paul. I don't have the time."

Keddie pulled the stick from the setter's mouth and threw it. The dog yelped, then ran off again.

"I need help," Rudin said.

"And I'm right at your side. Don't let Starkey worry you. I'm glad you came over to talk to me, but it's nothing to get so excited about."

"I'm scared."

"Paul," Keddie said firmly, "lawyers don't run roughshod over witnesses. Take my word for it. I've testified in fifty criminal cases. It doesn't happen. You have all the advantages. You know their minds. You know the questions they think are important. You control the examination, believe me.''

Rudin sniffed and blew his nose. He gazed off at Keddie's home behind them, then to the wide expanse of open fields where the dog cavorted.

''I suppose I didn't realize how worked up everyone was going to be. I should have known. He tries to escape, his mother pleads guilty. It's in the papers every day. They're all talking about it. I hear about the trial everywhere. Even from patients.''

''Try to relax. Feel confident. What are they all saying? They're saying Reece is insane. Well, isn't that what you're going to say?''

''Yes.''

''That's all. The D.A. is the one who should worry. He's flying in the face of conventional wisdom. Everyone agrees with us.''

Keddie smiled as the dog returned. The dog was the closest thing to him, as far as Rudin knew. He had almost no family. At that moment, Keddie pointed to Rudin. ''Go play with him, play with him,'' he said.

Rudin backed away as the setter returned, capering around him, poking him with the stick. ''Go away,'' Rudin shouted. ''Go away from me.'' But the dog only grew more playful as Rudin tried to shy back, flinging itself on him in such a rush of excitement that Rudin stumbled backward, fell down, and rolled onto the cold, spongy ground. The setter slavered over him. He shouted again.

''He's only playing,'' Keddie chuckled, calling the dog to him. The setter bounded up, put its paws on Keddie's lap. He grabbed the shaggy head again, rolling it as the animal growled.

''Woolly, woolly wugums,'' Keddie cooed, ''woolly, woolly, woolly wugums.''

TWO

For all its outward simplicity, the trial was a maze of details. They had to be properly introduced, woven together, and displayed as plainly as possible. From the Vale shooting to the death of Eileen Tippetts, Fraser brought his

231

scores of witnesses to the stand, each with a bit of the interlocking evidence.

It was work. Always work. From the first moments in the office at seven or earlier, to the time he left again at eleven or later each night, Fraser worked.

Other sections in the office cringed when he approached. Like a feudal lord claiming tribute, he dragooned other deputy D.A.s to work on various aspects of the trial—research, writing, cataloging, interviewing. Whalen, whom he talked to every week at most, had given him a free hand, and he took from wherever he wished.

He used more than people. Fraser felt very purposeful in all the bustling energies he directed. Graphics churned out a dozen charts and diagrams for him. He had his hundreds of exhibits noted and listed in a master index of the testimony for easy access. At the end of each court day he had a copy of the testimony delivered to him by ten P.M. He reviewed it closely. From it, he sometimes had charts made, research ordered, more questions written.

He and Ballenger still collaborated on that much of the trial, reviewing the day's proceedings, preparing to highlight obscure points that had arisen. But their relationship was different now. Ballenger didn't joke or tell stories. He left at seven for dinner and never invited Fraser to come home with him. He never talked about his other cases or his family. He remained professional, but aloof. From seven onward Fraser usually worked alone.

He ate simply in the morning, sometimes with Kate, often without her. It was alarming to him that her absence could roil him up for most of the day. Even in the midst of their ongoing tension, Fraser missed her. He fought down any feelings that made his work harder.

Starkey's cross-examination of Fraser's witnesses was disturbing in its blandness. He rarely challenged much of what a witness said or impugned the witness personally. Police officers, criminalists, civilians, all passed by with little argument. He signaled as loudly as he could to the jury that Reece admitted all of it. He denied nothing. Can you believe it, ladies and gentlemen, his questions asked implicitly, all of this is true. Someone must be able to tell us what this means, Starkey implied, an expert, a psychiatrist, who could make orderly sense out of this otherwise horrible, incomprehensible evidence. Mere people like us are lost.

In late April, as the gray scrolled clouds gave way to milder weather, Starkey began the defense. Fraser gave an off-the-record interview to several reporters, telling them that Reece was sane. The interview was paraded before McKinsey the next day.

"I'm requesting a continuance of the trial until we determine the effect of this prejudicial material on the jury," Starkey said. He held a newspaper up for the judge. His voice boomed out from his slender body, "Murderer Is Sane, that's the headline, judge. That's what these jurors can see."

McKinsey nodded. "It's big enough. What do you propose, Mr. Starkey?"

"I think we've got to question each juror, separately, of course, about these inflammatory headlines."

"You want a hearing?"

"Or a mistrial, judge. A juror sees this and he's got to be tainted."

Fraser heatedly pointed out that the defense had no evidence that any of the jurors had seen the newspaper. The judge had warned them about press accounts each day. It was Starkey's hearing that would prejudice them. He would force a mistrial.

"Well, I'll deny the request for a continuance," McKinsey said. "I don't want to impose a gag order. Let's police our respective sides, counsel? No talking out of court, or I will grant a mistrial."

Fraser spoke to no more reporters.

The defense case began as he thought it would. First came the old friends of Charles Reece, who said Reece was a normal, likeable, pleasant young man who suddenly, in the last few years, became withdrawn, subject to moods, anger, odd behavior. Fraser saw Starkey's plan. Reece had progressed from normality to lunacy, and he had mental illness of long-standing.

Next, the presentation of the psychiatrists to certify Reece's madness. On a Monday morning in late April Starkey began with Paul Rudin.

Ballenger had been right. The defense would lead up to

Keddie for a finale. Right now, Rudin was on, and Fraser had pinpointed every weak spot in him.

Marge swore Rudin in. "Be seated," she said adjusting the cushion in her chair so she was comfortable. "State your name, spelling your last name for the record."

Rudin sat down. "Dr. Paul Rudin. R-U-D-I-N." He looked nervously at the jurors.

Starkey strolled to the edge of the counsel table. He leaned on it. His arms were crossed. He was relaxed, folksy, twinkling. First, a genial recital of Rudin's medical qualifications. Then into the heart of the matter.

"Dr. Rudin, how did you get involved in this case?"

Rudin moistened his thin, dry lips. "I was asked by the district attorney to examine Mr. Reece."

"Not by Mr. Whalen personally?" Starkey asked with feigned incredulity.

"No, by Mr. Fraser, the gentleman sitting over there at the table." He pointed to Fraser, as Starkey wanted.

"When did you receive this request from Mr. Fraser?"

"May I consult my notes?" he asked, sorting through a welter of papers he had put on the stand.

"Sure." Starkey smiled.

He made a show of skewering the exact paper with the exact date, as though everything he did was as precise and methodical. "I was called by Mr. Fraser on December eighteenth, right after the Tippetts killing. I met Mr. Fraser at the Sheriff's Department. He instructed me to interview this man Charles Reece for the purpose of locating a missing child, the son of the dead woman. I was to try and win the confidence of Reece by offering to help him."

"I take it this offer was spurious?"

"Well, it wasn't strictly accurate, no. Mr. Fraser was clear that Mr. Reece wasn't a patient. I was only trying to win his trust."

Starkey nodded thoughtfully. "How long did you spend in there with Charles Reece, Dr. Rudin?"

"About two-and-a-half hours. I didn't learn much about the whereabouts of the child, but I did have a chance to closely observe Mr. Reece."

Here it comes, Fraser thought. Starkey was going to try to slip in Rudin's "expert" opinion on Reece's sanity.

"Describe him."

Rudin again studied his notes for effect. "He looked emaciated to me, and appeared a somewhat disoriented person. He was flat and withdrawn in his responses. He blocked many of his replies to my questions. He was not particularly communicative."

"Do you have any opinion after this time spent with him, whether Charles Reece is sane or insane?"

"Objection, your honor." Fraser's shout made Rudin start. A light film of perspiration suddenly appeared on his upper lip.

The judge fastened on Fraser. "What's the basis of your objection?"

"Your honor, this witness can't say anything about sanity. Sanity is a legal definition, based on legal principles. He hasn't been qualified in any way by Mr. Starkey to render an expert opinion on this legal question."

"He's a qualified psychiatrist, judge. Mr. Fraser didn't ask any voir dire questions of his qualifications. He accepted them."

"That's my point," Fraser pressed without waiting for McKinsey. "An ordinary psychiatrist can't come into court and give a legal opinion on the mental state of a defendant. Only a forensic psychiatrist can do that, and this man," his distaste was obvious, "isn't qualified."

Judge McKinsey faced Rudin with curiosity. "You know what it means when we say someone is insane?"

An uncomfortable tremor tugged at Rudin's neck. "Well, your honor, the word insane isn't used in psychiatry. It's a legal word. We don't think of our patients as sane or insane."

"So you can't say whether this man Reece is sane or not from your own knowledge as a psychiatrist?"

Rudin couldn't take his eyes off McKinsey's placid, rumpled face. "No, I really couldn't do that."

"Seems to me that answers this issue, Mr. Starkey," the judge said. "Sustained."

Starkey never sulked over his wounds. He recovered immediately, even though the ruling must have unsettled him. Fraser was impressed by that ability.

"All right then, doctor, did you make a diagnosis of Charles Reece?"

"Yes, I did do that."

"What was your diagnosis?"

"I found that Mr. Reece was a schizophrenic of the paranoid type."

Reece glanced up at Rudin, Fraser saw, and his head nodded very slightly.

"On what did you base that diagnosis?"

Rudin swallowed, but he seemed more confident because Starkey was unperturbed. "I used several factors. First, Mr. Reece was chaotic in his thinking processes. He could not follow my questions or reply to them. He was delusional. He had delusions that Mrs. Tippetts, for example, was a Nazi out to harm him. He didn't exhibit the kind of reactions you'd expect from someone talking about fairly hideous crimes. He showed no emotion about it. Sometimes he smiled at secret knowledge he refused to share with me."

Any of it explainable in ways that demonstrated Reece's sanity, Fraser knew. Rudin was interpreting everything one way. Fraser felt his distaste becoming unbearable. He took a deep, calming breath. Listen, note, be ready, he told himself.

"Dr. Rudin." Starkey now stood, but remained at ease. "Did you find any other delusions besides this Nazi one you mentioned?"

"Very definitely. Mr. Reece has a very complex set of somatic delusions. They center on his blood being poisoned."

"Excuse me . . ." Starkey turned to the jury. "Somatic?"

"Of the body. Bodily delusions. He believes his mother is responsible for his poisoned blood because she introduced viruses into his system. These result in the malfunction of his internal organs. His heart is failing, for example."

"Are any of these things true?"

"Not so far as I could tell that night. He seemed healthy."

Watching Starkey's act, Fraser saw how cleverly he was drawing everything from Rudin but the magic, forbidden word: *insane*. Even the legal definitions were filled in now.

"Well, doctor, this is very important. Do you think Mr. Reece understood the nature of his acts?"

Rudin cocked his head. "I would say he knew he was killing, but he didn't know who or what. At the various hospitals he's been in, he acted similarly toward animals."

"Could he conform his behavior to the law? In other words, was he compelled to kill Mrs. Tippetts even though he might have thought it wasn't right?"

"I would say that this man, Mr. Reece, believed himself in mortal peril. This was a delusion. These threats weren't human beings to him at all. They were just dangers to be fought." Rudin spoke to the jury, and it was plain he was pleased with this direct, firm answer.

Starkey asked about Reece's mental functions, finally coming to one Fraser had earmarked for exploration. "Did Mr. Reece have a delusion you observed as far as seeing things?"

"Yes, he did. He had visual hallucinations while I was with him. He seemed to be seeing someone or something else in the room. He moved as though trying to avoid this thing."

Starkey returned to his seat, reading down his legal pad while silence fell over the courtroom, like a drapery pulled into place. "That's all I have now," he said finally.

"You may cross-examine, Mr. Fraser," McKinsey said. He sat sideways, away from the jury and the witness. He was in profile to Fraser, a late Roman statesman on a coin.

Fraser stood. Rudin waited cockily for him to approach, but Fraser remained near his place at the counsel table. "Good morning, doctor," he said quietly. He was going to dismantle this fraud.

"Morning, sir."

"I want to clear up a possible misunderstanding, doctor. You said you think Reece is a paranoid schizophrenic. You've known a great many paranoid schizophrenics who kill, haven't you?"

"Not a great many."

"You've treated many paranoid schizophrenic killers?"

"No, I haven't done that."

"Charles Reece is the first person you've encountered who's been charged with murder, isn't he?"

Rudin nodded.

"Answer out loud, please, doctor."

"Yes, he is. I just meant that I've only treated a handful of patients who were paranoid schizophrenics."

"And most of them lead reasonably normal lives?"

"Some do. Some are hospitalized."

"But they all functioned, whether in the hospital or outside, didn't they, without killing other people?"

"Yes."

"Some even hold jobs, raise families, things we all do, don't they?"

"Yes, if they're treated. Some require medication to function that way, and I have no indication Mr. Reece was on medication," Rudin added waspishly. He coiled himself up, arms and legs crossed.

"My point, Dr. Rudin, is that merely because someone suffers from paranoid schizophrenia doesn't mean he must go out and commit murder, does it?"

"No."

"And because you have delusions, you don't have to commit murder, do you?"

"It depends on the nature of the delusions," Rudin scolded. "That was my testimony, sir, because obviously people have all sorts of delusions."

"No, I understand that," Fraser said. "I wanted it clear that delusions and abnormal mental states do not equal murder, even for people with the same disorder as Charles Reece."

"Objection to counsel commenting, judge," Starkey said.

"Ask a question, Mr. Fraser," McKinsey said laconically, turning his back on the witness stand after facing Rudin briefly.

"You also agree with me that Charles Reece killed Barbara Ellis and Eileen Tippetts?"

"Yes, yes, I assume that."

"While he killed them, he knew what he was doing? Cutting up living, feeling human beings?"

"You're saying that. I don't know."

Fraser now stepped to Rudin, his voice coldly brutal. "Did he know what he was doing? Look at me. I'm now killing a human being." His hand slashed the air in front of Rudin. "I'm cutting a human being, not thin air. Did he know that?"

"Well, I had information about his time at Sunnyslope, the information you gave me," Rudin pulled back in his seat, "when Reece killed rabbits and squirrels. They were inanimate objects to him. They had no life. He talked about dogs the same way. I concluded he felt the same about killing human beings."

"Do you honestly believe he didn't know he was killing human beings, Dr. Rudin? Is that what you're telling this jury?"

Rudin's whole face had a sheen now, and he daubed at his lower lip with a forefinger.

"This woman, Eileen Tippetts, doctor. Picture her. He shot her. He cut her up and sodomized her. Do you think he thought she was an illusion?"

"Well, I really can't say."

"Isn't it true, doctor, that Reece went to all that trouble and did all those monstrous things because he knew exactly what Eileen Tippetts was, a living, breathing human being?"

"I really don't know."

"You don't have an opinion whether Charles Reece would take such time and trouble with an illusion he didn't think was alive, do you?"

Rudin rubbed his lower lip once more. "No, I don't. No." He had the awful impression that sweat stains were spreading under his armpits for everyone to see.

Fraser shifted nimbly so that Rudin couldn't collect his thoughts. "Did you receive any assistance or advice in the preparation of your report, doctor?"

"What do you mean?"

"Did anyone tell you what to write?" Fraser held Rudin's report at his side.

With genuine anger Rudin said, "Absolutely not. Not one word."

"Where is your original copy, Dr. Rudin, the one you later had typed up?"

"You mean the physical document? The pages?"

"Yes, where is it now? Can you bring it into the courtroom? Can I see it?"

"Objection. Compound," Starkey said quickly. "He asked about a dozen questions."

McKinsey waved a hand. "Sustained."

"Doctor?"

Rudin nodded.

"Where is your original report, the one you wrote right after seeing Reece?"

"You have it, sir. You've been waving it in my face for the last few minutes."

Fraser had not, though. "You know this isn't what I'm referring to, doctor." Disdainfully he tossed the report in front of Rudin. "I mean the handwritten document you took with you from the Sheriff's Department, the one you say this later document is based on. Where is it?"

"I destroyed it . . . I—"

"Didn't you realize it would be evidence?"

McKinsey interrupted Fraser. "Counsel, hold on, let him finish his answer. Go ahead, doctor."

Gamely, Rudin continued. "My practice is to destroy all reports or notes of patient meetings after having a typed report made. I review the two together for accuracy and then destroy the original. It's a space problem more than anything. I can't store all the paper."

"And you didn't think that your first notes, the very first things Charles Reece said to anyone about these crimes after his arrest, would be of interest later?"

"No," Rudin said.

"We have no way of comparing this," he again picked up the typed report disdainfully, "this document, with what you claim it's based on, do we?"

Rudin shifted in his seat as if to evade Fraser's presence. "No, we don't. I mean, you don't."

Fraser nodded. Well and good. The jury now suspected Rudin of trying to conceal his report or of being incompetent, neither suspicion adding to his usefulness as a defense witness.

Rudin asked for a drink of water and gulped it down greedily when the bailiff gave it to him.

Fraser waited, then bore in once more. "When you heard Reece talk about all these legions of persecutors at the Sheriff's Department, you thought he was a dangerous man, didn't you?"

240

Rudin wore a tight, lonely smile. "Since you told me he'd killed four or five people, I did consider him dangerous."

"Based on your observations, his delusions, his demeanor in general, didn't you consider him a threat to the safety of others?"

"Yes, I would say so."

"The way he looked to you, that supported your diagnosis? His withdrawn, flat, disoriented behavior?"

Rudin nodded.

"Answer please, doctor."

"All of those things were factors."

"Aren't they as consistent with any person, you or me, for instance, being arrested for first-degree murder and taken to the Sheriff's Department? Wouldn't we act the same way?"

"I suppose we might."

"Then what you observed also fits normal behavior, Dr. Rudin, doesn't it?"

"It could."

Fraser now carefully leafed through the pile of hospital records that rose like a small white spire on the counsel table. "Dr. Rudin, weren't you employed at the Sunnyslope Hospital approximately two months prior to the killing of Clarence Vale?"

A detectable unease spread over Rudin. "For a time I served temporarily on the staff."

"Oddly enough, Charles Reece, this dangerous man you described, was also at Sunnyslope at the same time. Do you remember him?"

"I do not."

"You didn't see him?"

"I don't remember seeing him at Sunnyslope, no." Rudin primly folded his hands. A raging headache pulsed behind his eyes. He had to get off the stand somehow, but nothing offered hope.

"Didn't you certify Charles Reece for release two months before Clarence Vale was killed?"

"I said I don't recall him if he was there. I don't recall seeing him."

"He was," Fraser said rudely. "Here are the records. Here are your records. You certified him for release."

"I don't recall."

Fraser liked the way Rudin kept looking at Starkey, at the clock, anywhere but at him. He could feel Rudin's discomfort emanating outward in jangling currents. Rudin was hooked. "If you certified Charles Reece for release just two months before a killing, doesn't that mean he didn't manifest any of these symptoms that alerted you to his dangerousness?"

"I can't say."

"Perhaps he didn't talk about Nazis being after him at Sunnyslope," Fraser prodded. "Perhaps that came only after he saw you, at the Sheriff's Department."

"I can only report what I saw and heard," Rudin said shortly.

"Would you agree with me, Dr. Rudin, that everyone has some prejudices?" The time was at hand to cap off Rudin completely.

"I suppose we all do, but—"

"Did you approach the interview with Charles Reece with any prejudices?"

"I most certainly did not. I am trained to remain neutral." But Rudin's voice was not steady. The question about prejudice worried him that the district attorney might know something about his talks with Keddie. What would this wild man do to me? he was thinking.

"Neutral? You mean he killed several women, chopped them up, drank their blood, did unspeakable things to them—and knowing those things you didn't go in there thinking he might be crazy?"

"I didn't, no."

"Didn't these indicate to you that the person who had done crazy things like that had to be crazy?"

"No."

"Why *not*?"

Rudin rose to the challenge. "Because," he replied hotly, "people can do that kind of thing without being, well, to use your word, crazy. People can do what I had been told Charles Reece did without being psychotic or delusional or out of control."

"Isn't that precisely the point here, doctor? Isn't it entirely possible for someone to commit a ghastly string of sadistic murders and not be criminally insane?"

"Of course it is."

Even as he reacted without thinking what he was saying, some instinct tried to pull him back from the brink. But the answer was out. He had destroyed his own testimony. The jury had heard the damning admission. He twisted toward Starkey for help.

But Fraser sat down, and the moment for objections passed.

It was over. Over, over. Starkey attempted to rehabilitate him on redirect examination, but who was listening? Rudin left the courtroom in a clammy daze. What was he going to do now? What was going to happen? He forced his feet to move, to carry him away. What had Keddie done to him?

Starkey called another witness as he left.

And Fraser picked up another notebook, another witness. One down.

THREE

At six-thirty, when his last patient of the day had gone, Dr. Keddie's receptionist heard the phone ring in his office. He answered it, then gently closed the door. She had put on her coat already, but debated briefly whether to stay longer in case he needed her. Hat, purse, and gloves were gathered up in the meantime.

Then Dr. Keddie came out. He wasn't going to stay late.

"We'll lock up, Mary. I've got to run an errand of mercy."

"I hope it isn't anything serious."

He shook his head, but seemed to be looking off to the side of her, almost staring. She glanced in the same direction but saw only the wall. "No," he answered, "a colleague is a little excited. He had a very bad day, apparently. I've got to nurse him along a little."

Mary knew enough not to pry further. It took them quite a bit longer than usual to leave the office. Dr. Keddie seemed to be forgetting everything. He put his keys in one pocket, then a moment later changed them to another. He couldn't find his briefcase when it was sitting right there in front of him. And he would stare off at anything—the desk in the reception room, a vase of flowers—as he talked. The telphone call must be bothering him, she thought. He was rarely so bemused, so off in another world.

They locked the office finally and stepped into the cold April evening. It was very dark.

"Walk you to your car?" Dr. Keddie asked. He was always a gentleman.

"Why, no thank you, doctor. I can manage."

She said good-bye and went to her car, parked halfway up the block. It was cold out, stingingly, brightly cold. She got in with a shiver and started the engine to warm it up before driving.

Down the block, she could see Dr. Keddie pausing for some reason at the intersection. She shivered again and rubbed her hands together as the engine spluttered. Why didn't he cross the street? He just stood there as the light changed from red to green and then yellow and red once more. He didn't seem to notice. The seconds fled, the light went through its cycle again, and he still hadn't moved, as though he was still thinking about the call.

Mary adjusted the heater as Dr. Keddie stepped slowly from the curb. She could see him, even from the distance of a half block away, with complete clarity. She could almost see the preoccupied set of his mouth. My, he was going against the red light. He obviously didn't see it. It was right there in front of him, but he was still off someplace, as he had been before leaving the office. Lights, signs, warnings didn't mean much to him anyway; he always did what he thought was best, she thought.

She was going to honk her horn in warning when she saw a car speed into the intersection. Its horn brayed twice loudly. Dr. Keddie shook his head and jumped backward a step. Angry shouted words rose into the cold night. She relaxed for a moment. Why wouldn't he watch where he was going?

He was still shouting after the car, still in the intersection, when she saw a second dim shape, like a crouched animal, rush down on him, horn squawking frantically. He was illuminated in the flash of headlights, then catapulted into the air when the car struck him. To the shriek of brakes and tires, Mary saw him crumpling to the street in the path of oncoming traffic.

She suddenly heard herself shrieking.

FOUR

Kate got to the phone first. Fraser saw her jump up from the dining room table, strewn with committee reports, and hurry into the living room to answer it. He watched her from where he lay on the sofa. Particularly at certain times on certain nights, Fraser knew she would be near the phone, ready to pick it up before he did. And then she would speak softly, her back to him.

But Fraser saw Kate become unexpectedly frozen after speaking a few words into the phone. She turned to look at him.

"It's for you," she said, holding the receiver toward him. There was an accusatory look on her face.

Wearily he got off the sofa. "Who is it?"

"Mr. Reece."

"Who?" he said in surprise.

"He says it's Mr. Reece. He wants to talk to you. Take it." She pushed the phone into his hands.

Fraser put the receiver to his ear. "Yes?"

The whining, querulous words seemed to scuttle over the wire as if alive.

"You can get me moved to another cell. I have to get a new cell. I want a doctor to come see me because they're putting stuff in my food—"

"Listen to me," Fraser broke in, aware of Kate watching him. "I don't want you ever to call me again. Do you understand that? If you call me again, I'll make sure your telephone privileges are revoked."

The whining voice rose. "I can tell you things."

Like what? About the Tippetts child, or other crimes? That was the lure.

"Not over the telephone. I'll come to the jail tomorrow with your attorney. You can tell me whatever you want to then."

"No. You listen to me now. I'm offering you information. I'll tell you about everything you want to know."

Everything. Fraser was struck by Reece's horrible shrewdness. The defendant calls him at home. The defendant offers him secrets, but without the defense attorney present. It was a jailhouse tempter he heard. If he listened to even one disclosure, used just one bit of information, he had entered into a deal with Reece. He had listened. That was enough to slow the trial down when it was discovered, as it would be. It might be enough to have him removed from the case.

"No," he said over Reece's entreaties, "I'm not going to talk to you. It won't work. I'm not going to tell your lawyer that you called. I'm not going to say anything to you so I can be taken off this trial."

Fraser hung up and stared at the phone.

"That was the killer, wasn't it?" Kate said.

"Yes."

"He came in here, into our house? He can call me whenever he wants to?"

"He has use of a phone sometimes. I'll make sure he doesn't call here again."

The idea revolted her, as though a contagion had traveled in among them. "How could you let this happen? How could you let him talk to me? My God, he was speaking to me. He knows my number."

Fraser was at a loss. "I didn't know. I couldn't help it."

"That's your favorite excuse. It's never anything you've done. But I'm always the one who has to deal with it. I'm the one he talked to."

"Because you were so damned anxious to talk to . . ." Fraser let his surge of anger dissolve. He tried to turn away. He was tired.

"To who? Who do you think I talk to?" Frustration and fear mingled inseparably in her voice.

"Forget it," he said in blunt dismissal, his back to her now.

"I'm trying to carry on my life," she said without moving from where she stood, angry and frightened and guilty.

"Then do it. Do it, Kate. I honestly don't care right now. I don't care what you do."

She shouted once. His name was thrown at him. "So what did he mean when he asked me if you were enjoying yourself?"

"I don't know what you're talking about."

"Him. Reece. The killer you spend your time with, Tony. He asked me if you were enjoying yourself. You are, aren't you? You enjoy this trial more than you enjoy me."

For a moment the restraining image of Kate at the hospital when Molly died fell away. "Right now," Fraser said, "I do. Yes, I do."

CHAPTER XIX

ONE

The judge belched slightly from the luncheon enchiladas served by the Sociedad Santa Maria at their charity bash. He promised to eat one and ended up with three. Some charity. The fire stoked itself in his belly.

"I'm open to suggestions," he said to Fraser and Starkey.

"Judge, the doctors tell me Dr. Keddie is going to be in the hospital for some time. Maybe seven weeks."

Standing calmly against the bookshelves, Fraser knew what Starkey would ask next.

"So as I see it," Starkey went on, "I need a recess in the trial until he can get here to testify."

The judge whistled. "Seven-week recess? I can't do that."

"I'd oppose it," Fraser said.

"I know you would," McKinsey said with a wry smile. "Well, look, Al, don't you have any other witnesses you can call?"

"I do. I don't like jumbling up things, though."

"Well, I sympathize, but I've got to keep things rolling."

"Would you go for a three-week continuance?"

Fraser waited until the time was right for his suggestion. It was a sign, this overturning of Starkey's carefully planned build-up to Keddie. Now a chance appeared that could complete the upset. "I have an idea," he said.

"Shoot."

"How about if I put on one of my psychiatrists, like Gables, out of order? That will take some time, and we can see how things stand afterward."

The proposition would appeal to Starkey, who was plainly annoyed that Keddie had been so thoughtless as to nearly die in an accident. Starkey saw no harm in putting Gables on because Keddie could easily attack his testimony later. It was almost a consolation prize.

"Sure," Starkey said, cleaning his glasses again, as he did so often the lenses must have been worn down. "I'd go for putting Gables on. Then Keddie goes after him."

McKinsey agreed and suppressed another rumbling from his gut. He wouldn't have to wrestle with unwieldy continuances in the middle of a volatile trial. He could rest his tummy. "Gents, I think we can congratulate ourselves on a most productive afternoon. Now, if you two can get out of here quietly, I'm taking a nap. I'll see you tomorrow." He lay down on the couch wearily. His eyes closed even as Fraser turned away.

They were not in session that afternoon. Fraser and Starkey began picking up their papers at the counsel table, the leftovers from the morning.

"Tell Gables to be ready in four days. Maybe a week if I stretch the next guy," Starkey said.

"Okay, Al. Thanks for the consideration."

Starkey shook his head in wonderment. "That silly bastard. They always manage to do it to you when you don't need any more trouble." He knew Fraser understood his lament about errant witnesses.

Fraser was so busy planning how best to present Gables that he was already at his office before noticing Sally Ann crying at her desk.

For a moment, he thought something had happened to Kate, and dread formed inside him. Since Reece's call last night he had felt protective toward Kate, more so than in several months of their mutual silences. But Sally Ann was crying for a different reason.

"Harry's quitting," she said, blowing her nose into a tissue limply crushed in her hand. "He's packing up."

Fraser went to Ballenger's office. Already it echoed with the strange loudness of vacancy. Pictures, decorations, books, all the vases and lamps and clutter that Ballenger nested with were stacked in boxes. Down to his shirt sleeves, Ballenger tugged away at a picture caught on its nail.

"What's going on, Harry?"

Ballenger puffed. He wiped his forehead. "I'm leaving. I told Infeld just now I'm quitting. I'm out. By three o'clock you won't even know I've been here." He went back to work on the recalcitrant picture.

"Why the sudden move? We're in the middle of trial."

"You don't need me," Ballenger said, and the next words were unspoken.

"Can't you wait a while? At least hold off until the trial ends."

"I've got nothing to keep me here, boyo. Not one thing. I don't much want to stay on this trial anyway." He succeeded in loosening the nail. He held the picture in his big hands.

Fraser was suddenly swept with feeling for Ballenger. He asked, quietly, "What happened?"

"Infeld had me upstairs a little while ago." There was gall in his words. "To show me some surveillance reports. He had me followed. He had these assholes tailing me. I thought I knew those guys. Well, they found out a big secret. I've had a little law practice. Wills mostly, sometimes I do dissolutions, landlord-tenant stuff, but I never let it interfere with my work here."

"No, you didn't."

"But what's the point now? Infeld's going to the Civil Service Board with this stuff, and I'm going out. I can't prove it didn't affect my work. How can I prove that? They'll just say I was out of line with the law practice and kick me in the can."

Without thinking, Fraser said, "I'd be willing to tell them what I think of your work. I can tell them how valuable you are."

Ballenger chuckled. "No, no thanks. I can see what's coming. They want me out. I might beat this; but there'll be something else. This way I'm leaving on my own terms, when I want to, not when those assholes force me.''

''I'm sorry, Harry,'' he said, and he meant it, for all of their old friendship and shared trouble. It wasn't unalloyed, though. Mixed in with the realization of loss was an impatience to have Ballenger and his embarrassing knowledge removed. It was a relief in a way.

''Me too,'' Ballenger said, going about his packing quickly. ''After I'm gone there won't be anyone around here who was around when Gleason was D.A. I mean the guys who were here before you came even, before Infeld. Now Whalen and this asshole Infeld are going to act like they started the world, and no one's going to know what it was like before them.'' Ballenger looked at him steadily. ''That's the only thing that makes me mad.''

It was an awkward time for them both, so they simply shared the room as Ballenger worked, neither speaking. Fraser helped Ballenger load the packed boxes into his car.

After shutting the trunk, Ballenger stood looking around him, at Sally Ann, and then at Fraser. He had told no one else of his leaving. A sadness tugged his face into strange folds. Finally, he said to Fraser, ''Starkey's got a trump, you know. You may convict Reece of everything under the sun. The jury may say he's sane. McKinsey may abide by their verdict and sentence him to death, but as sure as the sun comes up, the Supreme Court is going to void the sentence. I don't know how. I don't know what they're going to say, but Starkey's sitting back waiting for that. You won't win, Tony, even if you win. They'll take it away from you. It's all going to be for nothing.''

Ballenger meant more than he said by his last, nihilistic comment. Fraser didn't say anything. He couldn't deny what Ballenger saw in the future. He simply couldn't afford to think about it.

''All for nothing,'' Ballenger said, taking Sally Ann's hand. ''You're like ice.''

''It's cold out here,'' she said miserably.

''Take care of yourself,'' Fraser said.

Ballenger let go of Sally Ann, saw her standing so dispiritedly, and gruffly said, ''I'll tell you what it all comes down to, Tony, my leaving, your trial, the whole ball of wax. It's choice. You make your own choices in this life. Just like Reece. He made his. You've got to make yours.''

"I have."

There was nothing more to add, and Ballenger couldn't draw his farewell out any longer. He hugged Sally Ann, shook hands with Fraser, and mumbled about future dinners, lunches, phone calls.

Then he was gone. Sally Ann took Fraser's arm. "Am I going to miss him." She shook her head sadly. "It's just you and me now."

TWO

The message was slipped to Fraser by the bailiff two days later, during Starkey's midmorning questioning of the last of Reece's high school friends. Fraser read the message twice. He rose to request a recess and hurried out of the courtroom before the jury left.

Kate stood with her coat on just outside the door in the busy hallway.

"I have to talk to you," she said. She was carrying a large handbag.

"We're only on a short break," he said, trying to keep brusqueness out of his voice. "Is this anything that can wait until tonight?"

Kate shook her head. People brushed by her, and her eyes briefly followed the milling groups and families.

"I never realized there were so many of them," she said as Fraser brought her to an empty courtroom near the end of the hallway. "It's a little like a cattle auction at the county fair."

"This is just an ordinary day."

They went into the courtroom, quaintly antique in appearance because it hadn't been touched during the remodeling of the courthouse. Unlike the other courtrooms, it boasted windows all along the walls that let in the April morning's sun.

Kate sat down at the oak counsel table where hundreds of lawyers had pleaded for clients who had drunk too much and driven too far.

"What's the matter, Kate?" His voice was gentle because he saw how tightly she held the handbag. In the flood of morning light he was startled at how much weight she seemed to have lost. Her face now had an angular quality. Her skin was more tightly drawn. He hadn't noticed the change at home.

"I've made some decisions. Some of them are selfish, some are just the best I could do," she said, letting go of the handbag. She unbuttoned her coat with fingers that fumbled and caught unnecessarily. "I'm leaving Santa Maria. I don't know for how long, so don't ask me. I'm not going to stay, so don't ask me to."

The words overwhelmed him. "I can't do anything now. I've got to be back in court in a few minutes. Can't we take care of this tonight? That's only a short while to wait."

"I can't wait anymore."

"I said this was my last trial. I promised you that."

"Months ago you promised me that. Months more might go by. I'll tell you what happened, Tony. When that man called the other night, when he just came into the house more or less and was talking to me, it all fell together. I didn't want to face up to it before, I suppose. He's just part of your world, all those people I just saw, all the terrible, ugly things that happen. You bring it all in with you like muddy footprints. I can't even pretend to myself anymore that you'd ever be happy doing anything else. I used to think, Tony will be satisfied working for a law firm. He'll have our marriage and that. But after all that's happened, I can't keep lying and telling myself that. It's not true. And you know it's not true."

"Kate, Kate." He shook his head. "I love you. I've decided I'm going to resign. We can have our marriage and a family. We can have children—"

"I don't want any children," she said with violence. "I don't ever, ever want to have another child."

There was a very long silence. Finally Fraser spoke, very gently.

"You loved her. I know you did."

Kate drew herself together again. "I don't honestly know what I felt then, not now I don't. But I know that I could never have another child with you. And I know that I can't pretend anymore about that, either. For me it's enough, it's everything to have a life just together. I like that life. I like doing things for you and being with you. I like it when you do things for me. But we don't want the same things now, Tony.''

She stood up. She held the handbag again.

"Where are you going?"

"Salinas for a while. My dad said he could put up with me. After that, I'm not sure. I haven't made any plans except what had to be done."

"No Frank or whoever else you've been with?"

Kate was impervious to the accusation. "No. Not him. Nobody. I pretended someone else was the way out. He's attentive, he likes me. But, it's you, Tony. That's the whole point. That's why I have to leave. I love you."

She kissed him on the cheek. "Please take care of yourself."

Fraser let her leave. He didn't move in the chair for several minutes after she disappeared into the crowd in the hallway. He formed the thought in his mind, trying to see each word distinctly. She's gone, he thought, she's gone.

He was late. He looked at his watch, then got up and hurried out the door.

When he got back to McKinsey's courtroom, it was evident that more time had passed than allowed for the recess. The judge sat on the bench, the jurors in the box, the guards and Starkey and Reece at the counsel table, waiting for him. He passed through the ranked chairs of spectators to the counsel table and sat down.

McKinsey stirred from his impatient watchfulness. "We're reconvening following the recess. Jurors are present. Defendant is present. Ready for the People, Mr. Fraser?"

"Yes," he answered, "ready."

THREE

Dr. Gables took the stand less than a week later. Like the jurors who fluttered at the prospect of something different—a psychiatrist for the prosecution—Reece became restive when he saw Gables. The sharp muttering to Starkey increased, and Fraser thought Reece was going to go off his good behavior. He had been too good before the jury for too long.

Gables was round-faced and sandy-haired in a gray, shiny suit. He was mild-mannered and genial, about as fearsome as the family doctor or the principal of an elementary school. One or two observant jurors, Fraser thought, would notice that his socks were mismatched.

Early in his direct examination, Fraser set out the path he wanted to follow. "Dr. Gables," he said, "I'd like to direct your attention to the chart nearest you. Do you recognize the legal test for sanity written out there?"

They had spent hours over the last weeks framing questions. The chart was an old friend.

"Yes, I do. That's the California jury instruction for insanity. It's the standard I used."

"Were you asked to determine whether Charles Reece was sane or insane at the time of the killings?"

"Yes, that was the directive."

"Let me read the jury instructions aloud, doctor, and then ask you about it. It says, 'A person is legally insane if, as a result of a mental disease or defect, he lacks the substantial capacity to either appreciate the criminality of his conduct or to conform his conduct to the requirements of the law.' Based on that standard, how did you answer the question of whether Reece was sane or insane at the time of the killings?"

Gables said mildly, "My conclusion was that he was sane."

Just as Ballenger promised he would, Fraser thought.

"Did you give Reece any sort of physical examination before you interviewed him in the jail?"

Gables nodded and got off the stand, coming down in front of the jury. "I gave him a neurological examination to show that all the major functions of the central nervous system were intact. I tested the cerebellum by having him rapidly alternate movements of his legs and arms." Gables capered briefly, his arms flapping, his legs stomping in a spastic dance. He quickly grew breathless. "I had him do deep knee bends, which test balance, coordination, the functions of the spinal cord." Gables grunted, wobbling down in a froglike position, rising up. "Also on one foot." He teetered dangerously toward the jurors, then regained his balance.

"You may resume your seat, doctor." Several jurors were about to laugh.

"I found him normal in all respects," Gables said. "There was no organic dysfunction of his central nervous system."

Fraser had a little trouble concentrating. He was not well rested, and his separation from Kate had left him unsettled and hurt. Only the trial remained for him. He wasn't going to give any advantage to Reece because of what was happening outside the courtroom.

"You reported several reasons for the opinion that Charles Reece was sane. What were they?"

Gables ticked them off on his fingers. "First of all, I found a complete absence of any evidence that Mr. Reece is a schizophrenic. He did tell me he'd killed some people. He knew he'd done it. Something that impressed me was his shift in manner whenever we turned to topics that were sensitive. He became evasive."

"What did that mean to you?"

"Well, it's very inconsistent with a psychotic state due to schizophrenia. If this man were globally psychotic or his thought processes were severely disrupted, he wouldn't be able to decide which things he would talk about and which things he would not. I concluded he was making very deliberate, conscious choices about things he would talk about."

"What sort of things"—Fraser noticed Reece's eyes on him—"didn't he want to talk about?"

"Oh, anything that was dangerous," Gables said breezily. "Why he killed people, where evidence might be found, things that would hurt him legally."

Starkey waved off another rapid muttering from Reece, pulling Reece's clinging fingers off his arm.

"How did Reece demonstrate a lack of psychosis in his thinking, doctor?"

"Well, the best example is that he was employed. He had a steady job. He was somewhat erratic at work, according to his employer, but he did work steadily. This shows a coherence and logical pattern over time. He also

255

had the foresight and coherence to build the generator at his home. His mother needed it for air purification. And he kept cages of pets, which he fed and tended. These things all point toward someone who is definitely not schizophrenic.''

''They also bear on his mental capacity, according to the insanity standard?''

''Of course.''

Reece countered his anxiety by smoothing back his hair slowly, with the absorption of a woman after a shower. Since his escape attempt he was in a belly chain until a few moments before the jury appeared and a few moments after they left. He had two new guards.

Although he could not see the jurors at all times, Fraser knew they were watching Reece often now, much as their forebears had watched a witch or warlock when priestly adjurations were hurled against them. Small reactions—a lowered gaze, tightened hands, whispers to counsel—counted almost as much as what Dr. Gables was saying. The ceremony and mystery of a trial came down to those human actions, the gestures people understood in themselves and their neighbors. Does he *look* guilty? they all asked. Looks told all.

''Did he show any other signs of sanity?''

''He knows right from wrong. He has a very specific sense of it where his own treatment is concerned. He demands a transfusion. He wants to see a doctor. He was worried that these pets I mentioned were being kept alive. This all indicates to me that he is capable of making judgments about what should or should not be done in given situations.''

Choice. The core of Fraser's case concerning Reece's mental state. It all hinged on the ability to know and to choose.

Gables had cemented Fraser's own belief in Reece's actions as purposeful rather than random. The jury also had to understand that perceptions of events turned on interpretations, not scientific truth.

''Dr. Gables, the insanity test involves an ability to 'appreciate the nature and quality' of one's actions. What is your estimation of Charles Reece's ability to do that?''

The psychiatrist flicked at some lint on his pants, to

256

Fraser's annoyance. "There was clear evidence to me that Mr. Reece committed these murders exactly because he knew the nature and quality of his acts."

"What do you mean?"

"He wanted the blood of these people. He wanted sexual contact with his female victims."

"He knew he was killing living human beings?"

"That was the point. That's why he killed them."

"Do you have an explanation for these murders, based on Reece's mental state?"

Gables sat up quite straight and looked over at Reece for a moment reflectively. "I certainly do."

"What is it?"

"This man," he pointed at Reece, who stared back at him, "has a very powerful belief his body is failing. He is infected. He has thought about it for several years. He is also convinced that blood will repair him. So he carries out a whole series of acts in accordance with his belief. First he obtains the blood of rabbits, the blood of birds, the blood of dogs, and then he kills people so he can get fresh human blood."

"You've described an almost religious devotion to an idea, doctor."

The analogy appealed to Gables. "Yes, very much so. You could say that Mr. Reece is the adept of a blood-thirsty god who demanded human sacrifice and had to be propitiated. He genuinely believes in the efficacy of blood, Mr. Fraser, that it has curative vitality."

"All adepts don't go out and kill, do they?"

"Of course not. We have in Mr. Reece a very selfish individual who was determined to get what he wanted, in this case blood, regardless of the harm he did or the suffering he caused to others."

"Because he has this belief, doctor, does it follow that he is insane? I mean, does a bizarre belief that motivates murder automatically excuse that murder?"

Gables vigorously shook his head. "No, no, no. I just said that this man," he again pointed at Reece, "wanted human blood. He knew what he was after. He took elaborate steps to get it. Bizarre, yes. Insane, no. At every step I concluded he had a full sense of what he was doing, and that determines sanity."

Fraser delved into Reece's hospital stays, all the people Gables had interviewed, and murmurs began among the audience and reporters. McKinsey, who had been stoically quiet, rapped. "Keep it down. I can't hear the witness. The jury can't hear. I'm going to clear the courtroom if the noise keeps up."

The judge turned restlessly to Fraser. "Is this a good time for you to break, Mr. Fraser?"

McKinsey was rattled by something and didn't want to stay on the bench. It wasn't the stirring in the courtroom, either. Fraser nodded. "Yes, I can stop for now, your honor."

"All right," the judge said briskly. "Ladies and gentlemen, we're going to take the noon recess. You should know the routine by now. Be back here by one-thirty on this clock. Remember my admonition not to discuss this case among yourselves or with anyone else until it is submitted to you for your consideration." He rose, unbuttoning his robe and turning toward his chambers. "Back here by one-thirty."

Fraser and Dr. Gables watched the courtroom come to life again. Jostling reporters hurried out first, and Fraser saw the camera lights blaze on outside. He decided to take the back stairs again.

Slowly, Dr. Gables lumbered off the stand. "That was fairly painless," he said gaily.

"You're going to have Starkey's cross this afternoon. I don't think you should eat a big lunch."

"I'm on a strict new diet," Gables replied. "Lettuce and green onions only."

"That's rabbit food."

The inner door of the tank clanked shut, shutting Reece in safely, and McKinsey coughed hoarsely in his chambers.

"Yes, rabbit food," sighed Dr. Gables.

FOUR

Spring cleaning meant dust—which meant a headache from the dust—and a strain in his lower back. But Monroe Allen, a cranky bachelor at sixty-one, still felt a strong obligation to clean his house and garage each spring because when he'd been young his mother and father had. He grumbled about it. He cussed. He fumed among the boxes and dirt that had miraculously accumulated, and he hauled the junk out to the driveway. The April air was crisp and invigorating. By noon he hadn't even worked up a sweat. The neighborhood was quiet. Damn kids were away at school. Wouldn't be any noise until three-thirty, when they came yowling by on their bikes and skates. Monroe stooped and carried out another box.

Excitement was high again with the trial going on. Everyone was scared as birds when that woman got killed less than a mile away. Some claimed to know her. He doubted it. Nobody knew anybody anymore. Too many people moving in, moving out. Tippetts was her name. Now everybody on the block was chittering about the trial all the time. Foolishness, he judged it, plain old foolishness. Watchdogs, guns—the place was more dangerous after the murder than before. Monroe wanted a gun, but only to scare off the damn kids who taunted him and threw garbage on his lawn sometimes. A far cry from the way his mother and father raised him. Nowadays they let the kids run wild. Found some rooting in his garbage, in his toolbox. He scared the willies out of them, he recalled fondly.

About noon, Monroe craved a beer. His green work shirt was dirt-smudged, and his gloves were filthy, but the garage was almost empty, like the hull of a ship in dry dock. He'd get it all in safe before three-thirty and the damn kids came.

He stooped over another box. The top came open.

Damn kids, he swore. In the garage again. On top of his old picture albums, the family shots from forty and more years before with mother and father, they'd hidden a broken doll. Stolen it probably, and stashed it here. Monroe set the box down.

Strange doll, too, like a dried-up old orange, very pruny, very . . . well, funny. The face was boyish, crinkled and sere. The eyes were shut. The once pudgy arms were shriveled. Doll's head was all broken in, a big hole gaping. Damn kids.

He yanked the doll up. The shriveled arm came off in his gloved hands.

A human arm bone protruded from the dried arm. He looked again at the doll's contorted face, a child's face. He cried out for his mother and father. The great black hole torn into the skull gaped open for him, and Monroe fell into it, falling down, down into a pit darker and deeper than he had ever imagined existed.

CHAPTER XX

ONE

It was a pleasure to see Starkey so upset in McKinsey's chambers after lunch.

"Judge, you can't let him put that evidence in."

"Like hell. I can. I'm going to. It's newly discovered evidence and it's damn relevant. Nobody's going to reverse me on this one."

Fraser had started the brawl by announcing his intention of presenting evidence on the discovery of Aaron Tippetts's body.

"We don't know it's the kid's yet," Starkey said.

"It is," Fraser said.

"I'll have to object."

"Go ahead. Go ahead," McKinsey said merrily. "I'll let you reopen your case, or you can put it on in rebuttal," he said to Fraser, "but that little boy's body is coming in."

McKinsey was unaccountably livelier, more feisty than before lunch. He was itching for a fight of some kind, and this set-to fit the bill just fine.

"Okay, but it doesn't change anything," Starkey said. He stalked out.

Unfortunately, Fraser agreed with him. The discovery had shock value. It made certain what had been suspected. But the shock value was no greater than the other evidence against Reece.

Back on the bench, color flowed in McKinsey's cheeks

260

as he called court back into session. Gables took the stand again. One more body did not a conviction make. No miracles here. Step by step, Fraser knew, by inches; that's how the trial would be won. If at all.

"We're reconvening again. Record will reflect all parties present and in their respective places, defendant and counsel, People are represented. The jurors and alternates are all seated. Go on, Mr. Fraser."

Why was McKinsey so jolly? Fraser didn't think it was the delight of watching Starkey squirm. It was something else. The question stayed with him as he turned again to Gables.

"This morning, doctor, I asked you about Reece's mental processes. Was his memory intact?"

"Yes."

Why not drop it now? "Is it your opinion he would remember where he had hidden a body, for example?"

Starkey muttered, then rose reluctantly. "Objection for the record, your honor. As we discussed in chambers."

"Oh, no. We're not doing that. What do you mean? Say it out loud, counsel."

The jury watched the judge and Starkey and, finally, Reece again.

Starkey's small hands gestured. "I'm objecting to any reference, at this point, to a child's body discovered over the noon hour by the police. I'm also moving for a mistrial based on a lack of discovery to the defense, lack of notice to use this evidence, and prejudicing the jury. The evidence is unduly prejudicial and not probative now."

McKinsey appeared to relish the confrontation. He was quite spritely. "Objection is denied. No, overruled. Your mistrial motion is denied. You knew about this as soon as Mr. Fraser did, isn't that so, Mr. Fraser?"

"I informed counsel and the court immediately, your honor."

"And the court wants it clear on the record that is what happened," McKinsey said. "Now, Mr. Starkey, nobody told you any faster or slower than we were told, so you don't have any gripes about lack of discovery as far as I can see. Mistrial motion is denied on all grounds."

"Thank you, judge," Starkey said.

"Now you can answer that question, doctor," the judge said to Gables.

"I think I have it in mind. Yes. He could remember where he hid a body. I can't think of any reason except sheer dissembling that would make Mr. Reece unable to tell you where a body was."

"Dissembling?"

"Lying. He'd be lying if he told you he couldn't remember."

"Do paranoid schizophrenics lie?"

Gables answered wryly. "The ability to systematically choose self-protective statements is not the kind of organized thinking characteristic of a schizophrenic, no."

Fraser recalled the first time he saw Reece at the Sheriff's Department and the momentary fear when he realized Reece had been around psychiatrists before. "Do you believe he is being selective when he recalls certain aspects of killing his victims, but not others? Is that your testimony?"

Gables nodded. "He picks and chooses what he wants to tell you. He's very cunning and self-protective. From his hospitalizations he's acquired a lot of the jargon of psychiatric practice. He uses it."

"Are you saying this defendant understands the criminality of his actions and attempts to hide it?"

Gables crossed his legs so his mismatched socks were clearly seen. He hadn't noticed them, however. "This is exactly why he does it, as I said before." Gables's stomach rumbled insistently.

"Didn't you get any lunch?" McKinsey inquired.

"I'm on a diet, your honor."

"You sound like you're starving down there."

"I'm sorry, your honor."

Fraser disliked having the rhythm of his examination broken. It interfered with the jury's attention. "Your honor, I've got to object to the court's interruption."

McKinsey raised his eyebrows. Another fight. He seemed to want one from anybody, either side, on any point. "He's your witness. Your witness's the one starving down there."

"I'd like to complete my questions, your honor."

"Fine by me. I wanted to make sure your witness

wasn't going to keel over. Go ahead.'' McKinsey giggled to himself. The horrible possibility that he was drunk rose in Fraser's mind.

Fraser asked more questions about Reece's thinking and other possible explanations for his actions. Gables's diagnosis boiled down to Reece having a mental disorder, but being sane.

Fraser came to the summary of his direct examination. It was the essence of what he wanted the jury to remember.

"How about a stretch in place?" McKinsey asked abruptly.

"Judge?" Starkey said in puzzlement.

The judge stood, raising his arms. "Just a little stretch to get the blood moving. We'll go straight through without a break this afternoon. Okay, everyone stand where you are. Stretch. Stretch.'' He barked out the commands while people in the courtroom groaned and twisted in their seats. Only Reece, his guards, and Fraser remained sourly seated. McKinsey sighed as he flexed his back. Fraser was angry at this new interruption. Dr. Gables, on the other hand, stretched himself enthusiastically in the witness stand.

"Better? Okay, settle down again. Let's hear the rest of this.'' McKinsey waved at Fraser to resume.

"Dr. Gables," Fraser said, standing to emphasize this phase of the examination, "in your opinion, did Charles Reece have the substantial capacity to know and appreciate the moral wrongfulness of his actions?"

"Completely and absolutely," Gables said with a genial smile. "He always carried out these acts, the murders, the sexual acts, in private. He took pains to avoid detection and observation. He apparently took one woman, Mrs. Henderson, I think, from an exposed living room into a bedroom. He made distinctive changes in his appearance. He wore clothing designed to be noticeable, bright-colored jacket, the sunglasses to hide his upper face. He deliberately was disheveled, unshaven when he murdered," Gables used his hands, pointing to Reece, shading and sketching as he talked, "then he shaved, dressed, and looked quite different. I believe this was done to avoid being recognized."

"Did his delusion—"

Gables held up a pudgy finger. "One further thing. He gave the name of a victim when the police came for him at the garage where he worked. This was to conceal himself because he knew he'd done something wrong. And, of course, he ran from the police. Now, if that doesn't demonstrate a substantial capacity to know wrong from right, I don't know of anything that does." Gables's double chin undulated emphatically as he spoke.

Fraser liked this assertive refutation of Starkey's claims that Reece acted impulsively and without control. "Reece has delusions about blood and Nazis, doctor. Do those delusions put him in a position that he must have been irresistibly compelled to commit these crimes?"

"No. Not so."

"Are you saying that when he killed, Reece had the substantial capacity to control himself? He could have refrained from killing?"

Gables nodded emphatically. "Yes, very definitely."

"Did he also have the capacity to form a complicated criminal design and to carry it out?"

"You simply have to look at the manner of his crimes to answer that question. Yes. He did. He brought a gun. He brought along all the tools he would need, gloves, a bag, the clothing I mentioned. He parked a car nearby, for a getaway, I assume, in the first killings. He showed the same ability to plan and carry out that plan as he did when he, oh, when he built that generator."

"He had the capacity to form an intent to kill, as well?"

The psychiatrist's head bobbed up and down. "I'd say far more than that. There's a scientific curiosity in his activities. He begins with the postulate that blood will cure him. He tested this postulate by collecting blood, the blood of beasts, and drinking it. He observed the results and reached the conclusion that he needed the blood of human beings."

"Are you describing the scientific method?"

"Completely. Mr. Reece conducted himself like a scientist."

It was a sharp, unforgettable image for the jury. Every person in the courtroom saw Nazis at work on cruel, inhu-

man experiments. A steely-eyed army of Dr. Franken-
steins trooped through every mind.

Reece did not like the image. He made odd doodles on
his notepad, dropped his pencil suddenly, then let his head
sag.

Fraser didn't care about these antics. The law required
only that Reece know what he was doing and act out of
deliberation. It made no demand that the acts or their
motives be comprehensible to ordinary people. The rest of
the trial was babble around this irreducible proposition.

"Thank you, doctor. I have nothing further."

McKinsey coughed. "You can cross-examine the witness," he said to Starkey.

"Well now, judge, I see that it's gotten fairly late in the
afternoon. Perhaps this might be a logical time to take the
evening recess so that we can all start fresh tomorrow
morning?"

"You need more preparation time?"

Starkey blushed at the jab. "No, judge. I was thinking
of the doctor and the jurors."

"You don't think about them," Judge McKinsey said,
"I do. It's my courtroom. I know what time it is." He
swung to Gables and said sharply, "You tired out, doctor?"

"I'm willing to remain as long as the court wishes, your
honor."

"Okay. The jury looks fine. We'll continue. Ask your
first question." McKinsey let Starkey fumble. The courtroom was charged up by the judge's inexplicably testy replies. He had been alternately jolly or somnolent all
afternoon. Fraser had no idea what was going on.

He wasn't alone. Starkey had counted on a recess to
gather his wits for the assault on Gables. He rearranged
himself, then finally said arrogantly, "Now, doctor,
you've told us about what a scientist this man is, how he
plans and figures things out. When we get through all
that," he flung his arms as if dispelling noxious vapors,
"you still believe Charles Reece is suffering from a serious mental disorder, don't you?"

"Yes, I do. I've said so several times." To be diplo-
matic, he added, "Perhaps I didn't make myself clear."

"We'll try to take care of that now." Starkey paced confidently up to Gables and stood less than three feet from him, in imitation of Fraser's examination of Rudin.

"You referred to Mr. Reece's delusions about Nazis. Do you believe he has delusions of persecution involving Nazis?"

"Yes and no."

"What does that mean?" Starkey asked swiftly.

"Yes, in the sense that he has evidence in his room, swastikas and Nazi books and so on. This suggests something to do with Nazis, I suppose. I can't say in what way. I found little, if any evidence to support a delusion of persecution prior to his arrest, but a great deal afterward."

"Are you saying the police made this up?" Starkey pointed at the files and papers on the counsel table.

Gables remained unruffled. "I'm saying Mr. Reece had seen other psychiatrists by then. I think he knew what to say."

Starkey dropped that line of questioning and walked back to his seat. "Now then, doctor," he murmured, picking up a file folder. Immediately there was suspense about what Starkey held so confidentially in the folder. His head was bent to it. He raised his head and strolled back to Gables. "Doctor, you are being paid by the district attorney for your testimony, aren't you?"

"I'm being paid for appearing here as an expert witness," Gables said, "but that doesn't buy what I say."

"I understand that. And please just answer the question. Mr. Fraser will give you a chance to make any corrections."

"Well, I simply wanted it clear—"

Starkey cut him off. "There isn't a question before you, doctor. You can't answer."

Something was coming. Starkey wasn't talking about what Gables had said on the witness stand.

"How much do you expect to make here from your testimony as a witness for the district attorney?"

"I'm really not sure. My office handles the billing. I am paid by the hour."

"Let's take a ballpark figure, okay? Four thousand dollars? More? Five? What would you estimate?"

"I'd estimate somewhere between four and five thousand dollars for my testimony and pretrial work."

Starkey went on gently. "Speaking of your financial affairs, doctor, you've had some trouble there, haven't you?"

"I'm not certain of your meaning." Gables's suddenly white face was rigid.

"You own five rental properties in Santa Maria, don't you, doctor?"

Fraser began objecting but Starkey suddenly called to Fraser, "Weren't you sued in this county for breach of contract, fraud, and various other things involving those properties?"

"I was *acquitted*," Gables said loudly. "I was exonerated entirely."

Shouting over Fraser's objections, Starkey held the file in front of Gables like an avenging sword. "Didn't the judgment in that case include findings by a Superior Court that evidence of bad faith existed in your financial dealings with renters?"

"Your honor!" Fraser called again.

"How did you get that?" Gables cried. "How did you get that record? That was a sealed court record. You can't bring that in here."

McKinsey looked down at the spectacle, the cacophony floating upward, the attorneys squabbling, a witness shouting, jurors squirming, and he let it go on for what seemed an endless moment. Grinning down at them all, he inquired innocently, "Is there some problem, gentlemen?"

Fraser took the initiative. "Your honor, Mr. Starkey has raised an entirely improper issue deliberately in front of the jury." He fought to be heard over Starkey's shouts of "It's impeachment. It's legitimate impeachment." Fraser called out again, "This ought to be gone into outside the presence of the jury."

"Judge," Starkey said, a deep frown of indignation creasing his small face, "it's really a case of Mr. Fraser being stuck with this witness. What I've presented is valid impeachment going to this witness's honesty and veracity." He smirked at Gables. "Or his lack of them."

"I don't want to discuss this now," Fraser insisted. "We can only take this up properly without the jury."

The jurors looked askance. They spent some time being moved in and out of the courtroom in order not to hear certain matters. It happened at least once or twice a day, as though they were very impressionable children.

McKinsey regarded the posturing Starkey. "You got your recess after all, counsel." He smiled at the idea. To the jury he added, "Well, you can see what's happened. The lawyers are at it again. We'll take a recess and straighten this out, my friends. So with that said, I'll let you go for the evening. Remember my admonition. Be back here at nine forty-five in the morning. Have a good evening." He bathed them in sudden goodwill.

In silence, Fraser saw them go, one after the other, followed by most of the spectators. On the stand, Dr. Gables sat frozen, mute, in an anguished pose.

Only four idle people stayed in their seats. Reece constantly darted his head back and forth to Starkey. He sucked on the back of his hand.

"That means you," McKinsey said to the remaining people. "Scoot. Out." They left, and the bailiff shut and locked the courtroom doors. The wall clock plunked mechanically to the next minute.

"Record reflect all parties present, defendant, counsel; and the jury excused for the night. We are outside the presence of the jury. Mr. Fraser has something he wants to do, I suspect." The judge tee-heed oddly.

"I do, your honor. I object to any further attempted impeachment of Dr. Gables based on this suit against him last year. It must be stricken. The Evidence Code permits impeachment based on bad character for truth by use of a felony conviction. Dr. Gables wasn't even *charged* with a felony. This was a civil lawsuit. What's more, he was acquitted. I want the whole matter dropped and Mr. Starkey admonished for trying to disrupt this trial."

"It may hurt," Starkey began snidely.

"Cut the cracks, Starkey," the judge said. "What's your position on the People's request?"

"Judge, what I have here are the documents filed in Superior Court showing there was bad faith—that's the court's finding—in the way Dr. Gables handled his renters. Now, I think this finding reflects on his judgment. That makes it admissible impeachment. He's testifying as an expert, and I'm permitted to test him.''

Gables listened in anxious silence and then broke in. ''I've got to be heard. This is my career you're talking about. My professional life. I've testified in dozens of criminal cases, and this is the first time, the very first time anybody has sought to attack me like this. Smearing me. Innuendos. That's a sealed record. I was told it could never be used like this.''

''Anything on that, Mr. Starkey?''

''It's public, judge. I got copies by merely requesting them.''

''That does not deal with the question of using them, your honor,'' Fraser said, ''as Dr. Gables noted, in a deliberate attempt to smear him, not his testimony. Mr. Starkey has now gotten this smear in front of the jury.''

Starkey wheeled to point at Reece, who watched with intense interest. ''The prosecution is trying to send this man to his death. It's my job here to do everything I can to prevent that.''

''Okay, hold your horses, gentlemen, we're outside the presence of the jury. I can get things very well if we all speak normally. Let me read the Evidence Code here.'' McKinsey propped his head in his hands and slowly read. He smacked his lips.

Fraser didn't know how he was going to mollify Gables. The psychiatrist burbled up again. ''I don't know how I can go on in this case. My work is at stake.'' McKinsey waved him down.

''Quiet, doctor, let me finish my reading.''

They all subsided into a grim, heavy silence. Only Reece seemed to be enjoying himself. He was delighted that someone else, an adversary no less, was being sorely tried.

Slamming the book shut, McKinsey slipped it back into a stack on the bench. ''I'm satisfied. What you've got are final orders of the court saying Dr. Gables was not guilty in the lawsuit, but there was some funny business in his other dealings?''

''That's right, judge.''

''Since that isn't a finding of criminal liability, or even

civil fault, I don't think it's admissible impeachment. Drop it.''

Starkey bowed slightly. "I will, judge. I thought it was worth the effort.''

The judge said to Fraser, who was still thinking and worrying, "Now what do you want me to do? Admonish the jury to disregard the last couple of questions? That'll drive it right into their minds. I'll do it, but you tell me if that's what you want.''

Fraser knew what might happen. The effect of such a judicial admonition was to sharpen the smear, make it more real even as the jury was told to forget it. If he simply let the matter drop, he could hope that the continuing shower of facts would overwhelm this brief attack. But jurors picked out single moments, treasured them as found jewels, and they might fasten on this one.

"I know the risk, your honor. I have to ask for an admonition, though.''

"Doesn't bother me. I'll give it," McKinsey said. "Okay. We're in recess until the morning. I'll caution both of you that if you've got any other little whoppers hidden away, I want to hear about them first so we don't go through these monkeyshines in front of the jury again.''

"Court's in recess until called," said the bailiff.

Gables remained on the stand while Reece was chained up and taken back into the tank with Starkey. Only he and Fraser were left in the courtroom. The bailiff began methodically snapping off most of the lights so the room was submerged into a purple darkness. Stiffly, Gables groped his way from the witness stand.

"You told me this wouldn't happen," he said accusingly.

"I said it was unlikely.''

"You gave me assurances.''

"I gave you no guarantees, doctor. I said I'd do everything possible to make sure the incident wasn't brought up.''

Gables was excited and angry. "But it was brought up. They heard it. All of them. It's out." He gestured toward the vanished audience and reporters.

"I'll make sure it's corrected tomorrow.''

"No. No. I don't think I can continue testifying here. I only agreed to appear becuase of your assurances.''

270

"Dr. Gables, you know your testimony is vital. You could do my case irreparable harm."

"I have to think of my career, too. This is my whole life. I'm being pilloried."

Fraser was calm. "I can't excuse your appearance tomorrow. You have to appear."

"Is that an order? Are you giving me some kind of order?"

"If you don't come to court, I'll have a marshal arrest you. Believe me, I will."

Gables fell silent, studying Fraser.

"All right. I'm in an untenable position. This has never happened to me before. Never. In all the trials, with all the lawyers. This is the first time."

He was ready to stampede blindly. Fraser spoke soothingly to him. The judge would chastise Starkey for being intemperate, and the jury would be directed to ignore the whole matter. It was Starkey who would seem foolish, not him. The psychiatrist listened in silence. Then he nodded more calmly. "I see what you're getting at. I'm sorry, I'm a little worked up."

"Understandable."

"Well," Gables managed a small smile, "I do have a practice, and it hasn't gotten any attention since I've been here all day."

"I'll see you at nine in my office."

"Yes," Gables said faintly, wandering to the courtroom doors, tugging and jerking at them.

"They're locked," Fraser reminded him. "You'll have to go out back."

"Yes. Yes. Thank you." Gables walked past him and to the rear corridor. His footsteps faded with the growing distance.

Fraser gave a sudden, weary sigh.

He heard McKinsey moving back in chambers.

He went back and found the judge in chambers as dark as the courtroom. McKinsey was at his desk with a bottle and a plastic cup. He slopped half a cup of the bourbon out of the bottle.

"Have one," he curtly offered Fraser.

"No thanks, judge."

"Have one."

"I'll pass."

"I'm having one," McKinsey said with satisfaction. He gulped down the greater part of his cup. There was something unspoken, pregnant in the antique, musty darkness of his chambers. The framed wartime pictures were rimmed outlines. "I'm even having another." He drank the remainder and poured again.

"I don't want to make too much of it," Fraser began, pausing at McKinsey's baleful stare.

"What?"

"You interrupted my witness."

"You didn't like my conduct?"

"I didn't think it was right."

"You didn't like the way I ran my courtroom today?"

Something loomed now. "I didn't like the interruptions."

"I'm entitled to them. I'm entitled to a couple of interruptions in my courtroom any goddamn time I want to interrupt any goddamn witness."

"Good night, judge." Fraser turned away.

Then McKinsey grunted, his head lowering a little. "This is my last trial, for chrissake. Found out for sure today. My very last goddamn trial."

Automatically, Fraser said, "I'm sorry. Is there anything I can do?"

"If there was, pal, believe me, I'd tell you. I'm not trying for a Purple Heart."

Fraser had known McKinsey for a long time. He did feel sorrow at the news. At another time, under different circumstances, he would have shown it, and he would have felt more of McKinsey's suffering. But a more immediate, more selfish concern filled him, a frightening prospect he tried to raise casually. "Can you finish the trial?"

Moodily, McKinsey put his feet up on the desk. His tight little potbelly pushed against his wrinkled white shirt. He was so indistinct now in the shadows, it was as if he had already begun to fade away. It was like questioning a shade. "Well. It was hearing it that got me. Threw me, I guess. I can't say it was a surprise, it was hearing it out loud. That was what got me. Got to tell my wife." He

272

took off his glasses and looked at Fraser for the first time. "You said something?"

"Can you finish the trial, judge?"

Suddenly McKinsey laughed hoarsely, slapping his cup down, knocking it over, spreading a shimmering pool of bourbon over his desk blotter and papers. "That's what I like, the old mad-dog D.A. I know what's eating you. You've got witness troubles. I heard you with that guy out there, and now you're worried I'll fold up. You think I'm going to blow your trial, right?"

"I want to know what's going to happen."

"Let me tell you, pal," McKinsey was a bit unsteady as he poured another cup, "you're going to get the most scrupulously squeaky-clean trial you ever saw. No errors. Perfect record all the way. I'm not having my last goddamn trial reversed. I let off a little steam today, but that's all it was. You bastards are getting a clean trial."

"I am sorry, judge."

"Yep. Yep. I'm not going to mistry my last goddamned trial." He drank. "Why don't you get out now? Close the door."

Fraser nodded.

"I don't want Starkey to find us gabbing together so he can ask for a mistrial." The judge winked at Fraser.

"I'll see you tomorrow."

"You won't say anything to Starkey, right? This is between you and me and whoever." McKinsey raised his cup slightly in the air.

"I won't say anything." He closed the door.

Fraser left him there, thinking of ashes.

His own thoughts were ashes now. Would McKinsey have the nerve to sentence Reece to death? Suddenly McKinsey was freed from all earthly worries about reelection, currying favor, even conscience. He could be whimsical if he chose. He was bound by nothing, and that made him unpredictable.

Sally Ann gave Fraser three phone messages. "She's called you all day. You should call her back."

He held the messages without looking at them. "I don't know."

"Take it from me, divorce is no fun, no fun at all."

Sally Ann shook her head. The bracelets she wore jingled as she shook her hands, too.

"We're not getting divorced."

"You're on that short little road. Take it from me, honey, it's no fun at all." She looked at Fraser. "Don't be an asshole. I call Ralph every day, and we're not even married."

"Maybe that's the difference."

"I warned you."

He tossed the messages to his desk. Starkey hadn't been really disturbed by the discovery of the body today. Oddly, Fraser wasn't either, even though it was an awful confirmation of his own failure to find Aaron Tippetts.

He had to think about Kate, too, but McKinsey was everything now. He was an old friend and he was dying and all Fraser could think about was McKinsey when the time came for passing sentence on Reece.

CHAPTER XXI

ONE

Dr. Gables returned the next morning, rested and sharp-eyed. He regarded both Fraser and Starkey with equal wariness. Before they resumed, McKinsey, a trifle pouchy, a little rough-voiced, but sober and in control, cautioned the jury.

"You're to entirely disregard the last two questions asked by Mr. Starkey yesterday afternoon. They are stricken from the record. You are to act as though you had never heard them. Remember what I told you, that what lawyers say or insinuate isn't evidence, and you aren't to infer anything from the unanswered questions Mr. Starkey posed." He was cologned, starched, upright on the bench. "Mr. Starkey, you may continue your cross-examination."

Starkey began without any preliminaries. "Doesn't the

bizarreness of these crimes suggest the disease of schizo-phrenia to you?''

With deliberate frostiness, Gables said, "In my opinion, no. If that was the only criterion, I think any violent crime would be classed as the result of schizophrenia.''

Starkey shrugged. "Doctor, doesn't psychiatry recognize that a mental illness can leave a person's intellectual ability unaffected, but cripple his emotional balance so he can't help but commit forbidden acts?''

The old irresistible impulse, conjured up again. Fraser didn't think Gables was quite so relaxed or jovial today.

"This question," Gables said, hunching forward in the stand, "is a perfect example of what psychiatrists cannot do in a courtroom, or anywhere else for that matter.''

Starkey shook his head, and his black glasses glinted as the sun hit them. "I didn't ask you that question, doctor. I asked you—"

Gables had turned to the judge. "May I be permitted to complete my answer, your honor?''

"Judge, direct the witness to be responsive.''

Fraser stood. "Your honor, Mr. Starkey won't allow the witness to finish his answer. If Mr. Starkey doesn't like the answer, that's a shame, but he asked the question.''

McKinsey turned to Dr. Gables. "Complete your answer, sir.''

Gables cleared his throat and spoke to the jury. "When psychiatrists are asked to state whether someone could or could not resist an impulse, we are asked to make judgments about events that have already occurred. It's a tautology.''

"You don't believe in an irresistible impulse?''

"It isn't a question of belief, it's a matter of proof. Proving such a thing as an irresistible impulse is the same as proving the number of angels in the air.''

Reece was drinking water and looking at Starkey.

"You think Mr. Reece is in control of himself because he makes other choices?''

"Yes.''

Starkey pointed up at the chart of the events in the case. "Everyone who talked with Mr. Reece thinks he acted in a random manner when he picked his victims. Are you saying these murders show choice on his part?''

"Perhaps not wholly in the manner of the killing, although he did plan for them, but the decision to kill, yes." Gables returned Starkey's truculent stare. "You left out Mrs. Tippetts. He chose her as a victim because he was angry that she reported him to the police over a dog incident."

"So you don't think he acted in a random, disorganized manner during these crimes?" Starkey demanded, his voice toughening.

"I considered it. I rejected it."

"Wasn't it disorganized to shoot a gun in the daytime in all the killings?"

"No. He used a gun at night in the first one."

"Leaving slugs in the house. That wasn't disorganized?"

"I don't think so."

"Wearing a bright, bright red parka, that wasn't disorganized?"

"I said he did that in order to make himself more visible. People recalled the clothing, not him. I believe this demonstrates conscious planning."

"His bedroom at home was a pigsty, doctor. Wasn't that disorganized, chaotic, the result of schizophrenia?"

Gables smiled at the jury. "Being very untidy, even as thoroughly untidy as Mr. Reece, doesn't indicate schizophrenia, absent all the other symptoms I could not find."

With the disgusted noise he made, Starkey conveyed to the jury his opinion of Gables's answers. They dithered along for some time over other issues. During it all, Reece continued to watch Starkey, not the psychiatrist who was testifying against him.

"Dr. Gables," Starkey finally said caustically, "so nobody has any doubt, you do agree that there's a difference between the ability to make a moral judgment—to distinguish right from wrong—and the emotional ability to control one's behavior, don't you?"

"Yes, I do."

"And isn't that distinction what this trial is all about?" Starkey swung his arms wide, embracing the whole courtroom. "Deciding whether Charles Reece saw moral right and was unable to act accordingly because of emotional pressures? Isn't that the sole reason we're all here?"

"I gather so."

"And you do agree," Starkey walked up to Gables, "that Charles Reece has great emotional pressures working on him?"

"His delusions impose great stress, yes."

"Thank you, doctor." Starkey bowed slightly, as if he had wrested an obvious fact from a fool. He sat down.

McKinsey called for any redirect examination, and Fraser went over several points, clearing up what Starkey had obscured or made confusing, arriving at last at the essence of Gables's testimony. "Did Reece have a compulsion to kill?"

"He wanted to kill all his victims, of course. He did have a compulsion, a desire. It was the only way he could get what he wanted."

"Because he had such a compulsion, does that relieve him of the responsibility for his actions?" Fraser pointed to himself. "I feel strongly about killing you, doctor. I really, completely want to do it. I do kill you. Does the strength of my desire to kill you excuse me?"

"I should hope not." Gables chuckled. "But, no, of course not. As long as you understood that you were killing me, and I wish you'd picked another example, and that it was wrong to do so, it makes no difference whatsoever that you felt very strongly about doing it. Even if it was all you thought about for days or weeks before."

"Thank you, Dr. Gables," Fraser said. "I have nothing more."

"Recross?" the judge asked.

Starkey didn't look up. He feigned disinterest in Gables. "Not from me."

"Can this witness be excused?"

"Yes, your honor," Fraser said.

Gables, when McKinsey politely excused him, bounded swiftly off the stand and hurried from the courtroom.

McKinsey peered at Starkey. "The case is back to you, counsel. Can we proceed with the defense?"

"I do have witnesses," Starkey said.

Fraser heard mumblings and mutterings from Reece and

277

one of his guards. Reece cried out, "I want another lawyer."

The judge said sternly, "Be quiet, sir. We'll take up whatever you want to talk about when the jury leaves."

Starkey turned to talk to Reece. Reece stood up, towering over the smaller man, and struck him in the face. Starkey's glasses flew toward the jury box, and a woman juror screeched.

The two guards behind Reece quickly pinned his arms behind him as he leaned back to hit Starkey again. The defense attorney had been knocked halfway onto the counsel table, and he now drew away as Reece, angrily yelling at him and the judge, was taken toward the tank. It was impossible to remove the jury because the guards had to cross in front of the bench.

"They're all trying to kill me. They're trying to kill me," Reece cried, imploring the jurors as he was pushed away. He yelled when the guards bent his arms backward painfully, trying to restrain him. "Help me. Help me," he squealed, his voice carrying as he was shoved back into the tank, where more marshals waited. Even through the thick door, the sounds of his scuffling and cries came into the courtroom.

"Ladies and gentlemen," McKinsey hadn't moved from the bench, quite in contrast to Judge Donelli, "we've had a small problem. I'm going to excuse you. Same rules. Don't discuss this or the case. Meet back here tomorrow morning at nine forty-five."

The jury was taken from the courtroom by McKinsey's bailiff. When they were out, the judge said to him, "Close the doors." The bailiff moved too slowly. "Now!"

Fraser went to Starkey. "Can I get you anything, Al?"

A coat sleeve was pressed to his nose, staunching a copious flow of blood that had already spattered onto his papers on the table. Starkey shook his head. "Can you find my glasses?" he said, his voice almost muffled by the sleeve at his mouth.

Fraser walked to the empty jury box and found them. One of the marshals from another courtroom had come in and was ministering to Starkey. Fraser put his glasses on the table. Starkey's nose was bent inward, hard to see in the rapid swelling and the blood that smeared his face.

McKinsey still hadn't moved. "Where's the court reporter?"

A hand went up from the side of the bench, pressed against the wall. "Here, your honor," she said, timidly returning to her machine.

"I propose we take a recess and see what's going on in a few minutes." He began to rise.

"Please, judge, I'd like to get some things on the record," Starkey said. The marshal who was trying to tend to his injuries told him to stay seated.

"It can wait, Mr. Starkey, until you're in better shape," the judge said gently.

"I'm fine," Starkey insisted, as a large white bandage was taped over his nose. "I know I'll have to leave in a minute to have this looked at. I do want to state that I'm requesting a hearing to determine what effect this incident has had on the jurors."

"Not again," Fraser said involuntarily.

Starkey persisted even though his nose continued to bleed. "This outburst can't help but prejudice the jury against my client. It shows his disturbed mental state. I'm entitled now to determine just how much damage has been done to the jury."

Fraser was going to argue, though Starkey's injuries moderated the temper of his comments. But the judge moved first. "You should be seeing a doctor, counsel, but I'm going to rule right now in light of your interest in having this decided quickly. Your client caused the incident. It was his doing, start to finish. Now, if I go along with your request, I'll reward him for that kind of behavior. He'll be running this trial," McKinsey said firmly. "And he is not going to run this trial."

"You're denying my request?"

"I just did."

Starkey groaned slightly. Fraser had to give the man doggedness.

"I'm also moving for a hearing," Starkey said, "to determine the effect the district attorney's facial signals to the jury have had."

Fraser started out of his seat. "My what?"

"His what?" the judge seconded.

"My client informs me that Mr. Fraser has been making

various kinds of faces for the jury, your honor. I haven't seen them myself. My client says these consisted of raised eyebrows, frowns, smirks, and so on. I believe this is an attempt to prejudice the jury."

"This is ridiculous," Fraser said heatedly. "Your honor, I haven't made any faces to the jury, much less tried to signal them."

The marshal spoke up. "Judge, I can't really stop this bleeding. I think this man ought to see a doctor."

"Hold on," the judge said with a raised hand. "He wanted a few minutes to make sure all this was on the record, and now it is. Here's my ruling on *that* request, counsel." The hand went down. "Also denied. I'm not going to have this trial manipulated by either side. I've been sitting up here, and I want this record to reflect that I haven't seen Mr. Fraser make any faces at the jury."

"You're refusing a hearing?"

"I certainly am. Now get him fixed up," McKinsey said. Starkey was helped to his feet. Fraser pushed Starkey's glasses into his hand.

"Thanks," Starkey said. He walked slowly away. "We're in recess?" he asked at the door.

"We are in recess," McKinsey said with a bemused wag of his head as Starkey pushed open the door. The court reporter tapped out the end of the transcript and jumped up from her seat.

It was all of a piece, Fraser thought, the weeping and the surreptitious wink, the escape, and now hitting Starkey. Even the phone call. It was part of Reece's instinctive twists and turns to get away from him. Call the prosecutor and provoke him into saying something so he is removed from the case for misconduct. Try to escape from jail. Try anything, Fraser thought. I know you.

McKinsey was still sitting on the bench. He said to Fraser, "You know what that's all about, don't you?"

"Al wanted to make sure his appeal issues got on the record right away," Fraser said sourly. "They can't accuse him of waiting too long to raise them."

"Dammit, they sure can't," McKinsey said with a tinge of admiration that angered Fraser. "Tough little jackass."

TWO

The genial nurse fluffed his pillow for him, trying by a forced smile to convey a cheeriness she didn't feel. "Does something hurt more today?" she asked brightly, with a solicitous bounce of her head.

"No, nothing hurts more today," he said. "Get out. Shut up and get out."

Her smile faded. Doctors made lousy patients. This one was a psychiatrist and even lousier. She mopped up the last of his overturned breakfast tray, congealed custard and milk, sticky bits clinging to his blanket. He acted like he was in a pigpen or something, like he could just throw his food anywhere. "I can get the doctor if you need some medication."

"No, no, no medication. Just get out."

She finished fluffing and being pleasant. Here was this guy, all broken up from a car accident, and he should have been doped up, asleep, dead to everything. But he got mad every time he saw the newspaper at breakfast. Today's lay thrown to the floor, the headline turned up, FIGHT IN MURDER TRIAL. His tantrums had gotten worse lately. He was a coffee-break legend already. If you want a thrill, go see the psychiatrist in 367.

"I'll be in at eleven for your change."

"Get out. Go away."

Something was rubbing him wrong. Instead of lying quietly and recovering, he tossed and turned like a kid being made to take a nap.

"I'll turn on your TV if you want."

"I don't want you to do anything. I want you to get *out.*" His bandaged arm, connected by tubes to several bottles of fluids hung above the bed, dismissed her angrily.

Gratefully, she eased out of the room. Inside she heard him cursing and rattling the metal side bars of his bed.

CHAPTER XXII

ONE

The dark-suited mourners were easy to spot, though they were almost outnumbered by reporters. From his car down the street, Fraser counted the camera crews as the service ended and people straggled slowly from the small Catholic church.

It was a one-story building, flat-colored, with a large lawn and a large, entreating statue of Jesus. Fraser saw most of the mourners leave for their cars. Only a few stayed to be interviewed by bustling young men and women with cameras lurking behind them.

One man came toward his car. He was solemn, dressed in a three-piece black suit. A tiny green sprig was pinned to his lapel.

"It's over," the man said to Fraser.

"I can see everyone leaving."

The man turned to look back at the small congregation gradually breaking up. "Well, it was a real nice service. Father Quiones did a very nice job." He paused, leaning against Fraser's window. "He didn't show up, you know. I looked around on the chance he might have heard, someone called, he read. But he wasn't there."

Fraser nodded, still watching the mourners in their slow departures. "The last time I saw Tippetts was before the grand jury met. I had to get a warrant issued for him when he didn't come in to testify. I hoped we might have found him in the first couple of months, but I don't think so now. Too much time has gone by." The trial was in its fifth month.

"Well, I tried to find him." The man sighed. "I used our personnel records, checked with his friends, but he and his wife weren't from around here. Nobody here really knew anything about them."

"I know," Fraser said.

"The house got sold three months ago. He got the check, I guess, then nothing. He could be anywhere."

"It was kind of you to go to this trouble, Mr. Cerrutti. You must have thought highly of him."

"Them both. Real nice family, all of them. It's just

terrible. Terrible shame." He shook his head. "I didn't know what Gene would have wanted, so I picked my church for the service. I don't think he was Catholic."

"He wasn't," Fraser replied. More people came slowly across the church's lawn, past the statue with its frozen arms trying to embrace them. The funeral of two children was enough for anyone. He remembered that other one, the earlier funeral in a large downtown church, ending in a cemetery near the airport, with the mountains standing whitely frosted on the horizon. The casket was so small, such a poor measure of how much had been lost, all the hopes and promise that had come to so little. Fraser had trouble remembering this was the funeral of someone else's child, a man he didn't know at all. Yet, in a way, he did.

"I don't think he'd mind having a Catholic service. Father Quiones did it very nice. Everything looked perfect. Flowers, the church, the casket." He bent to Fraser. "Thanks for the hundred bucks. We took up a collection at the plant, but it helped."

"I was glad to."

"You could've come in. It was all right."

Come in? Fraser shook his head. He told Cerrutti a partial truth. "We're still in trial. Too many reporters around here. It might have caused some trouble."

Cerrutti looked up at the cameras and microphones. "They like that bastard, I bet. They go anywhere he's been, don't they?" Then his face softened. "It breaks my heart about Gene. You couldn't find him, I couldn't find him. How's he ever going to find out about his little boy?" Cerrutti trailed off. "That goddamn bastard. I hope he gets hung from a streetlight."

TWO

He called Kate that afternoon.

They met in the same park where he and Sanderson had corrected the problem of the missing gun. Winos, perhaps the same ones, were still there. He and Kate met at the grand, dry stone fountain in the center of the park. She sat on the edge of the fountain's leaf and branch filled pool.

"Why didn't you tell me you were back?" he asked.

"There didn't seem much point."

Around them the traffic moved inexorably. The same windless sky hung damply overhead as it had the day with Sanderson. It had become very important to him to see Kate again after the Tippetts funeral.

She held her hands in her lap. Then she said, "I read about his mother going to prison for trying to get him out of jail. It sounded a bit harsh for a woman her age."

"It wasn't. I wish there was more we could have done. She pled guilty, she claimed it was all her idea, but I think she's protecting him. She's protected him all his life, no matter what he did." The mystery of children, the dead and living, he thought.

"Where are you living?" he asked after they had sat quietly.

"I've got an apartment. I couldn't stay in Salinas. It's not home. So I came back here about a week ago." The leaves in the dry pool rustled as some small animal moved beneath them.

"I should have returned your calls," he said.

"I wanted to talk to you."

"Kate, I miss you."

"I've been thinking that we should make this a permanent separation. I need to put my life on a firm footing, Tony. I need to know where I stand."

"No divorce."

"I think it's the best way out for both of us."

"No."

Kate sat with her gloved hands on the stone fountain. Her palms pressed against the cold, unyielding stone.

THREE

For Judge McKinsey, the courthouse cafeteria now prepared the same breakfast each morning of the trial. He ate it at nine-fifteen generally, as soon as he finished his morning calendar. He had almost twenty-five minutes before going back to Department 7 and Starkey and Fraser and Reece. The breakfast consisted of very weak coffee, because of his bladder, and two unbuttered slices of raisin toast, on which the judge dusted sugar as a treat. He also had a small glass of reconstituted orange juice. It was thin fare compared to what he had eaten for breakfast before this trial.

He sat near one large window, smoking his first cigarette after court, munching the toast, sipping the thin, bitter coffee, and holding forth with his cronies.

Very few people understood the language he spoke to these men of his age and background in Santa Maria when they sat together and swapped jibes. They gathered around him more often lately, as if they sensed time was short.

"Saw Arnie Saltz yesterday," said one.

"Saltz? That bastard still alive?" McKinsey exclaimed. "Jesus Christ, I thought he was long gone." In the course of the Reece trial, McKinsey had developed a small tic in his right cheek, and his lip made a faint smacking sound. He didn't notice it.

"Sure he's alive." The three of them sat crunched together at the small cafeteria table. "He's got tubes up the butt and nose, but he's alive."

"Saltz," the judge muttered.

Younger men and women circled through the cafeteria, paying homage to McKinsey as they walked by. It was the politic thing to do. None of them had ever heard of Saltz, or the dozen other names McKinsey's crew floated that morning; and as for the crew itself, they were old men whose names were, to the city and its new lawyers, little more than letters on fading signs. The world these men and McKinsey knew was passing away. But for now it existed at their tight little table.

They talked about Saltz and another favorite, now successful as a federal judge. They recalled some drunken sprees, and the time the future judge had pointed a loaded gun at a rival suitor as they teetered on the balcony of a woman neither man had married. They joked about how he had become a judge. Their voices dropped when the trial came up. As it always did.

"They should've just shot him. You don't arrest these guys, you just shoot." One of McKinsey's pals looked around the table for agreement.

McKinsey toyed with a crust and watched his friends drink real coffee. "The D.A.'s got a real burr under his saddle for Reece. He's going after him right down the line. I don't think poor old Starkey sees how mad the D.A. is.''

"Just shoot the guy. No problems later.''

McKinsey looked at the man thoughtfully.

"He's a mad dog," the man said. "That's the way you have to do it.''

Another elbowed closer to McKinsey. His voice became soft and conspiratorial. "What're you going to do? When they say he's guilty, what're you going to do, Sammy?''

McKinsey looked at them all, his tic going again. "I'm going to do the right thing. That's what I'm going to do.''

CHAPTER XXIII

ONE

On a Tuesday morning, after a three-day recess, there was a special excitement in the courtroom. The trial was nearing its end. An unusual witness was going to testify.

"I thought you said he was going to be in the hospital for a couple more weeks,'' McKinsey said to Starkey.

Starkey took the cigarette the judge offered. Only a small square bandage over the lower part of his nose remained to show where he had been struck. "He insisted. I met with him over the weekend, and he looks pretty battered up," Starkey touched his own bandage, "not as lucky as me. He said now was the time.''

"I'm glad he made that decision,'' Fraser said. Reece's attack on Starkey had bought the defense something from one or two jurors, he was sure of that. There couldn't have been a more perfect demonstration of Starkey's arguments about Reece's "irresistible impulses.'' Now Fraser was going to have a chance to go after Keddie himself, the mainstay of the defense.

Court reconvened. Starkey and Reece sat with about four feet between them. Three very attentive guards watched Reece constantly. Reece had lapsed into pathetic dejection now. It was more in keeping with his portrayal of a helpless victim.

"The defense calls Dr. Benjamin Keddie."

Fraser heard the courtroom doors open, and Dr. Keddie limped into view, assisted by a deputy sheriff. Keddie slowly clumped his way on crutches to the front of the room.

He balanced awkwardly while Marge gave him the oath, then he hobbled over to the witness stand.

"Dr. Keddie, would you prefer a chair down here in front of the jury? You look like you're going to have some trouble getting to the stand."

Keddie gave McKinsey a ferocious grin. "Thank you, your honor, but I'll manage."

Fraser watched his adversary clamber slowly up the small stairs to the witness stand.

He was hurt. The more constraining bandages on his face had been removed, leaving long red scars, still vivid and moist, covered with an antiseptic gel. His face was fuzzy where whiskers sprouted through the scars. One hand was still swathed in white. His leg was still in a cast up to the hip. He breathed cautiously because another layer of cast bound his chest. He was thinner than Fraser remembered.

For all that, he was obviously eager to talk. He settled himself and signaled his readiness.

Starkey spent a great deal of time painting Keddie's background. On its face, it was impressive. From prison psychiatrist to expert criminal psychiatrist, panelist, author, lobbyist for reduced criminal penalties and the expanded use of psychiatric evidence in court, lecturer, founder of two prestigious psychiatric clinics, a man of ideas and apparently indefatigable energy.

He was formidable in spite of his injuries.

Keddie made the other psychiatrists seem dry and academic by comparison. He joked. He smiled often for the jury, although it took on the quality of a grimace. He was bright and witty, yet his answers to Starkey's questions were precise. It was a powerful performance, as Fraser knew it would be.

"Is it your opinion that one of the reasons Charles

Reece killed these people is because he was afraid they were going to kill him?''

Keddie gestured with his bandaged hand. ''That was his primary reason—a misguided, frantic effort at self-defense.''

''His delusion about Nazis existed before he was arrested? Before he saw any psychiatrists?'' Starkey made a point of looking at Fraser.

''I have no doubt of it at all. I noted it in my report to you. He mentioned this delusion at our very first meeting. He repeated it constantly.''

The jury listened to Keddie, following his hand when it gestured. Reece, said Keddie, was like a drug addict, driven by his need to do things he would otherwise never consider doing. The power of his delusions, that his body was sick and he was being poisoned by Nazis, overwhelmed his freedom of choice.

Starkey finished, and Fraser started his cross-examination. Dr. Keddie looked a little woozy on the stand, but he braced himself when Fraser approached. Only the most monumental egotism, Fraser thought, could drag a sick man into court for a difficult cross-examination. This egotism was Keddie's weakness.

''This delusion of persecution by Nazis,'' Fraser said brusquely, ''that you say Reece has. You based your opinion of its existence on the statements he made to you and the items in his home?''

''Yes, I did.''

Fraser remembered that room as sharply as if he had just walked out of it. ''Excluding the statements made to you as perhaps unreliable, doctor, aren't those books and swastikas just as consistent with Reece admiring Nazis as fearing they were out to get him?''

''That is another inference, I suppose. You could draw that inference.''

''You did not? You chose not to?''

''That's correct,'' Keddie replied.

Fraser picked up Keddie's thick report. ''Does a psychiatrist have the right to distort facts like a storyteller and say he's merely interpreting those facts?''

''Definitely no. No one has that right, Mr. Fraser.''

''In your report, doctor, you say that Reece had hallucinations, spiders and so forth, when you interviewed him in the jail—"

"Yes, he did."

"Let me ask a question before you answer, doctor."

"I'm sorry." Keddie shut his eyes for a long moment, and when he opened them they seemed opaque.

"Explain to me, Dr. Keddie, how you can tell if someone is standing quietly and looks preoccupied, that he is therefore seeing things?"

"Well, you can't by merely looking."

"You had to add your own interpretations to decide what Reece was doing?"

"He spoke about these visual hallucinations."

"Do you have an explanation for the fact that Charles Reece never mentioned these spiders, or whatever you say he spoke about, until after he saw you, Dr. Keddie?"

"No, I don't, frankly. I'm puzzled. I recollect he mentioned these things to someone else."

"Who? Give me a name, one person besides yourself."

"I'll have to check my files."

He wouldn't find any mention of visual hallucinations in Rudin's report. Rudin introduced Reece's Nazi persecution delusions, Keddie his hallucinations. Fraser understood the design. It might have appeared too convenient for Reece to display all of the symptoms needed to declare him insane at once. So Rudin and Keddie divided them.

"We'll have to move on then for now," Fraser answered, turning from Keddie. Starkey was jotting notes down with rapidity, glancing over at Reece every so often. Reece looked away from Fraser.

"How do you define a delusion, Dr. Keddie? You've said Reece has various delusions."

"Well, sir, a delusion, and here I'm employing the current definition within the psychiatric community, a delusion is a belief contrary to proof. It is not ordinarily accepted by other members of a person's culture. It is not a commonly believed superstition."

Fraser paced to Keddie. "You wouldn't call a belief in God a delusion, would you, doctor?"

"No, I wouldn't."

"And that's only because in our society it isn't one, is

it? So many people believe there's a God that it's a 'commonly believed superstition'?"

"Yes, that's true."

Starkey's frantic catch-up writing increased in fervor. Fraser had managed to get Keddie to insult all the churchgoers on the jury.

"What if you lived in a community of atheists?"

"In that case, Mr. Fraser, a belief in God or gods would be something else again."

"Would you call it a delusion in that circumstance?"

"It might be. In any event, the religious practices of people are normally and properly outside the scope of psychiatric inquiry, I think." He shifted painfully in his seat, readjusting his legs. One of his crutches clattered noisily to the floor. He made no move toward it.

"So the nature of a delusion depends solely on how many people acknowledge a superstition? Is that what you're saying? It's a numbers game?"

"There is also the question of proof. In Mr. Reece's case, for example, we can medically demonstrate that his belief in the efficacy of human blood as a curative is false. Hence, it's a delusion."

Keddie's answers stayed confident, and Fraser was certain the psychiatrist had no forewarning where he was being led. His egotism was uppermost now, as he lectured the jury.

"Delusion is a matter of perception, Dr. Keddie?"

"Yes, in a sense."

"It's a matter of viewpoint, interpretation? Someone doesn't see things correctly?"

"Yes."

"Someone's actions can seem enraged, frenzied and disorganized, and actually be the result of carefully thought-out planning, can't they?"

"Objection," Starkey said, "that question calls for speculation. It doesn't follow the district attorney's other questions."

"Speculation?" McKinsey said. "Aren't you saying it's vague? I thought what this witness said was speculate."

Starkey reddened. "Well now, judge, I object to your characterization of the witness's testimony."

"Go ahead. I'm telling you the objection was improperly put. It ought to be on grounds of vagueness. We've listened to the honorable doctor all morning and all he's done is speculate.'' The judge turned a fatherly manner on Keddie. ''You don't mind me saying you speculate, now do you, doctor?''

''The court may say what it pleases, sir. I might only add that I'm engaged in informed speculation. That is my profession.''

''There.'' McKinsey turned back to Starkey. ''Even your own witness isn't bashful about it. I'm not being critical of anyone. But I want you to make an objection on the right grounds.''

Caught between the judge and Keddie, Starkey muttered, ''Okay, I withdraw the objection. My objection is that the question is vague.''

''Overruled.''

Starkey sat down with a thump. He tossed his notes angrily from one pile to another to occupy his hands.

Judge McKinsey gazed innocently out at the audience.

''Do you remember my question, Dr. Keddie?'' Fraser asked as soon as he could take charge again. Keep the witness moving, never let him pause to think. Never let the jury pause, either.

''I honestly don't.''

''My question,'' Fraser said, ''was whether behavior can seem enraged and frenzied when it's really the result of careful planning and forethought?''

Keddie sensed the trap. ''I'd have to think about that. It would depend.''

''Can it or can't it, doctor?''

''I'd need some reference points.''

''I don't care about your reference points. I'm asking you, can it or can't it?''

''The question is too abstract for me.''

''Objection,'' Starkey called out, ''vague and argumentative.''

''Are you saying you can't answer that simple hypothetical question?'' Fraser went on.

''Just a second, counsel. I haven't ruled on the objection,'' the judge broke in. ''Let's keep some decorum here. Objection's sustained.''

Reece slumped unhappily in his seat.

Fraser folded his arms. "Dr. Keddie, some behavior is truly frenzied, isn't it?"

"Of course."

"Some is merely frenzied in appearance? By how we look at it?"

"A lay person may make that error."

"But not a trained person like yourself?" Fraser asked quickly.

"I hope not," Keddie replied. The grimacelike smile appeared again.

"How many times did Reece shoot Barbara Ellis?"

Keddie looked up, briefly perusing the ceiling. He said after a moment, "I think three or four times, all told."

"Wasn't she shot once in the chest, followed by two shots to the head? A total of three shots?"

"As I said, I thought it was three to four times," he said, as if it didn't matter.

But it did matter. "Wouldn't that kind of execution-style murder suggest purposeful behavior, Dr. Keddie?" Fraser asked forcefully. "If he shot her once to incapacitate her, and then shot her twice more, carefully, in the head?"

"It might, sir."

"That's not frenzied, disorganized behavior, is it?"

Keddie kneaded his bandaged hand. "I believe it is. The overwhelming impulse to shoot Mrs. Ellis occurred several times."

"Do you mean this man," he flung his arm toward Reece, who flinched back, "got into a car, drove it some distance, parked it, got out, took his gun and trash bag and gloves, wearing his disguise of sunglasses and a red parka, gained entry to the Ellis home, shot Mrs. Ellis in a frenzy, then shot Mrs. Henderson and her husband in a frenzy?"

"Mr. Fraser," Keddie said didactically, "when I said frenzied, I meant in the grip of a disorganized, delusional state. I'm not certain, based on my own information, that Mr. Reece fully comprehended what he was doing."

"You mean he didn't know he was shooting and cutting up living people?"

"I mean he didn't know the full effect of his actions. He didn't realize the tragic consequences."

Fraser's disgust was evident when he barged up to Keddie. The scarred, raw face looked back at him. "Are you saying that he thought these people wouldn't be hurt by what he did to them?"

"I think that's the most likely explanation, given the information."

"It's your expert opinion he took such time to kill his victims, shooting them, then cutting them up, because he didn't think they'd be affected?"

"My opinion is that he was in the grip of a powerful delusional state. He didn't fully know what he was doing. In the legal sense," he added.

Reece had pressed both of his hands to his eyes. His head slowly moved from side to side, denying what Fraser asked.

Fraser leaned over the counsel table toward Keddie. The psychiatrist yawned suddenly from fatigue. He closed his mouth quickly.

"Dr. Keddie, you think Charles Reece killed his victims in order to obtain human blood and to destroy his persecutors?"

"I have said so. That was his delusional structure."

"Do you consider, even now, that he could have had any other possible motive for these gruesome murders?" Fraser looked over at the solemn jury and Reece, slouched in his seat. No more phone calls in the middle of the night from you, he thought, no more winks across the table or weeping to save yourself. I know why you did it, Fraser thought. So do they; he glanced at the jury.

Keddie shook his head with sluggish movements. "I did consider other possibilities, but I rejected them. Blood, his delusional need for blood, was the primary motive for what he did."

"Dr. Keddie, as an honest human being, as a trained psychiatrist, can't you admit that Charles Reece killed his victims because he enjoyed inflicting cruelty? Didn't he kill these people in this grotesque manner because his purpose was also sadistic?"

Keddie rallied at the suggestion, his sluggishness falling away. "No. That is not in accord with the evidence." His white hand lay like a dead fish on top of the stand. It twitched slightly. He waited for Fraser.

"As a trained, 'honest psychiatrist,' are you saying a

293

man who commits sodomy on the body of a woman he's just killed isn't driven by a sadistic impulse?"

"Objection, judge, I object." Starkey's voice was filled with righteous annoyance. "Mr. Fraser keeps saying 'honest psychiatrist' as though it's an insult."

"I think it is, applied to this witness," Fraser said.

"Oh, that's incredible," Starkey shouted. "Your honor, I must ask for a recess. The district attorney is clearly biased." He rose to his feet immediately.

The pause gave Fraser another chance to rein himself in. He wasn't going to join Starkey in shouting or posturing.

"I apologize for that last comment, your honor," he said.

McKinsey drummed his fingers on the bench. "I'm not going to have any more editorial cracks or theatrics, gentlemen."

"I want my objection noted clearly in the record, judge," Starkey said, sitting down.

"Noted. Continue, Mr. Fraser."

Keddie had listened with faint attention. He yawned several more times. He was plainly losing the energy to fend off Fraser's questions. "My answer to your question, sir, is that I found no evidence Mr. Reece was motivated by sadistic feelings."

"Then did putting feces in the mouth of Mrs. Ellis have anything, anything at all to do with Reece's delusions about Nazis being after him or his need for blood?"

"It wasn't part of his delusional structure, no," Keddie replied carefully. "But I attributed it to the overall chaotic thinking of Mr. Reece at the time."

He needed to keep Keddie on the stand until the very last minute before noon. Keddie would have time to think and recuperate over lunch. Time was growing short. The opportunity to discredit him might be lost after lunch.

He had to cripple Keddie now.

"I want to explore your use of psychiatric words, doctor. I'm going to use an example from history. You've written about history, haven't you?"

Starkey looked up with a bewildered frown.

"Yes, I have," Keddie said.

"Didn't the Nazis have a delusion about Jews causing the world's problems?"

"We get into that problem of defining a delusion again, sir. When a whole culture or even a very large group of people believes in something, I doubt that we can psychiatrically label it a delusion. It may be wrong, it may be a mistake, but it is not delusional."

"So if I say I can defy gravity and float to the ceiling, you would know it was a delusion on my part?"

"Oh, yes."

"And if the whole courtroom believed I could do that, is that a delusion for everyone here?"

"Yes, it is. Physics says you cannot float to the ceiling."

"But, likewise, aren't there more of us who believe Jews aren't the authors of the world's problems?"

"I hope so. I count myself in the number who don't."

"Then doesn't that mean we can confidently label this belief contrary to proof on the part of the Nazis a delusion?"

"It does turn into a matter of perspective. One man may have delusions. But I don't know about whole nations or cultures."

Millions could be put to brutal death and it was a question of perspective whether to call their killers deluded or not. Keddie could not seem to disentangle himself from his desire to help Reece avoid execution. The ultimate display of his derangements was at hand as Fraser bore in.

"Direct your attention to the jury instruction on insanity, doctor, and tell me if you would find the Nazis insane?"

Sideways, Keddie read the instruction on the chart. "In the first place, we aren't talking about any law. The instruction says 'the law' and for other nations we're not talking about the same thing. It may be apples and oranges."

"I don't want to hang you up on that. Substitute morality or decency or whatever you want. It's always been wrong to kill, hasn't it?"

"Generally, yes."

"Well, would you find Nazis who killed because of this belief in Jewish evil insane using the California standard?"

Keddie acted confused. "It's difficult. It's so hypothetical. But since they operated on this belief, and I think it fair to call the belief a disease, then I would find the Nazis, generally, insane.''

''Because they didn't refrain from acting on their belief in the evil of Jews? Because they went ahead and killed Jews?''

Keddie frowned and his white, bandaged hand rubbed across his head for a moment, ghostlike. ''Well, by our sanity test, the Nazis knew the requirements of law or ethics, and yet they were so dominated, so obsessed by the image of the perfidious Jew that they had to commit these horrible crimes.'' Keddie ended weakly. He was quite tired now.

''Whether or not you classify it as a delusion, doctor?''

''Yes, either way. They would be insane by our standard because of what they did, regardless of the underlying truth or falsity of the belief.''

''It was an irresistible impulse for them?''

''I suppose so.''

A snap again from Fraser. ''You would find them insane even though they were organized enough to set up gas chambers, whole extermination camps, to run railroads carrying Jewish victims, in fact, to organize a whole apparatus of government around the idea of killing Jews?''

''I think most people,'' Keddie looked to the jurors, not Fraser, ''would agree that those Nazis were insane. I don't have any qualms about saying that.''

''And you find Charles Reece insane for about the same reasons?''

''Well, very loosely the same.''

''He believed blood would cure him, they thought Jews were evil. Both killed for their beliefs, didn't they?''

''That was part of my diagnosis.''

''And like the Nazis,'' Fraser now spoke to the jury, ''Charles Reece was able to organize his own transportation. He drove his own car. He hid it. He brought tools of death with him. He performed his deeds in secret. He wore a disguise. He practiced killing,'' Fraser said slowly, ''before going into the Ellis home. All these things don't point away from his being insane?''

''No, they don't.''

''Just as the Nazis' efficiency doesn't point away from theirs in your mind, Dr. Keddie?''

"To be fair, Mr. Fraser, I don't find Mr. Reece as organized as you do."

McKinsey's mouth had hardened into a thin line. He tapped very softly on the bench with a closed fist as Keddie talked about the Nazis.

Starkey rose smoothly. "Judge, Dr. Keddie is obviously tiring. I wonder if we couldn't break a wee bit early for lunch?"

The judge glanced at the clock, then at Keddie, then at Fraser. "Is this a good place for you to break, counsel?"

No. No, not yet. There was more to do and Keddie must not have the respite of the luncheon recess. "Well, no, your honor. I don't have much more and I'd rather cover it before we adjourn for lunch." It was partly true. He needed the time now.

"We'll go on then," McKinsey said. Fraser thought the judge might have granted Starkey's request but for the last things Keddie had said. He excused the Nazis as he excused Reece. If you could not punish the Nazis, which was perverse, you could not punish Reece, either.

It was monstrous. It was absurd.

Starkey kept a vigilant eye on his wavering star witness.

"You do understand the effect of your opinions, don't you, Dr. Keddie?" Fraser asked. "Both the Nazis and Charles Reece would be freed from criminal responsibility for their actions."

"I didn't say that. I don't think that's my concern here. I'm only here to give you my opinion based on the questions put to me."

Now it was time to drive a wedge into the fissures in Keddie's whole view of Reece. Fraser went at it vigorously. "Earlier, Dr. Keddie, you talked about free will and irresistible impulse. That is the crux of this case, isn't it, whether Charles Reece had free will?"

"Yes, it is," Keddie smiled wanly.

"If he was possessed by some irresistible impulse, as you say, he couldn't premeditate or deliberate as the law requires, could he?"

"No, he could not. That's what I've been trying to make clear."

Keddie leaned heavily against the side of his chair.

"Aren't you aware, doctor, that the foundation of our legal order is free will?"

"Yes, I am aware of that."

"Are you aware of a differing philosophical view about a human being's capacity for making choices?"

Keddie nodded heavily. "You mean determinism."

"Doesn't psychiatry speak in the language of determinism and not free will, Dr. Keddie?"

Keddie shook his head. "It doesn't use the terms of either philosophical model, sir. Psychiatry is a scientific discipline."

Fraser didn't want to lose the jurors on this most significant point. He walked toward them so Keddie was forced to follow his movements. "What do you understand determinism to be, doctor?"

"It's a concept that supposes that after birth we have little or no choice in what happens in our lives. All things are predetermined for us. We are not the masters but the prisoners of our fate. A determinist would say that you and I and Mr. Reece and Mr. Starkey have to be in this courtroom. It is inevitable. We have no choice in the matter. It was decided in advance."

"Well, Dr. Keddie," Fraser asked pointedly, "do you personally believe in the idea of free will?"

Starkey grunted as if to say, what's the point here?

"Do I?" Keddie repeated. "Yes, I do. I believe we all have the initial capacity to make choices."

"To choose right from wrong? Good from evil?"

"Free will includes that capacity, of course. It's bound up with our social and ethical sense," he said slowly. He swallowed and asked McKinsey for a cup of water. He produced two small tablets and sipped the water while taking them.

Fraser came close to Keddie, close enough so the moist face glistened in the courtroom's hard lights near the bench. "Didn't you compare Charles Reece to a drug addict, though? You said he's unable to make choices."

"Yes, I did use that analogy."

"But isn't that analogy one of determinism rather than free will? Doesn't your analogy preclude anything but this idea of an irresistible impulse forcing Reece to act?"

"I only meant to illustrate that, like a drug addict, Mr.

Fraser, Mr. Reece had to do what he did. He had no capacity for full, mature reflection on his actions.''

"But that's determinism, isn't it?''

"Yes, it is.''

"Were you trying to mislead this jury by giving an example of determinism when you knew the model in our law is free will?''

"I wasn't trying to mislead, sir, I was trying to illuminate.''

He blinked his eyes frequently. Fraser suspected he was having trouble seeing.

"Illuminate?'' he threw back at Keddie. "By saying a drug addict doesn't have the ability to make choices about his actions?''

"I don't believe there is such an ability. I don't believe there are many choices.''

Fraser stared coldly at him. "Can't an addict decide to quit?''

"We all know that withdrawal is a very painful process,'' Keddie chided him.

"Answer me, doctor. Can't an addict decide to quit?''

"He can want to.''

"Can't an addict who steals to support his habit, decide he won't steal from his family or friends?''

"Yes.''

"Can't an addict make a decision about the kinds of crime he'll engage in?''

"To support themselves, they have no choice but to find quick ways of getting money.''

"Some will choose to be armed robbers?''

"Perhaps.''

"Some will choose to be burglars?''

"Yes.''

"Some will choose to be simply shoplifters?''

"I imagine so.''

"And some may even decide to kill for money?''

"Yes.''

"Aren't all those examples that even in your deterministic illustration there are many, many chances for the exercise of free will and choice?''

"Well, within a very limited sphere.''

"The law doesn't measure that, Dr. Keddie,'' he said.

"Do you think our law does more than measure the basic ability of someone to pick from two different alternatives? You don't think we should try to figure out how much better it is to be a burglar as opposed to an armed robber, do you?"

"Objection, judge," Starkey said, noticing Keddie's uncharacteristically submissive replies. "That's incredibly compound."

"Sustained."

"I'd like to renew my request for an early break," Starkey went on. "I can see Dr. Keddie is ready for one."

The clock moved as Fraser spoke. "Your honor, I'm nearly finished. I can end this very soon."

McKinsey nodded dubiously. "If you're sure you can."

Starkey remained standing. He had just lost and didn't know why.

Fraser didn't wait. Keddie had a distant look, as if he was falling into a reverie, and Fraser spoke gently so as not to startle him out of it. "Dr. Keddie, would you modify your opinion of Charles Reece's capacity to choose between distinct alternatives if you knew he had tried to escape from jail?"

Starkey recognized the danger. "Objection," he declared, and Keddie, surprised by the interruption, blinked again.

McKinsey ruled, "No, I'm going to permit him to answer."

The jury now knew that Reece had tried to escape. In front of them, Reece wrote rapidly on a page; perhaps witnesses he wanted, or his own musings.

"Answer please, doctor," Fraser said.

"No, I would not change my opinion. Trying to escape is something expectable in these circumstances." Keddie blinked several times, trying to clear his vision. "It has no real bearing on his overall inability to choose."

"What do you mean it's expectable? Why is it expectable for someone to want to escape from jail when they're being held for murder?"

Keddie tightened his mouth. "I think it's natural. It's . . ."

"Normal?" Fraser interrupted too hastily.

"Let him finish," McKinsey ordered.

"It's almost instinctive, a desire to get away from an unpleasant present and an uncertain future. There's little choice involved."

"Isn't the mere fact of an attempt to escape from jail proof to you, doctor, that this man knew what he had done was wrong?"

"It is not. It is not. Any person in this room would try to get out of jail in a similar situation whether they were guilty or not."

"Will you admit that this is merely your own interpretation of that event? Charles Reece might know he was guilty and want to escape for that reason, couldn't he?"

"He isn't capable of free will. I've said that. I've said that time after time after time."

"Who is freer, the soldier who kills under orders or the man who decides in peacetime to kill for his own reasons?"

"I can't answer."

"Why not?"

"I don't know the reasons. You're asking me silly, unfathomable things," Keddie snapped. His other crutch fell over and he swore loudly. "I won't let you provoke me. I won't permit that."

"Your honor, direct the witness to answer."

The judge said to Keddie, "You must answer if you can."

"I can't."

"He can't," McKinsey said calmly.

"Haven't you done everything you could to protect Charles Reece?"

"No. Nothing like you imply. I carried out my professional obligations scrupulously."

"Haven't you just now tried to mislead this jury? Haven't you coached this defendant in his insanity defense?" Fraser saw Keddie's angry denials forming. "Haven't you suggested psychiatric tricks to him and lied over and over in this courtroom to protect Charles Reece?" He raised his voice as Starkey strode forward shouting, heading to the stand as if to physically pull Fraser away from Keddie.

"Objection. Objection!" Starkey called out.

Fraser went on over the shouts and the judge's calls for

order. "Haven't you done all this to save Charles Reece?" He leaned within a few inches of Keddie.

Keddie swore again, shoving Fraser away.

"Objection," Starkey barked.

"I want to answer." Keddie quivered with anger, clenching his bandaged hand. "I want to answer this. I want to be heard."

McKinsey finally shouted, "Quiet! I'm going to hold everyone in contempt if I don't get some order now!"

Starkey addressed the judge. "This is the most flagrant kind of badgering, utterly unconscionable. I've never seen anything—"

McKinsey cut him off, rapping his knuckles on the bench. "Okay. No speeches. Objection is badgering. Argumentative."

Keddie burst out, "I want to answer, I want to be heard." Again everyone talked at once. McKinsey rapped heavily.

"Hold it again, I said. Mr. Starkey, you want to withdraw your objection? The witness doesn't mind, apparently."

"I do not withdraw it. I'm repeating it, judge. I object vigorously to the D.A.'s tone and his questions."

"Well," the judge said with a grim smile, "if the witness isn't bothered, I'm not. As long as we can have order, I'll let him answer." He pointed at Fraser: "But, don't you interrupt him, Mr. Fraser. You understand me?"

"Yes, I do, your honor." He was watching and waiting for Keddie to speak.

The psychiatrist seemed to steady himself. "I resent the charges you made," Keddie said. "I haven't compromised my ethics or done anything, anything . . ." He suddenly drifted off.

"But you do want to save Charles Reece, don't you, Dr. Keddie?"

Reece now looked up, a worried pout forming on his lips for an instant.

Again Keddie seemed to steady himself. "Save him? That sounds terrible. How can you want to save a murderer? I'm a human being. I understand the revulsion you have to feel in the presence of brutal murder. But I see him, too"—he gestured vaguely toward Reece—"he shouldn't be killed. He should be treated, studied. Why is he so selfish? What turns a respectable young man into a killer? Save him? I want to save him because he has those secrets." Keddie slowed. "The next time, perhaps some-one like him can be treated. We can vaccinate against murder. I don't know." He sighed tiredly. "We need to understand him for our own benefit."

Fraser spoke very softly now. The courtroom, so bois-terous a few moments before, was still. "Even at the price of six lives?"

The psychiatrist had trouble seeing him. He squinted slightly. His neck was limp. "Yes . . . no. That is terri-ble. That may be the most terrible part of all, that price of knowledge."

Keddie smiled suddenly at Fraser, at the jurors, a smile from far away. There was silence in the court.

Finally, Fraser released Keddie. "I have nothing fur-ther," he said.

From the bench, McKinsey stopped staring at Keddie. He tore himself away when Fraser spoke. "Okay. Okay. We'll have redirect examination after lunch. We'll recess for luncheon." He excused the jury.

He stood up. The jurors stood as well, and a path was opened through the audience for them by the bailiff.

"I'd like to stay in session after the jury leaves," Star-key said.

McKinsey stopped unbuttoning his robe. He sat down again. "Okay. We'll stay in session."

At his own seat, Fraser was drained and, at the same time, elated. He had done all he could. He had shown the jury everything he wanted them to see.

When the room had been cleared, Starkey began prowl-ing back and forth in front of the jury box. "Judge, after what Mr. Fraser did, I've got to make a motion for a mis-trial. He's now totally bollixed up this jury. They can't possibly render a fair verdict now."

"What are your grounds for your motion?"

"Prosecutorial misconduct," Starkey announced, "pure and simple."

"Mr. Fraser? You want to be heard?" McKinsey leaned

in his chair, sucking on the end of a pencil. He glanced sideways at Keddie, still in a reverie on the stand.

Fraser collected his phantom thoughts. "Your honor, what Mr. Starkey refers to is a single question. The question was the subject of a ruling by the court. The court overruled defense counsel's objection. I don't see the basis for a mistrial based on misconduct."

"Oh, judge, when the D.A. yells like that, waves his arms around," Starkey waved his angrily, "says all kinds of irrelevant and prejudicial things, and in bad faith, I might add, because he doesn't have one bit of evidence to support them, he's engaging in misconduct. I want that on the record."

Which means he doesn't think he can get a mistrial, Fraser thought.

McKinsey sucked, then put the pencil down. He raised his eyebrows as he added up the arguments and the scene just played before him. "Well," he said slowly, "the question was definitely out of line. I would have sustained an objection if your witness hadn't gotten into it. Now I'll chalk it up to energetic cross-examination. Motion for mistrial denied." He smiled faintly at Starkey. "One thing you've got is a great record, Mr. Starkey. Can we go to lunch now?"

"Not yet, judge. Since you've denied my motion for a mistrial, I'm moving now to have the court strike the last part of Dr. Keddie's testimony. I think the jury should be told he's sick and not completely in control of himself."

At the sound of his name, Keddie looked up uncomprehendingly.

"Why should I do that?" McKinsey asked.

"Because it's obvious Dr. Keddie is still weak, he's still sick, he's tired, he isn't up to Mr. Fraser's objectionable tactics. He didn't know what he was saying."

Keddie shook his head. "I know exactly what I'm saying," he said unconvincingly.

McKinsey ignored him. "Well, I'm not disposed to strike testimony. You can go ahead and rehabilitate him after lunch. That's what redirect is for."

"Strike? Why strike my testimony?" Keddie kept saying.

McKinsey's reply was icy. "Mr. Starkey is under the impression you did some harm to the defense just now, doctor." The judge didn't take his glance from the psychiatrist.

"I did?" Keddie looked pained. "How could I harm the defense? How could I? How could I hurt him . . ." His voice whispered away faintly and he slumped forward on the stand, pitching face down.

"Oh, Christ," McKinsey said. A deputy sheriff was already darting toward Keddie. The judge gave Fraser a look that was inscrutable.

"What's wrong?" the judge asked the deputy loosening Keddie's collar.

"He's fainted, judge. I better get him out of here."

"Notify the paramedics, Marge," McKinsey said. A gong boomed distantly, and in moments, three deputies, as anxious as hounds with a scent, hurried into the courtroom carrying oxygen canisters, a stretcher, and a medical kit. Starkey and Reece watched like spectators at an accident as they worked on Keddie.

"Are we in session?" the court reporter asked.

"No, we're at lunch," McKinsey said. He stood to supervise Keddie's departure.

Keddie was rolled inertly onto the stretcher. McKinsey said, "Bailiff, get the doors." Then under his breath, but loud enough for Fraser to hear, he added, "Take the bastard out."

CHAPTER XXIV

ONE

Each night it got a little worse. It was worst that night after Keddie's immolation.

The disquiet would start when Fraser drove up to the unlighted house, as dark against the night sky as the land beyond it.

When he went in and turned the lights on, his feelings of unease and incompleteness always got stronger because he could see the furniture and rooms, all of Kate's work and their shared lives, and he knew she wasn't there. They hadn't talked since that day in the park. It was impossible to think of a divorce. He would not let her go. He loved her and a divorce would be an admission of defeat, a concession of victory to the currents trying to pull them apart.

Sometimes he started to call her, but he never finished dialing. After the trial would be time enough, he would have a better grip on himself. Half the time he walked into a room and expected to hear or see her. Her presence was everywhere in the house, yet as poignantly distant from him as Molly. It robbed him of any pleasure he had in the day's success over Keddie.

I'm not going to let her go, he thought resolutely, the lights casting their false brightness on him in the bedroom. Most of her clothes still filled the closet. On the dresser and bureau sat her brushes and teak boxes. Kate, like a wraith, tormented him. Kate, he had come to realize, was a line tying him to the world. She felt and reacted as an ordinary person, and Fraser now knew that after the Reece case he would desperately need that link.

The final few days of the trial had passed without Reece ever testifying. Starkey had saved this surprise cleverly. Until the moment when he announced, "The defense rests, your honor," Fraser had thought Reece would take the stand.

But it was apparently too great a gamble. Reece stayed in his seat while Starkey and Fraser argued to the jury for five days.

McKinsey called the court to order earlier than usual on the day he instructed the jury. It was eight-thirty on a humid, edgy Thursday. He was cranky and snapped at the jurors who rushed in late.

"We've got a lot to get through, and I'd like to do it today, ladies and gentlemen. You must pay attention because I can't go over this again."

A clear space lay in front of Fraser on the counsel table. His books and papers were gone. He put the thick stack of instructions down.

The judge was also prepared with Kleenex and mints

and water all easily at hand. He began reading at eight-forty, licking his fingers to turn the pages. What was premeditated? "Considered beforehand . . ." How long? "The test is not the duration of time, but rather the extent of the reflection. A cold, calculated judgment and decision may be arrived at in a short period of time, but a mere unconsidered and rash impulse, even though it includes an intent to kill, is not such premeditation and deliberation as will fix an unlawful killing as murder of the first degree." It was catechistic, McKinsey both asking and answering the questions for the jury.

The hours passed. McKinsey sipped from his ice water, sometimes garbling his words when the mint he was sucking on got tangled in his mouth. Fraser was drowsy, lulled by the procession of convoluted words. Every argument had to be anticipated. The judge read the definitions of all the lesser crimes Reece could be found guilty of, second-degree murder, voluntary manslaughter; he read instructions on diminished capacity and irresistible impulse; and when the clock strained toward eleven, Fraser heard the closing words. His eyes burned and his back was knotted from the effort of sitting there tensely.

McKinsey held up the sheaf of verdict forms for the jurors to see. "There are over one hundred possible verdicts in this case. It is your duty to decide each count in the indictment against the defendant separately. Your finding as to each count must be stated in a separate verdict. The case now remains with you. Madam Clerk, swear the deputy sheriff to take charge of the jury."

Marge swore a squarely built deputy who then led the jury from the courtroom by a side door to a rear corridor, taking them out of sight and hearing to a room at the far end of the courthouse where they would be locked in and guarded while they deliberated.

McKinsey recessed court, and Reece was taken away to wait by himself. Fraser and Starkey went back to chambers. The judge stood thoughtfully at his high bookshelves of gilt-bordered state court decisions, one hand in his pocket, the other holding a cigarette. He coughed into his hand. It was an unpleasant, mortal-sounding cough.

"I think they're going to cut him loose," he said.

"I wish." Starkey sank to the couch with a sigh.

"They won't," Fraser said, supressing the fear he felt. "They won't cut him loose after this evidence."

The judge took a breath. "I figure juror number five, and number one . . . Eliot?" The judge looked for confirmation to Starkey, who nodded. "Those two'll vote for manslaughter on the first ballot. I've seen them do it."

"They're going to be out four days on this, figuring out which verdicts to use, arguing. I say four days."

"They've already decided," Fraser said.

McKinsey coughed again. "I bet they have," he said wearily.

Now Fraser waited.

It became impossible to do any work or to be far from the telephone. Things accumulated in the office, but he only gave them a passing look. It didn't matter what they were. Police reports he passed to another deputy, warrant requests he stacked up, phone messages he threw away. No word from Kate, and he didn't want to call her if the only reason she would see for the call was his apprehension about the verdict.

He got word that the jury wanted to hear once again the testimony of a criminalist who had said that the saliva found on Mrs. Ellis could not be conclusively matched to Reece. More requests followed—eyewitnesses, police officers, Mahon. Why were the jurors listening to this again? Had they forgotten it? Were they unsure that Reece had even committed the crimes?

Or the most terrifying question, did they have such deep disagreements among themselves that they couldn't even reach a verdict?

Fraser felt close to despair. Each day, at least twice, he saw the twelve solemnly sitting in the box before going out to deliberate, or going home, and no sign from them. No hint. Another day passed. Then another. What were they doing?

Attorneys in the office stopped by to chat. Infeld came, although Whalen still stayed clear. Fraser missed Ballenger very much then.

And each time the jurors came to sit in the box and he heard a merry word, a laugh, Fraser's brain froze.

If Sally Ann's telephone rang more than twice, he almost shouted. He couldn't even go out for a walk to relieve his tension. He was chained to the courtroom. To Reece.

On the fourth day, near ten in the morning, the phone kept ringing; Sally Ann was off feeding the copy machine. Angrily Fraser snatched it up.

It was McKinsey.

"You might want to come over," he said. "We've got a verdict."

He put the phone down slowly.

However many times he walked from his office to the courtroom to get a verdict, time still stretched out. All sights became magnified, all sounds grating and enormous, and he was seized by the idea that it was a verdict on him. Mounting the steps to the plaza was like climbing toward a scaffold whose outline would shortly come into view.

On the way over he forced his teeming mind to still itself. He must think of nothing. Numbness, quiet, the bottom of a frozen lake.

The noisy swirl around the courtroom was frenetic. Men and women pushed each other, and cordons of marshals and deputies pushed back. An incoherent jabber of exclamations, questions, and curses skirled out everywhere.

"What do you think the verdict's going to be?" asked a woman with a television camera at her side.

"I don't know." He kept moving.

"Are you going to do anything if he's not guilty?" came another question out of the barrage of shouts.

"No comment." He was led by deputies through the last part of the shifting crowd. He went immediately to his place at the counsel table, arranging it with complete self-absorption. Like a Japanese craftsman in paper sculpture, he ordered his papers and files. He waited. Marge scurried back to tell McKinsey.

Starkey bustled in a moment later. Reece was brought out, his thin neck gleaming with perspiration.

The fourth day, Fraser hopelessly realized, was the day Starkey had said they would come back. A verdict on Starkey's day.

McKinsey's bailiff stepped out. The courtroom doors opened wider as the audience spilled inside. The seats filled quickly with people who had been searched, checked, and approved.

The bailiff announced McKinsey. The judge on the bench wore his mask, too; a cold rigor held his features. His voice was barren. When he looked down at Fraser it was without recognition or warmth.

"The record will reflect all parties are present and in their places. Defendant is also present and the People are represented." He coughed. "Gentlemen, I'm informed by the jury foreman that a verdict has been reached. I propose calling the jury in. Is there anything to take up before I do that?"

Fraser shook his head. At the other end of the table, Starkey did the same.

"Fine. Bring the jury in," McKinsey told the bailiff.

From a distance, Fraser heard the jury coming, a thin tromping of feet, no voices.

The bailiff appeared at the doorway at the side of the jury box, leading a small procession. He went ahead to Marge, handing her the jury's daily parking validations. Verdict or not, jurors had to be compensated for parking near the courthouse. The jurors filed into the box, and Fraser looked for any sign of the decision they had reached. But they were slate. Impenetrable slate.

McKinsey said, "Have you reached a verdict, Mr. Bales?"

The foreman, his hair swept back in an obsolete block cut, stood awkwardly. "Yes, we have, sir."

"Thank you. Before you hand the verdict forms to the bailiff, I want to tell everyone seated in the courtroom that when the verdicts are announced, I will not permit, I won't tolerate, any outburst or any demonstrations of any kind whatsoever. Any outbursts and I will clear the courtroom. If anyone cannot abide by this restriction, I'm directing you to leave the courtroom now."

A pause. Fraser sat immobile, and beneath his hands, which rested on a thin page of notes, the paper was wrinkling as he sweated.

"Everyone is apparently able to abide by the instructions I've given. Mr. Bales, will you please hand your verdicts to the bailiff?"

Bales, serious in his tangerine leisure suit and black tie,

gave over a stack of papers. The bailiff conveyed the papers up to the bench, an acolyte presenting an offering upward. McKinsey read slowly through the first few forms. His face remained a mask.

A rushing cataract filled Fraser's ears. He felt his heart speed up, and time slowed for the moments it took the judge to read the verdict forms over for errors.

"All right," McKinsey announced. "Madam Clerk, please read the jury's verdicts."

Fraser repeated, let it be over, let it be over.

A plump little woman began reading nervously. Her gray-framed glasses slipped and she quickly pushed them up again. "In the Superior Court of the State of California in and for the County of Santa Maria. Case number four-seven-nine-nine-five, the People of the State of California versus Charles Edmund Reece, defendant," her voice subtly shifted, "We the jury in the above-entitled cause find the defendant Charles Edmund Reece guilty of the crime of murder in the first degree of Barbara Ellis, as charged in count one of the Indictment."

Fraser felt an embarrassing elation. He carefully lifted his hand from the moist page and drew a measured breath. Barbara Ellis.

Marge said to the judge, "Should I read the verdicts about the special findings and allegations, or do you want me to poll the jury, your honor?"

"Read everything I gave you, Madam Clerk."

She nodded and resumed. "Special findings. We find the allegation that the defendant Charles Edmund Reece personally used a firearm during the commission of said offense to be true. We find the allegation that the defendant Charles Edmund Reece used a weapon, to wit, a knife, during the commission of said offense to be true."

What about the rest? What about the special circumstances?

"We find the allegation of special circumstances, to wit, that said defendant Charles Edmund Reece committed such act or acts causing death, and that the murder was willful, deliberate, and premeditated and was committed in an especially heinous, atrocious, and cruel manner, to be true."

Fraser closed his eyes. Marge continued reading each

special circumstance found to be true. The language was archaic, prolix, but glorious.

"Is this your verdict?" she asked the jurors. They nodded, giving their affirmations.

"So say they all," she informed McKinsey.

"Does either side wish to have the jury polled?"

"No," said Fraser.

"Yes," said Starkey.

"Poll the jury, Madam Clerk."

Marge took her name cards out. "Robert Eliot, is this your verdict?"

Juror number one, his arms folded protectively, said, "Yes." On she read and questioned, twelve times, each finding, each of the special circumstances. It took fifteen minutes to poll all the jurors. Fraser leaned back in his chair. He was ready to explode.

When she finished polling McKinsey said to her, "Madam Clerk, record the verdicts."

She took a mechanical stamp, identical to the ones used throughout the courthouse to validate deeds, parking tickets, and wedding licenses, and clunked it onto the verdict forms, one after another. Date and court, date and court. The simple mechanical sound was final, awful.

Throughout the procedure Reece made noises and directed clouded, threatening stares at the jury.

They were excused for a week until the sanity phase of the trial began. I did it, Fraser thought blindly, I convicted him.

McKinsey finally spoke to him when the courtroom was empty. "Guess I didn't call that one."

"You weren't even close," Fraser said with satisfaction.

"Don't count your chickens yet, my friend. Could be a compromise they worked out. Guilt for insanity. Or guilt for life in the joint."

Fraser looked at McKinsey. "No, I don't think so."

He left the courtroom, finally ready for the reporters and the noise and the questions. He was not prepared to see Spencer Whalen in the center of it all, lights on him, talking earnestly into the camera. The reporters saw Fraser at once.

312

"And speak of the devil," said Whalen, turning his head, a great, sappy smile on his face. "Here he is. He's right here."

He held out his arm as if to shake Fraser's hand or grab him, but Fraser walked by Whalen, past the reporters and the lights.

"Tony?" Whalen called. "Tony? Hold up a second . . . Tony!"

The reporters, torn between the two men, fumbled uncertainly for a moment before gravitating back to Whalen.

"Well, he's worked day and night," Fraser heard behind him, "he's tired, he's ready for a little rest. I'm sure he'll have something to say later. This is exactly what I meant when I ran for District Attorney of Santa Maria County. Hard cases won by hardworking prosecutors. The people are finding out I live up to my pledges to them . . ."

Fraser shared his victory with a small party in Major Crimes. They had a cake Sally Ann had kept in the refrigerator for two days.

CHAPTER XXV

ONE

They sat quietly in chambers, he and McKinsey, chatting as easily as they had before the trial. Except for the fact that McKinsey was more frail, the whole year and a half might have passed as a dream. Fraser wished it had been.

McKinsey's facial tic made soft sounds as he spoke. "It doesn't matter if I mention it now. I had a call from the governor's legal affairs secretary the day before yesterday."

"What are you up for?"

"It wasn't about me, my friend. It's about you. Your name's been floated for a judicial appointment. They wanted my thoughts."

Fraser's thought was immediate. I'll be a judge. He looked at McKinsey's spidery limbs. They'll make me a judge, and I'll sit on the bench like some of them, half asleep, listening to lawyers I know tell me things they half believe, or don't believe at all. Or believe because they believe everything.

A judge is out of the ugly world Kate hates. He sits above it, making a show of his imperious rulings and manners. I know what a judge is. There is no secret to it now, he thought.

He said to McKinsey, "Should I take it, if they offer it?"

"It's good duty," McKinsey said. "Good hours. Good pay. I'd give it serious consideration if it's offered. Might be the only time they'll offer it to you." He laughed. "They're looking ahead to some vacancies now."

It would be the kind of reward, Fraser thought, that Kate would appreciate. A judgeship could be a way to keep her from a divorce. She would like being the wife of a judge.

"I'll think about it," Fraser said.

McKinsey ground out a cigarette. He was down to smoking four a day. This was number two. "You gave a damn fine argument out there. You're sitting pretty. They said Reece was sane last week. They'll come back with a good verdict today."

The sanity phase had come and gone with many of the same psychiatric witnesses—minus Keddie, who was back in the hospital—and the jury had taken only four hours to come back with a verdict.

Reece was sane.

The penalty phase now starkly presented the choices remaining. Would Reece die in the gas chamber, or spend the rest of his life in prison without possibility of parole?

Starkey brought on every possible witness to Reece's good character as a boy, his friendliness and industrious efforts to help others.

The only moment of doubt came when Starkey finally called Reece to the stand. He rose from his seat, followed by two deputy sheriffs, and went to Marge, who swore him. Fraser noted Reece's nervousness as he got the hands wrong for taking the oath, and how he primped on the stand, smoothing his hair with fingers held stiffly together. Here he was at last on the witness stand.

It was Starkey's turn first.

"You understand that these folks," he gestured to the jurors, "are going to decide whether you live or die, Charles?"

"Yo."

"Is there anything you want to say to them about that?"

Reece's thin left hand went into his coat pocket and came out with an irregularly folded clutch of papers. Reece opened them like a stage-frightened high-school student about to recite a Veterans Day poem.

He began reading. "I know I've done very bad things. I must be punished for them, and I want you to know that the people who told you I wasn't sorry are wrong. I am very sorry for what I did. I think about it all the time. I don't know why I did it, except that I had to."

He turned a page; the papers crinkled dryly like burning leaves. "I will try to make up for what I did the rest of my days. I have been helpful to people when I was in school, and I will try to be helpful again to make up for what was done. I can change in prison and I would like to have the chance."

He stopped, his head downcast.

Starkey's hand gently slapped the counsel table. It was a gesture of finality. His case was over.

McKinsey said, "You may question the defendant, Mr. Fraser."

And that was the moment of doubt. There had been a growing babble sounding in his head as Reece read. Reece would not look at him or the jury. He sat defeated, sorrowful and downtrodden.

Fraser hated him. He felt hatred as purely and cleanly as any emotion in his life at that instant. What is there left to ask?

"Mr. Fraser?"

"Yes, your honor?"

"Do you have any questions?"

"No questions."

There was a mild stir in the courtroom. Fraser let Reece return submissively to his seat.

*　　*　　*

The jury had been out two hours this time when the call came from McKinsey, and Fraser went back to Department 7. In court, all the preliminaries passed in a moment. He gave a small wave to Sally Ann, sitting in the middle of the crowd. She smiled and waved back. Four or five other deputy D.A.s sat in the courtroom to hear the last verdict.

"In the Superior Court of the State of California," Marge read, "in and for the County of Santa Maria. Case number four-seven-nine-nine-five. The People of the State of California versus Charles Edmund Reece, defendant. We the jury in the above-entitled cause find the penalty at death."

Starkey let out a long, tired breath, and Reece made small choking sounds.

Fraser's head jerked upward. It wasn't finished. He focused on McKinsey, who watched from the bench as the jury was polled. The sick old man was the one who had to pass sentence on Reece. He could undo it all as a last, spectacular fanfare.

And if he didn't, there were appeals to follow. Starkey had years of appeals to pursue.

"We'll reconvene in four weeks," McKinsey was saying, "for the consideration of a probation report and sentencing."

"June ninth," Marge said, consulting her desk-blotter calendar.

"June ninth at ten o'clock in the morning, Mr. Starkey and Mr. Fraser. And thank you, ladies and gentlemen, for your services on what has been one of the most difficult and complex cases I have presided over." He began a summation to the jurors for the last time. Fraser's hand clenched spasmodically, and he hid it under the table.

He stayed seated as the jury left and the courtroom began to empty. McKinsey left without further word to him or Starkey. People came to Fraser; Sally Ann was at his side, patting his shoulder, congratulations beat against him from other deputies and spectators. He was immovable in the chair.

The guards had come, and a strangely silent Reece was shackled again, lifted to his feet and pushed forward to the corridor behind the courtroom for his journey back to the isolation section of the jail.

From that corridor, over all the congratulatory praises flowing over him, Fraser heard a guard's boisterous call, "Dead man coming." It was the warning shouted when death-row prisoners were moved at San Quentin.

Fraser's eyes traveled back to the deserted bench where McKinsey would decide everything in four weeks.

"Dead man coming," the guard shouted again.

PART THREE

CHAPTER XXVI

ONE

Kate walked down the sidewalk, past storefront windows displaying spring fashions. She kept thinking, what if he hadn't called? And then: What do I do now?

Tony had called less than a half hour before. They had talked with a candor and intimacy long missing from their conversations. He had told her about the probability of becoming a judge. He had told her the trial was almost over. All that remained was the sentencing. He was free. Their lives were about to be utterly different.

At first Kate had not felt or suspected the turmoil his news would throw her into. She was just pleased.

But as soon as she thought about having to leave the apartment, it reminded her of how far apart she and Tony still were from each other. She drove for a short time, but her restlessness seemed to be unsatisfied unless her body itself was in motion. She parked downtown and began walking.

On impulse, she went into the next store. She moved absentmindedly among the hanging ranks of dresses, running her hands over the soft folds and hard buttons and buckles. What do I do now? she thought again. Her hands moved past dress after dress, her eyes assailed by designs and colors but dead to them all. Abruptly she turned away, unappeased. Nothing's simple anymore, she thought, if it ever was.

With the same hurried steps that had brought her into the store, she went back out. On the sidewalk again, her steps slowed. I'll talk to my father, she thought; he'll know what to do. She let herself be carried along in a stream of shoppers, pleased with the idea. I'll talk to my father.

CHAPTER XXVII

ONE

Two weeks later, he realized the problem was in him, not McKinsey. The old judge could do whatever he wanted to do at sentencing, and the unsatiated appetite would remain. Fraser had to extirpate it himself. In the end it was Keddie who convinced him that McKinsey's decision was irrelevant to the terrible yearning he felt.

Keddie showed him the way.

They met accidentally, or so he assumed, in the courthouse lobby one morning. It was busy and crowded. Fraser was on his way to see McKinsey, ostensibly to check on his condition, but more to glean his thoughts on the verdict.

Keddie was abruptly at his side.

"You're a hard man to pin down," Keddie said genially.

"Am I?" Fraser was startled by Keddie's sudden appearance. Where had he come from? He was off his crutches, only lightly bandaged, and otherwise restored. People eddied around them in the morning rush.

"Well, I understand your schedule."

"I don't think I have time to talk now, doctor." He started to move away.

"It's about Charles Reece." Keddie saw he had Fraser's attention. "I'd like to take a minute of your time about him, if you can spare it."

"Yes, I can."

"How about upstairs? I'll buy you a cup of coffee." Keddie pushed the elevator button.

"All right," Fraser replied. They got into the packed elevator and Keddie chatted affably as if they were old acquaintances.

"I should tell you I don't hold any grudges," he said, his eyes following the glowing numerals as they rose floor after floor. "You have to be ruthless sometimes. I wish Al Starkey was as ruthless as you are." He chuckled, "Of course, we both got pretty banged up.'' He indicated his scars.

Fraser watched the numbers ascend.

"Al doesn't want to discuss Charles with me," Keddie said with a trace of chagrin. "He won't say so, but losing hurt him very much."

Last floor. They spilled out with other people, then headed for the cafeteria. It was just nine in the morning, and everyone who had a court date or wanted one had gravitated to the cafeteria for rolls and a newspaper.

Keddie got a tray and two cups of coffee. He found a glazed roll for himself, asked if Fraser wanted one, added sugar and cream to the coffee, and paid for them both even as Fraser took out a dollar bill.

"No, I said I was going to take your time," Keddie insisted. "I'll pick this one up."

As if there were going to be others.

They found a half-empty table and sat down. At the far end of the room, with a small circle of people, was Judge McKinsey. He looked very small.

"I didn't think he was well," Keddie said.

"No, he's very sick."

Keddie nodded and ate some of his roll.

"Now what about Reece, doctor?"

Keddie patted his lips unnecessarily with a napkin. "Well, something has come up, and Al wouldn't be as much help as you. Charles tells me he's teased—well, tormented—by the guards at the jail and by the other inmates when he's moved for meals or exercise. I have to demand that you look into it and make sure it stops."

It was said in the same affable manner as everything before.

"He'll be transferred in two weeks, after sentencing." Fraser glanced over at McKinsey again.

"But he's in your control now, Mr. Fraser. This kind of abuse is particularly upsetting to him now. It's inhumane."

He wanted Fraser to dispute the charge.

Fraser stirred his coffee. "I'll talk to the jail commander."

Keddie smiled. "There is another problem. It's actually

323

more pressing. Charles is very low right now. His spirits are down, as you might imagine. I've just prescribed a new tranquilizer for him. He tells me that the guards sometimes withhold his medication. That is totally impermissible. He has to have his medication."

"A new tranquilizer?"

"For depression, for a variety of things. He's under tremendous stress. Al told him what to expect. I told him. He knows what will happen when he's sentenced."

Fraser looked at Keddie. "I don't have any control over the jail, doctor."

"I'm informing you of these problems, Mr. Fraser, so you can personally see to it that Charles gets his medication as prescribed, when prescribed. I don't want to have Al draw up a federal petition to force you, but I will do that if necessary."

Almost an echo of his words to Tippetts and Gables. "I'll look into it."

"Thank you," Keddie said agreeably. "I told Charles not to have any illusions about his sentence. Your judge," he looked back toward McKinsey, "will give him death. I told him the appeal to the Supreme Court is automatic and nobody's been executed in this state for . . ." He fumbled. "Do you recall how long?"

"No," Fraser said.

"And I told him there are federal remedies after that. I tried to explain his appeal possibilities to him, but he's still very depressed." Keddie finished the roll.

Fraser's blank facade dropped suddenly. "You're spending a lot of time trying to protect Reece," he said harshly.

"He's my patient." Keddie looked genuinely surprised by the intensity of Fraser's words. "No matter what you said in court, he needs help. I'm going to give it to him."

Fraser pushed his cup aside. "I have to go, doctor."

"I'll be keeping watch on this."

Fraser wheeled away, away from Keddie and McKinsey, out of the cafeteria, away from the courthouse.

He spent a along time in his office, thinking. The appeals were endless. The *thing* was endless. Reece would go on forever, no matter what McKinsey decided was best. The law would gently enfold Charles Reece and carry him along for however long it took to find an error in the trial. Any reversible error. And there had been months of hearings and rulings and testimony.

And there was the gun. The gun was in evidence forever, sealed in a box with the tagged clothing and photographs and dried blood. Some year, some day, when another court was convened to protect Charles Reece, the gun would see light once more. It would be brought out of the sealed box and examined. In a very short time, someone would realize it was not the gun Reece had used.

That had been Fraser's gamble. Now he had to coldly face its consequences after the trial was over. The gun lay waiting to free Reece.

And there was his own testimony, too. He remembered his own testimony.

Somewhere there was one judge, one lawyer who might unearth the things he had done and said. His own acts would topple everything.

Now there was more medication for Reece, who was very depressed. The other inmates hated him. The guards hated him. In two weeks he would be gone to another place, away from the scene of his crimes, out of Fraser's jurisdiction.

He picked up the phone and called Sanderson. Sanderson would understand the situation. He had contacts and friends in the county jail. They made Reece's food and watched his cell. They moved him. They tended him.

Fraser also found himself thinking of Kate as he talked with Sanderson. She was on the edge already. She would pass a point of no return if he was caught up in this case any longer, for any reason. The uncertainty of appeals. The certainty of what would happen when the gun and his testimony for Sanderson came to light. The secret waiting he would have to endure. Sooner or later it would end any possibility of their marriage being saved.

Fraser held nothing back from Sanderson. He reminded Sanderson of everything, from the very first phone call that dark morning, to the suppression hearing, and the meeting in the park. It wasn't as though he came to Sanderson unheralded. The detective had offered to help, to do anything special.

So Fraser told him what had to be done with Keddie's complaint. Sanderson was quiet, but he understood.

Fraser hung up.

TWO

Wednesday. Two days to payday.

Sanderson met him outside the watch commander's empty offices on the fourth floor. Signaling for quiet with a finger to his mouth, he led Fraser down the short, dingy hall to another room. He went in; Fraser followed and shut the door.

Dusty shafts of late-morning sunlight lanced into the spare little room. Sanderson stood, hands pointlessly checking his pockets, eyes looking out the window. He was sweating a little.

"I'm here to see an old pal in security," he told Fraser again.

"That's right. I'm not logged in. I came in another way. I'm not here."

Sanderson whistled tunelessly, softly. He rocked on his heels, then back. "Give it a minute."

"How long has it been?"

"I think about fifteen minutes."

They waited. The jail around them was quiet.

"Lunch. It's always quieter up in isolation. They feed them early. Before the others eat, the guys up here eat. He gets fed by himself." Sanderson repeated the drill of jail procedure as if he were talking to a rookie who had been rotated to the unwanted detail. Fraser was silent. He waited.

"That's enough time, Mel," he said after ten minutes had passed. "I've got to be back in my own office soon."

"Yeah. Yeah," Sanderson agreed, coming away from the window.

"Lead the way."

"Yeah." Sanderson went to the door. They walked down another short corridor. Voices trailed wisplike in the air, rowdy, laughing voices. Utensils clattered somewhere. Fraser stiffened for an instant when he thought footsteps were coming toward them. The terror passed. The footsteps faded.

326

They passed a lavatory and Sanderson ducked into it. Fraser went in after him.

"Come on, Mel," he said impatiently.

Apologetically, Sanderson said, "Gotta go," and sidled up to a urinal. He stood there, staring at a spot on the wall. He simply stood there.

"We don't have the time."

Sanderson stepped slowly from the urinal, zipping himself. He brushed by Fraser and went to the sink. He washed his hands, lather frothing over them. He dried them slowly.

"Let's go," Fraser said.

Sanderson didn't move.

"You've done it before," Fraser said. "This isn't anything new."

"It's not the same."

"No," Fraser agreed, "it's not. But we can't wait."

Sanderson closed his eyes, then they left the men's room. They came to a steel door. Sanderson produced a large key and opened it. There were three cells inside. Two were empty. In the center cell, a dank, shiny gray cubicle, Reece lay on his bunk, one skinny arm dangling onto the floor. There was a curiously graceful bend in his wrist. He was snoring.

A metal food tray sat on the floor. Half the food had been eaten.

"In the lunch. That seemed best, enough to put him out," Sanderson stammered. "Jesus. Jesus," he said.

"Where are they?" Fraser asked.

"Here. Here. I've got them. Both prescriptions, the old one and the new one." He fished out a plastic bottle, handing it shakily to Fraser.

Fraser uncapped the tranquilizers and poured some of the capsules into his hand. Most were red and white. A few were deep blue.

"How many went into the food?"

"Three. Four, I think."

"Only the old tranquilizers? He didn't get any of the new ones?" He held up one of the blue capsules.

"No. I made sure. Just the old ones, those there." Sanderson pointed at the red and white capsules.

"This should work out right, then. He was given two

capsules a day for eleven days of the old tranquilizers. He got one a day of the new ones for three days.'' Fraser shook several more of the capsules from the bottle into his hand. Reece's medication since the verdict. The capsules glistened in his hand like bright seeds. ''Minus the four in the food, I've got twenty-one here.''

Reece snored more loudly, gagging once. ''Hobart was mad,'' Sanderson said, ''when I called him. He says, I've given the son of a bitch his medicine every day. I haven't held any back. The son of a bitch is lying. So like you told me, I said, Okay, go search his cell. Sure enough, the guy was hiding his medicine for two weeks in a hole in the mattress.'' Sanderson grinned fearfully, reciting the story to comfort himself. ''So I said, You give me all the stuff you found in Reece's cell, and I'll take care of it. He gives it to me yesterday and says, You cover me, I'll cover you. I don't care what happens to the son of a bitch.'' Sanderson couldn't take his eyes from Fraser.

''I know there won't be any trouble.''

''He might throw up.'' Sanderson looked at Reece quickly.

''We'll stay long enough to make sure he doesn't.''

''Oh, Jesus,'' Sanderson breathed once more.

Fraser thought for a moment that it had never been determined how Naomi got the knife to her son. It might well have been a guard. He thought there was a satisfying reckoning, a balance struck, in the arrangement Sanderson had worked out with a guard of his own.

''Hold him up,'' Fraser said. Hesitantly, Sanderson put his arms under Reece's armpits and drew him into a sitting position, head forward. Fraser looked at him. Was this what he had seen in that blue bedroom? Was this what he had seen all this time?

Outside, coming through the window, were the sounds of the happy, ignorant city.

Fraser opened Reece's mouth.

CHAPTER XXVIII

ONE

The entire dining room of the Bel Air Country Club was given over to the celebration. It was a large room, papered in gold and blue, but the cacophonous crowd spilled outside onto the golf course, across the wide lawns, around the iridescent blue swimming pool in the rear. When twilight gave way to true night, the floodlights and illumination indoors gave the haughty building an icy white splendor in the summer evening.

The crowd inside was made up of people who had been stalwart enough to last through the speeches and the swearing-in ceremony at the courthouse, and of others who came later for the food and fun. Across the rear wall of the dining room, a serviceably lettered banner was hanging: CONGRATULATIONS JUDGE ANTHONY FRASER. Below it was a buffet table around which swarmed a constant throng, spooning food from table to plate, plastic cups of liquor held precariously or dropped with cries of annoyance, fingers going after morsels when the toothpicks and forks ran out.

A five-piece band alternated big band medleys with pop tunes, all of it sounding remarkably alike.

Passing through a stream of goodwill and heartiness and handshakes, Fraser made his way to Kate. She stood with Donelli and several other judges at the far side of the buffet table, an oasis of calm in the turbulent party.

"I can hardly hear myself," Fraser said happily. He admired her again, dressed in a white, belted skirt and blouse, elegant and attractive. It was something like seeing her for the first time. "Can I get you anything?"

"No, I'm fine." She held a small glass of white wine. The bar at the other end of the buffet table was surrounded forbiddingly by people holding their glasses out to the bartenders.

Donelli sipped from his bourbon. He was damp but bright-eyed. "I was just telling Kate you shouldn't worry 'bout this Keddie thing." He twisted slightly to take a toothpicked sausage from a plate at the end of the table. "Nobody thinks he's going anywhere."

"It obviously didn't affect your appointment," Kate said.

"A lawsuit doesn't worry me," Fraser said. Kate was charming. Gone for three months, and then back with him, for another month, painfully sorting out their wounds, she nevertheless looked untouched by the recent turmoil of their lives. It was, he knew, slightly miraculous that she was here. That he was here, too.

"I know it doesn't," she said, "but the gall of that man bothers me." The judges nodded. The band swung into a syncopated rhythm, and Kate had to raise her voice. "He's been saying things about you for months. I think there should be some way to make him stop it."

"Professional panic." Donelli sucked in a breath when the next sausage was too hot. "Keddie obviously feels he's got to lay the blame for Reece's suicide off on anybody but himself."

Fraser saw how polite, even ingratiating Donelli was to the new Superior Court judge and his wife. There was always the chance that getting off on the right foot might help Donelli rise to the same exalted position.

"Well, it's still wrong for him to go around saying Tony's responsible."

"He did tell me Reece was despondent."

Donelli fanned his mouth and took a swallow of liquor. "That's supposed to mean you knew this guy was suicidal and should have had a watch put on him. Keddie's mad because he blew it. Plain and simple. He prescribed the drugs, and Reece hoarded them."

"I knew there was nothing you could be faulted for," Kate said, looking at him. For a fleeting second he wondered if her trust existed because he was now a judge, out from under the D.A.'s office, or because of the shared anguish of the separation they had gone through. He wanted to think it no longer mattered. They had both changed.

He spoke over the noise. "I don't think he'll file a lawsuit."

"No, he won't file one," Donelli said. "He's making his record, that's all."

Fraser saw Judge Strevel working his way methodically around the buffet table, stopping at every dish. He was followed by his wife, who seemed to be guarding the rear of his advance. "Excuse me," Fraser said, "I better head him off before he gets over here. I can keep it short this way."

Kate wished him luck.

"How are you, Pete?" Fraser said when he reached Strevel. He put out his hand.

Strevel looked up. "Well, the new boy on the block. You've met my wife before? Helen, this is Judge Anthony Fraser. He's coming on the bench."

Mrs. Strevel, who had a very small saucer piled with food, shook his hand. "Oh, yes. I remember. You convicted that man who killed himself."

"That was murder," Strevel said, helping himself to cantaloupe. "The jury killed that man. He should have been put in a hospital."

"It's over now."

"That it is. Have they given you your assignment yet?"

"Monday. I get the word from the PJ then. I'm supposed to wander from court to court for the first few days."

Strevel munched fruit and nodded. "The Flying Judge. They're moving me from criminal to domestic relations." He smiled at his wife. "I need a change of pace. Don't want to end up like poor old Sam McKinsey."

"That was very sad," Mrs. Strevel said. "It was a very moving service."

The return of feeling had started at McKinsey's funeral, as if a pall were being lifted from him. Kate had come with him, and that night the numbness began to recede. But at the funeral he hadn't been able to say anything to Iris. Poor McKinsey. The judge had held out for a long time, hoping to see Fraser sworn in. He'd almost made it.

"I'm going to miss him," Fraser said.

"He was quite a character," Strevel agreed. "Speaking of characters, I thought I spotted your old boss making the rounds."

"He's been and gone."

Three hours before, when Whalen had arrived, Sally Ann had been laughing heartily in a small cluster of deputy D.A.s and unattached men. She had headed right for Whalen, intercepting him before he even got a drink. Although it was impossible to hear her from across the room, her gestures and Whalen's fairly rapid departure shortly afterward suggested that whatever she said had not been friendly.

"Well, stop by and see me Monday when you're settled in someplace." Strevel turned to begin another slow circuit of the table.

Just as Fraser got back to Kate, Sally Ann pushed through the people and dancers and laid an arm over his shoulder. She was slightly soused, a notch louder than necessary. "There you are. There you are. Oh, boy." She grinned happily at Kate. "You two look good from where I was standing."

"You look like you're having a good time at my expense," he said.

Kate smiled at Sally Ann. "I'm glad someone mentioned it."

"Oh, Kate, let me tell you," she glared in false hostility at Fraser, "if this moron had blown it with you, it would have been the stupidest thing he ever did. I told him, too. Didn't I?"

"You did." He took her arm down and kissed her cheek. "You're a princess."

"Well, thank you. I don't know why old Harry didn't at least show up."

"You talked to him?"

Sally Ann screwed her face up for a moment. "Since you forgot to invite him, I did. He isn't making any waves in his practice, you know. Still, he said he didn't have the time. Something came up. Something was coming up . . . I don't know. You're supposed to understand."

"I do."

"Well, I sure don't. He could've at least come over." She smiled at Donelli, who was alone that night. "How about a dance?"

"If Judge and Mrs. Fraser join us."

"Come on, judge." Sally Ann grabbed Donelli's arm and pulled him toward the parquet dance floor. Fraser took Kate's hand, and they held each other easily.

When they got to the dance floor, chanting began immediately. The music picked up, the other couples fell back to the edge of the floor to watch him and Kate move alone.

After a few bars of polite clapping along, the people nearest them cheered and began dancing again.

"I haven't been here since my father brought me the last time," he said.

"We could join."

"I hate this place."

Kate looked at him in surprise. The other couples swirled around them. "You really didn't like him. I always thought you did, a little anyway."

"Not very much."

She leaned against him. "That's a difference between us. I don't dislike my father at all."

He held her closer to him. "I know you don't." Her father was still the ultimate source of wisdom and comfort.

The music ended to applause, and he and Kate strolled outside like the new lovers they had turned into. The tennis courts in front of them were lit up garishly in red, green, and white. Couples walked slowly or stood on the grass, and as he and Kate moved away, the other people faded into shadows. The summer smells of cinnamon and mustard filled the air with dry pungency.

"My family was like yours," she said. They walked together without touching, their voices low. "I thought the whole world existed in Salinas and Monterey. I didn't think of going anyplace else."

"Kate, we were brought up alike. That doesn't mean we feel things alike." The tangy evening air tingled in his mouth. Light falling from the white front of the country club gave Kate's face a creamy softness, her clothing a delicate lambency.

"I know that," she said. "I just didn't realize it before. We coexist, Tony, that's it. We're not identical, even if everyone thinks we are. I've discovered that love is an accommodation."

"For us it is anyway." The past was finished, dead and gone four months before. Reece had rejuvenated the barren land, brought life where there was desolation and despair. Fraser took her hand again, almost shyly. "No matter what else has happened, Kate, there's always been that love."

"I knew that, deep inside," she said, looking out at the stand of elms and evergreens that bordered the edge of the lawns. "It feels like we're starting over again, almost a clean slate, a second chance."

"It is a second chance."

"Nothing will be like before."

"No, nothing."

Kate kissed him. "We won't hurt each other ever again." She made it sound like a pledge between children.

Over them, luminous, great and staring, hung a full moon, its plains and craters glowing in the blue black sky. The noise and music from the reception floated languidly upward toward it, drawn there as were Fraser's eyes.

"I wish everything from the past was wiped away," Kate said. "I'm sorry you've even got to think about this man suing you."

"I'm not worried. Believe me, it doesn't bother me."

"I don't see how he can possibly say you had anything to do with someone's suicide."

Fraser leaned to kiss her. "He can't," he said in a whisper that caressed her neck. "He can't."

Somewhere, he knew, the same pitiless staring moon gazed down on a man and son, exiled forever. Fraser straightened from Kate. The air around them stirred with a vagrant breeze, bringing the scents of summer to them. Kate turned to go back; he put his arm around her, and behind her, stretching into the darkness as far as he could see, was the endless celebration beckoning to him in the palace of nights.